THE CHRISTMAS WE KNEW

LIZA JONATHAN

Have a magical read!
Liza Jonathan

This book is a work of fiction. All events and characters depicted here are fictional. All real locations in the book, including The Greenbrier Resort, Snowshoe Mountain Ski Resort, and The New River Gorge Bridgewalk have been added with their permission.

First edition, October, 2020. Library of Congress ID Number: 2020917827

Paperback: ISBN 978-1-951209-04-9

Amazon ASIN: B08GZRYMKS

Attention Bookstores & Libraries:

Returnable paperback versions of this title can be ordered on Ingram Spark at a wholesale rate. Library versions of the paperback can also be ordered on the Ingram site. www.ingramcontent.com.

Created with Vellum

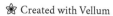

CHAPTER 1

CHRISTMAS EVE, LATE AFTERNOON

"YOU'RE A GOOD MAN. Do you know that, Hopper Vance?"

Mrs. Casto straightened herself up tall on her walker to tell him that, even if the old bird only came up to the center of his chest. Hopper grinned down at her. "I'll bet you say that to all the guys. Well, all the guys who show up with a truckload of presents, anyway."

She snorted and rapped him playfully on his arm. "Oh, stop it now. It's been fifty years since a man tried to distract me with gifts."

He winked. "Is it working?"

Mrs. C laughed for real this time, all the West-Virginia-tough in her softening up, just for a minute. But she wagged her finger at him anyway. "Don't you go changing the subject when a lady's tryin' to show her appreciation. I'm serious. Thank you. For all this."

"It's no trouble," he murmured, and gave her spindly hand a pat. He bent back to the work of unloading, feeling a sting of guilt for cutting the conversation short. But the praise made him feel itchy and uneasy somehow. Even here in this widow's trailer, surrounded by the results of the gift drive he'd organized, her compliment twisted strangely in his gut.

A good man? *Yeah, right. It's a little late for that.*

It was funny. Most days, he didn't feel like an ex-con. That life had been firmly in his rearview mirror for years. But sometimes, totally out of the blue, moments like this would remind him. He'd never atone for all the terrible things he'd done.

So he did the only thing he could do. He turned his focus back to the small boy's bike he'd been assembling. Seeing it all done put a wistful smile on his face. The shiny red bike was one of the Christmas presents he'd talked his employer, Holliday Hot Rods & Collision Repair, into donating for the Casto family. The whole team at the garage had pitched in with gusto, making the effort part of their company's Christmas celebrations. He was damn glad they had.

In a small town like Lewisburg, West Virginia, everybody knew everybody. And everybody knew, Mrs. Casto needed help. She'd never tell you that, of course. She kept her tiny white trailer all prim and perfect, flanked with vegetable gardens and flowers, set on a hillside that had been in her family for generations. She was a feisty, resilient, frizzy-headed old broad, and the type of woman who could pinch a penny until it screamed. But this year she'd had bad luck even she couldn't soldier through—having two grade-school-aged great grandchildren dumped on her doorstep, pretty much indefinitely, and a fall that fractured her hip.

He knew all too well what it felt like to be on the receiving end of that kind of parenting. So he was kinda excited he could make things come out right for the Casto family this holiday. It made him feel, well, almost Christmas-y.

He sighed with satisfaction as he took in the bitchin' custom flames he'd painted on the bike. No, he'd never be a good man. But a *better* man? Yeah, he could manage that.

The narrow trailer door opened with a clatter, and

Hopper's boss, Hunter Holliday, hulked his broad, athletic frame through, yanking at another big black bag full of Christmas presents. He stopped and glared back over his shoulder. "For God's sake, Ross, would you stop pushing? I worked hard on those bows!"

Ross may be one of the more junior members of their team, but he knew enough not to argue with his boss and his self-professed "mad wrapping skills." Hunter had probably been up half the night wrapping and tying and, most likely, cussing. The kid dropped the bag like it was hot at the base of the steps and pulled out a box. "Sorry, man." Ross cracked a sheepish grin, and scrubbed his hand through his shaggy mess of jet black, goth hair."The bag's too big for the doorway. Here, I'll just take them out and pass them through to you."

Eager to make room for the gifts, Hopper gingerly rolled the bike in front of the woman's battered pullout sofa—a pink-and-gray flowery number that was god-knows-how old. Adjusting the sheet and blankets, he rolled the bed back up. The rickety frame creaked ominously, and he jumped back a bit as it clamped shut with a shrieking snap. Mrs. C must not have used the pullout part of this sofa much. This old thing had turned rusty and dangerous. Seriously, somebody could lose a finger. Hopper made a mental note—*charity project after New Year's: build the kids some bunk beds. And find a new couch.* It would take a lot to make this old place suitable for kids.

Well, at least there was today's project—and that should get the Castos stocked up on most of their wants and needs, for a few months, anyway. Everyone had pitched in, dividing up tasks among them. Like Lita, their crazy, pink-haired auto-paint expert, who was currently balancing her tiny frame with catlike grace in the trailer's bay window, humming Christmas tunes while she painted a snowscape on the glass. Meanwhile, he worked with Hunter and Ross until one by one, package after brightly wrapped package of toys, books, clothes and candy were piled like a small mountain in the living room.

Funny how a team effort like this brought out parts of everyone's personality he hadn't seen before. Hopper and Hunter were the old guard of Holliday Hot Rods, both of them flirting with middle age and used to running things just so. Lita and Ross were their younger staff, twenty-some-things who brought their own unique, specialized skills to the shop. Everybody fell in line and knew their role. But today, they all were just a bunch of big kids.

Exhibit A: Ross, a broody, wiry, tatted-up engine and metalworking expert. He usually only smiled when he was needling Lita. But today he grinned from ear to ear as he pulled out a big, unwrapped box. "A Barbie townhouse?" he hooted. "Wow! This thing is huge!"

"Oh, yeah!" Lita called. "I bought that one. Didn't wrap it, because it needed to be put together. Somebody can do that while I finish this up, right?"

Hopper was already on it, pulling out big plastic rods and floor pieces.

Lita was a punk pixie, pint-sized but brash and loud and always the first to point out the BS in things. But she eyed the box with a sense of childhood wonder, still. "It's still got an elevator in it, just like the one I had."

Ross snorted and raised a pierced eyebrow in her direction. "*You* played with Barbie dolls?"

"What did you expect?" Lita huffed. "Barbed wire and poison darts?"

Ross gave her a playful wink. "*Yeah,* actually."

"Children, play nicely," Hunter warned, though he secretly enjoyed the two's sparring matches. The man had been telling Hopper for months that those two were really star-crossed lovers, destined to get together eventually. Hopper, for his part, didn't buy it. But then again, his experience in the love department didn't exactly qualify him to make a judgment.

But Hunter? That man had turned into a hopeless romantic after marrying his second wife a couple of years back—a fact that had disappointed all the single ladies in town, all of whom had tried, and failed, to bag "the broody widower" with the "sad brown eyes" and the "bulging biceps." Nowadays, his boss was so besotted, he saw hearts and flowers wherever he went. But Hopper had the feeling it would take years for Lita and Ross to learn how to be straight with each other.

Proving his point, Lita squawked and threw a spare pillow in Ross's direction. "Duhhh, everybody played with Barbie dolls. Barbie had all the cool stuff—the hot tub, the pink sports car—"

"The not-so-anatomically correct Ken," Ross offered.

"I dunno," Lita sang out, holding her hand over her heart. "He's pretty dreamy after you take off his stupid fedora. I may have gotten grounded once for tatting up my sister's Ken doll with permanent markers."

"Oh, ho!" Ross straightened up with interest, no doubt pleased, considering the boy was practically covered in them from head to foot. "You've got a secret thing for tats!"

Lita rolled her eyes. "The world may never know."

Hunter smirked over in Hopper's direction, as if to say, *See? I told you so.*

Hopper chuckled and shook his head at their bickering, tinkering away with the construction of Barbie's luxurious digs. He loved putting together things like this. In no time, he was snapping the last of the townhouse together, smiling with satisfaction as he got the elevator to go up and down. Attaching a big pink bow on it, he propped it in a corner with the dolls they'd gotten—Doctor Barbie, and a Barbie with blue hair and thicker hips. And Ken. With a man bun. He rolled his eyes.

These toys, they weren't just trinkets, were they? They represented something. Hope, maybe. Possibilities. Dreams for a bright, shining future where you could make the world whatever you wanted. Proof that the adults around you cared. Shouldn't every kid have that, especially at Christmas time?

Maybe this Christmas intervention would be the thing that really helped these kids. Maybe being dropped off with their granny...well, maybe they could help turn a tragedy into a blessing. Save those kids from going down a dark path.

Searching for another task to do, Hopper wandered into the kitchen area. Hunter and Ross were busy there, pulling the last of the fully cooked food out of the cooler and readying it to warm in the oven. When the kids came back, all Mrs. C would have to do is pull out the serving dishes to have one kick-ass holiday feast.

Hopper made himself useful setting out dishes, trying to remember which side of the plate the forks and knives were supposed to go on. Everyone was so focused on their fussing, they hadn't noticed that Mrs. C had gotten awfully quiet. When they paused to finally turn her way, they found the little sweetheart simply standing in the corner of the room, leaning on her walker, bawling her eyes out. *Oh...oh, no.*

Lita had been the first to notice the tears. She threw down her snowflake stencils and wrapped her arms around the woman's trembling shoulders. "Oh now, now," Lita cooed. "Don't cry. It's Christmas!"

"It's just—it's just that y'all are so *good* to me." the lady sniffled, dabbing her eyes with a crumbled up tissue. "And you didn't have to do any a'this, but you *did*. The kids, they won't be able to believe it. Their mama, she never did anything like this for them, neither. So, when I told them money was tight and I didn't feel up to getting a tree, they just said, 'That's okay, Nana. Santa's never stopped for us.' Can you imagine two kids in grade school saying such a thing? And now...and now...it just makes me so *happy*. And it's going to make them *so happy*. Thank you!" She hurried over and gave each of them a surprisingly bone-crushing hug.

"We're happy to do it," Hunter insisted. "Neighbors helping neighbors—isn't that what the season is all about? You'll be up and on your feet in no time."

They nodded in agreement and smiled at the woman. And she beamed right back.

But Lita twirled one of her long pink braids, studying the room through narrowed eyes. "Don't you think we should get her a tree, guys?"

Hunter pulled out his smart phone and checked the time. "Well, I suppose we could. We still have, what, two hours left before their friend's mom drops them back off? Right?"

Mrs. Casto nodded, then loudly protested that they all didn't need to go to any trouble. But none of them listened. Before long, the whole Holliday Hot Rods team was debating about who was going to take on the huge freakin' task of finding a live tree, dragging it back here, and decorating it good and proper.

But it seemed like everybody had somewhere to be. Lita needed to get on the road within the hour, so she could drive to her sister's house in Virginia. Hunter was hosting a big family dinner at his place. Ross was already running late for his mom and dad's Christmas Eve party.

Finally, Lita called it. "It's gotta be you, Hop. You're the only one without plans."

Hopper sighed resignedly. It made his chest ache a bit to hear it out loud like that, but it was true. At forty-one, he had no woman, no kids, and what family he did have was gone with the wind. Nah, his Christmas would be nice and quiet, with a couple of beers, old movie marathons, a nice long winter's nap—and this charity project, of course. Helping Mrs. C really was his Christmas, when it came right down to it.

Hopper raked a hand through his hair and blew out a breath. "Fine. I can do it. But where am I going to get a tree at this hour? It's half past four on Christmas Eve, for Christ's sake!"

"I'll bet if you just keep driving around on the outskirts of town, you'll find one of those pop-up places selling trees and ornaments," Hunter offered. "You know how they are. They'll stand out there until the bloody end if they have a tree left on the lot."

It didn't take much of a push to get Hopper in on this last-minute scheme. A Christmas tree was a luxury he'd never had when he was a child. But he'd loved them anyway. Back then, even a small, simple tree had seemed like a mystical, glittery wonder to him. How cool was it that he could give the Casto kids that little bit of Christmas magic, while they were still young enough to enjoy it? He silently gave thanks that he'd driven his banged-up work truck to this gathering. Everything would fit in the back with no trouble at all.

So, he said his goodbyes to his team and began his methodical drive through town, desperate for a tree—any tree. And it was taking *for-freakin'-ever,* his carefully mapped route yielding him approximately squat. But that didn't mean there wasn't anything to see. Everywhere he went, the hush of Christmas had fallen. Few cars were on the road. The quaint Victorian-era shops on Main Street were shut up tight, their lights gone dark for the sacred day. And nearly all the homes he passed had extra cars in their driveways, and warm lights glowing from the windows as friends and families gathered.

There'd be no lights glowing in the night for him. No, his house would be dark and empty when he got home tonight, just like always.

And whose fault is that?

Hopper curled his hands tighter around his steering wheel, willing the sadness back into its familiar, dark corners. Yeah, he'd turned his back on the love of his life, once upon a time. Now there was no sense cryin' over what could never be fixed. Time's cruel like that, always moving forward, and casting your worst decisions in cement. Sighing, he focused his mind determinedly on the world outside his windshield, and the open road in front of him.

On and on he drove, up into the Allegheny Mountains that surrounded this valley town. Overhead the trees shimmered from the remnants of a recent ice storm, their embracing branches making a sparkling tunnel that glittered like fairy dust in the setting sun.

But he didn't exactly have time to enjoy driving through this perfect little Christmas card. The snow was starting to blow around enough to make it hard to see. As the minutes wore on, he tapped his fingers impatiently on the wheel, mulling over his options. But there were none at this hour, at least not for regular retail stores, anyway. No, he'd have make this "find a roadside stand" strategy work, screwy as it was.

He checked his dashboard clock and let out a string of curses. Time was clearly not on his side. Weaving carefully down the mountain roads, he craned his neck and squinted his eyes to find a sign, any sign, that some rando had Christmas trees for sale.

Finally, he spotted a plain hand-painted cardboard sign hanging haphazardly from a stake in the road's shoulder. An arrow was scrawled on it in red paint, pointing down a winding, one-lane side road. *Stuck without a Christmas tree?* It said. *We're still open!*

Hot damn! Hopper let out a few whoops, hardly able to believe his luck.

Even though this stretch of highway was as familiar to

him as the back of his hand, he'd never noticed this side road before. It must lead to a private property or something. He yanked his wheel into the turn.

By God, he was going to get that tree. Maybe he'd get this Christmas back on track, after all.

CHAPTER 2

AS HOPPER RUMBLED ENDLESSLY down this rough, unpaved trail, his niggling doubts turned into worry. How far up into a holler was he gonna have to go? Shouldn't this tree place be right off the road?

No sooner had that thought crossed his mind, than he saw another strange sign: *Don't wimp out. You're almost there.*

He snorted. *Cute. Real Cute.* Turning in the direction the sign indicated, Hopper continued to mutter as he bounced over one rut and ditch after another, rolling ever deeper into friggin' no-man's land. Jesus, who would have a place of business so far out? Was he being lured out to some kind of psycho compound, or something?

But then there was another sign, written in the same red paint: *We're not psychos. Honest.*

Seriously, what the fuck? Hopper slammed on the brakes. And for a brief moment, he considered turning the truck around and going back. This was getting *way* too weird.

But he could see the store off in the distance. And he was probably being ridiculous. It was just a stupid sign. So, he put his foot to the gas pedal and motored off to the place, coming to a stop in the gravel lot out front of a countrified shop called Caine's Christmas Outpost.

And sure enough, there were fresh, beautiful cut trees surrounding the whole place. To his shock, it wasn't just a pop-up stand. This outpost was really a big, welcoming country store—set in a log cabin that had apparently been expanded by mismatched additions into a sprawling, timber-frame house. The place was trimmed in blinking, multicolored lights and fresh-cut wreaths with big red bows. Storefront windows twinkled with old-timey toy displays, and the whole place seemed all warm and glowy, with puffs of smoke curling out of the chimney.

He couldn't help but stop and stare through his windshield at the place. The Outpost was like some kind of glittery Christmas mirage out in the middle of a snowy, unspoiled wilderness.

A flash of alarm raced up his back as his truck door opened—from the *outside.* But he sighed with relief to see a harmless, rangy-looking old man with a straggly white beard standing on the other side of the door. Practically bounding up and down with excitement, the fella was obviously friendly, and kinda endearing, with his shit-eating grin, beat-up insulated overalls, and a fraying "Almost Heaven, West Virginia" ball cap.

"I knew it! I knew you'd come!" the man crowed, his sharp blue eyes dancing with an excitement far younger than his years.

Hopper carefully slid out of the truck, locking the door behind him. "You were *expecting* me? I didn't tell anyone I was on my way."

"But we *always* get someone on Christmas Eve. The later, the better. And look at you! Just look at you! You need us, don't you?"

Hopper shook the man's hand. "What I need is one of

your trees, and some lights and stuff to put on it, sooner rather than later. Can you get me fixed up?"

The man said he'd come to the right place and introduced himself as Earl. He puffed out his chest as he proudly showed him around the tree lot. They dickered a bit until they settled on a five-foot Christmas tree. And it was perfect—all crisp and fresh, and just the right size for Mrs. C's cramped trailer. It even came with a free stand. By the time they'd finished negotiating, Earl had already pulled out a rope and started binding the tree for hauling.

"You'll have to go inside to pay and get you some finery for this here tree." Earl smiled. "The boss will get you straightened out."

Hopper couldn't help but grin back at the old coot. "The boss?"

"My wife. Believe me when I tell you, she's the boss."

Hopper laughed and gave Earl a little two-fingered salute as he went in. The bell on the door clattered behind him, and he was immediately hit with a wave of warmth that carried the cinnamony smell of baking cookies and Christmas candles. The place was so oddly glowy with holiday lights, it was hard on his eyes, as if he was seeing it all through some kind of soft-focus filter.

Before he could even inspect the merchandise, an old woman was right up in his grill, holding out a plate piled high with cookies. "Snickerdoodle?" she asked, grinning so widely her face practically collapsed into a riot of laugh lines and deep wrinkles.

"Uh, sure," Hopper murmured. He grabbed a cookie off the top of the stack but stepped back a bit to get some more personal space. He felt kinda silly about it. The old lady was obviously sweet and welcoming, after all. But there was something about her hospitality that felt, somehow, *pointed*. Deliberate. It poked at his instincts.

"Wash it down with some of this nog too, boy." She

shoved a mug of the stuff in his hand. "I'm Candy Caine, by the way. And don't you go laughin' about my name. I can tell you're about to. I got the name when I married old Earl out there, back when I was too young to know better. There ain't a joke you can make that I haven't heard. 'Course, now that my husband's gotten to be a dried-up old fart, I've started calling him Raisin, just for payback."

Hopper stopped, cocked his head a minute, and snickered. "Raisin Caine? Oh, that's a good one." Candy may be odd, but she was a funny old buzzard. Hopper extended his hand and shook hers. "Nice to meet you, Candy. I'm Hopper Vance."

The woman set the plate aside and shook his hand, surprising him a bit with the strength of her grip. Then she fisted her hands on her hips, scanning him up and down like a drill sergeant eyeing a new recruit.

He wasn't quite sure what to make of the woman. This Candy was a skinny, wizened old bitty with a face as tanned and shiny as an old saddlebag. But the woman was dressed for the holidays in spades, what with her battered red leggings, flashing Christmas light earrings and an oversized sweater with a neon-green Christmas tree on it. Her frizzy, bright red hair was pulled back in a braid and showing more white roots than red. An honest woman, he'd bet, who obviously put in a lot of work to make the Outpost so super nice. To have a place this established, she and Earl had probably dedicated their whole lives to it.

So why have I never heard of this place?

Candy gave him the once over again and a knowing smile crept over her face. Honestly, the woman seemed more like a carney than the proprietor of a Christmas shop. A faint prickle of warning skittered down his spine. Hopper wondered if he was being sized up for a mark or something. But that was stupid, wasn't it? For Christ's sake, he was just here buyin' a tree, not checking into the Hotel California.

Since he really was pretty hungry, Hopper grabbed another sweet, buttery cookie and swigged down the nog. He'd never had homemade eggnog before, and the thick, creamy drink was just about the most delicious thing he'd ever tasted. "Mmmm…"

The old woman cackled. "Good, iddn't it?"

Hopper smacked his lips as he guzzled the last of it down. "It must be the rum."

"Naw, it's the Christmas magic!" She grinned.

He rolled his eyes.

Candy just kept smiling at him and moved behind the counter. "Don't you roll your eyes at me, young man. Whassa matter? You don't believe?"

"Christmas magic is better left to Hallmark movies and Christmas cards. I gave up believing in fairy tales long ago."

Candy rested her head on her hand and gave him a long, wise look. "And yet, here you are, late on a snowy Christmas Eve, risking life and limb to buy old Mrs. Casto a tree."

Hopper stepped back a step. "How did you— I don't remember saying—"

"Christmas magic network," she drawled, wiggling her fingers in the air. "Must've been the elves, or maybe a snowflake sprite who told me."

He chuckled a bit at her joke. And that's what it clearly was—a joke. Relieved now, he realized how she knew. He was wearing a mechanic's work shirt, one of his extras without the Holliday Hot Rods logo on it. Maybe she'd heard about the shop's charity project and put two and two together. Stranger things had happened. Lewisburg is a pretty small town, after all, and word tended to get around.

Shrugging off his unease, he began shopping in earnest. He didn't have much time, and the shelves were stuffed to bursting with just about every kind of Christmas decoration imaginable. The Outpost really was something to see, with all the neat bins of hand-carved ornaments, rows of oversized snow globes and toy train sets chugging along underfoot. In the end, Hopper chose to go for what was easy to hang and compact to store—tinsel garland, multicolored lights, and a couple of big plastic tubes of tree bulbs that glittered like glass but were really just painted plastic. Then he grabbed a matching tree skirt and a tinsel star that blinked with color-shifting LEDs for the top of the tree. And the best part was, he'd found what he needed in five minutes flat.

He checked his watch again. Hmmm, he had a just over an hour before the kids got home. By his calculations, he would make it back and have the tree up by the skin of his teeth. Rushing up to the counter, he plunked his finds down and swiped his card for the lady.

Candy handed him his bags. "I see Earl's got your tree all loaded. So, the only thing you've got to do is pick out your free gift. Go on, child. Pick out something just for you." She pointed to the middle of the store, to a tree so enormous its branches bowed with the weight of all its fancy ornaments and lights. Underneath it, wrapped gifts in every size and shape were piled high.

He grimaced. "I'm in a real hurry here. And I don't need anything, really. Save it for your next customer."

But Candy wasn't having it. She raised an impatient eyebrow and drummed her fingers on the counter.

He let out a helpless sigh, and gave the glittering presents another once over. It really was an intimidating stack, all wrapped up with shiny bows. "Where would I start? How would I even know what to—"

"Just go on over there." Candy pointed. "Once you get to the tree, you'll see exactly which one. It always works that way."

Hopper waved her off and started walking toward the exit. "Yeah but, I really don't have the—"

She stepped right in his way, blocking his path to the door, all crossed arms and narrowed eyes and rather intimidating matronly disapproval. "Good Lord. What's the matter with you, looking a gift horse in the mouth? Don't you know that's bad manners? Now don't give me any more lip. I'm not letting you out of here until you pick. If anyone needs a big fat dose of Christmas magic, it's you."

He wanted to argue with the woman, but sighed instead, set down his bags, and held up his hands in surrender. He walked over to the tree. He'd just grab something quick and open it up when he got home. Maybe something small.

He eyed what seemed like an endless stack of beautiful, professionally wrapped gifts in shiny reds and golds and greens. Yet, one gift stood out. It was a flat box, small enough to fit in his jacket pocket. The box was definitely shabbier than the others by comparison—the plaid paper seeming kinda dull and cheap next to all the gold foil wrap and fancy bows. But it had caught his eye, anyway.

Hopper held it in his hand for a second, and the strangest sense of déjà vu rolled over him. There was something familiar about this box he couldn't quite shake, like he'd seen it before. What an insane thought. How could that possibly be?

Silencing his strange misgivings, he stuffed the package in his jacket. "I'll take this one. How's that?"

Her eyes sparkled with mischief as she handed him his bags again. "Isn't it just like a man to pick *that* one. Well you make the most of it. Don't forget, Christmas is only as good as your memories."

He gave her a sideways glance. What in the hell was that supposed to mean? But Candy just shot him a weird, wise grin, again, like she knew something he didn't.

What is with that woman? Whatever it was, he didn't have time to figure it out. He had a deadline to meet.

He took the bags, turned for the door, and caught sight of Earl outside, strapping down the last of the bungee cords to secure the tree to his truck bed. The overhead bells made a racket as Hopper whipped open the door and stepped outside.

Into…*Nothing.* Everything was black. He couldn't see his hand in front of his face.

Jesus Christ! What the hell is—

I'm flat on my back. Why am I flat on my back?

Wherever he was, it was warm and…cozy? And it was dark. But not too dark. His eyes adjusted, and he could make out shards of light peeking through the blinds on the window, just across the room. He laid there feeling numb, his breath heaving in his chest as he absorbed the shock.

Where in God's name am I? How did I get here? Wait—am I in the hospital?

No, the place was too raggedy to be a hospital, and there were no machines or monitors. And there was definitely something *familiar* about that window. Hopper felt around, getting his bearings. He was in a bed. A backlit alarm clock blinked at him from the nightstand at his right hand side.

Holy shit—is that my old alarm clock? He ran his hand over the fake plastic chrome on the tacky old thing, a retro 1950s clock he'd bought on a whim at Goodwill, mainly because it had an antique car on it. Dear God, he hadn't seen that old thing since he'd rented his first house—the one just outside Douglasville, Georgia. What was that, more than *sixteen years ago?*

A jolt of panic fizzed through him and he shot up to sitting, rubbing his eyes. He was naked under the covers, like he always used to sleep back in the day. And if his eyes weren't deceiving him, it really was *back in the day*. Even in the near darkness, he could see it was all still here, just like it used to be—the same ratty black comforter, the same rock posters on the wall, even the same piles of battered jeans and briefs and hoodies on the floor. It wasn't just a dream. It *couldn't* be. He hadn't gone to sleep! Anyway, he could actually *feel* everything, touch everything…

A shadowy figure moved in front of the window. But before he could call out or jump up, there was a rustle, and the blinds flew open, flooding the room with the hazy white rays of morning. And the most beautiful woman in the world, the only woman he'd ever wanted, was standing there in nothing more than his favorite gray flannel shirt.

Delilah Jones. How in the world had *she* gotten here?

Holy hell, she looked so young, so perfect, just like she'd been when he'd loved her and lost her, so many years ago. No way could she have aged a day. Her pale, smooth legs gleamed in the morning light, and her gorgeous dark hair—black as midnight—tumbled in thick, rowdy waves down her back.

Jesus H. Christ. Am I really seeing this? He didn't have the brain cells to process the question. Hopper was paralyzed with awe, unable to speak, or move, or even breathe.

"Mornin' sleepyhead!" Delilah crooned. She sashayed her sexy ass over to his bed, peeled back the covers, and straddled his lap.

God damn. The heat of her, the closeness, after so long. Hell—it was friggin' *incredible.* Unable to stop himself, he brought his hands to rest on those perfect, silky legs, running his thumbs along the sinew of her muscles in mute fascination, in total disbelief.

What's going on? How did you get here? A thousand questions crowded his mouth. But before he could ask her any of them, she grabbed his face in both hands and laid a kiss on him. And not just any kiss. A *good morning* kiss. The Delilah special, she used to call it. It had been their running joke, how she could trot out a certain set of kisses and moves, and he'd be one hundred percent hard and aching by the end of it.

And she was doing it too. The scorching slide of her plush red lips against his...the sharp nip of her teeth on his bottom lip.

God. His heart raced with the sensation. She rolled her hips, sliding herself against him, skin to skin, heat to heat. And then she sucked on his tongue...

He groaned, long and loud, shaking with it, and gasping.

He swallowed the urge to laugh helplessly. *Holy fucking shit. It still worked.* His head buzzed and he actually felt a bit lightheaded, probably because all his blood had just been rerouted to his groin.

God it was so good, just like he remembered. *Better* even. Taking notice of his sudden raging hard-on, she pulled back, glanced down at his lap, and wiggled her hips triumphantly. "Works every time." She bit her lower lip while he simply gaped at her, dazed and bewildered and helplessly turned on.

"What—what are you doing?" he finally croaked out.

Delilah giggled—a sultry, lilting sound that lifted him somehow, practically sweetening the air he breathed. She idly traced her fingers in his chest hair. "Since it's the Christmas season and all, I thought I'd come sit in your lap this morning, Santa. Figured you deserved a reward for being such a good boy." She pressed the pad of her finger into the cleft on his chin, like she'd always loved to do. "I still can't believe you got me a motorcycle for Christmas."

He was so overwhelmed with her, he'd barely noticed she was holding a wrapped gift box. She opened it, pulling out a key chain with a Santa Claus on it and a big silver motorcycle key. Dangling it in front of her face, she kissed it. "Never in my wildest dreams did I think I'd be the owner of a BMW motorcycle. If I hadn't already known it, I would say you're the perfect man, Hopper Vance."

He swallowed hard and blinked stupidly. Whatever it was, it wasn't a dream. God, it *really was her.* Delilah, with her witchy gray eyes and that plush, sexy mouth and skin that felt like fine satin under his hand. Delilah—the only woman who mattered.

God in heaven, it really was. And she was looking at him

right now like he was her everything. Like he was the man he'd always wanted to be—a man who hadn't disappointed her. Whatever the hell this was, maybe he could be that man again, and relive it all somehow.

He kissed her again and almost laughed out loud for joy. Heaven tasted a lot like cinnamon toothpaste and her favorite cherry lip gloss. If he lived to be a hundred, he'd never forget how this woman had made him feel. He didn't understand how any of this was happening, but…

Choking back tears, he kissed her again, grabbing both sides of her face too, tangling his fingers in her hair, plundering her mouth as if she'd disappear. As if all this would end and she'd be snatched away from him again, just like before.

Holy hell, it's *impossible*. "Delilah," he breathed. "My God. You're really here."

CHAPTER 3

DELILAH SQUAWKED, but kissed him soundly with a big smack. "Of course I'm here, you big dummy. I've got a boyfriend who treats me like a queen and knows the meaning of teaching a girl to *ride*. And he looks like this. Mmmm." She slid her hands through his hair, curling it in her fist and yanking a little.

His head spun. Shit, he used to love it when she did that. And he loved it even more now. Hopper couldn't help but kiss her, a growl slipping out as he did. His hair was long again, down to his shoulders and jet-black, like it was before it had gone all salt and pepper on him. Gone was the trim undercut he'd had just moments ago. His body was leaner and less muscular than he'd become later. Christ, he must be in his mid-twenties again, like her. He glanced at his arms. Not so many scars. Not so many tattoos.

Oh yeah, I'm definitely younger.

Delilah dropped the key back in the box again. And the fizzy shot of lust that was coursing through his veins receded just enough for him to focus his attention on the box.

She shook it around in her hands with a grin. Gently, he took it from her, trying not to gawk at it like an idiot.

Because he recognized it now—the same plaid wrapping, the same-shaped box.

The. Same. Box. The one he'd picked up from under the tree at the Outpost.

"How?" Hopper croaked. Delilah reared back, brows scrunched up and obviously confused. So, he cleared his throat and tried to be cool. "Um...where did you get this box?"

She laughed and gave his shoulder a playful shove. "*You*, silly! You gave it to me last night! You do remember, don't you? Hmmmm." She narrowed her eyes. "I think maybe I was so appreciative last night, I might have fried your brain cells."

He chuckled a little bit, trying to play it off. But he couldn't help staring at that box. *God.* So that was why it was so familiar. He'd wrapped this very box himself—poorly—all those years ago.

How is that even possible?

What the hell is—

Could it be I've traveled through some kind of freaky time warp? Or maybe I've died and gone back to heaven somehow? Did I hit my head or get sick, and I'm having some kind of hallucination or something?

Shit! Was there something in that nog?

No... it couldn't be. No way was he high. This was way too crisp, too vivid, too unbelievably real.

Hopper sat the box on the nightstand. Trying to disguise his shaking hands, he wrapped his arms around the small of her back and pulled her to him. Because right now, he didn't give a flying fuck what was going on. Delilah had her sweet ass in his lap and her arms circled around his neck. And damn, her lithe weight was perfectly balanced over his rock hard, twenty-something cock, her eyes sparkling with the promise of things to come. Hopper didn't care if he had minutes, or hours, or days, he wouldn't let this pass by. Somehow, the universe was giving him another chance.

And he'd take it.

Oh, *hell* yes.

He dove his mouth to her neck, nipping and lapping up the taste of honey and coconut that always seemed to cling to her skin. And he popped open the buttons on the flannel as fast as he could make his fingers go. When he pushed it back off her shoulders, it was as if he'd been struck by lightning—incinerated by the sight of her.

He may not understand how he got here. But he did know that this, this right here, was the best thing he was ever going to get. *This* woman. *This* love. The woman who'd turned his whole world to the light. And here she was, with her pale glowing skin and tits that overflowed his hands and her tiny, cinched-in waist. She was impossibly perfect, a friggin' miracle of curves and sugar and mind-bending passion, there for the taking in his lap. And damn if she didn't kick up her chin and level him with a look that was Southern sweetness and fiery challenge, all at once.

Delilah Jones.

The woman whose face he saw every night when he closed his eyes. The woman he'd sacrificed everything to protect. He'd forced her from his life for her own good. But that didn't mean the ache in his soul ever went away. In the sixteen-odd years since he'd held her in his arms, the Delilah-sized hole in his heart had become a bottomless pit.

But here.

She.

Was.

This was sure as shit not a dream. He could feel the connection between them, alive and undeniable, pulling him tight.

It was too much. Everything crashed through him at once. Love. Regret. Self-loathing. Longing. And lust too, if you could call that an emotion. His body burned, and his chest heaved with every breath. If he were a better man, he'd lay Delilah out, ply her with kisses and perfect, tender foreplay, and tell her over and over again how much he loved her. How much he'd *always* loved her.

But he didn't have it in him to be good, not when everything he'd ever wanted was one thrust away. Hopper kissed her, hard and hungry, and pushed himself deep inside her, long and slow.

She gasped, but took him the rest of the way, grinding down hard to let him know she wasn't playing around. Just like always. Then she tipped her head back and let loose a groan, deep and throaty and so fucking sexy, it was like the most beautiful music he'd ever heard.

Awww yeah. Hopper grabbed her hips, and drove home...*home,* harder and harder into her slicked heat. God, so tight, so perfect...pure pleasure wrapped in heartbreak with every thrust. Scraps of words he'd held in his heart all these years flashed through his mind.

I miss you.

I need you.

I'm sorry.

Baby, please, I'm so, so sorry.

But they all jumbled in his head, scrambled by their journey up this peak. He couldn't stop, couldn't help himself. He was saying things now, groaning her name, begging—shit, he didn't even know what.

But Delilah just licked her lips and locked her gaze to his. She leaned backward a bit, one hand wrapped around his neck for balance, rolling with him like a dancer in perfect time. "Fuck yeah. Like that baby." She moaned, sounding more high-pitched and desperate with every breath she took.

It was sex. But sweet Jesus, it was so much more than that. In those eyes, he saw everything. Her pleasure, her—her *joy*. Yeah, that's exactly what it was. Her face lit with happiness as the flush crept up her neck, and her breath came faster and faster. It bubbled up in him too, rolling over him...

He shouted with it, couldn't stop as she shook and spasmed all around him, making him come too, milking the last bit of pleasure from him. When he could finally breathe again, he let out a shaky laugh. Holy fuck, he was trembling from his head to his feet.

God...

Thank you, little Lord baby Jesus. Had he ever thought he'd get to feel this with her again? It was some kind of *miracle.*

Damn, he felt boneless. He swallowed hard, gulping in air while his chest heaved. It had been too long. He'd forgotten how amazing. That was...that was...

God. He wrapped his arms around her, holding her tight as he could against him. She cradled her head on his shoulder, limp from effort, breathing hard on her way back down again. Delilah seemed so sated and sweaty and peaceful. He let that feeling in—let it creep into his bones, satisfying him in a way that nothing else could. His life had been one big, miserable mess. But not with her. No, with Delilah, he'd known real, true happiness, like the most beautiful firework that blazed through the dark and lonely sky, and then was gone.

Hopper wished with all his heart that he could stay right here, just like this, forever. He simply held her, nuzzling her neck and threading his fingers through the damp strands of hair at her nape. He breathed in deep, inhaling the smell of sex and spice that could only be Delilah Jones. And he kissed her again, soft and slow, tasting, remembering...

Lord, this girl was like no one else.

Delilah finally moved off his lap, breaking the spell. A strange kind of panic clutched at him then, gripping his chest. She was going to go now, wasn't she? What would happen then? Would he go back to his regular life? Would she disappear? Would he wake up?

Guilelessly, she padded across the room while he tried to act normal. You know, not like a man who might actually be losing his mind. She disappeared into the bathroom to tidy up. When she emerged, she was wearing over-the-knee lace-up boots, black tights, a plaid mini-kilt, and his flannel shirt again, tied in a knot to make a kind of halter top.

Oh, that's right—Delilah had dressed for her job as a server at The Sassy Lass, and showing off her killer body raked in the tips from their mainly male clientele. She quickly worked her hair into a braid. A woman like her barely needed makeup, or a fancy routine. She was so damn pretty…

Delilah stopped, wrinkled her nose at him, and grinned. "What are you scowling at?"

Hopper considered for a moment what to say. Part of him wanted to pepper her with questions. *What's going on?* chief among them. But the larger part of him rebelled. Because whatever this was, he wanted to stay here. With her. "It's the face I make when I miss you, sweet thing." Hopper pouted, pulling on a pair of jeans off his floor and tossing on a sweat-shirt. "Do you really have to leave so early?"

She sauntered over to him, at least making a show of sympathy with a quick kiss. "It's the day before Christmas Eve, babe. All the guys are out doing their last-minute shopping and they need to eat. Tips are going to be a-*ma*-zing. But don't worry. I'll be off at six and then we'll have the whole night."

No. No they wouldn't have the whole night. The pit of his stomach dropped out from under him. Because he realized, all at once, what day it was.

This was their *last* day.

The day everything had gone to hell. The day he'd been arrested and carted off to jail. The day he'd lost her, and the whole world with it. Was *that* why he was here? Was this a chance to change it all? Dear God…could he?

Could he?

Hopper's mind raced desperately as Delilah slid into his

old black leather moto jacket, popped on her helmet, and walked outside to get on the motorcycle he'd gotten her. He had to stop her. He had to change the course of events of this day and save them both!

She smiled up at him as she turned the key and revved the motor. But he blocked her, grabbing the handlebars and standing in front of the bike. Back then, he'd flipped her visor up and kissed her goodbye.

But not today. He turned off the ignition.

Delilah pulled off her helmet, scowling in confusion. "Hop, baby, what are you doin'?"

"Angel, listen to me." He grabbed her chin in his hand and bent his face level with hers. "You can't go in to work today. You can't even stay in town anymore. You and me, we need to get out of here, right now, and start over somewhere totally different."

Her mouth fell open. Of course, he'd shocked her. "What in the world?" she huffed, jerking away from him. "You want to tell me where this ridiculous idea is coming from?"

He opened up his mouth to tell her, but the words wouldn't come. How could he tell her that in less than twenty-four hours, she'd know the truth? That he wasn't the hardworking mechanic she'd thought he was. That he was a thief. A liar. And she'd be watching him getting led away in handcuffs. That one day, she'd bawl in bewilderment as he stood up and pled guilty to running a ring that stole luxury cars and sold them for their parts. A plea that'd earn him twelve years in prison.

Today, the bill would come due for every bad thing he'd ever done. And he'd be paying it, with interest. But it didn't have to be.

"Marry me," he blurted out. He hadn't planned to say it, but now that he had, he wasn't sorry. Marrying Delilah would change everything for the good—he just knew it.

Hopper shuffled on his feet, but he met her gaze square on and set his jaw.

Delilah, for her part, shook her head as if she hadn't quite heard him right. "*Marry* you?" she yelped.

"That's right!" he insisted, hoping to God she saw the seriousness on his face. "You're the only woman for me, Delilah, and I don't want to wait another minute. Let this be my Christmas present. Let me get on that bike, and we'll ride right up to the courthouse. And then we can pack up, and we can—"

"Have you *lost your mind?*" she sputtered. "You know how important you are to me, but I'm only twenty-three! I *like* my life like it is. I like my job and I like my roommates. I mean, what is all this nonsense about moving out of town? You've got your own business! You're doing great!"

"And I'd burn it all to the ground, baby. In a minute. Come on, let's just start over. Let's put our lives to rights. We can *be* anything. *Do* anything." The rightness of this burned inside him. He could clean the slate now before it was too late. All he'd have to do is dump the money, and destroy the evidence...

Yeah, he could start over, leave it all behind, and turn to the light, years early. God, what he'd change if only he could. They could change everything, together. His angel could make him a better man, beginning today.

But Delilah just shook her head and put her helmet back on. "I don't know what's gotten into you, Hopper Vance, but I'm not ready to settle down, or move, for that matter. Come on, baby. When I get back from work, we'll do our holiday baking and get ready for Christmas Eve dinner tomorrow, just like we planned. Whatever this wild hair is, I'm sure you'll be over it by then."

"I *won't* be over it." Hopper glowered at her, at a loss for what else to say.

She paused, searching his face for a long moment. Her

eyes widened a bit when she realized he wasn't kidding around. Her breath left her in a soft, shocked exhale, and she cupped his cheek in her hand. "Did you really just ask me to marry you?"

"Yeah." He nodded resolutely. "I really did."

She circled her thumb on his cheek. "I will, babe. Someday. I promise."

"But not now?" Panic squeezed at his chest again. "Would it help if I said please?" His voice cracked. But he didn't care if he sounded desperate.

She checked her watch and grimaced. "Hop, baby, I can't talk about this now. I've gotta go. They'll dock my pay if I'm late. We'll get to the bottom of all this tonight, okay?"

Before he could stop her, she'd flipped down her visor, revved the motor back up, and peeled off down the road.

Dammit.

Dammit!

He had to stop this! He could not—would not—make all these mistakes twice. Frantically patting down his pockets, he couldn't find the keys to his car or his bike. So he turned and ran for the house. He had to find her, catch her, *stop* her. He had to change the outcome of this day, and save them both!

Heart pounding in his ears, he took the stairs two at a time and threw open the door. But instead of being back in his old rented house, familiar bells rang as the door closed behind him.

The smell of snickerdoodles and the wink of Christmas lights greeted him. And Earl Caine handed him another mug of eggnog.

"Whassa matter, boy?" He cackled. "You lost?"

CHAPTER 4

For someone who grew up primarily in the South, Lila Cook—or Cookie, as her friends often called her these days—enjoyed the snow. She especially liked how the fat, fluffy snowflakes made everything on this scenic mountain road all majestic, like it was somehow pure and new. And as a bonus, the snow wasn't even sticking. She upped the volume on her classic Christmas music channel, feeling wistful for a reason she couldn't quite define.

Maybe this gorgeous drive was her Christmas present this year. Who needed piles of gifts and fattening buffets? No, solitude was what she needed. Crisp, white Christmas peace, boring as it was. She'd earned that, hadn't she?

The brisk ring of her cell phone snapped her out of her thoughts. It was her best friend and former employer, Dr. Kathryn Winslow, whom Lila had driven up from Roanoke to see today. Actually, Lila had been up to see little Ethan, Kathryn's incredibly cute, brand-new baby—the happy result of Kathryn's recent marriage to Hunter Holliday. Never in a million years had Lila thought cool, classy Kathryn Winslow would marry a man like Hunter, who owned a hot rod and auto body shop in the tiny town of Lewisburg, West-by-God Virginia.

Lila's stepfather, Randy, had suffered a massive heart attack the day before Kathryn's wedding nearly two years ago. Though it'd practically killed her to forego her duties as matron of honor, she simply couldn't abandon him during open-heart surgery.

Kathryn had understood her absence, and they remained as close as ever, in spite of living an hour and a half apart. She was glad to make it over here to Lewisburg to see how motherhood was treating her dearest friend.

Admittedly, she'd had her doubts when Kathryn announced she was moving to this mountain valley town. But her friend was happier than she had ever seen her, and who could argue with that?

She pushed the hands-free phone button on her wheel and answered Kathryn's call.

"Hey, Cookie, are you on your way back okay?" Kathryn's voice rang out.

"What, are you worried?"

"I don't like the way this snow is coming down, that's all. Are you sure you want to drive home in all that? We've got plenty of room. You could always stay here."

Considering that she'd just begun her trip across the mountains, she wasn't all that far away from Kathryn's place yet. Lila heard the baby cooing and snuffling on Kathryn's shoulder, and for one weak moment, she was tempted to turn back around. *Ah, those ten tiny fingers and ten tiny toes...*

But she steeled herself. No, she wouldn't intrude on Kathryn and Hunter's first Christmas with the baby. This holiday would be so precious. But sometimes being a fifth wheel at a celebration that important, that intimate, can make you realize all you don't have in your life. And she'd rather spend Christmas counting her blessings, even if those blessings were a quiet, classic-contemporary condo, boxed wine, and a stash of Godiva chocolates she'd been hoarding for the occasion.

Lila did her best to sound breezy. "No, Kathryn, I appreciate the invite, but I've got a nice long, relaxing night ahead. My Christmas movies and fuzzy socks are all set out, and waiting for me. I even have takeout in the fridge. It's gonna be great."

There was a long pause. "*Takeout.* Seriously, Cook?"

"What?" Lila gasped in mock horror. "It's Peking Duck! You can't get more Christmassy than that!"

"Girl, what am I gonna to do with you?" Kathryn drawled, her distinctive Southern rasp dangling somewhere between concern and amusement. "Do you really expect me to enjoy our dinner, knowing that my best friend in the world is probably in a snowy ditch, or *worse,* eating *leftovers* out of some sticky Styrofoam container on Christmas Eve? I can't stand it. I just can't stand it! You need to turn that car around and come back, missy."

Lila let out a long breath. She could practically feel her friend's concern—maybe even her pity—hanging there in the air. She paused. Should she turn back? She considered it, but then visions of her being there intruded, playing the awkward houseguest on Christmas morning when everybody opened their presents. She shuddered.

No. She couldn't. She just couldn't. Her heart squeezed uncomfortably just thinking about it. Most days, Lila loved the independence of her single life. Lord knew she'd fought hard for it, practically crawled across broken glass for it, given her difficult childhood and her uncanny ability to choose difficult men.

But she was *proud* of herself now, and that was no small thing. She'd paid for her education with no loans. And she had a terrific job working as an office manager and medical coder at the psychiatric offices where Kathryn used to practice.

Everything was going to plan. She'd already paid for her condo in full. And that red Audi she was driving? It would be paid off in three months, thanks to her double payments. Her 401K was piling up rather nicely too, thank you very much. Her life may not be exciting, or glamorous, or luxurious, but it was *hers*. She'd done it all on her own.

Yeah, when she faced herself in the mirror, she did it with her head held high. Maybe that's why this creeping sense of dissatisfaction had taken her off guard, tightening around her chest like a boa constrictor from the moment she'd stepped in Kathryn and Hunter's historic family farmhouse. Like a living Rockwell painting, the place was alive with the sights and sounds of an old-fashioned Christmas, from the fresh-cut garlands to the smell of anise cookies in the air. A sprawling red brick Victorian on a fabulous piece of land in foothills of the Alleghenies, the Holliday family homestead had been in Hunter's family for almost two hundred years. And then Hunter had come around the corner with Ethan in his arms...

Dear God, the devotion on that man's face for his wife and child was something to behold. The house hardly seemed big enough to contain all the love that was in it. It was practically in the air itself, wrapping around Kathryn, her husband, and her son in an invisible, unbreakable embrace. Even Wilson, Kathryn's son from her first marriage, seemed under its spell and totally over the moon to have a new little brother.

Yet, Lila couldn't bring herself to be jealous. Kathryn hadn't exactly had a good childhood either, or an easy road to finding this kind of happiness. No one could deserve it more. But being there in Kathryn's cozy family home, seeing all the perfect Christmas decorations and the four matching stockings by the fire...

It made her feel lonely, that's all. It reminded her she'd never find that kind of happiness with a man. After all, she was just a couple of years away from forty, and damaged goods, to say the least. No, the last thing she needed was to be faced with a great big bowl full of what she could never have. No matter how much she loved her girlfriend.

"I'm not turning around, Kathryn. Even when you use your mom voice," she assured her, determined to keep things light. "I can't wait to put up my feet up tonight. It's not up to you to take care of my Christmas. I'm going to have a perfectly nice holiday, and you know it."

"Mm-hmm," Kathryn hummed in a tone so sarcastic she could practically see the woman rolling her eyes. "You're going back to that cold condo without so much as a Christmas candle or cookie in it."

"I'm on a diet. And I'm *fine*. Stop worrying, and enjoy your holiday with your family, Kathryn. You've earned it."

Kathryn grumbled and put up a few more arguments, but Lila was glad to finally get her friend off the phone. Because she realized, all in a sinking, terrible rush, that Kathryn was right. The life she had fought for, that she treasured, was only half a life. She *really was* going back to a cold, empty condo.

In every way that really mattered, she was truly, profoundly alone. No one had ever looked at her the way Hunter looked at Kathryn.

Well, that wasn't *exactly* true.

Lila believed she'd had that kind of love. Once.

Back before she'd been "Cookie" Cook. Back before she'd changed her name. Back when a beautiful, beautiful man had woken her with kisses, and stroked her hair, and called her by her real name—Delilah. *Delilah Jones.*

Hopper had loved her. He'd never said it directly, but she could feel his love almost like a tangible thing—had felt it down deep in her soul. Or at least, she thought she had.

God, *Hopper Vance…*

Even now, she had to blink back tears when his face came to mind. All these years later, and you'd think she'd at least have the good grace to be angry with the man. Her mind drifted to memories of him more often than she'd like to admit. And thinking about him always hurt.

She and Hopper had practically grown up with each other, being each other's rock when times were tough. When they'd finally became lovers, and a strong committed couple, it had felt fated. *Right*. But Hopper hadn't been the man she'd thought he was. Had he ever told her anything that was true? He'd lied to her about everything—who he was, how he'd earned his money, and the crowds he'd run with, for starters. In many ways, he'd hidden his whole life from her, probably to protect her from getting sucked into his criminal schemes.

But had his touch lied too? Had his eyes lied when he'd looked at her as if she were the whole world, right there in his arms? And why the hell should it even matter? In the end, he'd pushed her away in no uncertain terms. No, she could do a lot better than stupid, misguided fantasies about Hopper Vance.

She sighed. Must be the Christmas season. It was making her weak.

Yeah, she was glad true love worked out for other people. But it wasn't for the likes of her. Not anymore.

She gripped her hands a bit tighter on the wheel and set her jaw as she wound down the road. No, she'd be charting her own course in this big world, and she'd be glad of it.

Just then, she came up on a cardboard sign on the side of the road with an intriguing message scrawled in red paint: *Make a Christmas tradition of your own. Buy a fresh cut wreath! Caine's Christmas Outpost, this way.*

Bit of a weird slogan, wasn't it? And yet, something about that funny sign grabbed her.

Lila slowed the car, giving in to the impulse to turn down the snowy gravel road and follow where the sign led. She almost never did anything like this anymore, did she—something fun and unexpected? But somehow, that silly sign made her feel like breaking her own rules and doing some holiday buying just for herself.

She wasn't much in the mood for a big tree or ornaments she'd have to store. But a nice fresh wreath would be perfect —not as messy as a tree, but enough to make her whole condo smell like pine. Maybe she'd even get a couple of Christmas candles, and cookies too if they had them. Like the sign said, she'd make her own holiday traditions. Who needed a family for that? Maybe this shopping excursion was just the adventure she needed, after all.

The ride may have been long and bumpy, but when she finally came to a stop in front of this crazy Christmas Outpost, Lila knew she'd come to the right place. The shop was darling, an adorable, almost idealized country store. And the Outpost was stuffed to the rafters with Christmas goodies. In no time at all, she'd picked out their biggest wreath, one with a pretty red silk bow, as well as apple-cinnamon candles, a jumbo box of white-chocolate-covered Oreos, and a bag of holiday blend potpourri. She'd even made friends with the country-fried couple who ran the place, Earl and Candy Caine. By the time she'd checked out with all her finds, she had actually managed to gin up a heaping helping of the warm Christmas fuzzies. Maybe this holiday wouldn't be so bad, after all.

With Earl running off to load the packages in her car, Lila turned to Candy. "Thank you so much for staying open today for late shoppers like me. I'll bet this is really starting to bite into your Christmas Eve plans."

Candy waved away her concerns. "Nah, not really. That's what we do, me n' Earl, we stay open for all the people who are lost."

Lost? Lila was taken aback by that strange statement, and couldn't shake uncanny feeling Candy was aiming that at *her* somehow. "Why would you think I'm lost? I mean, I just live over the mountains in Roanoke. It's one right hand turn and it's a straight shot to—"

"Whatever you say, hon," Candy broke in. "Doesn't matter anyhow. You can't leave until you pick out a free gift from that tree over there."

Lila protested that she didn't need a thing and the gifts were better left for someone else. But Candy was insistent there was a gift under that tree just for her and "only her." Finally, she sighed and gave in. The woman was sweet in her grizzled, hardened way. How could she say no? Her mama hadn't raised her to be rude.

Doing as she was told, Lila stepped over to the tree and inspected the gifts. They were so beautiful—all professionally done up with shiny foil wraps and hand-tied silk ribbons. But one box immediately caught her eye. The present was long and big, but it was wrapped with cheap, snowman-covered paper. The sight of it made her nostalgic for her younger, cash-strapped days, when she'd wrapped everything in flimsy dollar-store wrap. Maybe this would be one of the more inexpensive things under the tree. She should probably choose this one and leave the nicer things for someone else.

"I'll take this," she decided, turning to show the lady.

Candy's grin was full of mischief. "Aww, would you look at that? Goin' back to basics, aren't 'cha? Well, seeing as how it's Christmas Eve already, why don't you go on and open it?"

Lila almost insisted that she'd open it at home. But somehow, that didn't seem right. Candy was clearly excited to see her open it. So, she tore off the wrap, cracked open the lid, and...*gasped.*

A used motorcycle jacket laid inside. A black one, though age had made it more of a weathered charcoal gray. Men's size medium. She pulled it out of the box and held it up in front of her.

The same studded flaps that could be pulled up into a collar. The same black-and-white striped lining.

God, it was just like…

Just like the one she'd worn a lifetime ago. *Hopper's old jacket*—the one he'd given her when he'd grown out of it, saying, "You need it more than I do." The ratty old thing had been beaten down and broken up, and was way too big for her, of course. But it had been rugged and dear, and nothing else had felt like it when it'd been wrapped around her.

Her eyes misted up, a flood of the sweetest emotions pouring over her as she held the jacket in her hands. God, the feel, the smell of that time-worn leather. Was there anything better?

What a strange, uncanny coincidence. This jacket even had nicks all up the left sleeve—just like the ones Hopper had gotten when he'd fallen off his bike and onto gravel. *How odd.* Her breath caught and her head buzzed as the realization crept over her. This couldn't be the same jacket—like, Hopper's *actual* jacket—could it? She inspected the inside collar. Two letters had been written on the tag—H.V.

H—*oh my freaking God*—V.

"Where did you get this?" Lila choked out, her throat too thick to press out more than a whisper.

But before Candy could answer her, a terrible racket of banging and pounding erupted at the store's front door."Well damn," Candy shrugged. "Door must be stuck again. Could you answer that, sugar?"

Too numb to do anything else, Lila went to the door. It was stuck. But after a few jiggles and yanks, the door flew open in her hands.

And what she saw on the other side made her scream with shock. Because standing there in the doorway was a very young, very drenched Hopper Vance.

And he was wearing a beat-up black moto jacket.

CHAPTER 5

TEENAGE HOPPER HELD up his hands in surrender. "I'm sorry I scared you. Would you mind letting me in? It's awful wet out here."

Struck dumb in disbelief and alarm, Lila didn't know what else to do but step aside. Dimly, she began to realize that nothing was as it had been just a second before. The fluffy snowflakes and pretty mountain vistas were gone, replaced with the black of night and a mean, cold winter's rainstorm. She recognized the mid-century modern concrete porch just outside immediately. It was from the modest two-bedroom house she'd shared with her mama and stepfather Randy in Douglasville, Georgia. Still amazed, she realized the door handle she held in her hand was connected to Randy's door too. She even recognized the Christmas wreath hanging there—a homemade number she'd made entirely from origami cranes as a teen.

She spun around, shock hijacking every single one of her senses. The Outpost was gone.

Gone.

Somehow, some way, she was standing in Randy's living room. There was the same micro-suede beige couch with the

Atlanta Falcons throw over the back. The same Walmart area rug. The same family pictures. The same hooks to hold the car keys…

She caught her reflection in the mirror hanging near the front door and very nearly screamed. Because *she* was transformed too. *Dear God in heaven.* She touched her hand to her face, taking in her long, wild tangle of curly, jet-black hair, set over oily skin in bad need of the right skin treatment. Looking down at her clothes, she forced herself not to groan at the holey sweatpants and a baggy, paint-splattered T-shirt —her idea of loungewear at the time. God, how old was she? *Fourteen?*

Whipping back around, she half expected Hopper to evaporate, along with this whole weird hallucination. But the poor boy stood dutifully just inside the door, rain still dripping off his sodden clothes. He couldn't have been much more than sixteen himself. Hopper slicked back his long, shaggy mane of wet, black hair with his hand. And then those unmistakable, unforgettable blue eyes met hers. Butterflies erupted in her stomach, still.

God! How is this even possible?

Am I being forced to relive my past or something?

Because there was no doubt about it—this was most definitely *her past*. Oh yes, she'd remember this moment, to her dying day. Because this was the first time she'd laid eyes on Hopper Vance. And damn if he didn't take her breath away, all over again.

He was *beautiful,* if such a thing could be said about a teenage boy. This young Hopper was tall and lean, but in him she could see the clear promise of the man he'd become, with a strong, broad jaw and high cheekbones, wide shoulders, and the start of a line of stubble on his jaw. And oh, those eyes—the color of a clear summer sky, with a searching, intense quality that seemed to see her, right down to the bone, even at this age. He wore his usual uniform of faded jeans and a gray V-neck T-shirt that clung to his chest, revealing a ripple of lean muscle and the curve of his collar-bone. Lila thought about all the times those strong arms would wrap around her, all the times she'd kiss those lips in the future, cursing herself as she swallowed against her dry throat.

Hopper gave her a respectful nod. "I'm here to see Randy. He told me to come. Could you tell him Hopper Vance is here?"

"Yeah," she croaked, then cleared her throat. "I-I'll just go find him." Lila scurried away, tipping her head to hide her face under her hair, just like she used to do at that age. Except now it was to hide how overwhelmed she was. *Sweet Christ, how could this be happening?*

She quickly deduced that Randy was in the bedroom he shared with Mama. And the clock in the hall said it was only seven o'clock in the evening. She almost opened the door right up but decided to knock softly. "Randy? You in there? Hopper Vance is here to see you."

After a couple of seconds, the door finally opened a crack. Randy peeked through, and the sight rocked her back on her heels. She'd forgotten how tired he'd been back then. How wrecked and worried. "Ah, I wondered how long it would take the boy to come. Tell him I'll be out in a few minutes. You know how it is after the nurse leaves. Those treatments kick your mother's ass. I just want to make sure she's alright."

Lila nodded. But she wouldn't say what she already knew. That her mama wouldn't be alright. She quietly closed the door, and ran a shaking hand through her hair. Had she died and gone to purgatory or something? Why in the world would she be doomed to come back here—back to live through Mama dying of breast cancer, all over again?

Lila struggled to breathe against the hard knot of misery forming in her stomach, desperate to let it go as she padded back up the hallway to the living room. Someone or something was trying to torture her. *Why why why* was she here? There wasn't much that had gone unsaid or undone with her mother. She'd accepted Mama's death and release from the pain. Mama had too.

Did all this have something to do with the Outpost? Was Candy responsible for this somehow? If she was, the two of them were going to have words. *Oh-ho-ho yes* they were.

It was like she was in some kind of freaky time warp, trapped in a *Twilight Zone* episode. Was this like *Groundhog Day*, or *Scrooge* or something, where she had to go back in time to learn some kind of lesson from her past? But how did that make any sense? At this point, it would've been far too late at this point to "fix" her mother's cancer.

As she walked back into the living room, she was struck all over again by the sight of Hopper, standing there with his army surplus rucksack, dripping rainwater onto the hardwood. He straightened up his shoulders when she approached, his face guarded, but expectant.

Was *he* the reason she was here? Regrets, after all, were the hallmark of their relationship. The fact that the jacket she'd been holding just moments ago was on his back should probably be her first clue.

Look at him. He was soaked to the skin. And young—*God,* he was so young. How long had Hopper been out in that freezing rain? His jeans looked like they were stuck to him.

"Randy's ummm…busy helping my mom," Lila finally managed to say. "He said he'd be out in a bit."

"It's nice to meet you," Hopper nodded, holding out his hand for her to shake. "What's your name?"

Lila blinked and stared down at his hand, realizing that at this moment in time, she was a stranger to him. "I'm Delilah Jones," she answered him, trying not to let her voice shake. "But everybody calls me Lila."

Hopper cocked his head for a moment, grinning until she finally remembered herself, and placed her hand in his. "A pretty name, Delilah. Can I call you that instead? I don't want to be like everybody else."

Oh Hopper, you could never be like anybody else, she wanted to say. But Lila simply nodded, unable to get out the words.

There it was again, that zing when Hopper touched her, and that fluttery feeling hit her right in the stomach, whether she wanted it to or not. He held on to her hand far longer than he needed to. And that made her happy and lightheaded and somehow furious, all at once, rolling over her in a hot, itchy wave. Jesus, this was more than she could even process...old desire mixed together with pain and longing. And then there was the matter of being an adult, trapped in a child's body, with all those indecent memories feverishly rushing through her mind.

Honest to God, how am I supposed to act in this situation?

With a start, she realized she'd been standing here all this time, holding his hand, staring at him as if he might suddenly evaporate into thin air. Hopper finally pulled back a bit sheepishly, and she wiped her hand on her pants, feeling her cheeks burn.

"Uh, I'm—I'm making a mess here." He winced. "Is there a bathroom where I can change into some dry clothes?"

"Oh! Of-of course!" Lila walked him down the hall, kicking herself for not directing him there already. Grabbing a stack of clean towels from the linen closet, she got him set up in the tiny pink-tiled bathroom. When he shut the door, she groaned. "Holy crap," she muttered, sinking back against the wall.

This was more than she could handle. But Lila was struck by two things in this ridiculous situation: one, that she could still be so relentlessly attracted to Hopper, and two, how vulnerable and young the boy appeared.

When she was younger, she'd known he'd needed a job and a place to stay. But seeing him now...

He was truly desperate and alone, wasn't he? Yet even

here, at his lowest point, she could catch the outlines of the man he'd become—the flinty resolve and raw sensuality that'd follow him into his adult years. And she was still right there, falling into the same trap again.

Which brought her sailing right back to her original question: *why in the hell am I here?* There had to be a lesson in this, somewhere.

For lack of a better idea, she simply did next what she knew she had done back then. She'd made the boy a sandwich. While she waited for Hopper to emerge, she hurried to the kitchen and fished out the Christmas ham. She smiled when she found a loaf of homemade bread. This year, she'd made the whole Christmas spread herself, bread included. She'd done all the cooking and cleaning, in fact, while Mama had been sick. And she'd been more than glad to do so. Lila sliced off two thick, fluffy pieces and made a nice, supersized sandwich with all the fixins. And she set to work making hot chocolate on the stove.

By the time Hopper emerged in a clean, dry pair of jeans and a black T-shirt, she'd had everything spread out on the table, ready for him.

Hopper ambled into the kitchen and blinked with surprise. "Is that for me?"

"Yeah." Lila shrugged. "Thought you might be hungry."

Hopper grimaced for a second, like he might argue, but finally admitted, "I am. This may be the most delicious sandwich I've ever seen." He started stuffing it in his mouth before he'd even fully sat down. And the boy plowed into the food like he hadn't eaten in days. Maybe he hadn't. The thought made her gut twist in sympathy for him. Again, dammit. She poured the piping hot chocolate into a mug for him. Hopper groaned as he took his first drink. "Oh, this is really good. Did you make this with real milk or something?"

"Yeah." She snorted. "What's the matter, you never had hot chocolate before?"

"I've never had hot chocolate that didn't come from a gas station or a packet. This is, like, freakin' ambrosia." He hummed into his cup and took another long swig. Lila blushed from the compliment, but the confession made her feel a ping of sadness for him. Hopper had been such a fixture in her life. But he was a mystery she'd never unraveled. Could she even guess what had happened to him, before he'd come to her?

Hopper sat down his empty mug and considered her as he ate. "Randy's your dad?"

"Stepdad," Lila answered. "But he's like a real dad to me. He and Mom just got married this past year."

"He wants me to work for him in his body shop."

Lila could tell he wanted to learn more about the job, so she decided to use it as a chance to get more information out of him. She'd ask him some questions she'd been too shy and stupid to ask before. "He's a good man. And he could use the help. You got any experience?"

Hopper's eyes got round. "With what?"

"With *cars.*"

He shifted uncomfortably in his seat. "Yeah. Some."

"Where are you from, Hopper?"

Hopper flinched, as if he was at a loss for how to answer her. "A little bit of everywhere," he finally answered. "I moved around a lot as a kid. I'm on my own these days."

"Where were you born?"

"New Orleans, I think," he answered, chewing thoughtfully. That surprised her. He'd never told her that before. But his Southern accent was thicker than people's around here, so it made sense.

"You a Cajun?"

He polished off his sandwich and swallowed hastily. "Don't know. Doubt it. It was just another stopping place for my dad."

"What does he do for a living? Where is he?"

Hopper averted his eyes, a lost expression playing over his features, just for a second. "Anything that would pay," he answered her, simply, quietly. "Don't know where he's at. Don't care, either."

Just those three sentences were more than she'd ever been able to get him to say about his roots. And it was enough to make her remember why she'd never pushed. It was plain to see—whatever had happened to him had cut deep.

Uncomfortable now, Lila shifted her gaze to the floor and twirled a long strand of hair around her finger. "Yeah, I've moved around a lot too." She sighed because it was true. Her mother had moved them all over the Atlanta area while she'd done one low-wage job after another. Moving in with Randy had brought some stability to her young life, for the first time.

Stability. The idea picked at her. Maybe that was the reason she and Hopper had bonded so completely. They'd both needed that stability. Desperately. And they'd given it to each other all those years ago, hadn't they?

In Randy's house, the living room opened up to the kitchen and dining area. And Hopper took a minute to let his gaze travel around the space as he sipped his drink. "I like your decorations." He nodded over to the Christmas tree sitting in the living room.

She couldn't help but smile at the sight of it. The poor little tree was kinda pitiful, but she'd made it pretty, anyway. Randy had brought home a live tree for her. But after so many years of bachelorhood, he'd never bought decorations. With everything they'd had going on with her mama's care, she hadn't wanted ask the man to spend more money on the project. So she'd made her own. Construction paper garlands. Ornaments made out of pinecones, old buttons, and sugar cookies she'd baked. She'd found a galvanized aluminum bucket to hold it steady, and she'd jazzed it up with stencils. "Thanks. It's homemade, but I like it."

"You painted the scenes on the windows too? The sleigh full of people and all?"

She nodded.

"Wow." He whistled. "You're good. Like, really, really good."

Lila took a moment to consider the mural she'd painted on Randy's big picture window. It really was pretty elaborate, wasn't it? At the time, she'd been frustrated that she hadn't gotten the proportion right between the sprawling Victorian mansion on the hill and the children making snowmen and skating below it. But the detail and the joy in it couldn't be mistaken. And the pride on Mama's face when she'd seen it all? Well, that had made her feel like Leonardo DaVinci.

Funny how Hopper could still make her feel like that shy, fourteen-year-old girl at first. But as they began to talk, they fell easily into conversation like old friends. How she'd missed that. They talked about art, oddly enough, something they'd never really discussed before, at least on an intellectual level. Though he said he couldn't draw himself, Hopper loved the old masters, Vermeer and Rubens particularly, and even the modern artists Lichtenstein and Dali. He could even recall the names of specific paintings she'd studied in their unit on art history. It was shocking, really, for a sixteen-year-old boy who appeared more likely to sneak out to a biker bar than to spend his time in the library, reading coffee-table books on art history.

Why had they never discussed this before? All the times he'd seen her draw, and he'd never said anything? She wished she would've realized he liked art books. She'd worked at a thrift store her whole senior year. She could've bought them for him for pennies, and she would have too.

"Do you get good grades, Hopper?" she blurted out. It was another thing she'd never learned about him.

He raised his eyebrows as he sat back in his chair, smirking.

She bit her lip, suddenly embarrassed. "I-I'm sorry. I shouldn't have—"

"What's the matter?" He flashed her a lopsided, self-deprecating smile. "You only talk to the smart guys?"

"No, it's not that. It's just that...well...you seem like you do."

"Do what?" he whispered conspiratorially, leaning in to steal a cookie, and take a bite.

Oh...that bad boy vibe. He can't help it, can he? "Get good grades." She giggled a little and shoved at his arm. "You seem way too smart to get bad ones. I've never met a guy who's smart enough to actually understand Salvatore Dali. Even the guys in my class."

That comment seemed to please him. A lot. He straightened up in his seat, blushing. "I get good grades. When I can."

Lila decided she wouldn't push. Instead, she changed tactics. "How do you know you can't draw? Did you ever take an art class?"

"Just the standard stuff in grade school. But I took a sculpture class. Once." He sighed. "Had to leave in the middle of the semester, though. Moved."

"Did you like it?"

He cocked his head, considering that. "Yeah. I did, actually. Better than drawing. I think it's the putting things in three dimensions and working with my hands part that I liked. It's cool building things and making art useful."

Lila nodded, his admission choking her up a bit. There was a boy who could've been an architect or an industrial product designer. He had so much potential. Why had he never used it?

He got up and dutifully took his dishes to the sink. "So," he called back over his shoulder. "You going to show me your stuff or what?"

All the blood seemed to rush to Lila's face at once. "My-my *what?*"

Hopper turned around and chuckled. "Your *art*. Are you going to show me your *art?*"

Dear Lord. What a Freudian misunderstanding on her part. Cringing with both adolescent *and* adult shame, she went to the living room shelf where she'd always kept her art stash and retrieved her latest sketchbook. She set it down gently on the kitchen table.

Waiting silently, she observed him as he sat down again and began flipping through the pages. And there it was. His eyes lit up with amazement, just like they always had when he'd seen her drawings. Warmth bloomed through her—a sense of recognition, of one person seeing another person's light and being moved by it. How long had it been since she'd felt that?

The tablet in front of him was filled mostly with landscapes, and some close-ups of simple things like seashells or flowers that she'd copied from photos. There was nothing special about her style, really. She didn't have the kind of artistic insight that would make her a great artist. But she did have a pretty good sense of form, and the ability to capture the essence of a thing, even back then.

"You ever thought about being an artist?" Hopper asked her, snapping her out of her thoughts.

"Me?" Lila scoffed. "Oh, no. I could never."

Hopper fixed those perceptive eyes on her again. "Why not?"

He'd asked her that question before, in another day and time. She gave him the same answer she'd given him then. "If I did art for a living someday, then that puts pressure on it. I'd have to do the kind of art people would buy and worry about how much of it I sold. Or I'd have to teach other people how to do it. And I don't want to do that. I want my drawings to be just for me."

"But you showed them to *me*, didn't you?"

She gave him a shy nod, wishing she could give him a

more articulate response. But she didn't want to get into a big discussion about it. Truth was, Hopper was one of only a very small handful of people who even knew she could draw. And she'd *loved* to draw. In particular, she'd loved how Hopper had always made her feel when she'd shown him a finished piece—like he saw and understood. How long had it been since she'd picked up a pencil or watercolor brush? Twenty years? Had that stubborn creative spark in her really gone out?

She felt ridiculous all of a sudden. Had she really let her life grind all the originality out of her? The thought shocked her. Had she changed that much? She still had that sketchbook—one of only a few remaining of mementos she'd kept. How long had it been since she'd taken it out, and let herself remember? Not just Hopper, but her mother? Her young life? It was as if she'd been in such a hurry to get to her destination, she'd forgotten where she'd started. Maybe even why she'd started…

Hopper stopped dead center in the middle of the sketchbook, holding out a picture of a house she'd drawn. "Where is this place?" he asked, tapping the page.

Lila blushed. "It's-it's nowhere."

"Ah." He tapped his finger on his temple. "It's all up here, isn't it?"

Lila swallowed, not sure how comfortable she was to see him rifling through her teenaged dreams. The drawing was a picture of a fantasy house she'd concocted. The picture didn't even show a whole house, even. In the foreground was part of a white picket fence with a rose arbor arching over the entry to the yard. The arbor was bursting with fat red blooms. The house she'd drawn was no grand castle or anything. It was a simple, homey bungalow—one of the kind probably built in the 1930s or 40s, with a big, welcoming front porch that spanned the whole front of the house. In the distance, a girl sat propped against a porch column, one bare leg dangling over the side of the porch wall as she read a book. Hair obscured the girl's face, and her feet were dusty from walking barefoot in the yard.

"That girl." He stared for a moment, then pointed at the page. "She's you, isn't she? And this place, it's where you are when you need to get away, isn't it?"

Lila gasped, suddenly feeling the need to put the sketchbook away. She grabbed it out of his hands and pulled it to her chest.

Hopper hadn't said that to her before, even though he'd seen that drawing, many times. Was that something he'd always thought but had never had the courage to ask? She hadn't even realized it at the time. But the boy was right. She'd needed the escape that sketchbook offered, and the pretty, impossible worlds she could create in it.

Rather than be offended at her grabbing the book back, he gave her a soft, understanding smile. "Someday you'll have roses growing over your sidewalk and a neighborly porch. You'll have a house just like that, Delilah, and everything you've ever wanted. You'll see."

Lila snorted out a laugh. "As if."

When she looked into Hopper's eyes again, she realized he truly meant it. But it was just another dream.

CHAPTER 6

Randy came walking back down the hall, putting an end to their conversation. As he stepped into the light, she couldn't help but notice his harried expression and the bags under his eyes. Her heart swelled in appreciation for that man.

Randy wasn't particularly handsome, really. He stood about five foot seven. Mousy brown hair. Ruddy complexion. He had a bit of a ferret face and a little pot belly. His hands were a scarred mess from his work as a mechanic, and his fingernails were bitten down to the nibs. Yet, none of that mattered. In Lila's mind, he was Prince Gallahad, the man whose love had truly saved her mother. He'd been in love with Mama since their days together in high school, unrequited, of course. They'd been childhood friends. Mama had been the pretty, popular one back then, and Randy hadn't been. But when he'd taken her and Lila in at their lowest, most desperate point? He'd never hesitated. He'd married her and had given them both more care than anyone could've asked for.

Even today, after Randy had remarried, he still considered himself her dad. And he was, actually. He'd adopted her after Mama had died, to keep her from going into foster care.

And that had suited her. Still did, in fact. Her birth father had never been part of her life. Mama had always been a strong, independent single woman. She'd taken her father's name to the grave. But that was okay. Because in the end, Mama had given her Randy.

As an adult, she saw Randy all the time. But there was something about seeing the man like *this,* at *this* point in time, that made her heart squeeze painfully. All he'd been through up to this point...all he'd go through... She'd forgotten, hadn't she? She'd forgotten that a man could be such a rock.

"Oh good," Randy nodded when he saw her talking to Hopper. "I see you've been entertaining Mr. Vance here. We've got to be nice to our distinguished guest. I hope you fed him something."

"I did," Lila answered.

"Delilah's quite a cook." Hopper smiled over at her. "You're lucky."

"Yes, we are." Mama's voice rang out down the hall. "I don't know how we'd manage around here without her." Her slippers scuffed on the tile as she shuffled into the light of the kitchen.

Mama...

Another ache in her heart...another kick to the stomach. Lila swallowed hard, trying not to fall to pieces right here. Seeing her mother like this was almost more than she could bear.

Mama was dressed for comfort, of course, wearing faded Christmas leggings and an oversized V-neck T-shirt that exposed the chemo port still dangling from her chest. Oh, she was a sight—a pale, scary version of herself—with a silk scarf tied around her bald head, and her eyes all hollowed out and dark. Mama was smiling, though, and for just a moment, Lila could visualize the model-perfect beauty she used to possess—the long, wavy dark hair, the perfect curves…

God, how she missed her.

Randy turned around and scowled. "What are you doing up? The nurse told you to nap!"

"Nap, schnap," she replied. "I'm coming to get myself something to drink. The doctor hasn't banned me from tea too, has he? Besides, I've got a stack of movies to get through before they have to go back to the library."

"Here let me," Lila offered, jumping up to get the glass. She quickly found the pitcher in the fridge and poured her mama a tall glass of her favorite—sweet tea with a splash of lemon juice. Her heart throbbed painfully in her chest as Mama took a grateful sip. Lila's brain buzzed with all the things she wanted to say to her. But her mouth felt like it was full of sand. "You want me to come back there and keep you company?" she finally managed.

"No, just need some downtime," Mama replied, doing her best to sound like everything was all peaches and cream. She stopped and studied Lila, reaching out to pat her arm. "You sure there's nothing wrong, sweetie? You act like you've seen a ghost."

Lila almost sobbed. But she bit her lip. Mama would be dead in about eighteen months. Everything was wrong about this, wasn't it? Still, Lila managed a smile. "No, Mama. I was just thinking that I love you so much."

Mama smiled back fondly. "I love you too, peanut." She turned and shambled off down the hall. Lila watched her take every mincing step until the bedroom door snicked shut.

Randy indicated he wanted Hopper to come out onto the covered porch with him so they could talk over the particulars of working at the garage. "I'm obliged to you, Delilah." Hopper bowed in her direction. "That sandwich sure hit the spot. I hope I see you around."

Lila inclined her head and tried not to smile like a lovesick puppy. And Hopper left the room, Randy trailing along behind him.

When the door clattered shut, Lila let out a long, shuddering breath. *What in the world is all this?* But she didn't have time to think on all that, because Candy appeared by her side, somehow materializing in a haze of red-and-green glitter.

"Goddammit!" Lila squealed, quickly stuffing her hands over her mouth. She'd practically jumped out of her skin. "I can't take another shock, Candy."

The old woman cackled. "Relax. They can't hear or see you now."

And yet, Lila was still "out of time." They were still standing in Randy's kitchen. And Lila was still a gangly, pimply kid in second-hand sweatpants.

And this old bitty actually had the brass to tell her to relax? *Relax?*

Honestly, if the woman wasn't so old, Lila would've punched her in the face. "What kind of sadistic shit is this?" she spat. "Who are you? And for God's sake—why am I here?"

Candy crossed her arms over her chest, looking indignant. "The more important question is why do you *need* to be here? Me n' Earl are only called for people who really need it."

"Need it? *Need it?* I was doing just fine before!"

Candy rolled her eyes. "Obviously."

"How *dare* you." Lila glowered. "Who the hell are you, to be judge and jury of my life? And how can you do all—" she waved her arms around, *"—this?"*

"Aw now," the woman clucked. "Don't you go getting your panties all in a bunch. When you walked into the door at The Outpost, you walked into a place out of time. A place you can't get out of until you've found what you were missing.

We probably should call the place Stuckey's. Cause we get people unstuck. Me n' Earl? Just consider us your guides."

"Oh, I am *not* stuck, thank you very much. I've had some tough things happen to me, but I've moved forward. I've built a life for myself. So you can just let me out now. *Right* now."

Candy cackled again. "Well, bless your heart. It's not up to me to let you out. Only you can do that. I'm not the one still livin' in the past, girly girl. You are."

She let out an outraged squawk. "I am most certainly *not* living in the past!"

"Really?" Candy snorted. "When was the last time you kissed a man?"

"That's beside the point! And besides, if I'm not supposed to be living in the past, can you please explain to me why I'm here? *Actually* living in the past?"

"Ah, but you're not. Don't you see? You've asked the questions you were afraid to ask before. You and Hopper had a whole different conversation than you did first time around. People often say, *if only I knew then what I know now*. But I'm here to tell you, if you only knew now what you should've known then. Let me tell ya, honey, that'd change some things."

Lila just stared at the woman, mute with rage. Did she really think all that cryptic crap was an explanation?

Candy tsked. "Sweet child, you may think you know everything there is to know about all your heartbreaks. But you don't even know the half of it. And that makes all the difference."

"What is this, then? Some kind of messed-up Christmas story with magical elves teaching me the meaning of Christmas?"

The woman just grinned and gave her a patronizing pat on her shoulder. "Your words, buttercup, not mine. So you'd better get to work. And by the way, don't go calling Earl an elf. He'll take offense."

Incredulous, and absolutely smokin' mad, Lila started rushing all the doors. She'd get her own self out of here, all right. One of these doors had to open back into her life—her real life. She tried the front door, the back door, a few windows. But none of them would open. Lila frantically rushed from room to room. But Candy just popped a hip against the kitchen table and observed, calm as you please as she charged past her.

Realizing the futility of the situation, Lila slowed. There were no more doors, no more options. She was screwed—a prisoner in this crazy crone's melodrama. *Dammit to hell...*

Lila stood in the kitchen, chest heaving. "You're enjoying this, aren't you?" She moaned.

"Nah. Just letting you wear yourself out." Candy sighed. "Are you gonna stand there all day with your teeth in your mouth, or you gonna get this over with? Stop fightin' it. The only door you need to go into is that one." Candy pointed to the door to the sunporch.

Lila threw up her hands. "I can't go out there! They said they wanted to have a private conversation!"

"They won't be able to see or hear you. Go on." Candy nodded.

Lila stared balefully at the door, but finally screwed up the courage to open it. But her hand passed right through the doorknob, flickering as if it were a projection.

What in the world?

As if this day couldn't get any stranger...

She turned back to Candy, but the woman just waved her hand at her, urging her to literally *walk through* the door. Muttering prayers in her head, Lila pushed her foot out, and to her amazement, actually slid right through the door. She nearly landed right on Randy's back, and the man had no idea. Recoiling, she tiptoed off into the corner.

Hopper turned to face Randy and pulled himself up to his

full height. "You told me before you might have a job. That still true?"

Randy stuck his hands in his pockets and narrowed his eyes. "Maybe. You sixteen?"

"Yeah. Got a driver's license to prove it. I'll be seventeen in a couple of months."

"Got any experience workin' on cars?"

"Some," Hopper answered, shifting nervously on his feet.

"I'd say it's a lot more than some. By my estimates, you picked the lock and hot-wired my customer's car in under three minutes."

"You can't prove that!"

"Can't I?" Randy pulled out a CD case from the pocket of his hoodie. "That car you broke into was on my lot—a lot that's supposed to be safe. You think I don't have security cameras on that lot? I've got it all right here, nice and handy to give to the police."

Hopper paled. "I wasn't planning to steal it. I just wanted to warm it up so I could sleep in it overnight. I'm new in town and I didn't have enough money to rent out a place—not before I got a job, anyway. I never intended to take it off the lot. I *swear.*"

Randy crossed his arms over his chest. "Well, I guess we'll never know. Since I caught you first and all."

"And I came back here today, just like you asked." Hopper squared his shoulders and held his ground. "I could have run off and never come back."

Randy appeared to be weighing his options as he looked Hopper over. And to his credit, Hopper stared right back at him. "You a runaway?" he asked.

"Not exactly."

"Okay." Randy paused. "Let me put it this way. Is anyone out there wondering where you are? You got people, friends or someone you can go to?"

Hopper chuckled ruefully. "No. There's no one who wants me. I'm on my own. So, can we just cut to the chase here? I'm too young for the military. I'm *not* going into foster care. I'm *not* camping out in the middle of winter. And I'm sure as shit not going into another shelter. So stop playing around and just give it to me straight—do you have a job opening here or not? Because if you don't, I need to keep walkin' until I find one."

Randy nodded slowly, still fixing the boy with a steely, assessing glare. Another person might have concluded that Hopper had offended the man. But Lila knew that expression. It was grudging respect. "What kind of belongings have you got—just what's in the bag?"

"That's right." He turned his head from the man, squinting at the yard outside the screened porch.

"So you're homeless then. And you've been homeless for a while."

Hopper didn't answer. A tick worked in his jaw.

Randy let the statement hang in the air. But when he could see he wouldn't get anything else out of the boy, he let out a long breath. Then he walked over to a potted plastic Christmas tree Lila had used to decorate the back porch. He bent down and pulled a red ribbon off the tree, wrapped it around the CD case, and tied it in a bow. "Here," he said, handing it to a very surprised Hopper. "I believe when a man is down, you give him a hand up. So that's what I'm doin'. This disc has the only copy of the footage. It's yours."

Hopper curled his fingers around the disc, his teenaged brinksmanship disappearing. He flagged, seeming for a second like he might collapse in relief. Lila's heart swelled in gratitude for her stepfather. She'd had no idea any of this had occurred at the time. But it didn't surprise her. It was just like Randy, always taking in strays. He'd done it for her and Mama, hadn't he?

"Consider it my Christmas gift to you. Don't make me regret it. I got a one-time offer, take it or leave it. I need an extra pair of hands at the shop—someone who's willing to come in early and work late. I'll take you on as an apprentice at two dollars above minimum wage. I'll train you up in whatever you need. You can live above the shop for nothin'. It ain't much, but I've got a studio apartment up there with furniture that's not too terrible. After that, if you do good, I'll bump you up to eight dollars an hour above minimum wage, and you can live anywhere you please. We have a deal?"

Hopper looked at Randy like he was drowning and the man had thrown him a life preserver. She supposed he had. It was an incredibly generous offer. At that price, Randy could have easily found someone trained and ready to go. But her stepdad had never been one to take the easy way…

Honestly, this whole weird, magical, screwed-up trip was really doing a number on her. Lila found herself standing there with a lump in her throat as Hopper thanked Randy and shook his hand. The boy tried to hide it, but overwhelming relief was written plainly on his face. What kind of situation had Hopper been in? How long had he been living out of a sleeping bag?

Just thinking about it made her heart hurt. She turned to Candy. "I didn't realize he'd been homeless. He never said."

Candy's expression softened a bit at that, seeming sympathetic, for once. "Come on, child," she murmured, holding out her hand to her. Reflexively, Lila took it. With a sickening lurch, she and Candy stepped back into the Outpost—and back into her thirty-eight-year-old body.

The transition made her stagger a step, and collapse in the nearest chair.

"Girl." Candy clucked. "I think you need some more nog."

CHAPTER 7

HOPPER SKIDDED TO A HALT, blinking in surprise at Earl. Maybe he really was lost. "How did— What— How did I get back here?" he wailed. "I was just—"

Earl clucked his tongue. "You were gettin' too involved, trying to change the past, boy, and that's not allowed."

Hopper took a couple of stomping steps and scrubbed his hands over his face, so angry he hardly knew what to do. "What in God's name was all that? *You*. You were the one who made that...whatever that—"

"Hold on." Earl cut him off. "That 'whatever' you're talkin' about was your doin'. Not mine. You're the one who walked into this magical place. And you're the one whose memories took you back into your lost love's arms."

Hopper just stared at the man, too stunned to speak.

"Come on." Earl gave him a grandfatherly pat on the shoulder. "No one on heaven or earth can change the past. Don't you understand that? You're in a place out of time, a place where you can play around and relive moments from your past. You can change up a few things, ask questions and things like that. But nothing you do here will change anything in the real world, either in your present or your future—you got that?"

Hopper opened his mouth to argue with the man.

But Earl just held up his hand. "I know what you're gonna say. Once was enough. Why live something over again? You think you've moved on from your mistakes and you're doing better. But you haven't learned a damn thing. It's like you lived your life, but you didn't *see* it. Not what was important, anyway. And you're not getting back to your present-day life until you've figured this stuff out. You gotta unstick yourself."

Hopper strode up to the counter, leaned over, and glared at the meddling old fool. He was just about done with this shit. "And who the hell are you, to tell me that? You haven't seen what I've been through. You don't even know the half of it!"

"Oh, but I do," Earl crowed. "And all the halves you don't know too."

"And how can you possibly have all that in your head? What in the hell are you? An angel? Or demon? Is this some kind of trick?

Earl laughed so hard, he started to hack. "Oh, dang it," he wheezed. "Gosh darn them cigarettes. No, boy. Me n' my wife Candy, we're not angels. We live in the places in between—that place between what was and what could be. The place between where you are and where you're supposed to go. And sometimes, people get all tangled up in the in-between for too long. *That's* how you end up at the Outpost."

"'Cause I'm stuck?"

"Exactly."

"But I'm *not* stuck," Hopper insisted. And it was true. He didn't owe this freaky geezer an explanation. He didn't owe anyone anything. After twelve years in the pen, he'd paid his debt to society. And Hopper had truly moved on, landing an honest job he loved, working with people he both liked and respected. He was working with his hands again and helping build Holliday Hot Rods into a national name. And hell, Lewisburg was practically like living in a mountain Mayberry—so sweet and homey, it was a balm to his wandering soul. He had a clean life. A *good* life. That was more than he'd ever expected, and he was proud of it.

What in the hell did the Caines *want* from him, anyway?

Almost as if he read his thoughts, Earl grinned. "I want you to get the whole story, that's all."

"The whole story? I was there! It didn't end well."

Earl clucked. "Oh, it's a right tragedy, I'll give ya that. But don't you ever wonder what happened to Delilah? She was supposed to be the love of your life, wasn't she? But you never told her that. And the minute she found out what you were really doing with your time, you made damn sure to kick her to the curb. And she'd been prepared to forgive you, too. You broke her heart into a million pieces, Hopper."

Indignation spiked through him, and he clenched his fists. Did Earl really think he didn't understand? Shit, the weight of what he'd done had nearly crushed him. He'd never forget that jailhouse visit. He'd told her, to her face, that he'd never loved her. That he'd been using her, and she'd been too stupid to see it. He'd watched her tears fall, and the love in her eyes turn from confusion to outright despair.

But he'd been lying to her all along, hadn't he? What was one more? The thought of her hanging around, waiting on him to get out of prison—it had been more than he could handle. He'd already stolen enough years of her life. He'd been determined to set her free so she could live. Love. Achieve her dreams. Do better.

"I did what I had to do for her. For *her* life. Don't you get it?" Hopper pointed an angry finger at the man. "And I'd do it all again."

"You let her go so she'd be happy without you. But haven't you ever wondered what happened to your beloved?"

Just every damn day of my life.

Hunter swallowed against the knot that had formed in his throat. "One of her old roommates wrote me a letter while I was locked up. She said Delilah had found herself some rich guy and gotten married. That was twelve years ago. And I hadn't heard from any of them since."

Earl gave him a sad, knowing smile. "Yes. But you never heard what really happened, did you? How is she? Did she love him? Does she have kids? Does she still think about you sometimes?"

Hopper didn't answer the man, partly because Earl knew the answer anyway, and partly because Hopper couldn't bear to say it out loud. Oh yeah, Hopper wanted to see it all, even if it if hurt. Because now that he really had a chance to do it, he had to know she was okay. He needed to prove to himself that she'd moved on, that she'd recovered from the mistake of being with him. It would be the hardest thing in the world, to see her happy with another man. But it'd give him closure. Help him confirm that giving her up was a sacrifice that'd been worth it. If he ended up going through his whole life alone, he could live with that, as long as he knew he'd done the right thing.

Hopper closed his eyes and nodded. His throat was too thick with emotion to speak.

"Okay then," Earl urged. "You know what to do."

Hopper walked over to the tree and grimaced as he studied the presents. So pretty and perfect, there was nothing to tip him off about which one to choose. He finally just picked up a small, flat square box completely at random, even though it didn't seem familiar.

"Well, go on." Earl pointed. "Open it."

And Hopper did. The box was from a jewelry store, one of those big national chains. And inside was a diamond bracelet. Scratch that. It was a bracelet dipping with ten carats of diamonds and ten carats of onyx. It said so, right on the lid of the box. Black and glittering white, each gem was laid in perfectly uniform, alternating squares, one after the other in a single line.

He wrinkled his brow in confusion. "I thought these were gifts we'd given each other. Did somebody give this crazy thing to Delilah?"

Earl grinned. "You'll see."

And just like that, he and Earl magicked off to an entirely different place. Hopper shuddered a bit as they landed flat on a couch in a very elegant house, all unseen. He couldn't help but gape in wonder at what, apparently, was Delilah's home. This was the kind of place with white marble floors and expensive oriental rugs. A shiny white baby grand piano that probably never got played. Soaring ceilings. Uniformed servants too, he'd bet. And there Delilah sat, curled on the floor in front of a designer-perfect Christmas tree with a man he could only assume was her husband. She was opening the very box Hopper had been holding only moments earlier.

God, there she was, looking cultured, sophisticated, and so out of reach. His stomach churned. How had he ever thought he could aspire to this woman?

No, the man handing her that box had been the man who'd ended up deserving her. Hopper was trying to figure out what year this must be. Delilah appeared to be in her late twenties or early thirties.

Her husband seemed to be in his late forties. Hopper gave him a grudging once-over, a bit surprised she'd gone for the man, honestly. This husband of hers wasn't too unattractive, he supposed. He had the well-preserved look of the very rich: kinda jowly, yes, but not too fat overall. Steely blue eyes. Perfectly trimmed, silvery blond hair going white at the temples. He wore a crisp white dress shirt rolled up at the sleeves, a pair of flat-front khakis, and shiny black loafers with no socks. Hopper snorted. Must be casual Friday.

Hopper let his eyes travel around the room. A glint of metal and glass on the fireplace mantle caught his eye. He walked over, and saw it was littered with awards: "Roby Luxury Motors, best place to work," "Top-Performing Ford Motors Dealership," "Best Car Dealerships in Atlanta, People's Choice Award," "Humanitarian of the Year, PBS Atlanta," and too many others to count.

"It's beautiful. Thank you honey." She gave the man a bloodless peck on the cheek. Hopper studied her face, looking for some glimmer of happiness as her husband clasped the bracelet onto her wrist. But he found none. No, Delilah didn't act like a woman who was getting several thousand dollars of jewelry for a gift. She was smiling, of course, but he could see the sadness lurking in her eyes.

And honestly, Hopper was kinda surprised the man had bought her that overpriced bracelet. Obviously, Roby didn't understand the first thing about his wife. Lila liked hand-making her jewelry. And when she did buy something already made, she bought pieces that weren't expensive, or had unusual stones. This mass-produced, pricey bauble was pretty much the exact opposite of what she'd buy for herself, no matter how much money she had to spend.

He could tell Lila had her game face on when she offered to pick up all the Christmas presents and put them away. Her husband dismissed her, sending her hustling back down the hallway. Her designer heels clicked on the white marble foyer as she busied her way through what was obviously a McMansion. A glance or two out the windows revealed it was most definitely a too-big house on a too-small lot in a pretentious gated community.

Hopper passed by a fifteen-foot Christmas tree towering in the entry, one that had very obviously been professionally decorated with glittered poinsettias and big gold ornaments, and bit back a bitter laugh. That was quite a step up from construction paper chains and a tree in a bucket.

He supposed he shouldn't sneer. Wasn't this kind of wealth the brass ring opportunity most people were reaching for? Yet, he couldn't dismiss the uneasiness in his stomach. Something wasn't right—he could feel it.

As he and Earl trotted alongside her, Hopper found little to recognize of the Delilah he knew. No, this Lila *Roby* was so polished, she gleamed. Her wild, sexy curls had been straightened to a precise, blunt cut pulled back in a severe ponytail at the base of her neck. Even with no Christmas visitors in the house, Delilah was wearing a supple pair of bronze leather pants and a metallic-gold ribbed turtleneck that showed off her figure. Diamond studs glittered on her ears, and the marquis diamond on her left hand went practically from knuckle to knuckle.

By any objective measure, Delilah was a stunning beauty. Put together. Perfect, even. And yet…

She looked *terrible,* all the same. He knew the real Delilah, the girl with an easy, sexy laugh, flashing eyes, and a sweet, tender touch. And this wasn't her. This Delilah in front of him was obviously toned, but all her curves had turned to gaunt angles. Her jaw was too sharp, and her eyes were flat, their shine gone. Even her glowing skin had been ruthlessly covered up with a thick layer of expensive makeup.

He turned to Earl, shaking his head. "That man wasn't at all who I would've expected Lila to end up with. How did it even happen?"

Earl shrugged. "Met him at an expensive steakhouse she'd started to work at. He was one of the regulars. One day, he asked her out, and she said yes. He was charming then. A wealthy older man who showered her with gifts and attention. Mitchell Roby owns several successful dealerships and even a small business airport here. Everybody 'round Atlanta recognizes his face. He's on billboards all over town and he sponsors *Masterpiece Theater.*"

Hopper rolled his eyes at that. Following along, he finally

caught up with Delilah when she walked the boxes into the master bedroom closet. Jesus, it was big enough to be a small apartment, with a crystal chandelier hanging right in the middle of it. She pulled out several identical white shirts Mitchell must've gotten for Christmas and began steaming them carefully. Everything in there was so perfectly aligned, so perfectly coordinated; it seemed more like a fancy men's suit store, than a closet.

Delilah finished a shirt and hung it up on a cedar hanger exactly one inch apart from the others, worriedly inspecting the crisp creases to make sure nothing was out of place.

Then the phone in her pocket began to ring. She took it out and put it on speaker as she continued to work. It was Randy. After several overly cheerful Christmas greetings, Randy finally got down to the business of his call.

"Sweetheart, are you absolutely sure you can't come to our New Year's party?" he begged. "I don't understand. Are you ashamed of us or something? We haven't seen you since your wedding. And that was a year and a half ago."

Lila blanched. "I'm so sorry, Randy. I get it. It's been a long time. I probably won't be able to come with Mitchell, but I bet I can find an hour or two to come by sometime this summer, maybe."

"Not until the summer? Are you serious? You live on the other side of Atlanta, Lila, not the other side of the moon."

Lila made every excuse under the sun. Mitchell had her busy attending events with him. He needed her support because he worked so hard. *Blah, blah, blah.* Randy didn't act like he believed it, and frankly, neither did she.

After she'd finished her last BS excuse, Randy didn't answer her, and a long, disbelieving pause hung between them. "I'm going to ask you this question, baby girl, and I want a straight answer. Are you okay? The way you talk, it's worryin' me. Men who isolate their partners from their family and friends? That's abuse. Is Mitchell hitting you?"

If it was possible, Lila got even paler.

Oh, no. Hopper turned to Earl for confirmation, and the man nodded sadly. Hopper's heart dropped to his knees.

Holy shit. Roby was. He *totally* was hitting her. *Goddammit!* Was *that* why her clothes covered her up so much and her makeup was so thick? Was *that* why she was so thin? The thought pummeled him. He covered his mouth with a shaky hand, swallowing down the sudden urge to puke.

Lila made more excuses and finally got off the phone. But she was clearly rattled, her hands trembling a bit as she shoved the phone back in her pocket. She slumped in the corner of the closet with her head in her hands for a long, long moment. Then she rose, obviously lost to her thoughts, and stumbled to the farthest corner of the closet. It was where she kept her clothes—a runway-ready collection for sure, but a tiny one compared to her husband's. Crawling around on the floor for a minute, she pulled out a small suitcase with a miniature key padlock on it. Hopper walked with her while she carried the suitcase to the edge of their ridiculously large bed. Retrieving a key from her jewelry cabinet, she opened the suitcase, uncovering her old journals and mementoes.

Clearly, her call with Randy had made her feel nostalgic for her childhood, difficult as it often was. Apparently, that suitcase contained the only possessions she'd brought with her to the marriage. She smiled fondly at first, but as she rummaged deeper in the suitcase, her mouth drew up into a silent, furious O. Furrowing her brows, she turned the suitcase over, and dumped out everything. She frantically rifled around in the mess.

Hopper caught Earl's attention. "What's she's after?"

The corner of Earl's mouth curled up, the smile on his face too sly for Hopper's liking. "Just watch, boy."

Soon, she checked one of the suitcase pockets and found her quarry—a long, thin manila envelope. She grinned as she unwound the clasp and turned it upside down. But the only thing that fell out was a battered old keychain. Hopper recognized it instantly. It was a Santa Claus key chain—the one that held the key to the motorcycle he'd given her. But the key wasn't there.

She peered down into the envelope, shock registering when she realized it was empty.

For a second, he couldn't imagine what she was searching for—and then it hit him. *Shit! The title!* Ah, no no no. *Had the title been in that envelope with the keys?*

She rounded her eyes in panic and ran out of the house, through the frosty sod in the manicured backyard, and into the detached six-stall garage. He and Earl jogged along with her as she tore through the place from end to end, rummaging around under every tarp and behind every box. But there was no bike anywhere. It was gone. *Gone!*

And all Hopper could do was stand there in the shadows, grinding his teeth and clenching his fists as his poor angel got just as upset as he was.

What did that rich-ass mofo need with *her* bike? It was *hers!* Something Hopper had given her freely, with no strings. He let out a ferocious bellow, not that she could hear him. Earl just raised his eyebrows but didn't offer any commentary on his outburst.

But dammit, Hopper couldn't help it. The thought of her husband disappearing that bike made him want to smash something—preferably the prick's face. God, he remembered fixing up that bike, scouring the collectors market for months to find the perfect parts, and fantasizing while he turned screws about all the ways they could enjoy it. Long road trips. Back country picnics. Making love on it...

Yet more dreams that were stolen by his trip to prison. But after everything Hopper had taken from her, this was the *one thing* she could keep. *The one thing I could give her.*

Hopper took a long, shaky breath, and watched Delilah

process the news. Now that Roby's fuckery was plain, reality began to sink in for her. God, how it killed him to see that look on her face—so raw…so desolate…

He'd always wondered whether she'd just sell the bike and pocket the money. Had almost wished she had. But to see how important that bike was to her still…

Delilah stood there, biting her lip, the color rising in her cheeks until she began to sob. He'd seen her cry. But not like this. She was crying uncontrollably, like a lost little child, with big, shuddering gulps, the sound echoing off the concrete walls in the enormous garage.

His angel was alone. Totally alone. And he couldn't even touch her.

The sight and the sound of her tears stopped Hopper's rage in its tracks. All his angry venom drained out of him, replaced by a kind of helpless, heartsick dismay. This wasn't about him, or even the bike. It was about Delilah and the life she'd had to lead to get to this horrible point. And damn, how Hopper wanted to hold her, and tell her he was there.

It's just a bike, baby. It's only a bike...

But it wasn't just a bike, was it? Here in this place, it was a trail of breadcrumbs back to who she used to be.

He worried she might collapse right here. But Delilah's sobbing didn't last long. No, she wiped her eyes with her sleeve, the tears slowing to a stop. And her face morphed into an expression he didn't think she was capable of wearing. She thinned her mouth to a flat, tight line and balled her fists tight at her sides.

Oh yeah, it was rage he was seeing there—unholy, incandescent rage. It lit her up in every terrible, fucking magnificent way.

Delilah tore off full tilt toward the main house while he and Earl scrambled to keep up. Stomping from room to room, slamming doors as she went, she finally cornered Mitchell in the kitchen as he was serving up broiled steaks and sautéed vegetables onto crisp white plates. The table had been set for two, knives and forks precisely positioned on top of white cloth napkins.

"Oh good!" Mitchell crowed as he heard her approach. "I don't have to call you. Staff's off, so I made steak. Sit. Eat."

But Delilah only stood there, seething. "It's Christmas Day, Mitchell. And I don't *want* steak again."

"You'll eat anyway," Roby calmly replied, holding out her chair.

Her chin started to tremble, but only just a bit. "I h-hate steak. If you knew me at all, you'd know I've never liked it."

He rolled his eyes. "And yet, you were no more than a little waitress, peddling steaks when I met you. I won't tolerate any impertinence from you, Christmas Day or no, Lila. So *sit.*"

Won't tolerate any impertinence? Oh-ho. Hopper had never wanted to flatten anyone so bad in his—

"*No,*" she answered, her voice hard and clear, her gaze never moving from his.

Cold fury blanked Roby's expression. Apparently, the man wasn't used to blowback. It made the hairs stand up on the back of Hopper's neck. Roby stalked over to her, his eyes narrowed to suspicious slits, like a snake coiled to strike. "Dearest *wife,*" he spat, "what's all this about?"

"Where's my motorcycle? What did you—"

"I sold it," he jumped in, acting all smug. "Got a pretty penny for it too. Turns out it was collectible. Did you know that?" The S.O.B moved forward, smirking ever so slightly, getting all up into her space as if he dared her to do something about it. He raised an eyebrow in surprise when she didn't cower.

No, Delilah fixed him with a stony stare instead, a tick in jumping her jaw. "And my moto jacket? And the other clothes I had in my suitcase? You sold those too?"

"God no. That crap? Who would want it? I donated it." He

sneered. "I'm sure there's a homeless person somewhere enjoying that jailbait jacket."

"How in God's name did you even do that? I had it all locked away!"

Roby snorted. "And you kept the key stored in your jewelry cabinet. Good Lord, Lila. Even a small child could've figured that out."

Color flooded her face. "How *could* you," she choked out, her voice thick with fury. "They were *mine*."

Roby remained maddeningly, dangerously calm. And that scared Hopper even more than if he'd screamed at her. The man tried to wrap his arms around her in a possessive kind of hold, but Delilah just shoved at him, finally starting to slap at him. But he grabbed the tops of her arms tight. Way too tight. He shook her once. Twice. And she stilled.

"Did you really expect me to tolerate that, Lila?" he murmured, his voice full of enough lethal, banked menace to make a full-grown man blanch. He shook her again, harder this time. But Delilah stiffened in his arms, refusing to bend. "*Another man* gave you that bike," Roby grated out. "*Another man* gave you that jacket. Can you not see why that couldn't be allowed? Under *my* roof?"

"They belonged to *me!*" She quivered in his hold, but she didn't try to break away. "You had *no right!*"

"I had *every* right!" he screamed, the noise so loud and sudden it practically split the air in two. He shoved her, wheeling away, his face contorted with disgust. A sickening, charged kind of silence fell as he turned his back to her. He slowly, deliberately straightened his clothes, menace practically vibrating off him. Once he was satisfied they were smoothed, he rolled his shoulders, and straightened up. "It's time you apologized for this outburst."

But Delilah only laughed at the man—a bitter kind of laugh that twisted her face into a rueful smile. "Oh no.

There's only one thing I owe you an apology for, and it's this: I don't love you, Mitchell. I think maybe I never did."

Roby spun back around and raised his fist to backhand her.

But she caught his wrist in midair. "Don't. You. *Dare,"* Lila thundered.

Roby's eyes flared with shock, but he didn't move. And neither did Delilah as she stared the man down.

"I have carefully documented records, photos, and time stamps of every time you hit me," she told him, her voice icy calm. "I have it documented with my physician and my lawyer too. You hit me again, even one more time, and all that's going straight to the media. I'm sure your adoring public would love to know how Atlanta's friendliest car dealer really treats women."

Hopper whooped and pumped his fist in the air, not that anyone could see him. *That'll fix the bastard!*

Roby only sneered again, pushing his fist against her hold. But Lila planted her feet and held her grip firm, matching him in this epic battle of wills.

"I want a divorce," she ground out. "And you're going to give it to me."

"A divorce? *You?"* Roby laughed derisively, breaking away from her again. "And what are you going to do with that high school diploma? Turn tricks?" He tsked, and shook his head with a bitter, rueful smile. "You stand there, slinging arrows, thinking you'll wound me with all this talk about love. But wife number one quickly disabused me of any fantasies I may have had on the subject. Loyalty? Devotion? *Respect?* They're bought and sold, every day. And the difference between you and me, Lila, is I've always known what this is. In this big cold world, you've always needed me more than I *ever* needed you. So let's stop pretending, shall we? You wouldn't survive two minutes without my money." He stormed over to her place at the kitchen table and pulled out her chair, slamming it to the tiles with an explosive clatter as he did. "So come back to the table, *dearest.* The filet mignon is getting cold."

Lila canted her head in shock, as if she couldn't believe the words had left his mouth. As if she were really seeing him for the first time—a man who was nothing without a woman to control and money to control her with. She shook her head. "For the record, Mitchell, I didn't marry you for your money. I hate all this. And I liked myself way better when I was just that *little waitress.* So you don't have to worry." To Hopper's complete and utter amazement, she took off her ring. And the bracelet. And her diamond earrings. And she laid them on the table. "I don't want your money. Not one red cent. I don't want your cars or your clothes, or any of your fucking flashy *jewelry.*"

She grabbed her purse off the counter, her hands shaking with anger as she pulled out her driver's license and dumped the rest out on the table, her makeup, her credit cards, insurance card—everything. "I don't want alimony. Or a settlement. My lawyer will set everything in motion. I'm asking for nothing. *Nothing,* you hear? Only the money you got from selling that motorcycle. Because that was titled to me, and you sold it without my permission."

Roby stood there, staring blankly, as if he couldn't comprehend that she was defying him. But it was clear he couldn't say or do a thing to stop her.

Delilah stalked off to her bedroom.

Hopper could only stand there on the sidelines, dazed and completely amazed. He'd never been prouder of her. It was, without a doubt, the most spectacular display of badassery he'd ever seen. He clapped with glee when Roby picked up her plate and hurled it into the sink, shattering it to shards, his face all purple with impotent rage.

"Serves you right, you fucking monster," Hopper growled.

And he was about to read the man the riot act himself, even if the asshole couldn't hear him.

But Lila was back already. Somehow, she'd torn off her expensive clothes and changed into jeans and a sweatshirt. She yanked on a denim jacket and called an Uber. With her old suitcase in hand, she walked out that door without a backward glance.

Roby never said a word, only curled his lip in disgust as the door clicked shut behind her.

Idiot.

Hopper sighed and turned to Earl. "She's going to be alright, isn't she?"

"Better than alright." Earl nodded. "After her mama died, she'd gotten a big life insurance payout, set back in a trust that matured when she was twenty-five. When Lila got it, she didn't spend a dime, just put the money aside. Roby had no idea that account existed. Once she was out on her own, she used part of the money to get her associate degree in accounting and a certificate in medical coding. Soon she found a nice job as office manager for a medical practice. It took some doing, but she finally got free of Roby for good."

He gave Earl a curt nod, knowing the man was right. But his insides were still shaking with the furious desire to tear Roby limb from limb. *Too bad.* The time to protect Delilah had come and gone. No, while Delilah had been going through all that, his sorry ass had been rotting in jail. He hadn't been there to help her, and the regret ate him alive. "All I ever do is hurt her," he whispered. "If I hadn't gotten her that motorcycle, Roby wouldn't have had anything to lord over her. Maybe she could've—"

"Hopper Vance!" Earl cried. "What in the hell, boy? Is that what you're really taking away from this? It took losing that motorcycle for her to find her anger! It was losing the bike that was the real gift. You know how much Roby got for that

BMW bike? Forty grand. And that money was a big help to her once the divorce was done. You may not realize it, but you *freed* her and helped her find her way back to herself, Hopper."

"I wouldn't say that. Seems to me like she freed herself."

Earl just grinned. "Well, I'll tell you the real lesson in all this: that girl loved you. That's why all this business with the motorcycle counted like it did. She'll always love you, whether you like it or not, Hopper Vance."

CHAPTER 8

LILA STARED into the fireplace at the Outpost, unable to stop her brooding. "I suppose I shouldn't be shocked."

Candy smiled sympathetically as she cleared away their empty nog mugs. "Still doesn't make it any easier to hear though, does it?"

No, it really didn't, especially through her adult ears. She couldn't imagine what that would've been like for poor teenaged Hopper, having to get by with nothing more than what he could carry on his back.

Whenever she'd ask Hopper questions about his past back then, he'd say he'd "lived a lot of places" and his family was "gone." But that was all she could get out of him.

Lord knew she and her mama had struggled, trying to keep body and soul together. But no matter how many times they'd had to start over, Mama had always been able to find herself a decent job—manager at a retail shop, or a waitress in a fancy restaurant, or some such. They'd moved all around suburban Atlanta from place to place, school to school. But through it all, they'd always had each other and some kind of respectable roof over their head. Always.

They'd never had extras, compared to her classmates.

Pretty much everything they'd owned had come from some kind of secondhand shop. When she was young, she'd always believed she'd come from nothing. But Hopper? He'd truly had nothing. The boy who'd shown up on Randy's doorstep had been through things she couldn't even fathom.

"I think maybe the hardest part of this is realizing I was in love with a man I never knew. I was young back then, and I was just willing to accept him at face value. At the time, I thought it made me brave to love this mysterious man. But it only made me a fool."

"Did it?" Candy cocked an eyebrow. "A man is more than just what's happened to him. Seems to me you loved the real Hopper. Who he was way down deep."

Lila snorted sarcastically and shook her head, never tearing her gaze from the flames.

Candy scooted over onto the hearth so she could get right up in front of her. "Whassa matter? You don't believe me?"

Lila's heart throbbed painfully, as if it had aged a hundred years in the last few hours. She didn't have a clue what the woman wanted her to say.

"Fine. I'll prove it to you." Candy slapped her knee and jumped up to her feet. She circled the tree, rubbing her chin thoughtfully as she examined the gifts. "Seems to me like you need to see the past again, exactly as it was. You need to see the things you missed, first time around. I have something specific in mind for ya. But if you go back, you'd be on the sidelines, and not in your younger body. You'll be by yourself, and all you can do is observe. You okay with that?"

Lila squelched the urge to laugh derisively. Did she really have a choice? Candy was going to put her through her paces no matter what, so she might as well get it over with. "Yeah." she sighed. "Sure. Might be less tiring, anyway."

Candy snorted and rolled her eyes. "Now don't be so ungrateful, girl. I think you might actually like this one." She extracted a gift bag with a big red teddy bear on the front and rumpled green tissue paper that had clearly been used several times. She tossed it in Lila's lap, and it landed lightly.

Lila turned the bag over in her hands, trying to place it. She'd done a lot of the Christmas wrapping when she was a teenager, and this was one she'd recognized from that period. Most likely it contained a gift Randy had given her at one time or another. She held the gift back out toward Candy. "Why this one? I don't understand what this has to—"

"Child, don't you get it? The gifts we give each other are bigger than the gifts themselves." Candy shook a finger at her. "Go on and open that. It will take you to a time when you'll see Hopper. The *real* Hopper. As he truly is. You'll see how the boy felt about you. I promise."

Lila studied the package for a long moment. Could this strange magic really answer that question, once and for all? Dammit, it should all be ancient history, so far behind her it didn't even make it onto her radar. Yet, the thought of seeing Hopper again and getting answers…it made her excited and petrified, all at once. Didn't she deserve to understand her life, even if it hurt? Letting out a long, jittery breath, she decided to go through with this, before she changed her mind. She reached in the bag and…

A blinding flash of light, a surge of lightheadedness, and she was there.

She was standing in the shadows, observing her fourteen-year-old self. That gawky girl had dressed a bit better this time, wearing her knockoff Uggs, red crushed velour leggings, an oversized Christmas sweater, and a silly Santa hat. Teenaged Lila fiddled around nervously with her hair and brushed herself off, finally managing a timid knock on the back door of Randy's shop.

One look at the wheelbarrow and the piles of boxes at the girl's feet, and Lila knew she was there to help Hopper. A smile spread across her face, her heart swelling with emotion at the sweet memory. God, she'd thought she'd never forget this day. It was her favorite Christmas memory, after all. But how long had it been since she'd allowed herself to revisit it?

Sixteen-year-old Hopper opened the door at last, seeming confused that anyone would bother to knock on the door to the garret Randy had offered him.

He'd turned up at their house on the day after Christmas. And they'd all agreed Hopper should be shown some Southern hospitality. Since Mama wasn't really up to a big dinner around the table, Randy had sent Lila over to help him get settled in. Jarboe Transmission was a small operation, located in a rehabbed barn on his property. It had been a simple matter to load up everything she'd needed and roll it over.

God, Lila remembered how nervous she was, and she saw it now, written all over her fourteen-year-old face. How strange it was to see herself from the outside.

"Delilah," Hopper breathed, clearly shocked she was standing there. "What are you doing here?"

"What, did you think we were going to leave you all alone up here in the cold over the holidays?" Lila grinned, barging past him with an unusual show of teen bravado. She pointed to the overflowing wheelbarrow and pile of boxes sitting at the base of the steps. "I've got everything you need. Help me haul the stuff up."

Hopper scowled. "Hey, you don't have to babysit me or anything," he protested, but he grabbed a big stack of bedding and a cooler she'd brought, following her up the stairs anyway. "I could've gotten by. I had some food in my duffel—"

"Jesus. It's worse than I thought," Lila interrupted, scanning the place. "This apartment hasn't been touched in a couple of years. Well—" she clapped her hands, "—we'll just have to make it a home, won't we?"

As young Lila passed armload after armload of household items to Hopper, her older self let her gaze roam around this dear, familiar place. Hopper had lived here for a year. And she'd spent so much time up here with him that it'd felt like home to her too. The studio was nothing fancy—just one big room, really, over top of the garage. But it was cozy, with a queen-sized bed, a timeworn loveseat, a chipboard writing desk, and a kitchenette with smaller-sized appliances. The walls were crisp white, and the carpet was a tight-spun commercial gray. The only thing separated out was a small bathroom and a walk-in closet. Still, the space needed quite a lot to make it truly livable. Fortunately, her teenaged self had already thought of that.

Hopper flushed with embarrassment as all her boxes and bags piled up in his living room. "Seriously, you don't have to take care of me. I'm just grateful to have a place to sleep. You didn't have to do all this."

The girl executed a perfect adolescent eye roll. "Leaving our friends to shiver alone in the dark is not how we do things at Chez Jarboe, especially at Christmas time. So let's get to work!"

Lila could see by Hopper's stiff stance that he was wondering what to do with himself. But the boy overcame his discomfort, bit by bit, as young Lila chattered away relentlessly about this or that, making silly conversation to lighten the mood.

Together, they got a fitted sheet on his bed and unrolled a cheerful plaid comforter she'd found in a closet at their house. Thank God Randy was a pack rat. She'd found three space heaters in the basement—enough to keep this attic space toasty warm. By the time she'd laid out a couple of placemats on a card table she'd found, put some mismatched dishes and silverware in the cupboards, and stocked the bathroom with a a few nice, fluffy towels, this unused attic was starting to feel like a real, honest-to-God place.

Lila had to smile at the determination she used to have, and the breadth and depth of her foraging. Good Lord, how had she ever found all this stuff? Fourteen-year-old Delilah hadn't missed a thing. She'd brought toilet paper and a bathmat, and even a shower basket of travel shampoos and stuff her mama must've hoarded. And she'd had the foresight to bring a bucket of cleaning supplies over from the house too.

Up to her elbows in lemon-scented altruism, her younger self dusted and scrubbed while Hopper ran the sweeper. Horrified, Hopper blushed as Lila started cleaning his toilet. "I'll do that," he protested, taking the toilet brush from her.

"Okay." Lila shrugged. "I should start unloading the food anyhow. I brought ham. You like ham?"

Hopper's face brightened, and Lila's heart squeezed, seeing that. She could tell the boy was way too hungry. "You *know* I love ham." He beamed.

"Good," Lila continued. "When I asked Randy what he wanted to eat for Christmas, he told me to make up a ham and any fixins I wanted. I made some mac and cheese from scratch, and rolls, and green bean casserole with the little crunchy onions, and even some sweet yams—"

"Omigod!" Hopper exclaimed as he ripped back the foil on the yam container. "Holy smack! You made them with marshmallows. I had them like this once, and they were the best!" Poor Hopper was so excited. He started to spoon some right out of the pan, cold. "Oh, mannnnn," he groaned. "That's good."

Young Lila flushed with pleasure, but she whacked the boy's fingers. "Would you stop it? I intend for you to have an honest-to-God meal. It's still the Christmas season and all. Let's do it up right."

Hopper watched with amusement as she took pains to set the little card table properly, with their sparkling cider poured into mason jars, and the paper napkins and mismatched silverware set out just so. She'd even found a camping lantern in Randy's basement, and set it on the table with a few sprigs of pine branches spread out underneath.

With the red ribbon she'd put around it, it was really cute, in a rustic kind of way.

Her teenaged-self piled up his plate with double helpings of everything, and made herself a plate too, getting everything piping hot in the microwave. By the time the food was ready, they were both feeling the Christmas spirit. Grandly, Hopper whipped one of their cleaning towels over his arm like a proper maître d, walked around the table, and pulled out a folding chair with a flourish.

"Madame, your table awaits." His smile deepened as he pushed in her chair for her.

Lila giggled, the lantern glowing in between them. They settled in their seats and clinked their mason jars. "To Christmas," Lila declared, holding out her glass.

"And friends." Hopper grinned.

"And ham." Lila beamed back.

"And yams. Especially yams." Hopper laughed.

"And new beginnings!" Lila sang out.

Hopper tried to keep smiling, but a shadow passed over his expression. A shimmer of pain, perhaps. An unguarded moment. Her older self would've liked to hit the replay button to see it again, to read the clues in his face. But as quickly as it had come, the shadow faded. And his eyes warmed as they came back to teen Lila's face. "And new beginnings," he answered. He tipped his glass to hers with a hearty clink and took a big swig.

They both plowed into their food, all attempts at conversation postponed for all the ooing and ahhing and chewing.

"You really made all this yourself?" he asked. "They're, like, your own recipes and everything?"

Lila shrugged. "No, not mine. I got all these recipes from the Betty Crocker cookbook I borrowed from the library. They turned out pretty good, didn't they?"

"You can say that again. You can cook better than a lot of

country grandmas. This is the first Christmas dinner you've made, then?"

"Yep!" Lila beamed with pride. "It wasn't that hard, really. I just followed the instructions. I've been cooking since I was really small. Mama is so bad at it, I realized quick if I didn't want to grow up on frozen burritos and peanut butter, I'd better learn to fend for myself."

"Randy likes your cooking then too?"

She snorted. "You'd better believe it. I think the man has put on ten pounds. He's always begging me to make him cake. Sometimes I hear my friends complain about their chores. But I kinda like it. Mama needs the help, you know? And Randy, he lets me take charge, and that's fun. I plan out the meals, and he gives me money to go to the store, and *everything*. It's *so* cool."

"Except the part about your mama bein' sick."

"Yeah." Lila frowned, staring down resolutely at her plate. "Breast cancer. She was stage four before we even knew it was there."

When Hopper heard that, his whole face changed, his expression going soft and his eyes brimming with sympathy. He slipped his hand over hers and squeezed. "But you've made it nice. You've made your house feel like a home and given her a little bit of normal when she needs it most." The sincerity in his voice was real, and just as warm and reassuring as she'd remembered. He waited for her teen self to glance up at him again, and he gave her hand another squeeze. "Hey, you've stepped up. It's the greatest gift you could ever give her."

"Yeah." Lila grimaced uncomfortably at the praise. "I suppose you're right."

In the light of that lantern, Hopper's eyes shone as he regarded her. What was it Lila saw on his face? Admiration? Pity?

No, she realized with a start. It wasn't any of those things.

It was connection. He got her on a level no one else ever had, because he knew what it was like. God only knew the tribulations that had led him to this dingy garage on Christmas Eve. But whatever they were, Lila was glad. They'd led him to her, didn't they? And this girl before her needed a boy like Hopper, more than she could've ever dreamed.

Hopper spooned up his third serving of yam casserole. "So, did y'all have a good Christmas, in spite of everything?"

"Yes!" Lila brightened. "Randy got me a bedazzler and a bunch of stones and craft supplies for making my own jewelry. He got me all the pencils and watercolors and tablets I need for the whole year! Mama can't really shop. But she gave me some money to spend at the thrift store. It was the first time she let me go to the store by myself to shop for clothes. I took a bus there after school and practically bought myself a whole new wardrobe! Omigosh, it was the best thing ever, and I didn't even have to wrap anything. I got these earrings, and these new gray boots, and pink jeans—can you believe it? And..." Lila stopped abruptly. "I-I'm talking too much. I'm...I'm sorry."

Hopper quickly reached across the table and grabbed her hand in his. "It's okay," he murmured. "I like to hear you talk."

Lila's cheeks flushed, and God help her pale Irish skin, she was red all the way up to her hairline. He looked down at their linked hands then, his lips parting a little, as if he was shocked to see that he'd reached out for her again. He slowly, almost reluctantly, pulled back.

Lila still remembered the shock of his hand in hers that day. For the first time, she'd felt the raw power of the pull between them.

As a young girl, she'd been flustered by it. And sure enough, teen Lila jumped up and changed the subject. The girl walked over to the tiny kitchen counter, grabbed a gift bag with a teddy bear on it, and shook it at him playfully. "I almost forgot your Christmas present!"

Hopper gaped at her for a second and began sputtering. "But you didn't—I don't need you to—"

"Oh, don't be ridiculous." Lila waved away his concern. "I didn't have money to go to the store or anything. My mama's always telling me that the best kinds of *somethings* are the somethings you make from nothing. So, I made a little something from nothing." She proudly pushed the bag into his hands.

The tension that drew up his shoulders made him seem like the kinda kid who wasn't used to getting presents. But his mouth quirked up at the corner anyway, a subtle tick that gave away how much the kindness pleased him. When he reached in the bag, he pulled out a big stack of paper.

Confusion knit his brows. "What is this?"

"It's magic! Here, I'll show you." Eyes sparkling with excitement, the girl got down on her knees in front of him, pulled a hunk of paper off the top of the stack, and placed it in his hands. Then she put her hands over his, taking her time to get them positioned on the diagonal corners. Young Lila had her attention on his hands, so she didn't see Hopper's reaction to her closeness. But Old Lila did. She watched him close his eyes, dip his head toward hers, and take a deep breath in, as if he were memorizing her scent. He stopped just short of nuzzling her hair. Lila's older self laughed appreciatively. Why not? They couldn't hear her.

"Okay, Hopper. All we've gotta do is pull these ends away from each other. See? Nice and slow."

And they did, inch by inch until an elaborate paper spinner suddenly snapped to life, springing up and twirling in perfect three dimensions in their hands. Hopper whooped with surprise. With a few folds and artful slices with her scissors, she'd made it from a simple piece of paper from her large sketchbook. He grinned down at her, clearly awestruck.

"Something from nothing," he murmured, rotating the

curving paddles of the spinner in the light of the lantern. "I like that."

Lila got all flushed with pride again. "I made more! See?" She jumped up and started pulling at the pile, unfolding it until it reached across the room. "There's enough to decorate the whole place for Christmas! We could make two chains and criss-cross it over these open rafters."

"This is amazing," Hopper marveled. "How in the world did you get these done so fast?"

"Oh, I had them up in my room already. Made them a couple of weeks ago. But I think they're better in here, cause of the way these walls come up to a peak. Besides, I'm working on a chain of butterflies and lilies for my room, for the spring."

Excitedly, they both dug through the bag of folded paper creations she'd brought, along with some beat-up white Christmas lights she'd found on a dusty basement shelf.

One by one, she and Hopper popped up her cutwork snowflakes, spinners, and even her origami cranes for good luck, all made with snow-white paper. Tying them onto the string lights, they stapled it up in long, looping swags.

Then they turned off the lamps and turned on the lights. And oh...

It was *enchanting.*

Hopper and Lila cheered and clapped as they took in the scene. They'd turned it into a winter fairy's wonderland, with snowflakes and spinners working almost like lanterns against the bright white lights, casting soft, intricate shadows on the walls from the ceiling to the floor.

Lila beamed, held out her arms and spun in a circle. "Oh!" she squealed. "Look at it, Hopper! It's soooo beautiful!" Like the girl that she was, she stopped, closed her eyes and just soaked in the feeling.

"Yeah. It is," Hopper whispered. But he didn't even see the lights. He only had eyes for *her.*

Dear God…

Her heart swelled as she let the memory claim her. She'd demolished all the blank paper in three brand-new sketchbooks for this project. But she could hardly argue with the results. Young Lila had managed to conjure Christmas magic right here in this drafty studio with nothing more than elbow grease and stupid, stubborn hope. And it'd all been worth it, for the happiness on Hopper's face just then.

When was the last time she'd done something like that, just for the love of it? When was the last time she'd experienced real joy? Lila let the feeling settle in as the evening unfolded between the two teens. They'd stayed up until the wee hours of the morning that night, chatting about everything under the stars while Hopper taught her how to play poker. And Lila—the old and the young—laughed at his crazy jokes, and sighed as they talked about the constellations blinking outside the grimy attic window, and smiled with satisfaction as Hopper mooned over the fat slab of black forest cake she'd brought for him.

Finally, the conversation drifted away, and they simply gazed out the window, the moon falling on their young, smooth faces. They were quiet for a long time before Lila finally said her goodbyes.

"Thank you," he told her as she turned to leave. "This has been the best Christmas I've ever had."

"Yeah." Lila stopped in the doorway and beamed at the boy. "Me too."

The door snicked shut, and Hopper moved to his window, keeping tabs on her young self as she walked the moonlit path back to Randy's house. He stood there for the longest time. Lila realized he was making sure she'd made it back to her room and turned off the light.

Hopper walked over to the middle of the room, looked up at their crazy decorations, and smiled a soft smile. Reaching up, he picked off one of the origami angels Lila had given him and held it reverently in his palm.

Such longing stole over his face.

Oh my God. *Such love.*

It hit Lila right in her jaded, scarred-up heart. The boy was filled up to the brim with sweet emotion, and yet, he seemed almost bleak. Like he wanted something he could never have. Did he really think she was that unattainable?

Maybe it had appeared that way to him back then. She was so young. It wouldn't have been unheard of for a fourteen-year-old to date, in those parts. But he'd always held her at bay, probably in some kind of misguided attempt to protect her. She'd been twenty-one when he'd finally allowed himself to touch her.

She shook her head. All those years. He'd been in love with her that long? How much time had they wasted? Year after year, she'd laid under the covers in her twin bed, longing for him to touch her, kiss her, hold her…

Lord, he'd wanted her, from the very first day. The thought made her heart practically turn over in her chest.

Lila blinked back tears as Hopper placed the paper angel on his bedside table. And that was where it stayed as he curled under the covers, keeping vigil over it as the lights blinked softly overhead and he finally surrendered to sleep.

CHAPTER 9

As Hopper slumped in an overstuffed chair in Caine's Christmas Outpost, he wondered whether he was a greedy bastard or a glutton for punishment.

He'd gotten a taste of Delilah again. The good and the absolutely bad. Yet, somehow, he still wanted more. If there were things he was supposed to learn about her and their time together, he was ready to pull up a desk and take notes.

He wondered if he could get in another session like his first trip, one where he could be back in his younger body. It'd been fun to be younger again. And it had left him aching and empty too. God, the love and admiration in her eyes—it had been like a drug. He wanted more. Her cherry-flavored kisses, sweeter than any candy. His arms wrapped around her, and maybe even his bike rumbling between their legs...

Earl came out from behind the counter and clucked his tongue. "I see you're to the brooding stage. Realized what you been missin' yet?"

Hopper barked out a bitter laugh. "Yeah. You could say that." He turned to Earl. Surely he could figure out how to turn this strange exercise to his advantage. "Can you answer me this? Why Christmas? Delilah and I knew each other for years. Why can't I pick out a memory from the rest of the year?"

"Ah, well," Earl hedged. He shoved his hands in his pockets and rocked back on his heels a bit, acting circumspect. "I can't reveal too much about our methods except to say The Outpost needs Christmas for fuel. Most people can't see it, but there's a deep vein of magic that runs through all things. At Christmas, that magic intensifies. Some people say it's the goodwill around, and others say it has something to do with the Earth's magnetic fields—lay lines and seasonal energy pulls and such. All I can tell you is that it's powerful. And you and Delilah? You've got a special connection to Christmas, don'tcha?"

Hopper stopped to think about that. He supposed that was true. They had met during Christmas. And every year, whether they'd been dating yet or not, they spent Christmas together, almost like they were celebrating an anniversary. First, they'd celebrated around Randy's table. Then later, when he'd moved out, they'd cook dinner together on Christmas Eve. They'd make a big to-do about it, decorating the tree and opening up gifts. Lila loved Christmas. After his shitty, Christmas-free childhood, she'd taught him to love it too. Together, they'd drive for miles to take in the season's light displays. He'd happily binge watched every holiday movie on TV with her, sometimes more than once. And every year, she'd make him that awesome yam casserole with extra marshmallows, without fail.

Yams. *God.* He almost laughed out loud.

Somehow, he'd managed to lose sight of all that. Of how good they were together. He could never have it again, in real life. It'd been too long. But he could relive it here, couldn't he? Find the best parts of himself? See that pure, uncorrupted love, reflected in her eyes, one more time?

Yes. *Yes I can.* Dammit, he'd do anything for one more taste.

"I want another gift," Hopper blurted out, marching quickly over to the tree.

Earl clapped his hands. "Enthusiasm! That's what I like t' see!"

Hopper scanned the gifts, determined to find one that would take him back where he wanted to go. To one of the good Christmases they'd spent in each other's arms. He'd have to pick carefully. He scanned the piles until a Godiva bag caught his eye. A grin broke out on his face.

How could he forget giving her this gift? Yeah, this was the one. The *perfect* one. Excited now, he grabbed the bag and turned it upside down.

A bright flash exploded all around him...and he opened his eyes to Delilah, squealing with delight, sitting on the floor in front of his Christmas tree in his old rental house.

She had a big bag of Godiva chocolate squares in her hand. "*Eeee!* I love it! Oh my God, I've never had chocolate this fancy before."

Hopper let out a disbelieving *tsk*. "For God's sake, woman! You worked at the pretzel shop next door to the Godiva store. You mean to tell me that whole year you worked at the mall, you never once indulged?"

"No, silly!" She slapped his leg. "I couldn't. I was there to make money, not blow it on expensive treats."

She hurriedly opened one up and popped it in her mouth. "Mrrrrm," she groaned. She raised her hand in testimony. "All right. I get it now. Umm. So good. Srulsly."

Hopper was back in his twenty-something body again. He sent up a silent thanks to the Caines for not making him stay on the sidelines this time. Because just the sexy happy noises she was making were enough to make him lose his ever-lovin' mind. But he couldn't go there. Not yet. No, tonight would be for letting *her* come to *him*. For the first time...

Oh, yeah. He remembered this night really, really well.

Eager to get the show on the road, he grabbed the bag and

dumped the rest out on the floor. "The chocolate is not the only thing here," he crooned. "This here's a kit. You're the biggest hot chocolate fan I ever met. And we're going to make hot chocolate fit for a queen, angel. I've got whole milk in the fridge, and we're going to melt in this chocolate and add some of this." He pulled up a squirt bottle of salted caramel syrup.

"Oh my God. That's the same syrup they use at my favorite coffee sh—"

"And the same one you always order with your hot chocolate," he interrupted. "I made them sell it to me. You can have your favorite treat any time you come over here. From here on, *I* can be your coffee shop."

He'd also bought her a mug with an angel on it. When she pulled it out, she got the sweetest, dreamiest expression on her face. "It's amazing. I think you're the only person who notices those details about me."

When she'd said that the first time, he'd tried to pass it off like it was no big deal. Because he'd been trying to resist her at the time. But there'd be no resisting this time around. He decided to up the ante, tucking an errant curl back behind her ear and stroking her cheek. "I notice everything about you. I always have. And I always will."

He hadn't said it the first time. But he was glad he had now, because his words hit home. Delilah gazed up at him, her face shining with appreciation. It would be so easy to put on a full court press and really lay into this whole romance thing. But he didn't want to rush the fun he knew would be coming. He pushed up to his feet instead, offering a hand to pull her up. "Come on. Let's get that drink made. If you're gonna keep me company in the garage, you'll have to keep warm."

Hopper couldn't stop whistling on his way to the kitchen. How lucky was he, getting to revisit this night? Thinking back on it, this might be the best night of his life—the night they'd finally admitted they wanted to be together. And as a bonus, he'd have no problem sliding right into this magical do-over, because he remembered every single detail about this day.

It was the day before Christmas Eve. He was twenty-three. And she'd just turned twenty-one. She'd started working at The Sassy Lass that fall and was making great money and tips. But she was still driving an ancient, rusted out, piece-of-shit Jetta she'd insisted on buying without anyone's help. Fortunately, she'd let him fix it for her whenever it broke down. And this night, he'd rescued her, cold and shivering off the side of the road. She wasn't going to get to work tomorrow unless he fixed her car tonight.

Hopper shuttled her into the kitchen and they joked around, teasing each other about the presents they were going to unwrap tomorrow night. The easy conversation just kept flowing as they talked about their day, the cooking schedule for their Christmas Eve dinner, her funny stories from The Sassy...

He sighed contentedly as he stirred the melting chocolate into the milk. He liked how domestic she used to make him feel. It was a sense of home he'd only really had with her. He remembered, dimly, that he used to enjoy cooking. But since he'd gotten out of jail, his kitchen activities had been limited to his coffeemaker and whatever took less than three minutes to nuke in the microwave. And yet, the cooking itself wasn't what he missed. It was being in the kitchen with Delilah.

God, how surreal was it, being back at this house? The place wasn't much, really, just a two-bedroom cinderblock house on the outskirts of Douglasville. But this rental was the first place he'd ever lived that had felt like his. His landlady had let him make all kinds of improvements. He grinned as he checked out the kitchen again. He'd painted the cabinets black and poured a trendy concrete counter himself.

He could still remember every single thing about this place—where he'd stored the pots and pans, which records had been in his vinyl collection, the coffee table he'd made with glass and old hubcaps. He'd loved it. And he'd lost it all too when he'd gone to prison. Honestly, he was glad he'd asked his landlady to sell all these things, only saving back his motorcycle jacket and a couple of other odd mementos he'd requested. It had been a task, cleaning out this place after his sudden incarceration, and the woman deserved the money. Yet, regret still lingered. For all intents and purposes, these carefully curated possessions had been erased, and his young life right along with it.

Catching himself, Hopper shook off the ping of sadness. No, tonight was all about Delilah. And for just this moment, what was lost had been found.

He filled up their mugs, and Lila followed him into his well-lit, well-ordered garage. Popping the hood of her car, he dug in. Fortunately, only the battery was bad this time. Lila unfolded a lawn chair, positioning it so she could talk to Hopper easily while he worked.

Hopper scanned the intricate built-in shelving he'd created along the garage's back wall, hunting until he found a salvaged battery the right size and capacity for her needs. Hauling it to her car, he bent back over the engine to get to work.

He'd started turning screws and wrestling the battery free when it got awfully quiet in there. He glanced back over his shoulder to find Delilah's gaze fixed on him. She quickly averted her eyes, as if she'd been caught.

He turned back around and hid his grin. She'd been checking out his ass! Big time! He bit his lip to keep from laughing. He hadn't noticed that the first time around. Probably because he hadn't believed at the time that she'd wanted him. But tonight? Well, tonight he'd milk her ogling for all it was worth. He stood up, stretched luxuriously, and casually peeled off his shirt. He tossed it onto his work bench and turned around. "I'd better not get oil on that one. Hey, Delilah—would you mind getting my work shirt off that peg over there?"

He could tell she was trying not to, but she flitted her eyes over every inch of his chest. He glanced down at his abs, which, even though he was skinnier, were still pretty buff. Then he rolled his gaze back to her, nice and slow, throwing down a smirk for good measure. It took all his energy not to crack up as Delilah practically stumbled back into the workbench to get the shirt, a pretty flush rising to her cheeks. She handed it to him, and he held onto his end for an extra beat or two.

"Thanks," he murmured, and shimmied back into his grimy garage tee.

She settled back into her chair, and in minutes he had the new battery in.

He turned back around, wiping his hands with a towel. "Is something on your mind, Delilah? I've finished this whole thing, and you've just been over there, staring. What's up?"

She shifted in her seat, her gaze drifting to the floor. "I'm sorry. Lost in my own thoughts, I guess, after a long day."

Hopper grinned as he lowered the hood. "You should be tired, with the tips you're pullin' in. After seeing that envelope of cash peekin' out of the top of your purse, I'm beginning to wonder if they have any openings for sassy *lads*."

Lila tsked. "I dunno, Hop. I don't think you'd enjoy shaving your legs."

He raised an eyebrow. "Don't you go underestimating me. I could *totally* rock one of those short skirts." He slid her a teasing smirk as he walked by, ruffling a finger up under the edge of her kilt as he did. This was the joke that had set everything in motion, all those years ago. He lingered his hand over her knee this time, though, just to make himself crystal clear.

Now it was her turn to raise an eyebrow. He was making a play for her, for the first time. And by the answering spark in her eyes, he'd say the message had definitely been received. *Everything old is new again, right?*

All he had to do was sit back and wait.

"Really?" Lila rose from her chair, her smile seeming to say *it's on*. She strutted over to her car and leaned up against it, arms crossed, her foot popped up on a wheel to show her leg off to its best advantage. "I don't believe you've got what it takes to be *sassy.*"

"That so?" he called as he washed his hands in his garage sink.

"Mm-hmm," Lila teased. "Flirting on your downtime is a bit of an art. Flirting for money is commerce. It takes training, discipline, and most of all, marketing skills."

Hopper snorted. "Hanging all over a guy, they *train* you to do that?"

"Absolutely!" she insisted. "Though, probably not in quite the way you think. When you start at The Sassy Lass, you're encouraged to create your own persona—a kind of character you play when you interact with customers. We don't have lines or anything like that, but it is a way of thinking and being that makes it easier to create a consistent experience for our guests."

Hopper finished drying his hands and came over to lean against the car too. "Oh, that's interesting. What's yours, then?"

"I'm Brianna, the oh-so-innocent girl next door."

"In *that* get-up?" He ran a lingering glance down at what she was wearing—a torn-up T-shirt she'd tied into a halter, a mini-kilt that barely grazed her ass, and over-the-knee boots so smokin' hot, they should come with their own fire hazard warning.

"Ah, but you see, innocence is more an attitude than anything. It's a wide-eyed thing, where you laugh at all their jokes and act like the customers are so, so smart. Well, that and acting like you have no idea you're turning them on."

Hopper pretended to be upset about that, so she'd think she had him going. She was exaggerating for his benefit. And this little game she was playing was even more fun the second time around. So he raised his eyebrows. *"What?"* he sputtered.

"Oh, stop it. It's not that bad. No stripper poles are involved."

"But-but," Hopper wheezed, "you're actually *trying* to get them all worked up?"

"Mm-hmm. You know, to give them something to think about whenever they've got a cold bed. We're a bit more service plus than Hooters."

He bit the inside of his cheek to keep from snickering. The sound that sneaked out sounded more like a garbled growl.

Lila's eyes widened at that, and she laughed. "You don't believe me, do you?"

"I don't *like* it—that's my problem. I don't like the idea of you touching strange men."

"Don't be stupid. It's all harmless fun. Here, I'll show you." Lila grabbed the folding chair and sat it down in front of him. "Go on and get in that chair, and I'll give you the full Sassy Lass treatment."

Hopper did as she said and crossed his arms. "This better be good."

"Oh, it will be." Lila popped a finger in the air. "First rule of Sassy Lass—there's a lot of casual touching. Allow me to demonstrate." She reached over and got a car magazine off his workbench, brandishing it as if it were a menu. Then she trotted up to his "table," making sure her breasts bounced a little as she stopped. "Hi there, handsome, what's your name?"

"Hopper," he answered, rolling his eyes, but the corner of

his mouth still quirked up in amusement. God, his heart kicked up a fast beat as he remembered what she was about to do… "Nice to meet you, sugar." He swallowed, trying hard not to sweat. "What's a girl as sweet as you doing working in a place like this?"

Lila blinked down at him, all doe-eyed, and twirled the tip of her ponytail in her fingers. "Well hi, Hopper, I'm Brianna. And I work here because I just love taking care of guys like you." She slid one arm slowly around his back and handed him the menu over his shoulder with her other hand. "What's your pleasure?"

Hopper snickered as he groaned. "You're kidding. That's so cheesy."

"It gets better." She grinned. "Open the menu." He complied, opening up the magazine. Lila bent over his shoulder then, letting her breast brush his cheek ever so slightly as she pointed to the menu. "Gee, sir, I don't drink a lot of alcohol, but my customers tell me this IGA is good, and this single malt. See? The best part of this maneuver is I'm serving two people at once. You're getting a taste for how warm and soft I am, and your friend across the table is getting a real nice view down my shirt."

Hopper harrumphed theatrically. "So let me get this straight—you're actually *letting* customers ogle you?"

"Come on, Hopper. It's planned glimpses of skin. They're not stealing a look. I'm giving it to them." Lila moved around to the front of his chair. "See? I didn't cut up the neck of this halter top for the ventilation. When I bend over," Lila grabbed the back of the chair behind him and bent down right to his eye level, "they see the cleavage I *planned* for them to see."

Which, in this case, would be right down to the clasp of her pink hook-front bra. *Sweet Jesus.* Hopper almost laughed out loud again. He'd eaten at The Sassy before, and he knew damn well there was a "no-touching" policy there that went both ways. He was pretty sure they weren't allowed to dangle their tits in front of the customers quite like this, either.

But he wasn't complaining. Back then, he'd been warring with himself, trying to resist her and telling himself he shouldn't. But not this time.

Hopper riveted his gaze to the soft globes of her breasts. His fingers tingled with the memory of how perfect they'd felt in his hands, how heavy and hot. Goddamn, his mouth actually watered as he remembered how she'd moan when he'd run his tongue right there...

No way could he help himself. He'd hoped to draw this playact out longer, but the urge to touch her was just too strong. He slid his hand up the side of her hip, bringing it to a rest on the yummy little slice of stomach the halter top didn't cover. And when he drew his thumb in a lazy circle over that erogenous zone just over her ribcage, her goosebumps rose up under his fingertips.

God, the feel of her was like *nothing* else. He stared with wonder at the sight of his rough, calloused hands on the petal-soft perfection of her skin. When he met her dark, smoky gaze, she didn't look away.

"What if I don't want anything on the menu?" he murmured.

She batted her eyes prettily, slid onto his lap and straddled him. "Well, I hear the chef does take special orders." He sucked in a breath as she skimmed her palms up his chest and brought them to a rest at the nape of his neck. "What did you have in mind?"

"Something sweet." He pulled her to him. His head spun from the smell of her skin, her hair, the faint sheen of sweat that had gathered right here, at the base of her neck. Hopper nuzzled her there, letting his lips graze her jaw, her ear... "Something perfect. Something so good, I'd want it again and again, for the rest of my life."

Delilah drew her head back enough to search his face.

Concern creased her brow. "That's a pretty tall order, Mr. Vance."

He tipped his head to hers and landed a lingering kiss. Soft. Sensual. A tease of his lips against hers. Then he kissed that sensitive spot right behind her earlobe and ran his tongue along the delicate column of her neck. She arched into him, and her heartbeat raced under his wandering mouth. "Why is it then that I feel this way?" he hummed, never stopping the light, teasing nips her neck. "Like you're the only person in the world who could give it to me?"

She leaned up on her knees and straddled his lap, a position that had her eye to eye with him. The next move would be hers. He could feel her longing hanging in the air between them, heavy and real. Like he was holding her heart in his hands.

Maybe he was. Hopper swallowed hard, suddenly struck with the magnitude of this moment. Funny how he'd always thought she'd made a play for him because it was some kind of next step. A progression of their friendship, maybe. He'd always thought she'd had an itch, and he'd scratched it. But the wisdom of age allowed him to see more. And that made him suspect he'd been wrong about this night. Something more than fire burned in her eyes. Had she felt it all those years too? The hunger? The soul-deep need?

Maybe she had.

Damn, all those years of unrequited lust...

Yeah. He'd be requiting it. He'd give her all the requiting she could handle.

As he held her gaze, Hopper saw the moment she'd made her decision. The moment she'd found what she was searching for, staring her right in the face. She sank both hands into his hair, pulled him toward her, and kissed him.

Hot.

Hard.

Hungry.

She slid her tongue over his lips, and he opened to her with no freakin' hesitation. Oh no, he met her straight on, his mouth devouring her heat, her taste. He wrapped his hands around her perfect, round ass and hauled her tight against him, her softness the only thing that could ever soothe the raging ache underneath his zipper.

Hell yeah, all that wanting, banked up between the two of them. Years and years of it, pouring out. It was wild, ferocious—desire that was old, and new, twisting all around them.

Everything about this was desperate…deep and wet, his mouth clashing against hers, traveling over her collarbone, his fast breaths warm on her shuddering skin.

With one hard yank, Hopper pulled the ponytail holder from her hair, threw it to the floor, and buried his fingers in the cascading waves. He fisted his hand in it, tugging until she moaned helplessly.

Another smooth motion and he was on his feet, wrapping her legs around his waist. Three steps, and he had her perched on the hood of the corvette body he'd been storing for his next rehab. A second later, and he'd ripped off her tights and boots, and yanked his grimy shirt off over his head. He loomed over her, rocking himself against her. Just like he had before.

For a moment, he worried that he was gripping her thighs too hard, scaring her with the suddenness of it all. But Delilah only groaned and cupped his ass in her hot little hands. The heat of her mouth on his skin burned him, branded him as she rained down kisses on his chest, his neck…

And then the sharp snap of her teeth as they sank into his collarbone. *Ah hell, that's it, Delilah.* His cock throbbed against the confines of his jeans, struggling against the waistband. And God, she rolled her hips against him, like she had an ache only he could fill.

Desire fell over him like a red haze, drowning every other thought and sensation but her, her feel, her taste, the throaty, sexy sounds she made when he touched her. Delilah gasped, laid herself back on the hood, and actually *writhed* against him, her arms thrown over her head in pure abandon.

He was completely and utterly mesmerized by her, his breaths coming fast and short in his lungs. Dammit, he had to see her, had to get rid of the barriers.

Roughly, he began tugging at the knot in her halter top, finally loosening it with his free hand. He pushed it up to her armpits. God, that bra…it was so sheer that her tight, pebbled nipples were only hidden by a thin sheet of shimmery netting.

Sweet Jesus. Hopper flicked open the clasp. *Damn*, those breasts, God's most exquisite creation… Not able to help himself, he drew his head down, sucking the sweetness of her upturned, dusky red nipples while he rocked against her, harder, faster.

"More," she begged, sounding desperate. "Just more, *please*, Hopper!"

He shoved the kilt up to her waist and ran his fingers down the seam of her center. Unable to stop himself, he snuck a finger under the lace, then two, sliding them inside her quivering, wet heat.

And he couldn't take it anymore, couldn't stop, couldn't hold back. Hopper reared back and ripped those flimsy panties apart in one short, hard pull, tossing them on the floor.

Lila hissed with surprise but didn't protest, only gazed up at him breathlessly while he popped the buttons on his fly. He took his cock out, dragging it against her slippery, tight little pussy, back and forth while he reached around to his wallet for his condom.

This was going to be good. *Soooo damn good.*

"Oh!" Lila cried out. And Hopper stilled. Something about

her reaction niggled at him. He heard her desire, loud and clear.

But his more mature mind heard something else. An undertone that sounded almost like shock. *Surprise. Innocence.*

Good lord. She couldn't be.

Was she actually...

He laid a steadying hand on her stomach and gulped in a breath. "Delilah, babe. Are you a... Is this the first time you've..." He couldn't finish the sentence.

He didn't have to. The way she rounded her eyes and bit her lip? It told him everything he needed to know.

Holy hell. She was a *virgin*. She'd been a virgin this night, so many years ago. And back then, he'd plowed her like a fuckin' steamroller and hadn't given it a second thought. Like a goddamn animal, pounding her virginity into the dust. She'd never made a noise, never let on.

He closed his eyes, trying to catch his breath. Oh, he couldn't *believe* this. Here, he'd thought he'd been such a big man that night. But now he felt kinda sick to his stomach. "All those dates you went on with other guys. Even prom. You're telling me you never—"

"No, I didn't."

"Why not?"

She rolled her eyes. "You'll remember, I've never dated anyone all that seriously and—"

"But *why?*" he cut her off, his voice rising more than he'd intended. "Why in the *hell* didn't you at least experiment?"

"Because I was waiting for you, you dumbass!" she cried. She'd pushed herself up to sitting, eyes flashing.

And any urge he might've had to yell back at her died in his throat. She'd wanted it to be him. *Jesus*. Hopper felt like he'd had all the air let out of him. At the end of the day, it shouldn't matter how much or how little experience Delilah had. But it did. Dammit, it really did. Because he'd stolen from her, yet again. He'd taken this moment that should've been so perfect for her, so beautiful, and reduced it to popping her cherry on the hood of a rusted sportscar.

Isn't this just the story of my life?

A cocktail of emotions coursed through him—guilt, tenderness, a feeling of being responsible to her. He couldn't fix what had really happened all those years ago. But in this step out of time, this fantasy, maybe he could give her something perfect and good. The real Delilah, somewhere out there, would never remember this.

No, this little do-over would be just for him. To give him a chance to do at least one thing right. He gently wrapped his arms around her and tipped his forehead to hers. "We can't do this," he murmured.

Delilah let out whine. "Hop, no! I want to!" She ran her hand up and down his bicep. "Please."

"Wait babe. I didn't mean it that way. I am so, so honored you want me, especially to do what you're askin'. But I won't do this here." He began buttoning up his pants. "We're going to make this special. The way it should've been from the beginning. Do you trust me?"

She grinned down at her spread legs. "Does it look like I don't?"

Delilah giggled and whooped as he scooped her up quick in his arms. He'd be going off script, and he didn't give a damn. He was going to do something new, starting with something old. He was going to rock her world. "Good. 'Cause you're coming with me."

CHAPTER 10

"WAIT HERE." Reluctantly, Hopper stopped his kisses and set Delilah on her feet. "I have a better idea."

While she stood idly in his living room, he went back to his bedroom to inspect, quickly deducing it was no-seduction zone. Just as he'd remembered, there was shit strewn everywhere—T-shirts and jeans littering the floor, an unmade bed in need of fresh sheets, novels and magazines scattered around. He'd generally been pretty neat in the rest of the house, but the bedroom was the one place he'd always let go to hell, probably because he'd made it a policy never to bring anyone back there.

Hopper banged around, opening drawers in the bathroom until he found his box of condoms. He stuffed the entire contents of it into his back pocket. Then he opened his linen closet and barked out a laugh. There was the black-and-white plaid comforter Lila had brought to him the first night he'd stayed in that studio over Randy's garage.

It was a bit worse for the wear, but clean, and lovingly stored in this cedar-lined closet. He probably should've tossed it, or given it back, but somehow, he'd held onto it anyway. *All's the better,* he grinned, as he dragged it back up the hall.

"That old thing?" Delilah snorted. "You *kept* it?"

"I knew it would come in handy someday." He folded it in half and laid it down in front of the long glass-pebble fireplace he'd installed in the wall. "And I was right." Turning the knob, a long line of short flames sprang to life, instantly classing up the joint.

He offered to get her a drink, and after inspecting the choices, they settled on him pouring out two short glasses of Maker's Mark, on the rocks. Then he perused his album collection, selected a compilation of slower Motown tunes, and joined her on the blanket. They sipped their drinks, while he wondered what to say or do next.

Without warning, stupid, paralyzing awkwardness gripped him, and his heart was in his throat. This whole Rico Suave routine wasn't really him, was it? It didn't help that the pressure of Lila's first time was starting to rattle him. He wanted it to be special, perfect—tender, even. Yet, the whole idea of it had somehow stopped him in his tracks. He'd never been one to doubt his skills in this department, but how could any man ever do this moment justice?

Sensing his sudden nerves, Lila narrowed her eyes at him, putting down her drink, then his. "Dance with me," she simply said.

"But I don't really—"

"It's a slow song. No talent required." She pushed herself up to her feet and held out her hand.

Still, he hesitated. He was a terrible dancer.

Delilah put her hands on her hips. "What did you think we were going to do down there? Debate current affairs? Play scrabble? Get up here and wrap your arms around me. And don't make me tell you twice. I'm not wearing any underwear, thanks to you."

Chuckling, he let her pull him up. "So bossy." No sooner was she in his arms than the opening strains of "My Girl" began to play. He had to smile at the perfection of it.

Damn, it was a magic only she could weave, the way the color bloomed over her cheeks, and the fire's shadows flickered in her eyes. His heart beat wildly, dancing more to her spell than the music. He could see it all, her simple faith in him, her honesty, her open, giving heart, right there in those beautiful eyes of hers. Lord, how he could read them, and everything they seemed to be saying.

Hold me...

Stay with me...

Love me...

God, Delilah. How he wished he could. He'd give anything to have this in his life—his real life. But right now, this would have to do. He could make himself believe, just for one wonderful night, that she was still his.

For this moment out of time, the slate was clean, wasn't it? Anything he did right here was new. Perfectly, deliciously new—a self-contained memory he was creating.

He couldn't say how long this do-over would last, but he'd be making the most of it. He cradled her head against his chest. So small, and yet, she fit perfectly. All the tension and doubt drained from him as they swayed together. No matter what, they fit. They'd *always* fit. *My girl...*

He kissed her, slow and sure. A brush of lips that went exploring, tasting. But that need, that desperation rose right back up to the surface again, refusing to be banked. Suddenly, he forgot about the dance and this whole business about trying to be a cool, controlled kind of lover. Nothing about him felt cool or in control.

He needed her, all of her. He needed to strip away the last bits of the Sassy Lass off her and get the real, true Delilah underneath his hands, skin to skin. Right this minute. He shoved his hand up under her top and whipped it over her head, throwing it down God knew where. Hopper tipped her back to linger his mouth over her luscious breasts and her flat, smooth tummy. Soon, he was on his knees in front of her, unhooking her skimpy kilt and letting it pool on the floor...

And when he was done, he looked up at her and stilled with wonder. Goddamn, she was *perfect*—and everything good, and loving and hopeful in his life.

"Delilah...*angel,*" he managed to choke out. As he was kneeling here at her feet, it hit him—all of it. He remembered the love, and loss, and regret, and pain and lies and out-and-out *despair*. He remembered everything he'd done to her up to now, and everything, according to history, that he *had yet* to do to her.

Memories ran riot in his brain, choking him with bright, vivid detail. The distinctive rattle of the cell doors closing. The tears on her face as he'd told her she'd been stupid to love him. The desolation in her eyes when she'd searched for that motorcycle and not found it, devastated to lose that last connection between them...

Had she missed him like that, for fuckin' *years?*

It was too much, just too much.

Shame and heartbreak shook his soul, the horror, the *enormity* of it choking his throat. He wasn't fit to touch her.

And he couldn't even tell her he was sorry.

At this moment in time, she wouldn't understand.

But he *was* sorry, for everything. Hadn't his entire life become an atonement? An existence where "sorry" followed him with every footstep he took? Damn right it had. And if he lived a hundred lifetimes, it wouldn't be enough to make it up to her.

Trying not to break down and bawl like an idiot, Hopper flung his arms around her waist and buried his face against her stomach, furiously blinking back tears. Moments ticked by while he tried to pull himself together. At first, Lila simply let him stay there, and gently stroked his hair. It wasn't long before she bent down too, getting on her knees with him.

Hopper turned his face away. But she caught his chin, forcing his gaze to hers. "Hey. Come back to me. Wherever it is you've gone, please baby, *come back* to me. I *need* you."

"I— I'm sorry, Delilah," he finally forced out. "It's just—" He stopped for a moment as he tried to put words to the tangle he was in. "It's just that…you'll *never know* what you mean to me." And she wouldn't. That was the hell of it, no matter what he chose to say in this magical do-over. Because he'd already made his choices long ago.

Still her face shone with pure emotion as she caressed his cheek, layering on kiss after healing kiss. He'd never have the redemption his heart so desperately wanted, but he could have this—this woman, this love, right now. It was his own slice of heaven, a place out of time made just for him.

A soft exhale left her as Delilah traced her palms over his pecs and dragged her fingers through his thick, black patch of chest hair. And he could only watch, fuckin' hypnotized by the sweet, sexy way her hands lingered over him, exploring as if she'd never seen anything quite like him. God, the sweet torture of it… His heartbeat raced. She skimmed her fingertips over the work-related burns and scars on his forearms and hands, stopping to kiss each one.

And then she unbuttoned his fly, slowly, sensuously, each little pull ratcheting his desire up that much more. He couldn't get those jeans off fast enough. Delilah reached for him, but he grabbed her wrist. If she touched him, this would be over way too fast.

"Lie back," he commanded, and she obeyed, never taking her big gray eyes off his. He spread her legs wide with his palms. *Jesus.* He shook his head at the sight and scrubbed his hand over his watering mouth. Oh, he'd remembered her in all her earthy glory, when she was open and ready for him. But he'd forgotten how much it wrecked him, made him her slave, willing to follow her to the ends of the earth. Wasting no time, he dove into her, devouring her clit and licking up every last bit of her sticky sweet cream. Honey and salt, woman and need—damn, he could actually *taste* her desire, right on the tip of his tongue.

He groaned, deep and loud, lost in her. Shit, how he loved this, loved her taste, the heady smell of her arousal, the way she squirmed and bucked and dug her fingernails into his shoulders as he dipped his tongue deep inside her. He laved and pumped, nipped and soothed, the memories of their years together telling his mouth and hands exactly where to go. When his fingers began to feel the telltale quivers that announced she was getting there, he stopped.

Squelching Delilah's frustrated cry with a kiss, he rolled underneath her on the blanket, positioning her to straddle his hips. Understanding dawned on her face as he grabbed a condom. Ripping the packet with his teeth, he handed it to her and showed her how to roll it on.

And she lowered herself onto him, inch by ever-lovin' inch, so slick and wet and tight, the friction nearly did him in right there. Sensing a barrier, she stopped. But he rose up to push through until he was fully seated.

"Oh!" she cried out, wincing.

"Shhh—baby, don't worry. It only hurts for a minute. I promise, I promise, I won't hurt you. Just take it at your own pace."

She nodded, biting her lip as she rolled herself on him.

"Yeah," he purred, "like that. Nice and slow. Let the pleasure build over the burn."

She sat up fully, balancing one hand in the center of his chest as she took him slowly, carefully. He gritted his teeth, trying to pace himself.

He placed a tentative hand on her belly. "How does it

feel?"

Delilah let out a long breath. "Big."

He grinned. "That's cause it is."

She let out a breathy squawk and shoved at him.

"Come on, angel. Roll your hips." She complied, undulating so fluidly, the motion rolled all the way up to her shoulders. She licked her lips, and did it again.

*God so sexy...*He held his breath a bit to keep from losin' it right here. "When you come down, lean in a little, and grind against me, here," he told her, circling her clit with his thumb.

She nodded, and did as he said, her eyes widening with the contact. He felt the shudder tremble through her and she moaned.

"That's it," he groaned back, so in her thrall he could hardly do anything but watch. She rolled her perfect body over him, over and over, harder and harder, desire taking her to places she'd never been.

He pushed a hand between them then, rubbing his thumb in circles on her clit, fanning the flames. And soon, it was like she'd let the throttle out, and she was speeding along with him. Goddamn, nothing was better than this, to be one with her, to feel her all around him, pumping him like a velvet fist, those perfect tits bouncing, her wild curls tumbled over her face.

He tried to keep his shit together. But then she'd leaned forward to kiss him, and his last vestiges of control snapped. He devoured her with kisses, his fingers digging into her ass, pushing her down tighter, harder. Her moans became shouts, more high-pitched, more desperate with every thrust.

She clenched tight around him, and he couldn't hold on any longer. He came with a roar, and poured himself into her hard and fast, with everything he had. Delilah tumbled right after him. Shudders and screams, pulsing and pounding, pleasure tangled them together in a way that could never really be undone.

She cried and shook in his arms as she came, like some kind of miracle, an explosion of beauty and light he could hold in his arms. Shuddering through aftershocks, they floated back to earth together. And when they touched back down, it occurred to him that they hadn't just made love. They'd made a new world, a better world where he'd done right by her, if only this once.

He didn't care if it was all an illusion. He'd hold onto the atonement, the benediction with both hands. All was peaceful and still as they laid there, firelight flickering over their skin, spent and gasping.

"I never knew it could be like that," she finally whispered.

Yeah, me either, he wanted to say. But he couldn't exactly tell her all the reasons why *that* was, could he?

He gave her a playful nip on the neck instead. "Well, get used to it, darlin'. Because I'll be giving you a whole lot more of those orgasms in the future. It'll always be like this. Better, even." And it was true, of course.

She turned over onto her elbow and narrowed her eyes, a smile playing on her lips. "Oh, you've got a lot of confidence there, Don Juan. So sure of your future prowess 'cause of all the women you've taken to bed?"

"There weren't that many, angel. And they wouldn't matter anyway. None of them were you."

"Yeah, well." She sighed, pressing a fingertip into the cleft of his chin. "Let's hope you won't have anyone to compare me to ever again."

"Sounds good to me," he answered her. But inwardly, he winced. *Oh, Delilah. If only you knew how true that is.*

He gave her a peck on the tip of her nose and got up to go deal with the condom. He was only gone for a second, but when he walked back into the living room, she was gone.

Hopper quickly caught sight of her out his sliding glass doors. Good Lord. She was *outside?*

He scrambled into his jeans and went running out after her. But the woman was just standing there in nothing but his T-shirt and her boots, arms out, twirling in circles.

"Omigod, Hopper, it's *snowing!*" she squealed. "Can you *believe* it?"

God almighty, it *was* snowing. Big, fluffy flakes looped down through the sky, enough that there would be an accumulation.

"A white Christmas! It's a miracle!" Delilah stopped, turning up her face to let the snow fall on her skin. "Isn't it *fabulous?*" she called.

"Sure is baby. But hold that thought." He dashed inside and came out again, dragging the comforter behind him. He wrapped it around them both, a funny little cocoon in the middle of a snowstorm.

Delilah wrapped her arms around his bare waist and sighed. "It feels like Christmas, doesn't it?"

"Yeah, it does," he agreed. And he didn't even mind that it was the wee hours of the morning, that his bare feet were freezing on the cold ground, and she was out in his yard in nothing but his T-shirt. The light from his back porch lit up every swirling snowflake, and they were both standing there like goofballs, sticking their tongues out to catch them.

They giggled and hooted, and finally he kissed her again, long and sweet. "You're my Christmas. The greatest gift I'll ever receive," he whispered, resting his forehead against hers. "You feel me?"

"Yeah," she whispered back, "I think I do."

But when he bent his head to kiss her again, she was *gone,* his hands full of nothing but air. The blanket fell to his feet.

No. No-no-no-no! It can't be over...

"Bring her back! *Please!* I'll do *anything!"* he shouted, his bellow echoing uselessly around him. There was no one here to hear him. There was no house, no fire, no yard…only a hollow, empty plain, stretching out in every direction.

The stinging snow swirled around him, swallowing him up. And Hopper was all alone. Again.

CHAPTER 11

IN AN INSTANT, Lila found herself standing on shaky legs back in front of the cheerful, roaring fireplace at the Outpost. Honestly, she couldn't tell whether she was wobbling from the portal crossing or from seeing Hopper again. Feeling a bit like her knees might give out, she staggered to the well-worn wingback chair by the fire and flopped down.

Earl scurried over with another mug of eggnog, this time wearing a bright-green Rudolph sweater with an annoying, blinking nose. "Rough trip?" he asked, handing the mug to her.

"You could say that." Lila groaned and broke off a piece of cookie. "It was hard seeing how we were together...but then, you knew that."

Earl nodded but was quiet.

"You were right. I think maybe Hopper did love me all those years." She pinched the bridge of her nose. "But here's what I don't get. I knew the man for seven years before he made any kind of move. And that was after I'd practically thrown myself at him and dared him to. I could understand it at first. I was really super young. But I'd started going out with guys by the time I was seventeen or so. If he wanted me so badly, why didn't he just take me then, instead of friend-zoning me for years on end? He had to know I had a crush on him. Any fool could've seen it."

This should be ancient history, something that had happened so long ago as to not even earn a blip on her radar. But after seeing that scene? Somehow, it rankled.

Earl patted her hand. "Honey, the boy always knew he wanted you. But letting himself have you? That's another thing entirely. When a fella believes he's not worthy, he does a lot of stupid things."

"Isn't it up to *me* whether or not I think he's worthy?"

"Honey," Earl drawled. "There's a lot he never told you."

Lila narrowed her eyes at the man but didn't answer him. How could she argue with that? It was true.

The scraps of information she'd learned today notwithstanding, she'd really known next to nothing about his life before they'd met. Whatever it was, how bad could it have been, really? Back then, Hopper had been kind, hard-working, and respectful. He hadn't struck her as someone who'd been traumatized. Then again, he hadn't seemed like the type to run an auto theft ring that chopped up cars and sold them for parts, either. That had been going on for, what, two years, right under her nose, and she'd had no idea?

She stared into the fire and absently fiddled with the hem of her cashmere sweater. Catching her nervous tick, she stopped herself. But not before she noticed that the tiny rhinestone chip she'd added to her French acrylic nail tips had fallen out. She popped her hand up to inspect, suddenly feeling ridiculous.

God. When did I decide it was important to blow my money on this preposterous frill? The girl she used to be was stupid. Strapped for cash. And so trusting, she'd loved a man who'd made being an enigma his life's work.

Today she was older. Stronger. Wiser. But when she

considered this high-maintenance manicure of hers, she wondered how much of that carefree girl she'd lost in all this. The one who'd given her whole self to a sexy bad boy without reservation. Who was she really, under all this pretty armor? Maybe she was hiding herself too, in a way. From the world, from herself.

She closed her eyes and took a deep breath. "I just wish I knew the real Hopper. Who he was before he came to Randy's."

Earl cocked an eyebrow. "I'm surprised you're askin' for that. Wouldn't you rather learn why he did it? Why he turned to crime?"

She shrugged. "Maybe eventually. But I'd like to understand his past first. I think once I figure that out, more things will make sense."

Earl tsked. "Alright then, you asked for it. But I'm bending the rules some to make that work. The gifts are supposed to be between you and Hopper. But for this one, I'm going to have to pick out a gift Hopper got from his father." Earl walked over to the tree and grabbed a plastic ring box that didn't even have a bow on it.

She grimaced as he placed the yellowed, banged up thing in her hand. "Hopper's *father* gave him this?"

The man nodded gravely. "Just open it."

The look on Earl's face didn't bode well. But curiosity got the better of her. She cracked open the lid and…

Ugh…

Again with the bright, blinding light. Lila blinked until she finally brought her eyes into focus. No actually, her ears kicked in first. The staticky tinkle of Christmas music filtered through an ambient sound system above her.

The aroma of coffee and fryer grease scented the air. Ah, she was standing with Earl in a 1950s-themed diner, complete with neon signs and those retro tables with the colorful melamine tops. Cheerful decals of snowmen and Santas decorated a rotating cake stand full of meringue pies.

Okay, now she was confused. She'd definitely never been in this restaurant before. Checking out the window, she realized she didn't recognize this town either, though it appeared small and Southern.

Earl must've taken note of her nervous glances around the place. "Dothan, Alabama," he nodded. "About twenty-four years ago, if my calculations are right."

Lila couldn't imagine why in the world she'd be in Alabama. But then she spotted teen Hopper, wearing clothes very like the ones he'd worn the first day she'd seen him—the weather-beaten, black leather jacket, the combat boots...

Hurrying across the dining room, she staked out a place by his table, sight unseen, like she'd done at Randy's house. Hopper was sitting across from a man she'd never seen before. She turned to Earl. "Is that man Hopper's father?"

"Yep. That there is John Vance."

Seeing them together, it made sense. They both had oversized army surplus rucksacks and appeared to be traveling together. Hopper seemed right about the age he'd been when they'd met, and this was clearly Christmas time here, so...

Could this be what Hopper had been doing days before he'd come to Atlanta? She started to ask Earl again but the man shushed her, pointing back at the table.

Hopper hunched over his plate while his father rooted around in his pack.

"Ah, I knew it was in here somewhere." The man pulled out a small white ring box and shook it.

Hopper glanced up from his milkshake. "What's that?"

John gave the box a shake. "It's a gift. For you."

Hopper snorted. "A ring box? Really? You planning to propose, Dad?"

The man set the box down in front of Hopper's plate and

for a brief, flashing moment, he smiled. And there it was. A resemblance so strong, it almost took her breath away—the kind of sly sexy charm that could light up a room. Like father, like son.

The resemblance was uncanny, and yet, his father's entire demeanor was different. John shared the same shaggy black hair, but his was streaked with gray. Blue eyes that should have been bright were filled with a world-weary sadness. He had all Hopper's chiseled facial features. But on him, the angles seemed too sharp, and his face was covered in uneven, greying stubble. Still, the man sat there in the booth, regarding his son with fond amusement.

"It was the best I could find." John smirked. "And you're a real laugh riot, boy, you know that? Go on, open it."

Smirking too, Hopper opened the box. His eyes got wide. "Your St. Christopher's medal? But you never take it off! Not even to shower!"

"Well, that's how they work, you knucklehead!" John motioned for Hopper to tilt his head down so he could get it around his neck. "You're supposed to wear religious medals all the time. They protect you. This one here? It's supposed to protect you wherever you roam. St. Christopher is the patron saint of travelers and lost things too. You being such a young thing, I thought you might need it more than me."

The medal wasn't much. The pendant was simple pewter on an old pot metal chain, the design smoothed down from constant wear. Hopper gazed down where it hung, trying to be all cool and not too overly pleased at the gift. But she could see the boy *was* pleased. She could see it meant the world to get such a personal gift from his dad. "You didn't have to give me anything."

"I wanted to." John shook his head. "It's not right that a father can't give his son the world at Christmas. And I get how hard our...present situation has been on you. This was...well, it was the least I could do."

Hopper inclined his head. "It means more than any fancy thing you could've gotten me at the store. Who needs all that shit, anyway?"

John just smiled weakly.

Delilah turned to Earl. "Their *present situation?"*

Earl sighed. "To understand John Vance, you have to go back to the service. He was drafted young to go to Vietnam. When he came back, he never really was the same. He sustained brain injuries and had horrible PTSD. Even the Army brass could see he wasn't up to serving anymore. They sent him home, and he rattled around for years doing odd jobs. And then, he had a barroom hookup that resulted in Hopper. His mother just dropped him off when he was born, never to be seen again. And he and Hopper had been struggling along ever since. John would get a job and it'd last for about a year, until his mental health and substance abuse problems caught up with him. Hopper had always been the one who took care of everything—cooking, cleaning, and covering bills doing any menial job he could get. But they'd just been evicted again. They'd been on the street for days, by this point. And it ain't the first time, either."

Ah. So that was it. That was why...

God, poor Hopper. Lila blew out a shaky breath, vaguely ill at the news. Yet, her respect for that teenaged boy went up a few notches. How hard must his life have been, trying to hold things together for his dad? How resilient and patient must he have been to be there that day, smiling affectionately at his father, after everything the man had put him through?

"Seriously, Dad. You're making me feel all Christmassy."

John patted his hand. "I'm glad you like it. It used to be your grandfather's before he passed. He put a lot of stock in stuff like that."

"You believe all that? About saints?"

John blew out a breath as he thought that over. "I ought to. I certainly spent enough time in church as a kid. But whether or not it's all a bunch of bull, the St. Christopher's medal always seemed to me like a nice idea. I like to think of it as an insurance policy. Like somebody up there's got your back. It can't *hurt*, can it?"

Hopper shrugged. "I guess not."

"Good. Wear it, and don't take it off."

"I won't." Hopper nodded. And he hadn't. Lila knew for a fact—he'd worn that medal every day since. She'd always wondered about it but had never asked. Somehow she'd sensed he didn't want her to. And after seeing all this, well...

Maybe there was a good reason for that.

The contrasts between father and son were striking. While Hopper was strong and vital and quickly filling out with muscle, John was gaunt and rangy, his clothes hanging awkwardly off a too-big, too-bony frame. But it was more than that. Clearly, his father was troubled, harried even, like a man who was bearing the weight of the world on his shoulders, and wasn't strong enough for the task.

"Hopper said he'd been born in New Orleans. Why didn't they just stay there?" Lila asked.

Earl shrugged. "John started moving around a lot after his son was born. The two of them, they moved all over Alabama, Georgia, and even Arkansas. It was like ol' John was throwing darts at a map and deciding to settle there. There was no rhyme or reason to it."

"They had no one to take them in? No grandparents, or aunts or cousins?"

Earl clucked his tongue. "Nope. Small family. And what family John had was estranged."

Lila shuddered to think how terrible that must've been for Hopper. She'd moved around a lot too as a kid, but this? No friends, even? She couldn't imagine what it'd feel like to be that rootless.

Hopper tried to squelch his sigh of resignation. "So, where are we going this time, Dad?"

"Haven't decided," John answered, pasting on a smile. "We'll figure it out at the bus station. I'll let you pick the town this time."

"Really? You'll let me pick?" Hopper raised his eyebrows. "Cool."

Lila decided if she was invisible, she might as well sit at the empty chair at Hopper's table. Of course, the waitress picked that exact moment to swish up in her blue polyester jumper and pop her knee up on the chair, literally right on top of her.

Lila screamed and slapped at her, not that the woman could feel it. "Occupational hazard of being a snoop," Earl hooted, as he snickered away in a more discreet spot in the corner. Lila didn't give a right damn. She'd waited all her life for these answers, and she wasn't going to let being physically insubstantial stand in her way.

"Who ordered the extra sweet potato fries?" the waitress asked, smacking her gum.

"Me," John answered. "But they're for him. They're his favorite, and the boy needs to eat up. It's his seventeenth *birthday*."

That struck Lila as odd. She knew for sure Hopper's birthday was in March.

"Oh, really?" The waitress gave Hopper an indulgent smile. "One of those people with a birthday right before Christmas, huh? Well, happy birthday then, hon. Finish that up, and I'll bring you some chocolate cake on the house."

A flicker of upset rippled across Hopper's face, which he quickly hid under a mask of politeness. "Much obliged, ma'am." He nodded while his father smiled approvingly. When the woman sauntered off to cut the cake, he glared at his dad. "Really? What was that?" he hissed.

"Details, schmeetails. So your birthday isn't for a few months. That's not so long. And who's it hurting, really?

Sometimes you gotta bend the rules in this world to get what you need. Don't forget that."

Hopper executed a teenage eye roll but he didn't say anything else. Evidently, he was used to his father pulling stunts like this. Awkward silence descended on the table again as he worked on his fries, and his dad sat there, searching his son's face.

"I think it's time I apologized to you," John finally said. "If I was any kind of man, I'd be doing better than lyin' to get you free cake. I'd be giving you a big stack of Christmas presents—maybe even havin' a New Year's Eve party with all your friends from school."

Hopper snorted. "You don't have to do that, Dad. I've never expected that, or even wanted it. Hell, I don't have any friends from school."

"And whose fault is that? Mine! I keep screwin' up and hauling you all over the place. It's not fair to you."

"But you stood by me, Dad. That's what counts. Isn't that what families do?"

The words landed on John in a way Lila couldn't quite decipher. Honestly, the man looked like someone had just kicked him in the stomach. His cheeks reddened up, and his eyes were shining too bright with emotion. "Still," he answered, quickly schooling his expression. "I just want you to understand how sorry I am that I wasn't a better, steadier father. You know, the kinda dad a kid can lean on. Seems like I was always leaning on you, way too much. I have no idea how you've kept things up all these years, especially when I'm just liable to run off or check out. I don't *mean* to do it, son, but—"

"Dad!" Hopper jumped in. "It's okay. I can help. And I'm old enough that I can take on more hours and really make a dent in the bills. You'll see. It'll be better this time."

"No! No boy, there's nothing about it that's okay," John

countered, holding up a staying hand. "A man ought to be able to provide, to give his son a roof over his head without any help from anybody."

"It is what it is, Dad." Hopper shrugged. "I don't mind."

Hopper's reassurances only seemed to put John in a blacker mood. And that made Lila really, really nervous. Something bad was going to happen here, and soon. Something had to have happened to make Hopper so angry that years later, he'd barely even mention his father's name. It felt like the scene of a slow-moving train wreck. She considered telling Earl she wanted to go back. But then she decided no. She had to understand, had to see...

When the waitress came by, John glanced at his watch. He asked her to put Hopper's birthday cake in an extra-sturdy box with a fork and a napkin, saying they had to get to the bus station. Cake in hand, they left. Delilah and Earl followed while the two of them walked to the gas station next door. John insisted Hopper make room in his bag for handfuls of granola bars, bottled water, jerky and candy he'd bought, pointing out that Hopper would need them for their trip.

They walked a few blocks to the Dothan bus depot, and Lila followed them inside. It was a busy place, with travelers trailing stacks of brightly wrapped presents on dollies behind them, or dozing in corners until their bus came in. The smooth, modern, non-descript nature of the place was warmed up a bit by a half-hearted attempt at holiday cheer. Metallic tinsel looped along the ceiling, Christmas music played over the tinny sound system, and a bell ringer in a mangy Santa suit doled out waves and *ho-ho-hos* for donations. Hopper and John stood in front of the board marked "routes" to see what their options were and how much they cost.

John set his duffel down, letting out a breath of relief to be rid of the heavy weight, and plastered on another forced smile. "So whaddaya think, boy? We could go for the waterside charm of Mobile. Or what about all the Southern belles over in Charleston, South Carolina? Sounds like an adventure, huh?"

Hopper, for his part, scanned the board with a blank expression. The boy was trying to be cool, and not so overwhelmed with all the possible destinations. But Lila knew every nuance of Hopper's face. Years of studying him and longing for him from afar had taught her well. And right now, she saw a good son who was just going along with what his father wanted. No way was he happy to pull up stakes and turn his life upside down again. The more she thought about the whole sordid situation, the more it riled her. John was making a big show of giving the boy a choice, but really, it was no choice at all.

Hopper finally pointed to the board. "Atlanta. That's my call."

Atlanta—I was right. This is the trip that will bring him to me...

John grinned, a little too brightly. "A bold choice. The Big Peach. A major city like that will have lots of opportunities for a young man. You'll do great."

Hopper raised a finger in the air and smiled. "*We'll* do great."

"Right," John nodded, his voice trailing off. "*Right*, so, I'm going to go buy the tickets. Wait here."

Hopper obeyed, taking a seat on a bench, supervising their stuff while his father waited in line. Lila and Earl sat on the bench with him, though the boy couldn't tell.

Finally, John came back. But he appeared different—upset maybe—with a grim, almost scary set to his jaw. Her alarm bells went off for real this time, and it let loose a sick wave of dread in her stomach. "Oh, God in heaven..." She grabbed Earl's arm. "What is that man going to do?"

"Just watch," Earl murmured, putting his hand over hers to calm her.

It didn't work. There was a hollowness to John's eyes that brimmed with defeat, as if he'd given up. Completely.

Hopper must have seen it too. "Dad?" he croaked, his voice cracking a bit. "You okay?"

"Yeah," John insisted. "And you will be too. Here, I've got your ticket." He handed Hopper a bus station envelope that had been printed up special for the holidays. The design featured a big red bow to make it look like a present. *This Christmas, you're going places!* it said on the front.

The envelope was strangely overstuffed, and Hopper eyed it suspiciously before he finally opened it. In it was a ticket *and a big wad of cash*. Hopper eyed it in a kind of dull shock.

"There's your ticket," John told him, as matter of fact as you please. "You're getting a late start, but you'll get to Atlanta by end of the day tomorrow. There's an overnight layover in Douglasville, Georgia first. I put three hundred dollars in there too. I wish to hell it could be more, but it was all that was left after our last paychecks. If you're careful with it, it should be enough to get you started, though."

"Get *me* started," Hopper answered, his voice sounding so thin, so pained, Lila barely recognized it. "Don't you mean get *us* started?"

"No, son." He clapped a hand on Hopper's shoulder. "This is where we part ways."

Lila's hands flew up to cover her startled cry. The sight of Hopper's stunned face was more than she could bear. The poor boy couldn't have been more surprised than if his dad had knifed him in the chest. Lila supposed, in a way, the man had.

Hopper hesitated for a long moment and then he yanked himself away from John's steadying hold. His eyes blazed with too many emotions—love, fear, fury, disbelief, and deep, debilitating hurt.

Abandonment. Complete and utter abandonment. That was what Hopper was feeling. It didn't take much to figure that out. There was something about the last blood relative in your life disappearing. She'd felt it when Mama had died—that sharp, desolate sting of being left behind. But her mama hadn't *meant* to die. And she'd had Randy, and friends, and…

The idea that Hopper had had no one, absolutely *no one* in that moment…it broke her heart. Hot, furious tears rolled down her cheeks.

That *bastard.*

"Come on Hop, don't be like that. Anyone can see I'm nothin' but dead weight. I'll only hold you back from becoming all you're supposed to be."

"What I'm *supposed* to be," Hopper quavered, "is *with my father.*"

"No, Hopper, you're not." John's voice was hard, and stony. "You're sixteen. You're old enough to support yourself and keep what you earn. You can do a lot better on your own than you can with me. Maybe stay at the same high school until you graduate. Or get a GED and land a good job at a warehouse or somethin'. They've got programs that'll help you through college—scholarships and stuff for employees. It's pretty obvious I can't stay around for that. I'd just be a millstone around your neck, and you know it."

"But–but we're *family,* Dad!" Hopper cried, his voice ringing with disappointment. "We help each other. That's how it works."

"No, boy, that's *not* how it works. Dad fucks up. Son helps him. Dad fucks up again. That's how it works. I'm done. I'm making this a clean break. For your sake."

Hopper threw up his hands. "But where will you go?"

"Wherever the wind blows me. Maybe somewhere warm, like Florida. Or maybe I'll give the Midwest a try. I haven't done that yet."

Hopper stared down at his envelope and took a shaky

breath. "If I get on that bus," he murmured, his voice grim, "I'll never see you again. I'll never even *talk* to you. There'd be no address, no telephone—"

"I know," John cut him off. The man's voice was soft. But his eyes weren't. They glittered with finality, seeming to say, *please, son, stop arguing with me.*

Hopper simply stood there, frozen, his mouth hanging open. "God!" he finally gasped. "You really mean it!"

"I do," John answered. He wrapped his arms around Hopper's rigid frame and gave the boy a short, fierce hug and a sharp pat on the back. "I guess this is goodbye. Everything will be fine, son. You'll see."

And just like that, the man grabbed his bag, turned his back on his child, and began stiffly, deliberately walking away.

Hopper tried to stand tall, but he swayed on his feet as his father walked away from him. John had almost made it to the outside door before the boy finally found his voice. "Dad! Dad, *please!*" he begged.

John turned around to face him.

Hopper was truly vibrating with despair and panic, heartbreak etching every single one of his features. "Don't do this! You're all I've got!"

John gave his son one last, sad smile. "You've got yourself. And that's all a man ever really needs."

The man turned heel and walked resolutely for the exit.

"Dad…*Dad!*" Hopper screamed, his desperation ringing off the walls. Lila found herself letting out an involuntary wail too.

John winced, his steps faltering only for a moment. But in the end, the man simply kept going. The automatic doors whooshed softly shut behind him.

Hopper stayed frozen in place for several long, long moments. It was the only time Lila had ever seen him cry, tears streaming down his face as he clenched his fists tight by his sides.

This was the boy who'd shown up on Randy's doorstep. The boy who'd worked hard and had treated Lila, Randy, and her mama like family. The one who'd lied to get what he wanted, and had told her goodbye, for her own good. And all of it—every bit—had come from this. Lila wiped a shaky hand over her face, swiping at her tears. If the weight of all this was crushing her now, how could Hopper have stood it?

Eventually his tears slowed, and the boy stared dazedly down at his white knuckles, slowly opening his fists. In one was several bloody half-moons, where he'd dug his fingernails in. In the other was the envelope. He scanned the room, blinking as he slowly seemed aware of his surroundings again. A few parents who'd heard the goings-on were holding their shocked kids tighter to them. The Santa Claus had stopped ringing his bell, gawking at him outright. Hopper glared back at the jolly old elf, and the man turned away, embarrassed. Adjusting his filthy fake beard, the idiot rang his bell again and belched out another *ho-ho-ho...Meeehhhhrrrry Christmas!*

Hopper studied the bills in his hand again in numb amazement, as if he couldn't quite believe what he was seeing. Then he jammed the envelope in the pocket of his moto jacket, and quickly wiped his eyes with his sleeve. Shamefaced, he stole a couple furtive glances to see if people were still staring. They weren't.

An announcer with a cloyingly sweet Southern accent blared over the cheap loudspeaker, saying passengers for the Atlanta route could start boarding. Panic gripped his features, as if he had no idea what to do.

Forgetting herself, Lila jumped up off the bench and ran to Hopper, trying to throw her arms around his neck, trying to tell him somehow, some way, that he wasn't alone. That all he had to do was get on that bus, and they'd find their way to each other. That's they'd get through everything together. But her arms just slid through the boy like a shadow. It only made her sob more.

He picked up his bag and shuffled toward his bus. Lila lunged forward to follow him. But Earl grabbed her arm.

"No. Don't," Earl urged. "You already know right where that boy is goin.' If you want to find out what's really happening here, we've got to follow John."

CHAPTER 12

AS SOON AS Lila took Earl's hand, she was magicked off to a different place, landing with a thud on the back seat of some taxi.

"Earl!" she yelped, so queasy from tripping the space-time continuum, it felt like she'd pulled her stomach out over her head. "Could you warn a girl next time?"

He barked out an ornery laugh. "Where's the fun in that?"

Lila shot him a dirty look, wondering how he could find a sense of adventure in all this mess. Not much about this excursion down tragedy lane had been fun. And they were nowhere near done yet. Because John Vance sat slumped on the seat in between them, completely oblivious to their presence.

As she practically stared a hole into John, Lila knew she should feel the strong urge to slap some shame into the man. What kind of *monster* could do that to his own flesh and blood? But she couldn't quite summon the anger. The man seemed so desolate, so tired and worn, he'd clearly done a pretty good job of punishing himself.

John didn't offer a word of chitchat to the driver, simply giving him an address and settling in for the ride. He peered out the window, squinting against the sun as they passed by Dothan's southern charms—picket fences and porches, the low-slung, old-fashioned storefronts giving way to the busy business district. Everywhere there were glittering shop windows and light displays, ready to spring into service at dusk. But John was too lost in thought to even notice.

When the taxi reached its destination, Lila finally understood why. They'd stopped at a hospital. Sliding out of the van, she stood dumbstruck as John paid the driver and tipped him generously. Then the man gingerly hoisted his duffel over his arm and walked inside. From her vantage point on the sidewalk, Lila could see through the glass doors, as a nurse pointed him to the admissions desk.

She turned to Earl. "What's wrong with him?"

"*What's not* would be the better question. John has near total kidney failure, advanced cirrhosis of the liver, and a dangerously enlarged heart. He got his kidney diagnosis yesterday. This is his first dialysis treatment. But it won't go well. From this day forward, John Vance will spend the rest of his life in a hospital or a skilled nursing place."

"But how? The man can't be more than, what, forty?"

Earl tsked and shook his head. "Age duddn't matter when you drink too much, and smoke too much, and have terrible nightmares stealing your peace of mind on a daily basis. He drank like a fish and did a lot of drugs, especially when he was young. That probably didn't help him any."

Oh. My. God. Lila's heart felt like it was plummeting to her feet. Lord have mercy, what that poor man must have been going through. He'd been a dead man walking. "How long has he known?"

"He knew about his heart and his liver. Those conditions had been advancing for years, though he'd never told Hopper that. But his kidney troubles? That's new. He'd been feeling worse and worse but had put off going to the doctor for weeks. Once he went into the hospital today, he didn't last too long. The doctors said with dialysis he might live another year or two before his heart and liver condition caught up with him. But one round of dialysis was enough for him. John said no. He decided he wouldn't do anything."

Lila gasped. "My God! No dialysis? He would have been dead in a week!"

"A month, actually," Earl answered, shaking his head.

Her stomach pitched as she put two and two together, and all John's actions suddenly made an awful kind of sense. "That's what the whole business in the bus station was really about," she groaned. "He knew he was dying, and he didn't want his son around to watch."

"That's about right," he answered. "He died in a VA home. His body was donated to science."

Lila could see John's predicament. But to make Hopper think he'd just *abandoned* him? To refuse to let his son care for him, and hold his hand when he'd died? That was *better?*

"I can tell what you're thinkin', girl," Earl warned. "But he didn't want his boy spending one more day cleaning up his messes. He didn't want Hopper trying to talk him into getting years of pricey, painful treatments, either. John just didn't want to prolong the inevitable. The man truly thought he was being cruel to be kind."

"Kind. You call this *kind?*" she howled. "What could possibly be more devastating than what happened in that bus station? Hopper never got over it. He never will! You can't condone this, Earl. Tell me you can't!"

He held up his hands in surrender. "I'm not saying it was right or wrong. I'm just saying, John Vance made his choice. And to his dying day, he believed it was the right one."

She wobbled over to a bench at the hospital's entrance and gently sat down, her legs too rubbery to support her. God, she felt ill just thinking about it. Poor Hopper. He never knew. All this time, he thought his dad hadn't wanted him...

probably had wondered what he'd done wrong. It was all just so, so unfair.

I never knew him. I never knew anything about him, really.

Had anyone ever known Hopper? What he'd been through? All those years, and this is what he'd been hiding. The source of all his pain. His lack of place in the world…

A cold wave of nausea coursed over her. Something akin to shame. Embarrassment. Foolishness, even. She'd thought they'd had a love for the ages. A connection that could never be broken. But she'd been in love with a ghost, hadn't she?

Worse, she felt vaguely dirty. Like she'd had no right to ask these questions. How could she scroll through the worst moments of Hopper's life, like they were some kind of movie for her viewing enjoyment? They were his burdens, not hers. And what good would all this snooping do anyway? He'd made it clear he'd wanted her out of his life, and she needed to stay out.

God. I'm such an idiot...

Her stomach churned. *I have to put a stop to this.*

She stood up on shaky legs. "I'm done here, Earl. I've got all the closure I need. Please, just get me out of here."

His eyebrows shot up. "But don't you wanna learn 'bout—"

"*No.*" She held up a staying hand. "I want you to stop. I want to leave. *Right. Now.*" There were just some questions she never should've asked.

Earl paused for a long, hard moment, like he might argue with her. But in the end, he just shrugged. "Alright, sugar," he drawled, holding out his arm. "As you wish."

And the second she touched his arm, they were flashed right back to the Outpost. She landed with a thud, right on her ass, over by the cash register. And she was *pissed.*

Lila brushed herself off and jumped to her feet. "What the world, Earl? I told you I wanted out! Why am I back here?"

Earl threw up his hands. "'Cause you ain't done yet!"

"The hell I'm not!" Lila shook with anger. "I'm *done*. Why would I want to break my heart all over again? My time with Hopper is over. Ancient history. He doesn't love me, or want me, and that's that. So let me go!"

But Earl, the maddening old coot, just grinned at her. "You sure about that?"

Lila opened her mouth up to yell out her answer when she heard the heavy sound of booted footsteps. They weren't alone in the store, were they? She turned to see who was coming up behind them.

And she damn near fell on her ass again.

"Delilah? Is that really you?" The voice that came out of the man standing there sounded nothing like Hopper. It was gravelly. Deeper. Raspy.

But it was Hopper, all the same. Dear God. *Hopper.* The only person in the whole wide world who called her Delilah. She found herself furiously blinking back tears again. Because this wasn't some "point in time" Hopper from her past. No, this was *present-day* Hopper. She could tell that from the salt and pepper in his beard and hair. Could see it in the feathered lines around his eyes and the fine white scar that ran down the side of his temple.

He was dressed more or less like he used to—a pair of weathered jeans that pulled over his thighs just so, a black long-sleeved thermal pushed up to his elbows, a work shirt, and black square-toed motorcycle boots. But that's where the similarity ended. He was bigger. Ripped, even. So much so that his shirt molded over his pecs and biceps. His arms were almost completely covered in tats. Side of his neck too. To anyone else's eyes, he'd be a big, bad biker. An intimidating man.

But Lila couldn't find it in her to be intimidated. Because the way he was looking at her was the same. Clear blue eyes, holding her to the spot. Taking every last bit of her in. Seeing her, right down to the bone. *Oh, yes.* It was just the same.

. . .

Hopper stared in wonder. Delilah. The *real* Delilah. Right here. Right now.

He couldn't tear his eyes away from the woman she'd become. Because she looked good. *Really good*. Like, Delilah 2.0. She'd left her wild, Sassy Lass vibe behind, he was glad to see. And this older, wiser version of her was obviously doing well—a fancy sweater that fit her to perfection, dark blue jeans that hugged her curves, and black leather boots with a heel that came down to a precise little point.

He wouldn't have thought it possible, but the years had actually made her more beautiful than ever. She didn't have all that waist-length, wavy hair anymore. But surprisingly, he didn't miss it. Those gorgeous locks were cut to her shoulders but still the color of midnight, and combed back from her face, making the most of her pretty widow's peak. And yeah, she still had that kick-ass figure, but her contours were lush, and soft. She'd lost that doe-eyed freshness she used to have, and her naturally rosy cheeks. Yet, the years had only made her face more interesting—more honed, maybe—and her smoky gray eyes sharper and more discerning.

And she was *discerning* him now.

How in the hell had she gotten here? Was she "stuck" too? Holy shit, had she gone back? What had she seen?

He felt the sudden urge to shrink under her gaze. What would she think of him, after everything he'd done? He swallowed hard, trying to ignore the lump forming in his throat. He stuffed his hands in his pockets, cringing when he noticed he'd pushed his sleeves up, exposing a batch of prison tats. He quickly pulled the shirt down to his wrists.

God, what he must look like to her—like some kind of jacked-up monster. The kind of guy you wouldn't want to meet in a dark alley. An ex-con. He closed his eyes briefly, that old familiar shame creeping up the back of his neck.

“Yes,” Delilah finally breathed, her voice barely more than a thready whisper. “It’s really me. How-how did you get here?”

“Same as you,” Candy interjected. Hopper had been so focused on Delilah, he hadn’t seen their magical tour guides come up beside them. “He’s been on his own trip through your Christmases past. Though he picked out different gifts.”

Delilah peered steadily at him while the silence stretched on, and they both struggled for what to say. “What did you see?” she finally croaked out.

“You,” Hopper answered. “And us. *Together.*”

Delilah flinched. Actually *flinched*.

Hopper swallowed down the embarrassment, swallowed the bile forming in his throat. “It wasn’t like that,” he blurted out, before he could stop himself. “It was beautiful. *You* were beautiful. We were happy.”

He’d forgotten how tiny she was, the top of her head not even coming up to his shoulder—yet another fact that made him feel like some kind of towering monster. But she gazed up at him anyway, as if she might find something important in his expression. And maybe he was searching for something too. Some spark of recognition…the flame that used to dance between them, perhaps. But she pressed her eyes closed, shutting him out. Her cheeks reddened up, and she swayed on her feet. Instinctively, he reached out to steady her. But she stepped back a step, startling when her back hit the counter.

His blood ran cold. Dear Lord, was she actually…*afraid* of him? “Delilah,” he faltered, trying to keep the disappointment out of his voice. “I get it. I must look like a different man, but…you know I’m not going to hurt you, right? For God’s sake, what did they show you?”

She held up a staying hand. An errant tear sneaked down her cheek. Yet another tear he’d put there. “It’s not that, okay? It’s just— I can’t do this. I can’t just pretend like the past never happened. It's too much." She stalked over to the peg by the door and grabbed her bags. "I'm out."

Hopper wheeled around to follow her. "Wait! No—please! Can't we talk at least?"

Delilah didn't answer him as she hastily threw on her coat. She had that *you-can't-change-my-mind* look on her face. His steps slowed.

Candy slid in front of him, slapping a small, slim gift box into his hand. "Stop her," she urged. "And take this."

He'd barely had time to bound up behind her as she yanked open the door. He grabbed her elbow. "I don't know why we're here any more than you do. But we're supposed to be figuring things out with our past, and I'm pretty sure running away isn't going to accomplish that. Come on, baby, *please.*"

She stiffened under his grip. "Don't call me that. I'm not your baby. You told me that years ago, and I believed you. Whatever this bullshit is, it's a fantasy. So *get off!*" She squirmed, trying to break his grip.

"I pushed you away once," he growled, holding tight. "I'll be damned if I do it twice."

Lila growled right back at him, determined to wrestle her arm free. When she realized she couldn't, she heaved her way through the door anyway. Hopper staggered along behind her.

There was another one of those damn blinding flashes...

And they both landed with a thud in the back of a horse-drawn carriage, all decked out with red ribbons and sleigh bells. Hopper groaned when he recognized the box in his hand.

Candy. She'd engineered this Christmas paradise, of course.

He'd hoped they could have this conversation on the porch of the Outpost or something, like adults. But here they were both in their twenty-something bodies, back in one of their Christmases past. This time, they were in the Alpine-inspired tourist town of Helen, Georgia. Like a little Bavaria up in the mountains, this place was decorated to the nines at this time of year—a real Christmas mecca. On a whim, he'd taken her here for an extended holiday the year they'd first gotten together. They'd just been a couple for a few days at this point. But he'd booked time at a cabin up here, and they'd had an incredible time. Morning, noon, and night.

But the minute Lila turned to him with her eyes flashing fire, he knew this wasn't the twenty-something Delilah he'd encountered in his flashbacks. No, this was present-day Delilah, like him, trapped in her younger body. And she was none too happy with her predicament.

"Oh, for God's sake. Are you *kidding* me?" she yelped. "You *would* take me here. To *this* weekend."

Hopper rubbed his forehead. "I swear I just wanted to talk to you. It was Candy who put this gift in my hands. Here." He handed over the package. "I believe this belongs to you."

She opened it, a sarcastic sneer twisting over her face. "Just like I remember," she groused, then hurled the box out of the carriage and onto the street. *Of course.*

The box held the reservation sheets for their three-day stay in the cabin up here. He'd sprung it on her during their carriage ride all those years ago. He could hardly blame her for chucking it out now.

Delilah threw her hands up in the air. "Great. I suppose we're stuck up here for, what, three days?"

"Beats the shit out of me."

Lila whipped back around and plastered her back against the seat, sitting there in stony silence with her arms crossed over her chest.

And Hopper sat there too, without the faintest clue what to say to the woman. Finally, he screwed his courage up. "I don't regret it, going back. Those Christmases with you?

They were the best of my life. The only real Christmases I'd ever had."

Lila snorted. "And I'll bet the sex wasn't so bad, either."

He turned to her. "It was always good, wasn't it?"

She paused for a moment, frankly roaming her eyes over him from head to foot. "Yeah." She grumbled and forced her gaze forward again. "It was. I just don't know how I feel about it that you—that you..."

"Yeah." Hopper winced. "I see what you're saying. That was kinda bad, wasn't it? But you have to understand. I was in this weird magical space and it felt like the chance of a lifetime to have you back in my arms again. Like I could wipe away all my sins and start over. It was too much for me. I-I couldn't help myself."

She nodded, but still didn't say anything. To be honest, he was at a loss for words, too. Maybe he'd already said too much. His heart beat a ragged tattoo in his chest as the horse swayed along, its hooves clip clopping loudly on the street ahead of them. If their driver could hear them at all, he didn't let on. His top hat never bobbed, and his shoulders were ramrod straight in his flawless, Victorian suit. It was midday in Helen, a perfect, crisp December day in Georgia. There was a dusting of snow on the ground, but it was melting in the relatively warm midday sun. He and Lila were dressed up for the day in matching Christmas sweatshirts and knit hats they'd bought at one of the shops. Everywhere tourists were smiling, carrying armloads of shopping bags and eating street food like churros, fudge, and cones of sweetened nuts. Holiday music filtered out from the shop doorways.

It should've been idyllic. But it wasn't. The painful irony was definitely not lost on him.

Jesus, this is fuckin' uncomfortable.

Lila gently cleared her throat. "So you're out of prison then."

"Yeah," he answered, grateful for an easy answer. "I got out a little over four years ago. They let me out early."

She nodded. "You working anywhere?"

"Yeah. As a mechanic."

She arched an eyebrow. "So you're not—"

Hopper jumped in once he understood her meaning. "No. *God* no. I swear, Delilah. I swear to you, I haven't done so much as run a stop sign since I've gotten out of jail. That part of my life is over. I'm not that man anymore."

Delilah studied him for a long moment, then nodded. "I believe you."

He found himself letting out a long breath, and his shoulders relaxed. Thank Christ. At least she'd believed that much. "What have you been doing? You married?" he blurted out. "Or seeing anyone?"

She scowled. "No. I was married once, but… No. There's no man in my life these days."

Hopper was damn happy to hear that. He realized all at once that he was smiling broadly at her. Probably too eager. But it was too late now.

Delilah blinked, but held his gaze. "What about you? Is there someone?"

"Nah." He shrugged. "I tried Tinder, when I first got out. But it was such a let-down. After a while I just, I dunno. I just stopped. Nothing about it felt right."

And it was true. He'd already had the great love of his life. Everything else was a pale imitation. Yeah, he'd binged on the hookup buffet at first. But in the morning he'd wake up feeling more hollow and desolate than he did before. Being on his own hurt less. He couldn't tell her that, of course. But maybe she could see the truth of it on his face.

LILA SWALLOWED hard as she listened to his answer. The way he was looking at her, she'd swear it was like the stars and the moon had been returned to him. And in some weird way, it'd felt like they'd almost been waiting for each other, without even realizing it. It was a stupid thought to have, she knew, but it niggled at her anyway.

"So you're not waitressing anymore, huh?" Hopper asked, apparently trying to lighten the conversation.

"Absolutely not. Though I have to say, that job at the Sassy wasn't so bad. I made great money. But these days, I'm too old for that."

He let his eyes drift lazily over her. "Trust me, Delilah, you're not. Men would still pay good money to see those legs in a short kilt."

Lila snorted. He was actually *flirting* with her?

She searched his face, only to find him smiling down at her with such warmth and affection and utter sincerity, it took her breath away. And dammit, she fell right back into those blue, blue eyes again. Seemed she still wasn't immune to his charms. If anything, he was harder to resist. It was the damnedest thing. He had all the vitality of his younger self—the unmarred skin, the youthful glow—but his eyes were older, sadder, more...

Hell, she didn't know what. But he was too close to her, dammit, seeming to take up all the space in this little carriage. So big, so overwhelmingly male, his very presence seeming to radiate sex and Sunday morning kisses and...

And bad decisions.

Snapping herself out of it, she rushed to correct him. "Well, be that as it may, I'm hoping not to have to peddle shepherd's pie and expensive beers again. I earn my crust as a medical coder and practice manager these days. I really like my work. And I got rid of the Jetta, you'll be glad to hear."

Hopper barked out a laugh. "May the piece of shit rest in peace."

She laughed too. "Hey buddy, my taste in cars has

improved. I got a nice, used red Audi. Runs like a top. Have a sweet little condo too, all paid up. It's perfect for me."

"Sounds like you've set up a nice life for yourself," Hopper answered. Another man might've said it with a note of bitterness. As if he'd been disappointed she didn't "need" him. How many times had her ex-husband hurled that kind of barb? But Hopper's expression told another story. His gaze was warm. Proud. Happy for her.

Relieved, maybe? That too, probably.

"This is strange then, isn't it?" she mused. "Makes you wonder what's going on. I mean, if we're both so well adjusted, why are we here?"

Hopper leaned his head against his hand, giving it some thought. "Well, Candy did say we had to learn the things we didn't know before. So, what did you see?"

Lila's heart dropped to her knees. She'd walked right into that one, hadn't she? Aww hell, she was in no mood to admit how she'd pried. How she'd seen him at his lowest moments. She squirmed uncomfortably. "I dunno," she hedged. "I mean, what did *you* revisit?"

Hopper raised an eyebrow, as if he might press her to answer. But he didn't. "I'm not going to hide anything from you, Delilah. Not anymore. Any information you need, you can ask me, you understand? I owe you that much."

So she did. She asked him question after question. And as the carriage clattered 'round and 'round Helen's downtown, Hopper related his story about going to the Outpost to buy a tree, and how he'd ended up in his bed back in Douglasville, on the day he'd given her the motorcycle as a gift. How he'd figured out he couldn't change the outcome of anything and that he was "living out of time." He mentioned that he'd wanted to see what happened to her, and he was taken to the Christmas Day she'd left Mitchell. Gratefully, he skimmed over that lightly, apparently reading the shame and embarrassment on her face.

And then he surprised her. He said he'd gone back to that day at the garage, to revisit their first time together. He said, out of all the Christmases they'd been together, this had been the one he wanted to remember. But then he kinda stopped.

He simply got quiet, grabbed her hands, and held them between his. Lila found herself staring down at them. She'd forgotten what this felt like, having her hand in his. They were nearly twice the size as hers, and more muscular and calloused than she remembered. He circled his thumb on the top of her knuckles, sending a tremor of tingles up her arm.

"Can you tell me one thing?" he asked, the pained expression on his face telling her he had something very important to say. She nodded. "Back in my garage, when we got together, why didn't you tell me it was your first time?"

Delilah reared back, aghast, the moment lost. "Are you even serious? Why in God's name— What? Did you want to do a victory lap? Wave my cherry around like a flag or something?"

"No!" Hopper cried. "Goddammit, it's not like that, okay? It's just— It bothers me, that's all. Your first time shouldn't have been like that."

A sizzle of heat rushed through her as she remembered the hood of that car, but she quickly shoved it away. "I had the first time I wanted, Hopper. It was fine."

His mouth flattened to an outraged scowl. "No! It wasn't fine! You shouldn't have kept that from me. For God's sake, it was your *virginity,* Delilah. I should've never taken that from you like that. You should have said something!"

Lila yanked her hands away, her blood suddenly boiling. "Why?" she demanded. "So you could find another excuse to push me away? To stop?"

"Dammit, Delilah! I deserved to know if I was hurting you. I've never wanted to hurt you. Don't you understand?"

She let out a disgusted squawk. "It's a little late for *that,* isn't it?"

His face collapsed in a way she'd never quite seen before. As if she'd crushed him. That was pretty rich—*him* pretending to be the injured party. She'd had a belly full of men who tried to turn shit like this around on her. And she wasn't having it.

"Since you're so put out by my lack of total honesty, let's review all the things *you* hid from *me,* shall we? Let's start from the beginning. You were a homeless teen, struggling to keep a roof over your head your whole childhood. Randy was the only reason you weren't sleeping in a cardboard box. But you were stealing even then. And let's not forget how well you did after you left the haven of honest work Randy offered you. How much did the police impound again from your busted stolen parts ring? Two hundred grand? Or was it three?"

Hopper gave her a stony stare. "It was two-hundred fifty thousand dollars, pretty much on the nose. And for your information, I'd just told my partner I was quitting the day the sting happened. I was getting out."

Honestly, did he really think she'd believe that whopper? She stared at him, almost too incredulous to speak. "Even if I chose to buy that convenient story, how would that make anything better? The years of stealing? And lying—don't forget about that."

"It's true, Delilah. Whether you want to believe it or not. I really was getting out. I'd saved up what I'd intended to save. And I was ready. I wanted a better life for us!"

A-A *better life?*

Anger bubbled up in her gut. What was wrong with the one they'd had? They'd been happy. They'd been together. Wasn't that enough for him? Wasn't *she* enough? What, had he wanted some over-the-top life for her, like the one she'd had with Mitch? Oh, *please.*

She chuckled bitterly. "And that's how you build that life? On stolen money?" Her lip curled in disgust. "What did you think I'd do once I found out you had all that money? Did you think I wouldn't care? Jesus Christ, Hopper! Who was this man I was giving my body and soul to? Did I even know him at all? Did you ever think it was important to show him to me?"

His face twisted in anguish, true desperation gripping him. He grabbed her hand again and held it against his chest, trapping it there. "Feel that beating, angel? It beats for you. It always has. That was never a lie."

His heart thundered under her hand. The shock of touching his warm, broad chest sent a fizz of awareness through her. And somehow, that only made her madder. Did he really think he could manipulate her this way?

"Say what you want, Hopper," Lila answered, pulling her hand away. "But when I'd come to visit you after the trial, all prepared to stand by you? You told me you'd used me. Told me I was a stupid little girl. That you—and I quote—*never gave a shit*. And you come back here after all this time, and tell me I'm the love of your life? Tell me, Hopper, why should I believe a goddamn word you say?"

He sat there gaping at her like a deer in headlights. *Yeah, history has a way of biting you in the ass, doesn't it, Hopper?* His Adam's apple worked up and down, but no sound came out. Speechless. Of course.

In the silence, her anger churned and twisted inside her, years and years of it, crashing through the walls she'd erected to contain it. What was she doing, trapped in this stupid carriage with him? Did she really think he would just say some kind of magic word, and it would be all right? There *were* no words that could fix what this man had done to her.

God, she had to get out of here, had to escape the pain that threatened to drown her. She kicked the door open and balanced her foot on the narrow step.

"Angel, wait!" he called, trying to grab her arm again. "I had my reasons! I swear! I—"

"Stop, Hopper! Just stop!" She wrenched her arm away and lost her balance, falling off the moving carriage. Landing hard, she stumbled and fell. But she was surprised when her palms met coarse gray gravel, and not the smooth pavement in downtown Helen. She pushed herself up on her wobbling high-heeled boots, startling when she realized she was back to her 38-year-old self, and standing beside her red Audi. All her Christmas purchases sat carefully stowed in the backseat. the Outpost stood in the distance. One by one the lights blinked out, and an unseen hand turned over the sign in the door from "open" to "closed." The place was completely dark, and the smoke abruptly stopped puffing from the chimney.

Delilah didn't wait around to ask questions or wonder why. This was her chance to get out of this bizarre time loop she'd been caught in. Out of whatever kind of painful dream this was and back to the reality—the peace—she'd fought so hard for. And though her heart felt like it was cracking open, she got in the car, turned over the ignition, and flew back down the road as fast as those wheels would turn.

CHAPTER 13

HOPPER JUMPED out of the moving carriage, right behind Delilah, and tumbled to the ground. But when he rolled himself upright again, coughing and sputtering, he found himself in a dark, musty old building. He frantically scanned the room.

I haven't been here before, have I?

Wherever he was, he was all alone. The only sound was a whistling winter wind and the front door, loose on its hinges, banging open again and again.

His eyes adjusted to the hazy light of dusk and he began taking in details. A creek-stone fireplace covered in cobwebs. The carcass of a Christmas tree nearly turned to dust with decay. Display shelves knocked over and their merchandise scattered and broken.

He picked up a present from under the tree, blew off the dust, and opened it. It was empty, but he recognized the wrap.

The Outpost. He was in the Outpost. But why was it like this? Had he gone *forward* in time or something?

He walked out to the porch, but his foot went through the

decaying floorboards, and he nearly fell. Booking it down the steps, he didn't stop until he was on solid ground.

"Delilah?" he yelled out. "Candy? Earl?"

There was no answer, of course. He scanned the snowy landscape, completely at a loss to explain this. *Had any of this really happened? Was it all some kind of fever dream? A hallucination?*

He stalked around the house. The place was abandoned, alright. But soon he turned a corner and was almost shocked to find his red Ford pickup, in the side lot where he'd left it. And it was still loaded with everything he'd bought for their Christmas project. The tree, the ornaments—every bit of it was still there, all shiny, new, and perfect.

He bellowed in frustration, not that anyone would hear it. Dammit, where had Delilah gone? She'd just...*disappeared.* And yet, he knew their meeting in the Outpost had *actually* happened. At the least their meeting in the store, anyway. Surely she'd remember it, just like he did. He had to hold on to that and keep believing.

He had to find her, and that was the end of it. No way could he leave things like this. He had to see her again, if for no other reason than to make amends in a way she could understand. And *man*—now that he knew she was on her own again? He wanted to give her a lot more than apologies. He wanted her back. All of it. He'd prove to her that he'd changed or die trying.

But how?

Where could he even find her? Shit, did he even know what day and time it was?

He felt around in his back pocket and found his phone. Pulling it out, he spotted a text in his Holliday Hot Rods group stream from Lita.

(Today, five p.m.) **Hey Hop—found a tree yet?**

According to the phone, it was December 24. Five-fifteen in the evening. Practically down to the minute when he'd first parked his car in front of the Outpost—which apparently had turned into some kind of freaky end-times ruin. In a matter of *seconds*. He shook his head. *How is any of this even possible?*

He stomped himself around in a circle and jammed his fingers through his hair. Dammit to hell, he wanted to go after Delilah. Right this minute. *If only I knew where she was.*

He checked his phone again. It was two minutes later. He let out a long breath. Okay, so time was moving forward.

He truly was back in the here and now. And there was nothing to be done, was there? He had to snap himself out of it and get back to his life, he supposed. This Christmas tree wasn't going to get to the Casto place all by itself.

He answered Lita's text.

Found one. And some decorations too. All set and heading over there.

As soon as he hit send, a flurry of texts followed.

From Hunter: **Good work, Hop! You'd better promise me you'll get some rest and relaxation over the holidays!**

From Lita: **Awesome!! Thanks for taking one for the team! Merry Christmas, big man!**

From Ross: **Amazed you found something this late. How did you find all that so fast?**

Hopper hesitated over the screen, debating what to say. **Just an out-of-the-way stand, like Hunter said,** he finally typed, going for a "less is more" strategy.

Popping the phone back in his pocket, he hopped back in his truck, relieved to see it was still in perfect working order. He idled there for a moment, staring hard out the windshield. Conflicting emotions ate at him. He was half afraid to leave and half afraid to stay.

But Delilah wasn't here. There was nothing to do. No one to save. He was back to his life again, and the memories, the old and the new.

He'd have to figure all this out later. Determined now, he

jammed his foot on the gas and powered down the road, flying hard over every rut and pothole. He made a mental note to replace his shocks after this.

He finally turned onto the open road again and was back at Mrs. C's in no time. The sight of their decorations helped jolt him out of his brood. Lita had outdone herself again with the window painting. It looked amazing from the road—a friggin' masterpiece, as usual, with a big old columned house and a bunch of Victorian-era people dashing through the snow in a red horse-drawn sleigh. She'd even made the family a colorful wreath of plastic bells, ornaments, and netting.

As he turned off the ignition and lingered a bit, déjà vu stole over him again. Then he realized why. The window painting, the wreath—it reminded him of Randy's house, the Christmas he'd shown up on the man's doorstep. *My Delilah.* She always could make something from nothing. She'd been so full of hope and sweetness back then, she could practically conjure Christmas spirit from the thin air. The thought made him smile, but somehow a twinge of sadness pinched in his chest anyway. He brushed it aside. This tree wasn't going to decorate itself.

He locked up the truck, hoisted the tree over his shoulder, and made his way inside. Ah, the place smelled like it should at Christmas. Hot cider bubbled on the stove, and the scent of buttered rolls and glazed ham was delightfully strong in the small space.

When Mrs. C caught sight of him piling through the door, dragging the tree, she clapped and hollered. "Oh! You made it! And with a half hour to spare! You're a miracle worker!"

"Told you I would." He grinned back at her, his mood lifting a little too.

When he finished yanking the tree across the living room, he was ambushed by a big hug. "You didn't have to do this,

Hopper, but I'm so glad you did. The kids are going to love this! You're a real-life Santa. I hope you get that."

"Come on, you don't have to keep thanking me. It was a group project," he answered, feeling self-conscious. "We're all glad to help out."

"Don't you go being modest," she answered, dragging his bags of ornaments over to the couch. "This was all your idea. And I appreciate you thinking of us at this time of year. It means a lot to know I'm not in all this alone."

Hopper inclined his head. "Anytime, ma'am. It's no trouble." And it really wasn't. Because this charity project was the only thing keeping him from falling apart. If he couldn't solve his own problems, it sure as shit felt good to solve a problem for someone else. Someone who deserved it.

He set up the tree and strung the multi-colored lights on in no time flat. Once the tinsel was on, Mrs. C sat on the couch and passed him big handfuls of the ornaments. It was a small tree, so the whole operation was done faster than he'd expected. But it was six-thirty, and they both startled at the sound of tires coming up the gravel driveway. Eager to get out before the kids saw him, he lunged for his coat.

She pulled herself back up on her walker. "That's them!" she cried, practically shaking head to toe with the Christmas spirit. She grabbed Hopper by the sleeve as he darted by. "Aww! You don't have to go! The kids would love to meet you."

"No way! I want to make sure you get the credit for this one. Or Santa. Your pick. Y'all have a Merry Christmas, all right?" He gave her a quick kiss on the cheek as he dashed out the back door. Deciding to hide until he could make a clean getaway, he tiptoed out into the trees on the rise just above the trailer and settled in to spy on the kids' reactions. He could hear the whoops of joy even from out here.

The little girl, Savannah, was eight. She walked silently around the room in wonder, as if the entire thing was a mirage that'd disappear if she blinked. Dazed, she bent down to the Barbie townhouse, one of the few gifts that were unwrapped, and picked up each doll, marveling at them quietly. Her five-year-old brother Tristan was apparently her complete opposite. He was shrieking and cheering enough for the both of them.

"I got a bike!" Hopper heard him whoop. "I can't believe it! Woo-hooooo!"

Hopper grinned. The boy got a basketball hoop too, which he'd be installing at the end of their driveway come spring.

All the ruckus seemed to finally snap Savannah out of her trance. She turned to see her brother with his bike and she raised her hands to her mouth. Lord, the pure joy that shone from that child's face. Aw now…daggone it. She was starting to blubber—like, cry so hard, she could hardly stop. It made his chest get tight with emotion to see all this, but he couldn't turn away.

Savannah held her arms up for her grandma to hug her, and Mrs C. gingerly got down on her knees to do the honor. The poor kid practically collapsed in her arms in happiness.

And something else Hopper recognized. *Relief.* That for just one blessed day, they could be like every other kid on Christmas.

Yeah, he felt that—felt it right down to his boots. Because he knew exactly what that was like. To be poor. To bear that weight like a stone in your chest, every minute of the day. To feel like you had to carry your family on your own young shoulders, because nobody else was. Seeing that he'd taken all that rough stuff away from those kids, even for a minute? Well…

He chuckled and wiped away a tear that had snuck down his cheek. Aw hell, he was so glad he'd gone for that tree.

Hopper stayed for a few more minutes, banking and treasuring all those Christmas feels. And for a few precious minutes, the heaviness that had taken up permanent residence in his heart lightened, just a bit.

But when the family gathered around the table and bent their heads to pray, he began to feel ridiculous, like a peeping Tom or something. So he tiptoed off to the truck, which he'd pulled out of sight in the back, just in case. Killing the lights, he carefully coasted by the house, revving everything up to full speed once he'd gotten well over the hill.

He rubbed at his chest as he drove the familiar road back home. Damn, what a day. He was exhausted and heartsore. It was crazy, really, if he thought about all he'd been through since the last time he'd lain his head down to rest. It felt like it'd been longer than a regular day. Maybe it had been.

The trip back to his place was a short one with the streets being so deserted. When he finally turned the key in his back door and stepped into his kitchen, he found himself locking it behind him. He flipped on the lights and slumped with his back against the door, as if he could hold back every freaky-ass thing that had happened to him today.

He kicked off his boots and hung his coat on its peg, but he was so tangled up he hardly knew what to do with himself. He was home. In his house, his refuge. He should feel peaceful, like his ordeal was over.

But after everything he'd learned on that insane trip through Caine's, he doubted he'd ever feel peaceful again. How could he settle down, after he'd held Delilah in his arms again? After that carriage ride with her? He shuddered. God, the anger and the pain in those stormy gray eyes, even after all these years...

He scrubbed his hands over his face, wishing he could erase the memory. Had he ever been straight with her, even once? Would it have been so hard to tell her about his life, his dreams, and what kind of future he wanted with her? It was kinda nuts, in the harsh light of hindsight. He'd thought he'd loved her with everything he had. But he'd been hiding himself from her the whole time. Delilah was right about that.

All at once, it struck him how fucked up and tragic it was. He'd done those bad things, assuming he knew exactly the kind of future that would make her happy. But he'd been wrong. He'd been so wrong that nearly twenty years on, they were both alone and miserable at Christmas.

And right this minute, there wasn't much he could do about any of it.

Desperate to distract himself, he halfheartedly went through the stack of mail on his counter. Bills. Direct mail coupons. Christmas cards from the crew at work and a few of his friendlier neighbors. He opened each card and smiled wistfully at the sugar-frosted winter scenes and pictures of happy families.

If he hadn't been such a dumbass, maybe he'd have a family too. Maybe he'd have a card to send of his own...

He groaned. He really needed to stop doing this. It wasn't helping anything.

He propped up the cards, displaying them on the granite counter ledge that separated his kitchen from his great room. And he set about getting himself something to eat. The effects of all those fuckin' magic cookies were starting to wear off, after all.

He rattled around in the kitchen and found the spiral sliced ham slices he'd bought at the store. He made himself a nice, thick sandwich and washed it down with his last beer, but he was still friggin' starving. He decided to take a deep dive into the pantry. Surely to God there was something in all his stockpiles he could eat. He rustled around amongst the chips, bulk paper towels, and soap until he laid his hand on a can of yams.

When he pulled it out of the dark corner it had been hiding in, he barked out a laugh. Of all the days to find that. He'd bought it last Thanksgiving with the intention of figuring out how to make that damn casserole. But in the end, he'd just made himself a microwave dinner.

Well, no time like the present. Grinning, he peeled open the lid, drained it off, and started shoveling it in by the fork-ful, eating right from the can as he walked around his house. He wrinkled his nose. Okay, this wasn't like he remembered. The damn things were cold, and over processed, of course. Missing the sugar. And the marshmallows.

Still, he enjoyed his stupid little yams. He finished every bite and plunked the empty can down on his coffee table. It sat there, as proud as a piece of pop art.

A smile pulled at the corners of his mouth, though he could hardly say why. It should be depressing as shit, sitting in his empty house on Christmas Eve, eating out of a can like some derelict. But somehow, it wasn't.

Maybe because it brought back happy memories. Maybe because, in some bizarre way, that cheap can of yams made him feel human again. Made him feel like someone who was more than just a man moving along from day to day, keeping busy.

Ah, who was he kidding? It wasn't the damn yams. It was seeing Delilah again. It had been so hard. And so damn wonderful.

Even if this whole thing with the Outpost turned out to be nothing more than a hallucination, he'd still been given the greatest gift. Because he'd reconnected with the best part of himself. He'd been sent back to the moment when he'd been embraced by the purest, sweetest love. How crazy and disorienting it had been, like coming out of a deep, dark cave and seeing the light. But that was hardly surprising. Delilah had kickstarted his heart and made him *feel* something, for the first time in friggin' years.

So yeah, he was a dumbass. But he was a dumbass with hope.

He'd seen how she reacted to him, back there at the

Outpost. She'd been going on about him "not loving her" and "not wanting her" and shit. It had damn near killed him to hear her say it out loud like that. But he'd heard something else too—a note of longing in her voice, as if she wished it wasn't true. He had to hold on to that. He had to hold on to the belief that he could find her and tell her the truth. That he'd never stopped loving her. Not even for a minute.

Full of his yam-fueled energy, he took his can to the kitchen and chucked it in the recycle bin. Then he turned around and regarded his house with narrowed eyes.

As always, everything was orderly and clean in this three-bedroom brick bungalow. He'd fixed up every inch of this 1940s-era house until it shone, with his own hands. But it sure didn't feel like Christmas in here. After all the effort he'd made around this place, and he'd never put up so much as a holiday wreath on his door? How messed up was that?

And why? Because he didn't think he deserved it? Because he was all alone?

Screw that.

That was going to change, today. It was time he started creating the life he wanted to live. *All* of it.

Determined to dig up some holiday cheer, he went rooting around in his basement. He did a little whooping of his own when he finally found his quarry: his artificial Christmas tree. He'd bought it on sale when he'd first moved in, but in the end, he'd never had the heart to put it up.

Grinning like an idiot, he blew off the dust. The first glimmers of a master plan started to form in his mind. Oh yeah, *Operation Find Delilah* was kicking off, right this second. And Christmas just might be his secret weapon.

CHAPTER 14

LILA SAT ALONE at her dining area table, attempting to mindfully eat the remaining bites of her leftover Peking Duck. She washed it down with her last swig of boxed Cabernet, and swept her chocolate covered Oreo crumbs into the empty to-go box. *Great.* Now she had red, sticky duck sauce all over her hands. She grumbled as she carried it off to the garbage can and scrubbed herself down. Apparently, Kathryn's prophecy had come true after all. This Christmas, she really was eating out of a sticky Styrofoam container.

An uneasy jumble of nostalgia and sadness had been knocking around inside her since her trip through the Outpost, and she tried her best to will it all away. But as she shuffled back to the couch for her scheduled Hallmark Movie marathon, she found herself staring at her strange new Christmas wreath again. Her steps slowed.

She'd hung this little piece of Outpost merchandise over her dining area table, right in the middle of everything. And it really was a very pretty wreath—the biggest one the the shop had, studded with gold glitter pinecones and an oversized bow. The festive decoration filled up that broad expanse of white drywall rather nicely, and smelled like heaven, too.

But as she studied it, she realized something. It didn't belong here.

This adorable pine confection was old-fashioned. Sweet. Homey. And her condo? It was anything but.

That hadn't been her intention, of course. When she'd moved here, she'd wanted a fresh start. A clean slate with contemporary lines. The floors were grey-stained bamboo, the walls exposed, weathered brick. She'd chosen sophisticated furniture too—a rose gold velvet sectional, a fluffy flokati rug, and a dining room table made from reclaimed driftwood with turquoise resin accents, for starters. She'd anchored the room with a huge abstract painting with soothing, simple blocks of blues and pinks.

Yeah, there wasn't a turned spindle or a bright color in this place. How different this was from her hard-scrabble childhood. Everything they'd had back then was secondhand and mismatched, but you could always find a kind of ramshackle welcome at their house.

Lila scowled as she surveyed her place. This condo was pretty on the surface, but cold and uninviting once you'd lived with it. If homes are supposed to be a reflection of their owners, this place was pretty damning.

Lila snorted, catching herself. *Is this what I'm doing these days? Judging my character and my life based on my decorating?* Dammit, that whatever-the-hell she went through at the Outpost had really messed with her head. She didn't care if it was a dream, a psychotic break, or a full-on visit from the ghosts of her Christmases past. She wasn't going to wallow in self pity, questioning what might have been. She hadn't done anything wrong. And as for how her life has turned out, was it really so bad?

No, it really wasn't. As if to prove it to herself, she sank down into her luxurious sofa, cued up her movie, and checked her phone, which was delightfully full of Christmas wishes from friends and family. Kathryn had sent her some cute photos from her last visit. Lila replied, thanking her for her hospitality and telling her she'd gotten home safe.

She'd also heard from Randy's second wife, Amy, who was confirming their New Year's Day brunch. It was an annual tradition. He'd always celebrate Christmas with his wife and her children in the DC area, then swing by for a big to-do in Roanoke on their way home.

Looks like we'll be hitting your place about 1 p.m. on New Year's Eve. Is that good? Amy messaged.

Sure is. I'll make the reservations at the restaurant for 1:30. It's a little bit of a tight squeeze, but that'll give us time for a nice visit before you have to get back on the road, Lila messaged back.

She smiled. The timing would work out well, as it would still give her a few hours before she had to go to a company charity gala—the Mental Health United Ball. The psychiatric practice where she worked sponsored a table every year. Kathryn used to be on the board and was very involved. But since Kathryn's move to Lewisburg, Lila had taken over her volunteer work, organizing psychiatrists in the area to offer free care to the indigent. This year, the event would be hers to run. New Year's Eve was going to be *busy*.

Amy responded, **Sounds like a plan. How's your Christmas going so far?**

Quiet, just like I like it. Lila texted back. Then she sent through a photograph of her fuzzy-socked feet, propped up in front of her TV. The fireplace and her wine glass were also in the shot, along with her open Oreo container.

Amy sent back a laughing emoji. **Wish I had some quiet about now.** Then she texted a few pictures of Randy, whooping it up with her grandkids. There was Randy, crashed out and laughing at the bottom of a snowy hill, his too-small saucer sled still clutched in his hands. And Randy, spiking the egg nog. Followed not too much longer after that with a short film of him trying, and failing, to karaoke to the score from *Hamilton*. Lila laughed out loud at that one. And she couldn't help but smile to see him enjoying the holiday with such abandon.

Aren't you supposed to be keeping him out of trouble?

Are you kidding? Amy texted back. **I'm going to get years of blackmail traction out of that video.**

Lila snorted. Somehow, she didn't doubt it. They'd be joking about that for years.

Can't wait to see you, baby girl! Got lots of goodies for you!

Seeing you both is gift enough. Safe travels. And tell Randy I said to leave the rapping to the professionals!

Amy texted back a GIF of cats dancing around a Christmas tree. Lila turned her phone off with a chuckle. She was lucky to have a stepmother like Amy—someone kind, easy to talk to, and supportive. Pretty too. She was thrilled Randy had found her. Mama's death had been devastating for him.

She put her phone away, feeling reassured. Her Christmas wasn't so lonely, was it? She had family, even if they weren't blood. Mama's horrible, abusive family may be lost to her. But she had Randy, and that was the kind of family worth treasuring.

Burrowing back into her extra pillows and throw blankets, she settled in to enjoy a movie or two, nodding off once or twice as the hours ticked by. She woke up to some sweet little film involving a spoiled heiress trying to redeem herself with a Christmas cookie bake-off.

Normally, she loved these movies and their low-stress, darling storylines. Who didn't need more romance in their life, after all? But the more she drank, the funnier it all got. She never could hold her alcohol. Soon she found herself heckling the heroine's baking mishaps (*it's baking powder, not baking soda, you dumbass!)*, and creating scorecards for their chaste hugs and kisses. So far, this star-crossed couple hadn't gotten above a 5.5.

Hopper never kissed me like that. No, he kissed like he meant it —heated, hard and hungry. And sometimes gentle, searching. Cherishing, even. Like I'm the only woman who ever existed.

Didn't they always say you could tell how a man felt about you by his kiss? Hopper might not have said the words, but when his body did the talking, well…

Even here in the half dark, Delilah could feel the flush on her cheeks. Jesus, all these years later, and still the mere thought of his kisses raised her temperature.

Lila blew out a long breath. *Dammit I'm not going to win this fight, am I?*

She threw off her blankets and powered the TV down with a disgusted click. Well, if she was gonna brood about Hopper, she may as well do it properly. One more day. She'd give herself one more guilt-free day to obsess over the man, then she'd be done.

So she decided to pull out the big guns. Marching off to her walk-in closet, she located the suitcase she'd taken when she'd left Mitchell, the one with all her keepsakes. She flopped it down on her bed and carefully unzipped it.

When it opened, all her breath seemed to leave her. It wasn't so much that she was surprised at any of the contents inside. It's just that it'd been so long since she'd seen any of this. Ten years, maybe, at least? She'd hid whole sections of her life away, shoving it out of sight on the top shelf of a closet.

But here it all was again, rushing up to meet her and catching her unprepared. Was this handful of stuff, rattling around in this suitcase, really all she had to show for the first twenty-seven years of her life?

There was one small photo album in there with a scattering of pictures from when she was a baby. They hadn't had much extra money to get prints made back then. It was mainly school portraits, and a flash drive full of photos her mom had taken from her digital camera. Lila always told herself she would get an album made of those, but she'd never gotten around to it. She knew why. Lila swallowed hard, the itchy beginnings of tears threatening, and she chuckled ruefully. They were photos of happier times. But they were still too painful to revisit.

She shifted all the items around in the case—her high school yearbooks, a few favorite storybooks Mama had read to her when she was a child, an old teddy bear with an ear nearly loved off…

But then her fingers lighted on something she'd totally forgotten she had. She snorted out a laugh. Her teeny-tiny kilt from the Sassy Lass. How it had ever escaped Mitchell's wrath, she'd never know.

But she was genuinely tickled to see she that skimpy little thing. Playfully, she held it up to her hips and consulted her floor-length mirror. *Hmmm. Would it fit?* Smiling with mischief and just tipsy enough to not give a crap, she peeled off her pjs. And slowly but surely, she shimmied into the kilt. She squawked in triumph. It was a bit snug, but she was still killing' it! Who knew?

Excitedly, she rummaged around until she found its companion: the halter top she'd made from ripping up one of the Sassy's standard-issue T-shirts. Giggling, she peeled off her rather matronly flannel shirt and pulled the halter down tight over her breasts. *Uh oh.* This one was considerably tighter than before. Her jump from a D-cup to a DD in recent years had been a bigger leap than she'd imagined. The way her breasts spilled out of this thing was practically obscene. *Not that this is a bad thing.* She snickered.

She turned herself in a circle and whistled. Maybe Hopper had been right, after all. She still could pull off this look. It was an insane idea, of course. There wasn't a single place she could wear something like this. It was trashy with a capital T. And so totally not who she was anymore.

But maybe that was the point.

Lila couldn't stop grinning at her reflection. Dammit, she liked who she saw in this glass, this Delilah Jones. The crazy, carefree girl. The girl who didn't give a damn what anybody thought. The girl she'd been before she'd gotten herself hurt. She'd been fearless. Bold. And damn sexy, if she did say so herself.

Feeling nostalgic, she flopped down on her bed and opened up her sketchbooks. Most of the drawings she'd kept were from when she was in high school, when she'd started to get her skills up. Lord, it'd been ages since she'd picked up a sketchpad. She'd forgotten how good she'd been. She'd always poo-pooed Hopper when he'd suggested she go to art school. But maybe he'd been right.

Quite a few of these drawings were frameable. The portrait of Randy she'd done, sitting at Mama's bedside...the drawings of flowers and birds. And then the sketches of Hopper. Lord, she'd had a whole jumbo sketchbook of them, most of them done when he'd thought she was working on homework or something. But when she'd been hanging out with him, she was almost always sketching. She couldn't help herself. There were drawings of Hopper reading a book. Or napping. Or puzzling over a car part. She'd drawn studies of his hands. His eyes...

Chiding herself over her case of teenaged hero worship, she snapped the sketchbook shut and stuffed them all back in the suitcase where they belonged.

And yet, her memories of Hopper refused to be stored away. Something was niggling at her. Doubts, maybe. Earl had started to say something—*don't you want to know about*—but she'd cut the man off. She wished she'd hadn't. If the point of going through all that business at the Outpost was to learn important truths about her past, then what good had it been? Had she short-circuited everything early by calling it all off?

Lila chewed her lip, wondering if she'd been too quick to argue with Hopper. If she hadn't jumped out of that carriage, what would he have said?

More lies, probably.

No, it was time to put him behind her. She peeled herself out of her Sassy Lass clothes and folded them away in the suitcase too. Then she slipped back into her flannels. She scowled at her baggy, saggy-ass pjs, suddenly feeling repressed. She remembered the days when she hadn't worn anything to bed at all.

No, she couldn't go back. But she wished there was some way she could reconnect with the excitement of those adventuresome days without overturning the gains she'd made as a successful, well-respected professional.

She arranged everything neatly in the suitcase, preparing to zip it closed. But something caught her attention—her old motorcycle license. It was out of date, yet it galvanized her attention anyway. She grabbed it, marveling at her photo and the fresh face staring back at her, wide-eyed and innocent. Her hair had been long and wavy then, and unruly enough to be effortlessly sexy. She closed her eyes and remembered the roar of the engine underneath her and the feeling of flying free down the open road...

And a sense of giddy excitement bubbled up in her, like a mischievous child up to something. Maybe she could have a motorcycle again. Maybe she could even get herself a set of leathers and over-the-knee boots, like she used to have.

It would be...*wonderful*. Oh yes, it would. And though he'd never see her ride, she'd be flippin' a giant middle finger to Mitchell, in a way, every time she put her butt in the seat. And how perfect was that?

Racing for her laptop, she hurriedly got onto the internet and searched the new motorcycles for sale. The price on them quickly cooled her ardor for this idea. Then again, what if she found an older bike that just needed some rehab? She'd bet she could locate a fixer upper, probably for half the price of new. Maybe she could score something vintage and unusual, even.

A few internet queries later, and she'd spotted exactly what she wanted. Better yet, the seller was just around the corner.

Oh, yeah. This was gonna be cool.

And for once, she was gonna be cool too.

CHAPTER 15

HOPPER GROANED and rubbed at his forehead, still nursing a Christmas hangover two days after the holiday. Turned out, staying up half the night chugging coffee and searching the web for lost love could wipe a man out.

Chasing a ghost tended to do that. He'd scoured every nook and cranny of the internet for her, querying Delilah Jones and Delilah Roby, her married name. He'd also tried searching for her as Lila, the name most people had called her. Still nothing.

The last thing he'd been able to find was a listing of her and that Roby creep living together, more than ten years ago. And after that? Nothing. Like she'd deliberately covered her tracks.

And that worried him, dogging his sleep and his every step this morning. But brooding wasn't going to do him any good.

So even though the garage was officially closed today, he decided he may as well go in. There was nothing else he could accomplish until the holidays were over. At least he could get some work done on his personal rehab projects. It'd become a bit of a tradition at the garage, actually. They all brought in their fun projects to work on during the week between Christmas and New Year's Day. In no time at all, he'd showered and made his way in to the shop.

And sure enough, as soon as he'd unhitched the Corvair he'd hauled in, the garage bay door went flying up.

Lita stood there, one hand on a Red Bull, the other playfully cocked on her hip. She let out a low whistle. "Well, lookie here. Hop's out of his holiday hibernation already! Quick everybody, let's see if he has a shadow. Maybe we can figure out whether or not we're having six more weeks of winter."

Hopper just shook his head at her and grinned.

Hunter and Ross popped up from one of the engines they were inevitably bent over. "Hey, Hop!" they hollered nearly in unison.

He'd missed this crazy crew. Lita was here working on her Unicorn VW bus, and Ross was trying to get the final touches on the black Vincent motorcycle he was restoring. That bike was going to be worth a fortune when the boy was done. Ross was practically an artist with chrome. Hunter, for his part, was rehabbing an old Mustang—a weakness of the man's.

But they all rushed out front to help him roll in his latest bucket of bolts, the beat-up 1967 Corvair he'd bought from an old lady's estate for just a hundred dollars. His Christmas gift to himself.

Ross whistled as he looked in the windows. "Damn, Hop. This one's got potential!"

"Yeah, I thought so." Hopper nodded, unlocking the door so they could get in. "For the price, especially. It'll need a new engine, new upholstery, some door panel repair, and of course, paint. But there's no rust and the undercarriage and axels are still solid as a rock."

"Are you keeping it when you're done?" Hunter asked.

Hopper shrugged. He had no particular draw to the

project, really, but something inside him had told him to buy this car. "It was a good deal, no doubt. But naw, I'll resell it. Should make a nice profit if I market it right."

Hunter emerged from the interior, wiping his hands. "Well, no one can market like you, man. Who can say no to a mechanic with an MBA and killer fabrication skills? Whoever buys this will be eatin' out of your hand, that's for sure."

"You should let me work on the paint," Lita trailed her hand down the hood. "This is a girly car. I can just see it with iridescent magenta paint. And the upholstery should be bright white with hot-pink accents. It would be so cool!"

Ross cracked up. "Naw dog, don't listen to her. By the time she's done, she'll have you packing glitter bombs into the airbags. I mean, hot pink? Really?"

Lita bopped Ross in the back of his shaggy head. "Last time I checked, I'm the paint expert here. What would you do, goth boy? Let me guess—black paint, black seats, black dash."

"Black is the king of colors, babe, 'cause it's all of them at once."

"Don't you call me babe, you objectifying bro-boy!" she shrieked, and punched him in the arm again. Ross just grinned unrepentantly, and the two of them continued bickering as they headed back to their projects.

Hunter shook his head as they walked away. "When do you think they'll ever realize they belong together?"

"Never." Hopper grinned. "I'd put my bets on never."

"Yeah." Hunter grinned back. "You might be right."

Hopper moseyed over to his locker and slid on his Holliday Hot Rods work shirt—a black 1950s-style bowling shirt with red stripe down the front and a the Holliday Hot Rods logo on the back. He checked himself in his locker mirror and couldn't help smiling proudly at his reflection. The new logo rocked. Lita had drawn its main feature—a 1940sinspired pin-up girl in a Santa hat. Her hair was silvery white, with a streak of red, like a sexy Christmas sprite. He'd put the logo design and the shirt detail together himself after learning PhotoShop. They'd gotten so many compliments, he was considering creating a fan version to sell on the shop website.

After circling the Corvair a couple of times on the shop floor, he decided he'd check in at his desk instead. It'd been a few days since he'd read his email, and holiday or not, that made him antsy.

When he opened the door to their crowded paneled office, he found Hunter at the desk across from his, apparently doing the same thing.

Hopper fired up his laptop, and a quick scan of his inbox was promising. "Looks like we have two new customers wanting street rod makeovers," he called over to Hunter. "Want me to set some meet-and-greets for after the first of the year?"

"Sweet!" Hunter crowed. "Make it so, number one."

Smiling at the nickname Hunter often called him, Hopper did as the man said. And then he killed an hour or so responding to orders for the antique car parts business he ran for the shop. He took the time to reply to some of their fans on their Facebook page and blog too.

While he was at it, he breezed through their spreadsheets for the year, slugging in the last couple of weeks of their data. Their numbers were great. Over the last few months, they'd had several winning hot rod show entries, and they'd done wonders for the business. Hunter's regular project updates and how-to videos on YouTube had earned the shop an audience of two hundred thousand, give or take.

So, in other words, everything was running fine. He knew he should be tearing himself away from his computer and breaking that Corvair apart piece by piece. But somehow Hopper just couldn't manage to click his laptop closed.

For the thousandth time went back and did a search for Delilah on Facebook, LinkedIn, Instagram, Twitter, and Pinterest. As if somehow, a new profile for her would've magically appeared overnight. Then he circled back around to some of the public records search sites. Still, not a damn thing came up that he could use.

He let out a long sigh and sat there, glaring at the screen. There was nothing to be done at this point but to hire professional help. He typed in "private eye" and got a blue million results. He chewed his bottom lip as he scrolled through the list. Should he pick a PI here? Or in Georgia, her last known address? Could he even trust these online reviews? And how much did someone like this go for? How would he know he wasn't getting ripped off?

Uncertainty settled heavily on his shoulders. Hopper clapped his laptop shut and scrubbed his hand through his hair, feeling more tired and hopeless than he had in a long time.

Apparently, he must have been making too much noise. Because now Hunter was peering at him over the top of his computer, regarding him thoughtfully. "What's eating you, Hop? Something on that screen got you upset?"

Hopper shifted self-consciously in his seat, embarrassed to think he must've been grunting at his computer. He considered how to answer the man. After all, Hunter was his boss and also his dearest friend. But no way would Hunter ever believe what had happened at the Outpost. "Memories at this time of year can be tough for me," he simply said, leaving it at that.

"Anything you want to talk about?"

"No."

Hunter furrowed his brows for a second but finally said, "Fair enough."

Grateful he wasn't going to push him for more, Hopper forced his attention back to the screen, and setting appointments for the new customer consults. But he was at the task no time when a large white box van pulled into their gravel lot outside.

Hunter leaned over and looked out the window. "What in the world?" He let out a whoop, and a grin spread across the man's face. Immediately, Hunter barreled through the office and hit the button to send up the bay door. "Cooookie! Lord, girl! What are you doin' here with this big ol' truck? You movin' in?"

CHAPTER 16

HUNTER BOUNDED outside to greet the woman, but Hopper kept busy filing away the clutter on his desk. He wasn't in the mood to chat up customers today.

Still, he couldn't exactly focus on his work with the racket going on in the driveway. There was all the noise from the back door rattling up, not to mention Hunter's somewhat muffled hoots and exclamations. He could hear the man stomping around in the back of the truck. God only knew what was in there...

Curiosity getting the better of him, Hopper tipped his head to listen. He heard a feminine laugh, throaty and lilting. Bits and pieces of conversation too.

"Jesus Christ. A 1978 Triumph Bonneville?" Hunter called. "How in God's name did you find this?"

Then something-something "—had to have it," the woman answered.

Ugh. He couldn't quite make it out. What was it about that voice that was so familiar? Almost like...

Jesus, it couldn't be.

Nerves jangling, Hopper slid out from behind the desk

and settled into a discreet, shadowed spot near the entrance. A petite woman in ass-huggin' jeans and a short, hot pink parka stood with her back to the door, supervising Hunter as he rolled a beat-to-shit rusty motorcycle down the ramp.

"Be careful," she snickered. "Something's bound to fall off."

"You got that right. Judging by the rust on this, I doubt it has ever seen the inside of a garage. Why in God's name did you take this on, Cook? I didn't even know you could ride."

She shrugged. "My love life is such ancient history, it hardly bears mentioning. But an old boyfriend taught me to ride, way back when. He even fixed up a bike and gave it to me for Christmas. I was moving things around in my closet yesterday and found my expired motorcycle license. I guess it made me nostalgic. Before I knew it, I was scanning listings, and this one was for sale right up the road from me." She gave the seat a proud little pat. "When I saw it, I said to myself, who do I know who could fix this old thing?"

Hopper suddenly felt lightheaded, and his stomach actually fluttered, like that butterfly thing teenaged girls liked to talk about. *Delilah.* Holy hell...*could it be?*

The woman still hadn't turned around, and her hair was annoyingly obscured by a big knit cap. But the height, the short little nip of her waist, the slope of her perfect ass...how could he not have recognized her? *It had to be.*

Hunter grinned ruefully at the bike. "You're a sucker. This thing's a total rebuild. You could probably buy one totally restored on the vintage market for less than what this project will cost."

She shrugged. "Yeah, I figured that. But I like the idea of making something from nothing. It's kind of romantic, don't you think?"

Something from nothing.

Oh man oh man, it's her. His lungs squeezed like they were in a vise, adrenalin making him weak-kneed and jittery. But he stepped forward anyway. Gravel crunched loudly under his boots as he took a couple of shaky steps toward them.

Hunter gave her a bemused look. "Mm-hmm. So, what are you missing more—the boyfriend, or the motorcycle?"

She paused, as if she were going to make a joke, but decided against it. "Both. But if I can't have the man, I suppose I can settle for the bike. I mean, Christmas is only as good as your memories, right?"

Christmas is only as good as your memories...

His breath caught. Candy had said that.

Holy shit. That time at the Outpost had been real. Their argument in the carriage—she'd actually been there. That means she'd picked out magical gifts too.

Sweet Christ—what else had she seen?

Delilah turned around, smiling as Hunter took the bike from her hands. But her smile faded as she locked eyes with Hopper. She stuttered a step, like she'd been stopped in her tracks. And there it was. Instant recognition. A flash of something unreadable in her eyes.

She. Was. His. Delilah.

All those years of fantasies. All the things he'd imagined he'd do and say. They all skittered out of his mind, burned away with the sizzling shock of seeing her. He was completely, utterly speechless. And there didn't seem to be a word in the whole English language that was up to the occasion.

Because this was real. This counted—no fuckin' magical do-overs this time. He was rooted to the spot, stuck there like some damn fool. But somehow he managed to grind out, "Angel?"

Delilah didn't answer him. She simply looked up at him with wide, shocked eyes, her cheeks flushed from more than just the cold wind. Though it hardly should be possible, she was even more tongue-tied than he was.

Hunter looked back and forth between the two of them as he tried to make sense of all the weird vibes. Then realization crept over the man's face, and his eyebrows flew up. "Oh-ho-ho wow. *Jesus,* Hopper. *You're* the old boyfriend she was just talking about, aren't you? The one who got away."

"Yeah, I—" Hopper sputtered, swallowing against his dry throat. "I suppose I am."

LILA BLINKED at Hopper a few times to make sure she was actually seeing this. Her heart was beating so hard, she could hear the blood rushing in her ears. Dear God, it was him. Still so gorgeous, it was unnerving. And, damn her eyes, the man still looked like sex on a biscuit, just like he had at the Outpost.

She pointed to his embroidered work shirt. "You-you work here?" she squeaked.

"Yeah," he answered, sounding a little breathless. He lurched forward, as if he might draw her in for a hug. But he stopped himself, standing just inches away from her, searching her face for some kind of permission.

She didn't give it. No, she stepped back a bit.

A flash of hurt passed over his face, and that just pissed her off. What—did he think she'd leap into his arms after everything that had passed between them?

Her brain buzzed with indignation. But her traitorous body wasn't paying her brain any mind. Oh no, it had other ideas. It was lost in the simple shock of his presence, simmering with the sizzling current running between them.

"I've been here for four years," Hopper answered her, wrenching her out of her thoughts. "Ever since I got out."

He'd really been out that long? The news took her aback. "How did you get all the way from Georgia to here?"

"I can answer that," Hunter jumped in. "I put up a posting for a mechanic with a welder's certificate and machine fabrication skills on an online job board. Hopper responded and had more experience than I was even asking for. And he was willing to pay his own relocation costs."

Hopper snorted. "Glad to know you were so discriminating, boss."

Hunter clapped him on the back and grinned. "Best decision I ever made, man."

Seeing Hunter so at ease with his employee calmed her nerves a bit. And it helped to have that third person there, to cut the tension. To dull the impact of the pure, towering physicality of the man and the way he still looked at her...

Soon they were comparing notes about who knew who and their near misses. She explained that she'd worked with Kathryn for years, handling billing and administration for her old practice. And she also told him they were the best of friends, even though they lived in different cities now. Truly, it was amazing she and Hopper hadn't crossed paths already.

Hunter shook his head. "God, just think. If you hadn't missed our wedding, Cook, the two of you probably would've walked down the aisle together."

The image of that made an unwilling flush rise to her cheeks. Lord, could this get any more awkward?

Hopper turned her way and frowned for a moment before the realization hit him. "Ohhh." He snapped his fingers. "*You* were the missing maid of honor!" Then his eyebrows knit together again, in concern this time. "Wait. Hunter had said something about you having a pretty bad family emergency. But your family was— What would that have been?"

"It was Randy," she hesitated, wondering if opening this particular can of worms was a good idea. "He had a massive heart attack the night before the wedding. He was having a triple bypass that afternoon."

Hopper looked stricken, and that was surprising, considering the massive rift between the two men. Randy never had been able to get past what Hopper had done to land himself in prison. The man had seen it as a personal betrayal—like Hopper had thrown all his kindnesses back in his face. And when Hopper had been so cruel to her, there at the end? He could hardly say Hopper's name without spitting on the ground, even to this day.

"How is he?" Hopper asked, reaching out to rub her arm like an old friend.

"Better. He's remarried, and his new wife, Amy, is constantly on him not to cheat on his diet. He's had to cut back on his hours at the shop. But he's come out of it okay."

"Remarried." He raised his eyebrows. "Wow. That surprises me, after the way he was with your mama."

Delilah managed a wry smile, trying not to let lingering sadness color her expression. "What happened to Mama was terrible. But Randy was there for her when she needed him. He's a man who truly understands the meaning of loyalty. I don't begrudge him this—"

"That's not what I meant," Hopper jumped in, dipping his head down so he could look her right in the eye. "It's just that some men, once they love somebody like that, they can never find room in their heart for anyone else."

His words hit her in a small, unprotected part of her soul. He wasn't talking about Randy, was he? The way he searched her face with such an expression of longing… Well, his feelings were plain to see. Her heart felt too full and too achy, all of a sudden. She couldn't summon any words to say to the man. Tearing her gaze away from him, she toed the ground with her boot.

Trying to get out of the line of fire, Hunter circled around the back of the motorcycle and crouched down, pretending to give it a closer inspection.

Hopper lowered his voice and moved a step closer. "That

thing you said a second ago, how Christmas is only as good as your memories. That's one of those weird expressions of Candy's." Her face must've given her away, because the corner of his mouth turned up into a knowing smirk. "Ah, so you were there, at the Outpost. It was real. You remember it."

"I do," she simply replied, not wanting to give anything away with Hunter within earshot.

Hopper must have realized that too, because he glanced over his shoulder, then walked her a couple steps away. He pulled her close enough to talk privately. Close enough, too, to pick out the fresh, clean scent of the soap he'd used this morning. When they were younger, it had seemed like he'd always come to her freshly showered from the garage. How she used to love that. His hair would still be wet, and his shirt a little damp under her fingers. Her heartbeat picked up at the memory, but she ruthlessly pushed it away.

He still had his hand on her shoulder, and he used his position to force her to look him in the eye. "It was you in that carriage with me. Not some memory, right?"

She nodded. "And the story I told you in the carriage about how I got to the Outpost, that's all true."

"Same here. But you never did tell me what gifts you picked, and I can't figure out why you're being cagey about it. I need to know what you saw, Delilah."

Why? Was he afraid she'd caught him in more lies? It was the wrong thing to say, the wrong way to ask. She ground her teeth, and simply said, "No."

He let out a breath. "Okay, I get it. Maybe here is not the best place but—"

"I said no," Lila cut him off with her best steely glare. "As in I'm not discussing it with you. Ever."

Surprise and maybe a little hurt flared in his eyes, and a thread of guilt wound its way around her.

She ignored it. Why should she tell him? She couldn't make him understand, anyway. He'd never get why she'd needed to go back to those horrible, painful moments. Why she'd needed to get into his head. And honestly? She was afraid he'd be angry with her. Or worse, feel violated. But she didn't owe him an explanation, anyway. If he'd been more honest with her in the past, she wouldn't have needed to open up the darkest corners of his heart like that and shake out the contents.

"Come on, Delilah," he growled. "You can't talk to me about it? After everything we went through in that strange place?"

She yanked her arm away, stepping back. "Seriously? What about all the things you've hidden from me?"

He stepped forward into her space again, dammit, and reached out for her hands this time. "But we were supposed to come to terms with the past. Earl and Candy said—"

She wrestled out of his grip, fury making her movements faster. "Would you stop?" she cried, not caring how loud she got. "This isn't about what Earl and Candy said. Who cares what those old buzzards have to say about my life!"

Hopper opened his mouth to respond, but Hunter beat him to it. The man popped up from behind the bike. "Wait—you're not talking about Earl and Candy Caine, are you?"

She and Hopper exchanged a panicked glance.

"You know," Hunter pressed. "An older couple. Funny little hillbillies. Candy's got frizzy red hair, and Earl wears that Almost Heaven hat."

Yeah. Exactly those people. They both just stood there with their mouths hanging open, not sure what to say.

He clapped his hands and whooped. "I knew it! I freakin' *knew* it! They're not what they appear to be, right?"

Not knowing what else to do, Lila and Hopper just nodded again.

Hunter waved over to the garage, where Lita and Ross were mercifully out of range but still trying to make sense of the show without being too obvious. "Hey Ross," Hunter called. "Would you mind taking this bike in and getting an estimate together on the rehab?"

"Sure thing, boss," Ross answered, trotting up. "Afternoon ma'am." He tilted his shaggy head in Lila's direction, then silently slid a *what's going on?* look between the two men. "Don't worry about your bike. It'll look crazy good when it's done."

Lila was beginning to think the bike was the least of her worries at the moment.

Hunter pointed back to the garage. "Come on," he commanded. "Both of you. My office. Now."

Lila meekly followed them, wondering what in the world she and Hopper were going to say to the man if pressed. But when they walked through the big, open warehouse doors at Holliday Hot Rods, her mind blanked for a minute. This was her first time here, and she had to admit—the place was damned impressive.

A former factory, the space was bright and well-lit from windows that towered up two stories. Giant vertical ceiling fans gently circulated the warm air around the space which, though very well-organized, was filled with cars and vans strung out in pieces. In the back, fabrication machines stood for custom machining. To the side was a worktable and industrial sewing operation for upholstery. Beside that, the door was open to what she presumed was a paint room, with pressurized paint sprayers that came down from the ceiling.

Hard rock pounded through the speakers, and a giant mural on one long wall sported the Holliday Hot Rods Logo, modified to look like street graffiti. And of course, there were rows and rows of antique car parts, set up on long, orderly steel shelves.

It was no mystery why Hopper would love working at a place like this.

But Lila didn't have time to walk around, gawking. Hunter shuttled them both off into a private office, separated from the rest of the space by paneled walls, a plexiglass window, and a door.

Hunter sat them both down in two metal chairs facing his desk and popped behind his, smiling way too excitedly for Lila's taste. He tented his fingers and narrowed his eyes, as if he couldn't wait to give them the third degree. "You didn't get Mrs. C's tree at some random stand did you, Hopper?"

Hopper tried his best to stay cool. "Sure it was. Just an out of the way place, up off Route 60."

"Don't give me that." Hunter grinned like the Cheshire cat. "Come on, you can tell me. You went to Caine's Christmas Outpost. Don't try to deny it."

Wait, how did Hunter— *Good Lord!* Had he been to the Outpost too? Lila debated jumping in and peppering the man with some questions of her own. But it was probably best if she and Hopper didn't get into their whole freaky-deaky story. Not yet, anyway.

She glanced over at Hopper who, for his part, was still not giving up on his attempts to keep this all under wraps. The man shrugged. "Yeah. So? It was a nice store back off the road, on your way up to Potts mountain. Had just the right selection of stuff I needed for the Castos. I think they closed it up after Christmas, though."

"Yeah," Hunter pressed. "They closed it up after Christmas, all right. Because the whole place was run by magic. And you got sucked right into it. Put you in some kind of parallel dimension or something, didn't it?"

Hopper slid her a beseeching look and, not sure what else to do, she laughed. Even to her own ears it sounded tinny and strained, an *oh-you-silly-boy-aren't-you-funny* kind of titter.

But Hunter didn't buy it. He just sat there, drumming his fingers on the desk, waiting for one of them to crack. The silence dragged on. And to her surprise, it was Hopper who caved first. He blew out a long breath and threw up his hands. "How do you know about the Outpost? You been there too?"

"Not exactly," Hunter smirked. "But you're not the only ones to find yourself in a magical Christmas vortex in the mountains around here. It happened to me and Kathryn too."

CHAPTER 17

IF IT'D BEEN JUST Hunter telling him all this, Hopper might not have believed him. Because, honestly, his story might even be crazier than theirs.

Come on, really? Kathryn and Hunter had gotten caught in an entire Christmas town? That had just appeared on Potts mountain? Then had friggin' disappeared in five days? And somehow magically seemed to populate around all their wishes and desires?

But when Hopper had insisted they get on speaker phone with Kathryn, he had to listen. Hunter could be excused for being a little full of shit—he loved pranks and watched more reruns of *The Twilight Zone* and *X Files* than was probably good for him.

But Kathryn? That woman was as steady as they came. For God's sake, she was a psychologist—pretty much the authority on what was sane and not sane. If she'd been through something similar and swore it wasn't a hallucination, then maybe they'd managed to escape with all their marbles intact.

Hunter and Kathryn even claimed they'd been transformed by their brush with the magical.

It all had to do with how Hunter and Kathryn had met, they told them, over two years ago. He'd been told, of course, that Kathryn had wrecked on the way to The Greenbrier Resort, just up the way. Thankfully, Hunter happened to be driving by in the Holliday Hot Rods tow truck, finding her just in time to save her from plummeting over the side of a mountain.

And he also knew Hunter had been missing in action for a few days after that. When the man had shown up with Kathryn's banged-up SUV on the back of his tow truck, he'd said he'd spent the last few days at The Greenbrier with her.

"I knew it!" Hopper crowed. "I knew something about that story of yours wasn't right. Why in the world would you have left the tow truck loaded up in a Greenbrier parking lot for five days?"

Hunter rolled his eyes. "You got me, okay? But what was I supposed to do? Tell you the truth? We probably would've made the front of *The National Enquirer* in days!"

The way Lita and Ross liked to talk, Hopper wouldn't have doubted it. Not everyone could take this kind of paranormal development in stride.

Delilah, however, seemed to be having no problem. In fact, she started to giggle. First nervously, then outright guffaws, clearly feeling the bizarre humor of it all. "Let me get this straight," she waved her hand. "You're telling me you were trapped in a magic tourist town that was populating around your wishes and desires. Kinda like Brigadoon meets Fantasy Island. Wait-Wait. Was Ricardo Montalban there? Did someone say, 'da plane, 'da plane!' when you pulled up?"

"Very funny," Kathryn drawled.

"I dunno." Hopper smirked. "Populating around your desires, you say? Sounds like a pretty good time to me."

"I'm neither going to confirm or deny the conclusion you're drawing." Hunter grinned and wagged a finger in

Hopper's direction. "But stop it. You're visualizing. That's not allowed."

Hopper was snickering now, too.

"In all seriousness, though," Kathryn interjected. "Christmas Pass was a weird place. The magic in it wasn't completely obvious. It just seemed like a place with over-the-top service. All your Christmas wishes coming true and such. There was something weird and off about it, but it was like you couldn't put your finger on it."

"Let me guess." Delilah interrupted. "Everyone and everything there was a mirage. But they seemed totally real at the time. Like, completely solid."

"Pretty much," Kathryn replied.

"So how did you get out?" Hopper asked.

"The place just started to decay," Hunter answered. "It was as if there wasn't enough magical juice to keep it going or something. I never did figure out the source of it all. I think it may have been coming from Miss Holly Berry, the lady who ran the inn there, but I have no proof of that."

Kathryn tsked. "Sounds pretty similar then. An older person who's pulling the puppet strings. Incredible magic that seems to be connected to Christmas and on some kind of time limit."

"Here's what I don't get," Hopper interjected. "How did you guys hear about Earl and Candy?"

Hunter explained Earl and Candy had bumped into them in a convenience store, just after they'd escaped from Christmas Pass. The couple had noticed the cowboy hat he'd been wearing, one Kathryn had bought him in the magical town. "I cornered them then," he continued, "trying to pump them for information, because the whole rest of the world seemed to have no idea Christmas Pass existed. But they both said the town appeared only to people like us, who were lost in life."

Hopper stroked his whiskery stubble as he thought about

it. "Hmmm, Candy and Earl said similar things to me. That I was lost and had to get unstuck. Didn't they say the same to you, Delilah?"

"Yeah," Delilah answered, "but that still doesn't prove anything. They could have been a couple of old codgers spinning local lore."

Hunter scrubbed his hand through his hair. "I can't say why they made me so uncomfortable. Call it instinct. They were friendly but a bit creepy, too."

"You've got that right," Delilah grumbled.

Hunter nodded in agreement. "Their truck had the Caine's Christmas Outpost logo on it, and it was loaded with pine tree saplings. I turned away for a second and when I turned back, they'd vanished into thin air. It made the hairs on the back of my neck stand up—let's put it that way."

Hopper had no idea what to make of all this. He'd thought it was a mess before. But this just added a whole 'nother layer of bat-shit crazy to the mix. And honestly, as excited as he was to have Delilah right here in front of him, how it had gone down didn't exactly sit easy with him. After all, they'd been selected for this mind-bending experience because they'd failed some kind of test they hadn't even realized they were taking.

It was kinda insulting, honestly. He and Delilah were so royally fucked up that they needed a magical intervention? Really?

From the flash of annoyance in her eyes and the way she rubbed her forehead back and forth, he'd be willing to bet Delilah was thinking the same thing. Then again, maybe they were framing this this all wrong. Christmas Pass had turned out to be a real blessing for Hunter and Kathryn. They'd found happiness. Could the same be coming for him and Delilah?

He snuck another look. Delilah was rooting around in her

purse and muttering about needing an aspirin. Not exactly a good sign.

Still, he wondered. What if none of that business at the Outpost had ever happened, and he and Delilah had crossed paths some other time? Their lives were too interconnected for them not to have seen each other at some point, and probably some point soon.

What would've happened then? It sure as shit wouldn't have been all swelling violins and moonstruck looks. Most likely, Delilah would've slapped him in the face, stalked off, and refused to talk to him again for the rest of her life. And it would've been no more than what he deserved, honestly.

But the Delilah in front of him today? She was asking questions. She wanted answers. She was engaged.

And that? *That* he could work with. He'd get some precious time to prove his feelings for her and show her he was a better man. And Lord knew, he couldn't wait to learn every single thing about the woman she'd become. It could work. The same old spark was there. He could feel it. And this whole "solving the mystery" thing? This could be the fuel they needed to turn that spark into a flame again.

Hopper bit back the urge to grin triumphantly. *Operation Find Delilah* just might be transitioning to *Operation Get Her Back*, way ahead of schedule.

CHAPTER 18

HUNTER DRUMMED his hands on his desk with a resounding smack. "Well, I tell you what I think we should do about this. We should go out to where the Outpost stood and look around a bit. Maybe we'll run into Earl and Candy. And believe me, I've got some choice questions for those two."

Lila sent Hopper a beseeching look, trying to tell him with her eyes just how bad an idea this was. But dammit, the man actually seemed excited at the prospect. "I doubt you'll find those old codgers at this point. But it's still a good idea. I sure want some answers. Don't you, Delilah?"

Lila practically choked on her surprise. Why on earth would he want to dredge all that up again? God only knew what they'd find out there. But at this point, did she want to act like she was hiding something? Or worse, running away like a coward? She found herself sputtering. "Well, uh, I suppose—"

"Great!" Hunter beamed. "It's all settled then."

Lila sat there in a kind of suspended animation while everyone made plans. They decided to ride out on this fact-finding mission right this minute, before it got dark. Kathryn, who was working at the local Veteran's Hospital today, said she'd find someone to take her rounds so they could pick her up at work. Before Lila could even process the idea, they'd shuttled her to her feet and were rummaging around trying to find her warm things to wear from the shop.

She was just opening her mouth to protest that her coat was plenty warm enough when Hunter threw an extra scarf and gloves her way. Then Hopper came around the corner with a black motorcycle jacket in his hands. Her breath hitched.

Hopper held it out to her. But Lila hardly knew what to say. "My God, is that what I think it is?"

"Yeah," he murmured, his voice sounding gruffer than usual as he pressed it into her hands. "You gave me this at that last Christmas party you threw at your apartment, remember?"

"I remember," she answered, running her hand down the sleeve. Surprisingly, the jacket was in great shape after all these years, all smooth and well-conditioned. "I can't believe you kept it."

Hopper shrugged a shoulder, but she saw a tremor of vulnerability in his expression. "Yeah. Landlady said she'd keep one box for me while I was inside. I made sure this was in it. It's a good jacket."

Lila took note that he was wearing a different jacket for riding, this one dark gray. She wondered why he wouldn't just be wearing this old one if he'd gone to such pains to save it. She spotted the tag inside. Men's large. Ah, that's why. No way could he fit those arms and shoulders into this thing now, not with the skinny way it was cut. Lila misted up, thinking about how he'd kept it in his locker for years, even after he would've realized it didn't fit.

She rolled the familiar leather in her hands, resisting the urge to bury her face in it, and inhale the scent. It's only a jacket. That's what she tried to tell herself. But the memories still poked at her heart.

She'd bought this jacket for him their last Christmas together. God, she'd been so happy when she'd seen it in the store window. She'd known immediately that was Hopper's jacket, with its supple, double-thick leather and the stud work around the collar flaps and the pockets. The way the cut nipped in from the shoulders to a narrow waist had definitely gotten her motor running. It had been pricey though, and she'd had it on layaway for months before she could pay it off. But when Hopper had opened it up and put it on…*well.* He'd been a sight to behold. Like some kind of black-haired, rock n' roll dream.

He'd looked as excited as a little kid at Christmas, wearing this the first time. And he'd laughed, his deep, rich rumble warming her all the way through. *You just bought this so you could keep my old one,* he'd teased her, kissing her and lifting her off the ground with a bear hug. He hadn't exactly been wrong…

Damn, now the man was smiling down wistfully at her. Like maybe he was remembering it the way she was. Lila swallowed past her thick throat. "This is a lovely trip down memory lane, Hop. But why are you showing me this?"

He took the coat out of her hands and held it up expectantly. "Because you're gonna wear it. That flimsy parka of yours isn't safe for riding."

She stared at him. "You want me to get on the back of a motorcycle? With you?"

"Better do as he says, Cook," Hunter called as he threw a helmet her way. "You wouldn't want to ride in a car up there. If what Hopper says is true, those roads will be too rutted and washed out for anything with four wheels."

. . .

Delilah sighed, her reproachful expression screaming *this isn't fair.* But she still slid her arms through the sleeves and let him zip it up for her anyway.

Hopper studied her while she tried to maneuver in the enormous thing, rolling up the sleeves until she could find her hands again. The sight punched him right in the gut. Maybe he shouldn't be so surprised at that, really. Seeing Delilah in clothes of his had always given him a caveman kind of thrill.

But this was something else entirely. His heart brimmed full in his chest as he savored the moment. This felt good. *Right*—as if Delilah putting that jacket on created a connection to his lost past, no magic needed. And for the first time in, well, maybe ever, remembering didn't fucking hurt.

Hopper was glad when his boss trotted over, shaking him out of his thoughts. Getting philosophical wasn't going to solve any of these mysteries, was it? They headed to the motorcycles they both kept stored at the garage for safekeeping—Hunter's vintage Harley Hog, and the BMW he'd restored for himself a few years ago.

For a minute, he thought he'd seen Delilah's eyes get all shiny and emotional when he rolled up their ride. It wasn't quite the same model, but it was an awful lot like the one he'd rehabbed for her years ago. But she didn't say anything. And he didn't push. He simply got on the bike and motioned for her to hop onto the seat behind him.

She flattened her mouth into a thin line but did as he asked, popping on her helmet and sliding into place behind him.

And damn, she fit so perfectly, their years apart simply fell away. He revved the motor and she circled her graceful arms around his waist. Then she scooted herself tight against his back, finding the footrests.

He swallowed hard. Funny, he'd thought having her close would be a good idea, a way to ease back into their connection gradually. But there was no gradual about it. His whole body was responding to her, tingles of awareness spreading through him in thick, unruly waves. And of course, he was hard as a goddamn tailpipe in about half a second. Apparently, his dick hadn't gotten the memo that he was playing the long game here.

Fortunately, concentrating on the road and leading their party to the location of the Outpost helped him calm his shit down. They'd made short work of the trip up the winding mountain road after they'd picked up Kathryn. But as soon as they turned off the pavement, all that changed. What had been a gravel road when he'd first gone to the place was now a washed-out, barely visible trail. The ruts and unexpected potholes were so damn bad, he felt like he'd been kicked between the legs repeatedly by the time they finally spotted the structure.

"This has to be it," Delilah pointed. And he knew it was true. He'd been counting decayed sticks coming out of the ground on the way. There'd been four little signposts, as he recalled, the last one within sight of the Outpost itself. And those sticks, rotted down to nubs and missing any sign on them at all, were still in just the right positions.

He motioned for Hunter to stop. "Over there!" he yelled. They pulled their bikes over to a flat spot and powered them down.

Kathryn removed her helmet, running her hand through her short, golden hair, and unfolding her willowy, elegant frame from the bike. At moments like this, Hopper would often shake his head in amazement that a rough-and-ready guy like Hunter would end up with such a cultured, southern society belle. But Kathryn had adjusted so well to life here in Lewisburg, she'd even managed to be at home on the back of Hunter's old Harley. Love conquered all, he supposed.

Kathryn turned to him and narrowed her eyes. "Are you

sure about this, Hop? How in the world could this be the place you were describing?"

"I can't explain it." Hopper sighed, throwing up his hands. "But it is."

Hunter stalked over to the rickety ruin, peering at it with suspicion. "Well, there's gotta be a clue around here somewhere."

They all set about inspecting the place. Actually, "place" might be a generous way of describing it. What had once been a sprawling structure with several additions now appeared to be just an oversized shack. A shack missing its roof and most of its walls, that is. In places, all that was left was just the corner post. They managed to find a few floorboards sturdy enough to hold them and they ventured inside.

Delilah shook her head. "I don't understand. The Outpost was so much bigger than this. There was a big open space with a fireplace and this huge Christmas tree, right in the middle. And the counter, and...how could it be this small?"

Hopper was thinking the same thing. The building they were in was clearly a one-room log structure built probably around the late 1800s. Three-hundred square feet, tops. Not that you could really tell. There was hardly anything left.

Hunter unearthed a couple of thin metal beams, so desiccated they were nearly rusted through. "There's a whole bunch of these all over the place. Any idea what these are?"

"Oh man, it's the shelves," Hopper answered. "They were busting with Christmas decorations and shit. Hard to tell that now."

"And look at this!" Kathryn dug around until she pulled up a rusty, battered, metal item with four legs.

Lila took it out of her hands and her brows knitted for a moment. "Oh my God!" she gasped. "It's the tree stand, Hopper! The cut Christmas tree—it was in this!"

Kathryn rubbed the back of her neck as she examined it. "Wow. Not much Christmas spirit left in this place. You'd think it wouldn't be quite so decayed as all this, considering you were here just a couple of days ago."

"Why not?" Hunter answered. "That old coal camp Christmas Pass was superimposed on practically crumbled to dust the second we drove away."

Hopper gently took the tree stand from Delilah's hands and tossed it back on the ground. He handed her a bandanna from his coat pocket so she could wipe the god-knew-what from this place off her hands. "Yeah, when I left here, it had already seemed like it had been abandoned to the elements for decades. However it is that Earl and Candy mess with time, we'll never be able to figure it out."

They all agreed there was no more point in nosing around out here. Dusk was closing in, anyway.

"So that's really it?" Lila asked Hopper as he helped her down the last decrepit step. "There's nothing more we can do?"

"I 'spose not, angel."

Angel. The old pet name rolled off his tongue so easily, still. She hadn't braced herself for it. She wasn't ready to hear it, either. But it still warmed her from the inside out. Damn, this was more than she could process. Her emotions were so tangled up, she wasn't sure she'd ever get them unwound.

Lila rubbed her forearms as she braced against the wind. She wasn't thrilled to be commandeered on this group adventure. But now that she was here, the thought of somehow just being done with it all left her cold. What was she going to do? Go home to her empty house? It's what she'd planned when she'd woken up this morning. But somehow she felt strangely…disappointed.

"We should be heading home." Kathryn hooked her arm through her husband's. "Dad and Alice are back at the house with the kids. On the way back, we should probably pick up some take-out for dinner. Why don't you come back with us, Cookie? The guest room's taken, but I have a pull-out in the office you could use. There's no sense in you driving back in the dark."

Lila let out a long breath she hadn't realized she'd been holding. She should probably take Kathryn up on her offer. It'd be the sensible thing to do. But again, she didn't want to impose.

Seeing her hesitation, Hopper grabbed her hand. "Or... you could come with me. Not back to stay at my house or anything like that," he rushed to say, somehow managing to look hopeful and uncertain all at once. "No, I mean, maybe I could take you to dinner and we could see the lights at the Greenbrier or something. I could drive you back tonight, and the guys at the shop, they'll handle taking back your rental to the closest U-Haul around here tomorrow morning."

Lila found herself chewing her bottom lip, a nervous habit she hadn't had since high school. But she felt just as unsure as that young girl again. It didn't matter how many years and hurts had passed between them. Hopper Vance could make her good judgment vanish with a smile. And he not only was smiling at her so earnestly, but she was standing here wrapped up in his stupid old jacket, too. Like she was wrapped up in what she used to be.

It didn't matter that the man still revved her engine in just about every possible way. She should tell him no. What good could come of this? How long would it take him to start lying to her again? Lila opened her mouth to tell him as much when Kathryn grabbed her arm.

"I'm sorry to interrupt." Kathryn slid her a meaningful look. "I need to borrow Cookie for a conference. You know, girl stuff."

Hopper knit his brows in confusion but he stepped back respectfully, holding his hands up. "Yeah, uh, yeah. Sure." He moved over to where the bikes were parked, stopping to chat with Hunter while Kathryn hustled her off behind the remains of the shack to talk.

Kathryn dropped Lila's arm and took a peek around the corner, just to make sure they were safely out of sight. "Look, I'm sorry to be so obviously cloak-and-dagger about this. But I wanted to check on you, to make sure you're okay. Hunter filled me in on everything before he picked me up. Oh my God, girl, why didn't you tell me you'd had this whole great-love-lost thing going on? And with Hopper of all people! Here I thought you didn't believe in the concept."

Lila couldn't help but grimace at the way Kathryn had just portrayed her. Was she really that jaded? She groaned. "It's not that I don't believe in love, okay? It's just— I don't know. Every time I open myself up to a man, I live to regret it. Maybe it's me I don't trust."

"Especially with Hopper. You don't trust yourself with Hopper. Right?"

"Something like that."

Kathryn crossed her arms over her chest, and gave her one of those long, probing, sympathetic looks she often trottted out with her patients. She tsked. "Listen, you are clearly feeling it with this guy. If you want him, even a little, maybe you should be listening to your heart."

Lila let out a disgusted grunt.

"No, seriously!" Kathryn pressed. "Are you sure you want to write him off so easily? I see the way he looks at you—like someone has just given him his life back."

Lila rolled her eyes. "Oh, sure. That's what I want to be. His redemption project. 'Get good ol' Delilah to forgive me, and I can pat myself on the back and consider it all behind me.' Then what? Do you have any idea how many times that man lied to me, right to my face? I think back on our time together and I have no idea what was real. But he's here and he seems so different and… I just don't know how to react, okay?"

"Hey, I get it. I do. If I were in your shoes, I'd probably be thinking exactly the same thing. But speaking as an outside observer, and as friends to both of you, I think you might be missing the bigger truth here. That man over there? He's never stopped loving you. When you're around, all his gruffness, all his hard edges—they just fall away. And whether you want to admit it or not, you're reacting to him in much the same way. That's a rare thing. Don't snuff out that ember before it has a chance to catch fire."

"That's a lovely metaphor. But that doesn't mean I can trust the man."

"I trust Hopper," Kathryn insisted, patting her hand over her heart. "So does Hunter, implicitly, with nearly every aspect of his business, including the books. Hopper works his butt off, and there's never been a penny out of place. And it's not just us who feel that way about him. People in this town love him. He's constantly thinking of ways to help out his friends, his neighbors, and the whole community, even. He's a real softie." Kathryn gave Lila another reassuring pat on the arm. "If you won't trust him, trust me. You couldn't find a better man."

The thought of Hopper pining for her all this time hit her right in the heart. It sounded over dramatic, almost too good to be true. But it wasn't like Kathryn to gush about people like this. Normally her best friend was the first person to offer up a list of pros, cons, and every potential pitfall. Could what she was saying about Hopper really be true?

"That a pretty big turnaround, Kathryn. How did it even happen? Why in the world would Hunter have hired a man with a record like Hopper's?"

"If you ask Hunter, he'll say he was hired for his qualifications. But it really was because of the reference letter his warden sent."

Lila cocked an eyebrow at that. "They do that sort of thing?"

"They do when you've saved their life," Kathryn answered. "Have you ever wondered why Hopper's voice sounds so raspy and why he has that big scar on his temple?"

Lila suddenly felt nauseated. She wasn't sure she wanted to hear this. But she closed her eyes. "Go on," she murmured.

"The prison Hopper got sent to was particularly riddled with gang violence. One day, the warden made the mistake of going out into the yard to talk to someone, and he got jumped. Big time. Hopper put himself in between the warden and the crowd attacking him, just long enough for the guards to get the warden to safety. But Hopper sustained some stab wounds, and his head had gotten kicked. His throat was stomped too. That's why he has half the tattoos he has—to cover all that."

Tears pricked at Lila's eyes, threatening to spill. "Oh," she breathed. "Oh, God."

"I know that sounds bad. And it was. But it turned out to be a blessing for him. He got sent down to a minimum-security prison and was able to get an associate's degree in business, then a bachelor's, then an MBA. While he was doing that, he was also earning certifications in welding and machining. He's truly turned himself around, Lila. I promise you."

Delilah scrubbed her hands over her face. This put a whole new spin on things, didn't it? Lord, she wanted it all to be true, maybe more than she'd ever wanted anything before. Images played out in her head—Hopper holding her against his bare chest, like she was the most precious gift he'd ever been given. His kisses, so raw and sexy and wild. The way he used to smile at her, like she'd truly made him happy. They'd made each other happy once. Could they find that together again?

Her pulse kicked up, and that restless, breathless feeling jittered her nerves.

What was she afraid of, really? She was all grown up.

Surely she could dip her toe in the water? Keep her guard high and her expectations low?

Honestly, it'd been so long since she'd opened herself up to someone, she wasn't entirely sure how much her poor heart could take. And Hopper could hurt her more easily than any other man on the planet if he chose to. But would he?

Had he changed? Maybe she owed it to herself to find out, one way or another.

"Okay," Lila finally said. "It can't hurt to at least talk to the man again. I'm sure I'll be bumping into him all the time if I come to visit. We should at least be cordial."

A wicked grin spread across Kathryn's face as she tugged Lila back around the building. "Being cordial. Is that what we're calling it these days?"

They were both snickering when they rounded the corner and the men saw them heading their way. Both men lit up at their approach, Hunter beaming at his wife, while Hopper laser-focused on her. Poor Hopper. He straightened up self-consciously and looked like he was wiping his sweaty palms on his jeans. Maybe Kathryn was right. Maybe she had been getting to the man.

"So," Hopper croaked out. "What's the plan?"

"The plan is…" Lila answered, poking him lightly in the center of his chest with her finger, "Kathryn and Hunter are going home. And I'm taking you up on that offer to check out the Christmas lights at the Greenbrier."

He let out a relieved breath. "God, I'm so glad." Then he smiled. Lord, his smiles. Lila had forgotten how devastatingly handsome they made him—his full, sensual mouth pulled into a broad grin, his blue eyes flashing with happiness. Now that he was older, the effect was only magnified. Laugh lines around his mouth were deepened by his salt-and-pepper beard. The crinkles around his eyes only made his face more masculine and interesting.

To her surprise, Hopper grabbed both her hands and pressed a courtly kiss to the top of them, sliding a teasing wink in her direction as he did. And oh, those butterflies in her stomach kicked up for real, this time. Even her knees felt wobbly.

He grabbed their helmets off the seat and handed one to her. "Your chariot awaits, milady," he crooned. She climbed on behind him, settling in so easily it felt like she'd never left. And Lila circled her arms around him, hoping she was ready for whatever the road would bring them.

CHAPTER 19

One thing Lila could say for sure about The Greenbrier Resort: pictures just didn't do it justice. As maid of honor, she'd gone through plenty of the resort's brochures with Kathryn, helping her pick out menus and such before her wedding. But nothing could've prepared her for the scale of the place in person. When they'd rumbled to a stop in front of the resort and seen thousands of glittering Christmas lights, her jaw nearly hit the ground.

"Amazing, isn't it?" Hopper grinned, taking his helmet off and stowing it in his pack on the back of the bike. She did the same. "I don't get up here nearly enough to experience all this. And it's a shame. It's like, what—five miles from my house?"

"I'm glad I've given you an excuse to get your Christmas on then," Lila answered. Yeah, she definitely couldn't imagine a better place to be at this time of year. The Greenbrier was everything Christmas was supposed to be, all wrapped up in one unbelievably grand package.

He grinned in agreement and cocked out his arm for her to take. Together they walked arm in arm all around the outside of the property. The main building was beautiful—a white monolith that seemed to go on forever with its colonial-era columns and sweeping verandas. The front of the building was lit up, the shifting shafts of light glowing in the darkness, highlighting the building's magnificent Georgian architecture in shimmering reds, blues, and greens. Lila may be a southern girl, but she'd learned to appreciate the crisp snap of the winter wind. On this velvety dark, cloudless night, it made her feel alive, like the colors were brighter and the stars hung lower in the sky.

The sea of white columns at the front of the building were the perfect backdrop for the property's outdoor centerpiece—a towering live Christmas tree that was easily forty feet high, decorated with thousands of multi-colored lights and a magnificent sparkling star on the top. Practically every tree on the whole property was lit trunk to branch with magical, glittering lights. And there were plenty of other outdoor displays too—giant lighted candy canes, Santas, oversized stacked boxes, you name it. Just then, a horse-drawn carriage driven by a man in colonial red-and-white livery clattered by, carrying a load of chattering, smiling guests. As Lila and Hopper made their way around the side of the property, there was still more decorating, this time around an idyllic outdoor skating rink surrounded by blazing fire pits and lounge chairs.

Hopper entertained her with facts and figures about the place he read off his phone. "The Greenbrier has been open to guests since 1778. It features 11,000 acres of land with more than seven hundred guest rooms, twenty restaurants and lounges, fifty-five indoor and outdoor activities and sports, and thirty-six retail shops."

"Impressive. Wonder why it was built?"

"That's easy," he answered. "The water. White Sulphur Springs is kind of like Bath, in England. People came here for the sulphur spring water, hoping drinking or soaking in it would cure their ills. Everything just built up from there.

Here's a crazy fact—during the Cold War, they built a secret bunker under here, with an underground railroad that connects to the nation's capital. In the event of a nuclear attack, our federal politicians were supposed to be shuttled off to this place so they could run the country from underground."

Lila cocked an eyebrow. "Come on. You're making that up."

He grinned back at her. "No, I'm not! It's not in operation anymore, but you can book a tour." They finally found their way back to the entrance again, and Hopper stopped. "It's just as impressive on the inside. Let's go in. I can show you around."

But Lila hesitated. "But the way we're dressed! Won't that be a problem? It's awfully fancy."

Hopper chuckled. "You think they don't have people coming here to stay after motorcycle tours? Trust me, they're used to the sight. And besides, the dress code only applies to a couple of their nicer restaurants."

When they went inside, Lila realized Hopper hadn't been overselling the place. The Greenbrier was a full-on Christmas spectacle, with a towering tree made of poinsettias, and another one made out of hundreds of gifts, stacked up to the sweeping ceilings. The lobby was lined with black-and-white marble tiles leading up to an elaborate wrought iron staircase, painted white. Hallways led off in every direction, going to spas, stores, and attractions. After stopping to linger a bit over the enormous village the Greenbrier chefs had made out of gingerbread, they decided to head to the second level, which featured one huge ballroom leading to the next, each outfitted with waterfall taffeta-style wallpaper and beautiful colonial friezes over the doors and windows.

The middle ballroom, though, was set up to be more of a meeting space, with cozy couches, overstuffed chairs, and tables sitting around. At one end was a long, mahogany bar, where people were lining up to get drinks. Hopper pointed in its direction. "What's your pleasure?"

Damn, the idea of a drink sounded like heaven. She smiled gratefully at him. "How about something warm? I could stand to chase off the chill."

He nodded and in no time was back with a tall latte for her. It featured peppermint crumbles, great puffs of whipped cream, and a generous shot of peppermint schnapps. It was perfect. He smirked. "I made sure not to get any nog. As for me, I'll take my whiskey straight. After getting stuck at Stuckey's, I'm gonna make it a policy not to drink any more unfamiliar concoctions, you feel me?"

Lila snickered in agreement as a waitress stepped up, handing them menus. After some discussion, they decided they'd rather keep it casual and get a burger here, rather than book one of the more formal restaurants at the resort. They placed their order and began their first real attempt at making conversation.

Lila worried they might run out of things to talk about. But the conversation flowed better than she'd expected. They did have a lot of catching up to do, obviously. She told him all about her life in Roanoke—her job, her condo, and how she and Kathryn had become such good friends.

He filled her in about life at Holliday Hot Rods and some of the projects he'd been working on. She hadn't realized the national reputation the shop was getting under his watch. More shocking still, the key role he was playing in making that happen. She was so used to seeing Hopper under the hood of a car, it blew her mind to hear him bandying about terms like "digital marketing funnels," "return on investment" and "key performance indicators." He'd turned into quite the business mogul, and the man clearly loved his work.

Lila couldn't help but take in every detail while he talked —the ease in his expressions, the slow smiles and twinkling eyes. Maybe Kathryn was right. Maybe he had changed. He didn't have that flinty edge to him anymore, like he had something to prove. He seemed comfortable in his own skin. Settled, even. Whether it was age or bitter experience that'd brought him to this point, it was wonderful to see.

Their food came, and the conversation just kept flowing. Hopper listened carefully to everything she had to say, as if he were thoughtfully contemplating every word. She'd forgotten how much she missed that. No one had ever listened to her like Hopper. His gaze stayed right on her as she talked, eyes sparking with interest over this or that point she'd made. He followed the thread of her conversation so naturally, asking one follow-up question after another.

Hopper was unusual that way. In her experience, men only wanted to talk about themselves, or worse, talk *at* you and tell you how to feel. But when she talked to Hopper, he'd always made her feel like she was interesting. Smart. Maybe even special. To a lonely, stressed-out fourteen-year-old girl, that kind of attentiveness had been like catnip to her. And at thirty-eight? It was damn near irresistible.

He polished off the last bite of his burger and sat back in his chair, regarding her. "Sounds like you've got a pretty good thing going in Virginia. But here's what I don't get. Why'd you leave Atlanta? All your friends, and Randy—you left them to go hours away."

Lila had to look away from him for a moment before she could summon an answer. The truth was, there were more reasons than she could count. Embarrassment that she'd let herself stay with a man like Mitchell for so long. Pity too, from people who knew her. Everyone seemed to have some kind of idea about who she should be and what she should do after her marriage had fallen apart. It had all been well-meaning concern, borne out of love, of course. But in the end, she'd just felt like the walls had been closing in on her there.

"I needed a fresh start," she finally answered. "To get away."

"To get away from Mitchell, you mean."

"Something like that."

Hopper paused, his expression growing grim. "Did he come after you, after you left? Is that why you didn't just change your name back to Jones?"

She fiddled with the rim of her drink while she tried to figure out what to say. "There were a lot of threats at first," she finally said. "I filed a protective order. But I think once he figured out I truly didn't want anything belonging to him, or anything he'd given me, he stopped. His lawyer probably advised him to lay off. I changed my name to Cook as a bit of an insurance policy, just in case he got some kind of wild hair to reunite. Thank God, that's never happened."

"You have no idea what's happened to him since?"

"Don't know. Don't care. If he fell face-first into a volcano, it wouldn't be a day too soon."

He laughed.

"What about you?" she asked him, eager to change the subject. "What made you leave Georgia? And why Lewisburg, of all places?"

Hopper reached across the table and laced his fingers through hers. She didn't have the will to pull away. "Think about it, Delilah. The only real connection I had to Atlanta was you. When you were gone, why would I stay?"

"That's too easy, Hop. There had to be more to it than that."

"Well, yeah, I suppose. Job hunting wasn't easy when you've got prison time on your resume. So when I got the offer for Holliday Hot Rods? It was a dream come true for me, and more than I ever expected. I jumped at the chance. Money's good, and I feel like I'm doing some real good for the business. And you gotta love Lewisburg. The rolling hills are flat-out gorgeous. The sense of community here is something I never knew I was missing. And I'm hanging onto it, with both hands. Somehow, the place calms me down."

Lila felt a twinge of recognition at that. "Gives you peace, doesn't it? Makes all the noise in your head stop."

"Yeah," he said, rubbing his thumb along the top of her hand. "Something like that."

He went on to tell her about all the kindnesses the community had paid him when he'd first arrived. How Hunter had allowed him to stay in the garret above the garage rent-free, in exchange for him donating his labor to remodel the place. How coworkers and neighbors had offered him furniture to use. The boost had been enough to let him save the lion's share of his salary over the next couple of years and put down a hefty down payment on his house. "It's no palace or anything, but the house is just right as far as I'm concerned. I'm really proud to call it home."

Home.

When was the last time she'd ever felt truly, completely at home? When she'd lived at Randy's? When she'd shared an apartment with her roommates? Roanoke was a perfectly nice city for her to be living in. But it wasn't home.

No, home was a rare and wonderful thing. And she was so happy he'd found that. As she listened, Lila started to get that full feeling in her chest again, an overflowing feeling. She realized all at once it was pride—pride for that bewildered teen who'd been abandoned at a Greyhound station. After all that, he'd finally arrived at his destination. She unwound their fingers and sat back. "Sounds like the perfect situation for you. Like you've found your way."

"'Spose I have." He smirked at her over his beer, as if to say *it's not all wine and roses, honey.* "What about you, angel? Are you happy?"

It was a big question, one she hadn't a clue how to answer. "I'm fine," she found herself reflexively saying.

"Just fine?"

"What do you want me to say, Hop? I'm holding my own. It's enough, most days."

He scowled. "Holding your own. Yeah, and that's my damn fault."

The comment stopped her. "Your fault? What do you mean—your fault that I'm not deliriously happy or something?"

"It *is* my fault." He jabbed a finger on the tabletop, eyes and flashing with certainty. "Don't you see? Nearly all of the bad things that have happened to you were because of me. If I hadn't broken the law, you would've never been out there, ready to fall into the clutches of somebody like Mitchell Roby. I would've been there for you. I could've protected you."

He was so sincere, so contrite. But the words wormed their way under her skin, anyway. Was that what he really thought of her? That she was some little lost lamb that couldn't take care of herself? "Oh, I see. So when it comes to my life, my choices, all roads lead back to you! Is that it? I was so crippled by my heartbreak I couldn't possibly have had the presence of mind to make a decent decision about anything!"

He rounded his eyes in shock and held up his hands. "Delilah, wait. That's not what I meant."

"Don't you dare. Don't you *dare* take the responsibility for marrying Mitchell away from me. I was the one who decided to marry a man I didn't truly love. That's on me. And all those things he did to me? That's on him. Not you. And that's the last thing I'm going to say about that fucker Mitchell Roby. Are we clear?"

"Yeah," he answered, the sound so gruff it barely qualified as a word. He grabbed both of her hands this time and held them tight. "I just want to say I'm sorry, that's all. For all of it. Everything. I did so many things wrong, I can't even count them all. But you, angel? You were the only thing in my whole rotten life that was right. If getting stuck at the Outpost taught me one thing, it was that for one brief moment in time, I had a love that was sweet and perfect and true. That you're the only woman who's ever mattered to me. Who *will ever* matter to me. Do you understand what I'm saying to you?"

Lila was shocked to see his eyes get shiny with tears. He carefully blinked them back. But still...in all the years she'd known Hopper, she'd never seen him get even remotely weepy. Only once, at the bus station....

He means it, doesn't he?

She tried desperately to hold that revelation at some kind of emotional arm's length—so she could study it, judge it, or quantify it. But the idea still wrapped around her like an embrace.

She swallowed hard. "What are you trying to tell me, Hop?"

"I said it at the Outpost, and I'm going to say it again, for real. I want you back. All of it. Everything."

Wow. So there it is.

Words she'd never thought she'd hear, least of all from him. It was like the stars had aligned and suddenly she had a whole universe of choices. A whole menu of new expectations she could choose for herself. Maybe she was starting to feel weepy too. But she was getting ahead of herself, wasn't she? She cocked an eyebrow, trying to play it cool. "Just like that? You say a few pretty words, and all our past goes away?"

"No." He shook his head fiercely. "All I want is a chance, Delilah. So that maybe we can build something better, together. Something real, on a solid foundation this time."

After Kathryn's encouraging speech and the sweet way he'd been treating her today, Lila suspected something like this would be coming. Had braced herself for it, even. She'd been prepared to tell him no. But hearing the words out of his mouth? It was a balm that soothed something, deep inside her.

And there was that piercing gaze again, making her feel seen and somehow exposed, all at once. He had a way of holding her to the spot, making her feel…necessary. That was it. He made her feel necessary—like his life couldn't be complete without her. Maybe he was necessary to her too.

But if he thought she was just going to go running right back like nothing had happened, he was mistaken.

They were going to do this. But on her terms. In a flash, an idea occurred to her.

She swallowed down the surge of emotions pounding through her, sat up straight in her seat, and looked the man right in the eye. "Alright, Hopper. I agree, it'd be good for us to get to know each other again. But I'm not willing to pine away for months or years waiting to see if this is going to work or not. I've wasted too much of my life wondering what might have been. So I have a proposal. It's two days after Christmas, and I don't have to go back to Roanoke until the night before New Year's Eve. That gives me three days. I'll book a room here. And you have three days to convince me this thing between us could work. Are you in? Or out?"

A look Lila could only describe as sweet, happy relief passed over his face. But he quickly reined in his excitement. He stuck out his hand. "Angel, you've got a deal."

And they shook on it.

CHAPTER 20

HOPPER STOOD in the lobby of the Greenbrier, shuffling impatiently from foot to foot, waiting for Delilah to come down to meet him.

Today was "his" to plan, they'd agreed. Tomorrow would be hers. And the day after that, they'd decide on something they both wanted to do. He'd known immediately exactly where he wanted to take her. And as a bonus, he could show her more about his life and the man he'd become—proof he was sure she needed. He'd told her to eat a big breakfast and meet him at noon, dressed to ride.

He checked the time. It was twenty til. He felt kinda like an idiot, coming so early. But he couldn't help himself. He was betting everything on this day-trip, because he was playing to win. No way would he come peeling in here at the last minute.

Still, he paced, as jittery as some teenager on his first date. He stood around, reading the posters sitting on easels in the lobby, advertising all the excursions the resort offered. ATVing on the property. Falconing. Bowling. Dancing. Couples spa dates. Glass blowing. Bunker tours. His heart sank. Did he make a mistake, not going with one of these fancy options?

He used to understand every little thing about her. They'd grown up together, after all, and liked the same things. Elaborate dates were hardly even necessary, because just hanging out with each other had been special. Not to say he'd never taken her out or done special things for her. He had, but…

He blew out a breath and sat down on the edge of the steps to wait.

And worried still more. Delilah was a far cry from the wild, sexy girl she used to be. The woman she'd become was buttoned up. Professional. And probably had developed tastes for a more sophisticated man. Could he keep her satisfied?

When Delilah sashayed down the grand staircase, all his worries blew away like so many snowflakes. Because this? *This* was the Delilah he remembered. She'd taken his advice on motorcycle-appropriate wear to heart. And she looked fuckin' delicious.

Somehow, with not even so much as a suitcase at her disposal, she'd managed to find skin-tight black leather leggings and over-the-knee boots with big, chunky heels. On the top she wore a sparkly red sweater that was long enough to cover her rear, yet still caress every single one of her curves. She must've washed her hair and let it dry naturally, because her rowdy waves were back—not as long as before, but still begging for his fingers.

By the time she'd gotten to the bottom of the steps, his heart was pounding and his mouth was too dry to speak.

"What's the matter, Hop?" She smirked, coming to a stop in front of him. "Cat got your tongue?"

Hopper collected himself quickly enough to smirk back at her. "Pardon me," he purred. "I'm picking up my tongue from the floor. I hope you didn't do all this for my benefit. Don't get me wrong. Those leather pants are going to haunt my dreams. But I would've been just as happy if you'd been in jeans and an old T-shirt."

She kissed him on the cheek while he helped her into his old jacket. "Well, I didn't have an old T-shirt with me, did I? But I had a great time shopping for everything. The stores here are amazing. I've become quite the consignment store diva in recent years. But I decided to splurge this morning. I can't tell you the last time I've been on vacation. And this? With you? It's my vacation."

He popped out his arm for her to take and couldn't help puffing his chest out a bit as they walked out to his bike. "I hope I don't let you down too much. I've just got a simple day planned. It's supposed to be in the mid-sixties today—so unusually warm, I couldn't resist getting out on the bike. Thought maybe we could take a ride around and I could show you some of the natural wonders around here. And later I'll make you dinner back at my place."

Grinning with excitement, she popped her helmet on and climbed into her spot behind him. "Until yesterday, it'd been more than ten years since I've been on a motorcycle. But I think I'm catching the bug again. I can't wait for this."

"As you wish, milady." He revved the motor once or twice, just for effect. They rumbled out of the parking lot and took off. He didn't have any particular route in mind, so he started off by taking her on a guided tour of Lewisburg, his new hometown. She'd seen it, no doubt, on her trips to Kathryn's before. But he showed her the out-of-the-way places—driving past the Greenbrier River Trail, Carnegie Hall, the historical society, and such.

But he didn't linger long. His real objective was The New River Gorge, which was about an hour and a half from here. He could've gone on the interstate but opted instead for historic route 60 North. This stretch of road was one of the prettiest anywhere, in his opinion—all rolling hills and spectacular vistas, little farms with cows and horses grazing, historic old buildings, and quaint communities. The most peaceful, idyllic drive you could imagine.

Which made viewing it all from the back of a motorcycle even better. The excitement of the open road was not to be underestimated. But the pure thrill of enjoying it all with Delilah? That was as close to paradise as he could ever get.

He could hear her giggle over the roar of the engine as they leaned into those mountain curves, heard her exclaim in wonder as they rounded the corner into another shadowed patch of trees, still shining from the remnants of stubborn, melting icicles.

He thought he'd remembered every detail about Delilah, jealously guarding every single moment of their time together in his mind. But he'd forgotten just how much she loved the bike rides they'd taken together. The way the joy would transform her whole face, like a little kid on Christmas morning. The way she'd beg him to keep driving, just a bit longer, no matter what the weather. Sometimes on the slower straightaways, she'd stick her arms out just to feel the rushing wind, and let it pass through her fingers as if it were water.

And she'd throw back her head and laugh. Just like she was doing now, the sweet notes of it drifting in the wind. There was no two ways about it. Whether she was driving one, or on the back, Delilah was born for riding a motorcycle. And when they were riding together? She made him feel accomplished. Adventuresome. Like a man. And he couldn't stop smiling about it.

By mid-afternoon they'd reached their destination—New River Gorge National River. Specifically, they'd stopped at the Bridge Walk.

"How awesome is this?" Delilah cried as they pulled up. "I've always wanted to go to see the gorge. But what's this?"

"This—" he grinned, sweeping her off the bike, "—is your chance to walk across the bridge."

"But isn't the bridge just for cars?"

He shuttled her off in the direction of the tour center. "This is underneath the bridge. It's a catwalk that takes you across and allows you to see the river under your feet."

"Okay, so it's just off the ground then."

"No, angel. It's more than eight hundred feet up."

Lila skidded to a stop at this startling tidbit. "What?" she squeaked.

She must've paled, because she could almost feel the blood draining out of her face. Hopper's eyebrows flew up. "Oh. My. Lord. *Woman!* You never told me you were afraid of heights!"

"I'm not usually. Too much. It's just…" She swallowed, and squeezed her eyes shut. God, she could just see herself teetering on a flimsy catwalk, swaying in the wind. "It's just so high. A little too close to Jesus, you know?"

"*Awwww* no." Hopper groaned. He scrubbed both hands over his face, looking sick with dismay. "I can't believe this. Here I'm trying to take you out to do something special, and this is what I pick. The one thing practically custom designed to freak you out. I'm such a fucking moron for not running this by you. God, I'm so sorry."

Lila grabbed his hand. "Hey, it's okay. I'd never told you about this stupid phobia. And this was a nice idea—a fun little surprise."

"Hey, we don't have to do this. It's just a couple of tickets. There's plenty else around here to do." He gave her hand a little shake, as if to reassure her.

But Lila couldn't stop thinking about what he just said. "You already bought the tickets?"

He shrugged. "Bought them online yesterday. But it's no big deal, really."

But the idea of leaving didn't sit so well, despite her

queasiness. She was absolutely allergic to wasting money, a lesson drilled into her practically daily during her childhood.

He must've seen the gears turning in her head, because he barked out an incredulous laugh. "You're scowling. This is making your thrift alarm go off, isn't it?"

She growled. The man knew her too well, didn't he? "It's like I can see your money growing wings and flying out the window."

His chuckle seemed to rumble through his whole chest, and his eyes crinkled up with affection as he looked down at her. "What else would I expect from the girl who used to wash out sandwich bags just so she could reuse them?"

"Hey!" she slapped him on the arm. "Don't make fun of me! I was sustainable before sustainable was cool."

"What are you saying then? You want to do it? I, for one, am happy to bail. I mean, this is our first date n' all, after so long. It'd probably be a good thing if you weren't in fear for your life."

Something about the way he said that didn't sit well with her. Was it as bad as all that? She was making too much of this, wasn't she? Lila squared her shoulders. Cowardice wasn't a good look on her. She'd been afraid of too many things in her life. She'd hidden herself away, building this shiny shell around herself to keep from getting hurt. Hell, she'd even been afraid to call herself by her own name. It was more than past time she started acting like the badass she wanted to be, and not some scared little girl. Hopper would be here, so…maybe she could do this?

She narrowed her eyes at him. "You'll be right behind me?"

He gave her another one of those heart stopping looks, brought her hand to his mouth, and kissed it. "Always, angel."

She let out a long breath. "Okay then. I can do this. I-I want to try it."

He raised his eyebrows again. "You're sure? You're *abso-*

lutely sure? The last thing in the world I want to do is force you to do something that makes you uncomfortable."

Lila couldn't miss the ring of sincerity in his tone, and that warmed her. When was the last time a man had given a damn about what she thought? She pressed her finger into the cleft on his chin, a movement so natural to her that she hadn't even realized she'd done it until her fingertip met his stubbly beard. "Oh, Hopper," she breathed. "Somehow, I think you could never make me feel uncomfortable."

He broke out into the most adorable blush, and seemed so pleased, she was glad she'd made this call. "Come on." She grabbed his hand. "The bridge awaits."

Together, they went through the process of checking in, getting briefed on safety and assigned to their tour group. Hopper made sure they were at the end of the line, just in case. The bridge walk, their tour guide told them, was nearly a mile long, and the catwalk footpath surface was only twenty-four inches wide.

Her stomach protested at the thought. But Hopper kissed her on the back of her head and rubbed her shoulders. Her panic receded—some.

When they got out onto the platform, she was reassured. Yes, the catwalk was only one person wide, and there were open-air scaffolds all along the sides and bottom of it. But the steel platform didn't seem like it swayed in the wind, and two railings on either side gave you something to put your hands on as you crossed. Harnesses attached to safety cables above your head, and moved along with you as you walked. So, on the slim chance you put a foot wrong off the sides of the platform, you'd be safe. She was feeling better about this all the time.

Hopper gave her another reassuring squeeze as they got themselves harnessed in. And soon, they were off, walking along behind a group of chattering teens and a couple of families with young kids. She was fine. Really. She occupied herself admiring the way the steel beams were latticed into rows of triangles, stretching off into the distance. She listened to the tour guide. Something about "once was the world's longest steel arch bridge" and "nineteen thousand cars go over in a day and—"

Suddenly, she didn't hear another word that was said. And she couldn't take another step, either. Because, for the first time, she was looking down. Way, way *waaaaaaaaay* down.

Holy hell.

She stiffened, and her chest got tight. She could hardly breathe. Her knuckles turned white as her fingers snapped into a death grip on the railings. She'd done it now. *Shit shit shit.*

"Miss, are you okay?" The metallic sound of reverb from the guide's mic scraped at her ears, and it seemed every person in their tour group had turned around to look at her.

Fear had gripped her throat so completely, she couldn't get out a sound.

Thankfully, Hopper held up a hand. "She'll be fine. She just needs a minute. Go on without us. We'll catch up, okay?"

"All right," the tour guide answered, still clearly concerned. "We can bring up someone from the other side to help walk you back. You sure you want to keep going?"

"We'll get back to you on that," Hopper answered.

The tour group and all its prying eyes moved on, and Lila felt the vise-grip of panic recede a little. She could at least have her freakout in peace. Hopper moved close behind her and circled his arms around her waist. Lila leaned back against the hard, smooth warmth of his chest and turned her face against one of his arms. "I'm sorry," she whispered. "I can't believe I'm such a wimp."

"Hey," he murmured, leaning his head down to talk in her ear. "We've all got somethin'."

She snorted. "Really? What's yours?"

"Handcuffs," he replied, his growl going playfully low. "I'm just warnin' you, you probably shouldn't ever lock me to the headboard."

Gallows humor hit her, and she found herself laughing helplessly. "Well, shoot. I guess I'll have to leave those fuzzy pink handcuffs in my nightstand."

"Mmm…guess so." He nuzzled her ear and kissed her lightly on the neck.

"I'll have to return the mask and my leather whip too."

"Probably a good idea," he murmured, this time nipping her right behind the ear with his teeth. Tingles of awareness slid down her spine. God, he smelled so good…windswept and woodsy, mixed with a hint of sweat, no doubt from their ride. The heat of his skin warmed her as the wind buffeted them up here, soothing her. Making her forget where she was.

She turned to face him, and he smiled at the closeness of her, pressed hard up against him. She bit her lip, for effect, and sighed. "It really is too bad. I think that red leather catsuit I bought is probably non-returnable."

He chuckled again, a deep and mellow sound, despite his rasp. "You're just tryin' to torture me! I'm going to be picturing you in that catsuit every time I close my eyes now."

She buried her face in his chest and sighed theatrically. "Glad I could be of service."

He slid one hand to the small of her back, the other to the nape of her neck. "Angel, I see what you're doin.'"

"And what's that?"

"You're distracting me so you'll distract yourself, right?"

She burrowed her head in harder and tightened her fists in his shirt. "I suppose I-I just don't want to look down again."

"Fine then," he said, tipping her chin up. "Don't look down. Look up, at me."

And when she met his gaze, everything stopped. For just

one moment, the world itself stopped turning, and there was no bridge, no steep drop. There was only him, and the way he looked at her, right now. His gaze held so much…tenderness, amusement. But more than that—history. Intimacy, even. Her heart overflowed with it.

He tipped her head back and leaned into her, brushing his lips against hers gently, lazily, his mouth seeming to ask *do you need this? Do you want this?*

Yes. *Yes, she did.*

She parted her lips for him, leaning up on her toes to deepen the kiss and throw her arms around his neck. God, the taste of him. She'd forgotten. But her body remembered—the sensual slide of his mouth on hers, the way she molded perfectly against him… Nobody in this whole wide world could kiss like Hopper Vance. Like he put his whole self into it. Like his life depended on it. Deep. Savoring. Like she was the sweetest candy he'd ever tasted.

He groaned, trembling under her fingertips. And she trembled too.

"Ma'am?" A concerned male voice rang out from behind Hopper. "Excuse me, but are you alright? You've been stopped for some time."

They broke apart, both of them breathing hard. Hopper turned, and she peeked around to see a twenty-something tour guide standing there, twirling his lanyard uncertainly. The poor boy was slight of build and about a head and a half shorter than Hopper. When Hopper turned, all hulking muscles and tattoos, the poor kid blanched. Hopper must've looked like thunder.

"Yes, he's comforting me," she sputtered, trying not to snicker. "I just got a little freaked out is all."

"Oh! Don't worry about that." The kid smiled. "You're really quite secure here. We've never had an accident. But sometimes the distance to the ground can be a bit much for some people. Sir, we're about to cue up another crossing group, so you won't be able to stay here. Would you like to go on the rest of the way, or do you want to turn around?"

Since it was shorter, they decided to walk back the way they came. She was behind Hopper for the walk back, and somehow that kept her calm. She hooked one hand on the railing and the other on the back of his belt. And as they walked the hundred yards or so back, Hopper pointed out the pretty mountains, and the New River running like a ribbon on both sides of them. Always to the sides, and not down. When they finally got back to solid ground, she collapsed in his arms. The tour guide started lining up his next group.

"Well." She groaned, hiding her face in his chest again. "That was embarrassing."

He wrapped an arm around her. "Embarrassing? Are you kidding me? I just got to kiss the most beautiful woman I've ever seen over top of The New River Gorge. I hope they sell commemorative photos, 'cause I'd sure as shit be framin' that. Hell, I think I'd like to eat off the commemorative plate."

She giggled and shoved at him, at least making a show of being affronted. "I was supposed to be working on confronting my fears!"

"Well, can't say you made much progress against the heights. But maybe you're less afraid of us. I'll call that a win."

Lila had no idea how to respond to that. But as he offered her his arm again, she couldn't do a thing but wrap her arm in his and go wherever he led her.

CHAPTER 21

AS THEY MADE the last turn into Lewisburg, Hopper mentally kicked himself for the thousandth time. What had he been thinking, taking her to the Bridge Walk? Half the people in the world were afraid of heights! It'd been a stupid, rookie move. And he'd considered himself no rookie when it came to Delilah.

He'd thought he knew everything about her. What she liked and didn't like. What her moods and expressions meant. What she looked like lying in the moonlight. How the wind whispered through her hair. And all those thousands of physical details that haunted his dreams, from the delicate arch of her foot to the tiniest curve of her lips.

But he really didn't understand her anymore, did he? He was starting over from scratch with her—a fact that should be keeping his raging libido in check. After all, he had every intention of wooing her like a gentleman. But damn, that kiss...

He could still feel it, taste it.

Minus the cherry lip gloss maybe, but that kiss was every bit the Delilah he remembered. All that bottled-up sensuality and chemistry. It hadn't ebbed over the years. Not one bit.

Which presented an interesting challenge. Delilah was no random hookup. Sure, their relationship had always been explosively sexual. But he refused to lead with that. He didn't want to be her "bad boy," the kind of man who'd fuck her on the hood of a car, for Christ's sake. He wanted to be her man. The kind of man who stayed.

Their arrival at his house set his internal strategy session to pause mode. He pulled the bike around to the back and took Delilah's helmet from her.

She whistled appreciatively at the sight of his place. "Oh, Hop! It's adorable. You must be so happy living here."

"It suits me." He shrugged. But secretly, it pleased him to hear her say it. The woman had lived in a marble-crusted mansion at one time, after all. There'd been no telling how she was going to react to this humble house, which had to be, what—a third of the size of Roby's place?

But when Lila toured his bungalow, her eyes lit up. She truly seemed to love it. The compliments kept flowing as she took in the black granite counter in his kitchen, the freshly refinished hardwood floors, and the floor-to-ceiling bookshelves he'd built on all four walls in one of the bedrooms. He'd turned it into a full-on study with a built-in desk and a brown leather reading chair and ottoman set right in the middle of the room. He'd always wanted to be the sort of man who had a study, after all, and now he was.

She walked around, trailing her pretty hand over the books. "Wow. I see you've still got the reading bug."

"Ever since you started bringing me books from the thrift store all those years ago. I decided to make it a hobby when I got out. It felt good, to read anything I wanted again." He propped himself in the doorway, smiling with satisfaction to see her browsing his titles. He had a metric ton of books these days, in just about every type of genre. Some he bought new, but the majority were used, mainly hardbacks he'd hunted down at garage sales, the local Goodwill, and used bookstores. He'd spent the last couple of years carefully curating a collection he wouldn't mind reading again and again. Classics, thrillers, sci-fi, fantasy, and historical fiction, for starters.

Delilah stopped in front of one of his nonfiction shelves and let out an impressed little cluck. "I've never seen such a broad selection of books. Look at this! Steven Hawking, Thomas Friedman, Thomas Paine, even—your tastes have gotten a lot more sophisticated." She stopped, pulled out a book, and shot him a quizzical smirk. "Wow. The Analects of Confucius?"

He moved up beside her. "What can I say? There's nothing like jail to make you wonder about the meaning of it all. I found a book series on the great philosophers, used online, and I couldn't resist. That's the last one in the series, and I haven't gotten to it yet. But I've enjoyed reading all those, believe it or not. I've never been a particularly religious man, but philosophy? That appeals."

"Hmmm." She linked her arm in his, and together they walked back down the hall. "Hopper Vance. Mechanic. Philosopher. Renaissance Man. Not too shabby if you asked me. Having a study suits you."

He smiled down at her, warmed to his soul by the compliment. He still wasn't entirely used to being appreciated for his brain. But it was something he'd been slowly getting accustomed to since he'd gotten out of prison. Still, hearing her say it? It meant the world.

He motioned for her to come with him to the kitchen so he could start on dinner. Pouring her a glass of white wine, he started gathering his ingredients. Delilah raised her eyebrows at the sight of the ball of dough he pulled out of the fridge. He grinned at her. "It's pasta dough. So, I have a confession to make. When I found out we were doing this three-dates thing, I decided I'd better bring my A-Game. I stopped in and asked Kathryn for advice. She recommended I make pasta from scratch."

Delilah swirled the wine in her glass, and huffed out a little chuckle. "The woman practically has a catalog of all my quirks—one of which is depriving myself of carbs."

His face fell. "Oh, no. Did I make a mistake? Do you have that gluten thing? Or an allergy?"

She waved away his concern. "No. I'm usually trying to watch my weight, that's all. But now that I think about it, a bowl of pasta might do me good. I can't even remember the last time I had some. Kathryn's probably engineered this so I'll have a carb-gasm and imprint on you like a baby duckling."

"Does this mean you'd follow me around all the time if I carried bread in my pockets?"

She poked him playfully in the chest. "Probably." She peeked around at the dough. "Have you ever made homemade pasta?"

"Nope." He hoisted Kathryn's enormous electronic pasta machine out of the cabinet and plugged it in. "That's why we're going to use this puppy right here." Kathryn had showed him how it worked last night, but his brain had been buzzing with date prep. He'd promptly forgotten what she'd told him.

Luckily, Delilah was able to decipher the instruction booklet and get the machine going while he chopped up the mushrooms and fresh spices for the sauce. They ended up with gorgeous homemade linguini. While the pasta was boiling to a perfect al dente, he tossed together a simple cream sauce with white wine, fresh rosemary and thyme, mushrooms, onion, chicken and fresh peas.

He pulled out salads he'd made the night before, and crusty bread too. And before long, Delilah was beaming at him from behind her full plate.

"What?"

"You. You've come a long way from making me Chef Boyardee pizzas."

He snickered a little bit through his groan. "Oh, man. I made so many of those. I didn't even have the class to buy a pizza shell."

She rolled her eyes. "Oh come on. Don't be so hard on yourself. Those pizzas were snack crack. And besides, I had you scratch cooking soon enough."

And she had. Matter of fact, he could still make a pretty decent peach cobbler, biscuits, roast, chicken and dumplings, and a whole lot more, because of the lessons she'd given him in the kitchen. "That, you did." He raised his glass to her. "My stomach salutes you."

They spent the rest of the meal talking companionably, about anything and everything, really. Books. Movies. How he'd rehabbed the house. Why she enjoyed the details of running a medical practice. How he roped in new customers with social media marketing and sponsorships at car shows. He'd been in the middle of discussing the favorite philosophers he'd read lately—Thomas Merton and Sartre, to be exact—when she'd sat down her glass, looking bemused.

He stopped. "What? What's that look for?"

"You've changed."

He couldn't help furrowing his brow at that statement, but he still smiled back at her. "You say that like it's a bad thing."

"Oh no, it's not—not at all," she answered, still idly twirling a fingertip around the top of her wine glass, considering him in a way that made him feel a bit too…inspected. "It's just that…well, you look so different than the last time I saw you. You've easily picked up thirty pounds of muscle and how many tats? Your hair's gone so gray. And don't get me started about your voice. It sounds like a rocky road."

"Yeah." Hopper sighed. "Time has a way of marking a man."

"But it's more than that, isn't it?"

He frowned a little bit at that, and picked up their dishes. She followed. "I'm not sure what you mean by that. I'm still the same guy I always was. Just grown up, I guess."

"No. The Hopper I knew wasn't secure in his own skin. There was a restlessness. A simmering anger too, maybe. Like there was something you wanted, and you weren't taking no for an answer."

He snorted as he started loading everything in the dishwasher. "Shit yeah, I had something to prove. I was starting at zero. Less than zero, even. I had something to prove to the world, and I think more important than that, something to prove to myself."

"And yet, here you are, living a pretty good life, as far as I can see."

"I'm damn glad of that too. I walked through a mine field to get where I am today. You know, I didn't really even realize how angry I was until I was in prison. There's so much anger and hate there—and a whole lotta people blaming the world for all the bad choices they'd made. I realized, I didn't want to be one of those guys. I had to do some thinking about the sort of man I wanted to be. I had to let go of some things."

"Like what?"

He let out a long sigh. The list was almost too long to mention. His dreams? His ego? His fuckin' fantasies about how he could become a completely different person? Yeah, he'd had to wipe it all clean. Oh, he'd never been able to forgive himself, but at least he'd come to understand what he'd really done. He'd tried to cheat his way to an elusive goal —becoming a solid, stable, community man—someone so successful and useful, no one could ever deny that he belonged.

Back then, he'd banked every dime he'd stolen, certain he could use it to start off a new life with Delilah. One with a big house filled with little black-haired kids and a white picket fence. In his daydreams, he'd go off to work every day in a custom-made suit and come home to the kind of lifestyle where they never had to worry about money, the kids went to private school, and the family vacationed in nice places, like Martha's Vineyard or some shit like that.

Just thinking about it made him squirm. He was glad he'd never shared those boyish aspirations with Delilah back then. She would've laughed him out of the room at the time. Everyone would have. Because they would've known then what he knew now—he could never have been that man.

He tried to give Delilah the simplest answer he could think of. "I had to let go of this idea that I could be something I'm not," he simply said.

LILA TOOK a second to consider that. There was something he wasn't saying. But she decided not to pry. "This *real you*—the man you ended up being. Do you like him?"

"Yeah." He shrugged. "I suppose I do. Do you?"

The question caught her off guard. She gave him a long, assessing look while she turned it over in her mind. "Yeah, I suppose I do. It's easier to like what you understand. Since you're not hiding anything that I can see, I feel like maybe I've got a shot at knowing you again. And I'm not gonna lie. Those new muscles of yours are seriously off-the-charts hot. You're one of those men who's gotten better with age, Hop. It's totally not fair."

Lila would've never believed it was possible, but the man actually looked flustered for a second, blushing a little and shifting on his feet, as if he wasn't used to getting compliments. But he stalked forward anyway. He stopped right in front of her, right up in her personal space. He treated her to another one of his cockeyed smiles, and tenderly ran the backs of his fingers over her cheek. "So…you think I'm hot, huh?"

"I do," she breathed, not able to resist running her hand up one of his cabled, tatted-up forearms. His skin was rough, but a glowy kind of warm to the touch, and the underside of his arm was so silky. "I-I'm not that sweet young thing I used to be. I'm sorry if I don't look—"

Lila would've finished the thought, but his mouth was on her again, blazing and insistent. Devouring her like their years spent apart never existed. As if it were his right. *Filthy. Wild. Hard.*

He pressed for entrance with his tongue, and she eagerly opened to him, their mouths sparring, exploring. A wave of hot, prickly sensation poured over her from her head to her feet, and she felt the jab of the kitchen counter at her waist as Hopper pinned her. She wound her arms around his back, her fingertips traveling over all his fascinating planes and angles.

Lila was sure his next move would be hitching her rear end up onto the counter and having his way with her, just like they used to do. She had no problem with that. But he uttered a pained groan instead and pulled back. Gently, he wrapped her in his arms and tucked his head on top of hers, letting out a long, satisfied sigh. "Awesome how some things never change, huh?"

She chuckled breathlessly and buried her face in his chest. Apparently he was going to play the gentleman. She'd play along.

"Let me show you what else hasn't changed. Dessert." He broke away from her and rooted around in his freezer until he pulled out a very familiar bundle of pint-sized perfection.

"Cherry Garcia! I don't believe it!" she cried.

He fished out two spoons from the drawer. "From the days when Ben & Jerry's was five-star dining."

She swiped the spoon and picked out a big cherry piece

right off the top. "Do they give six stars? 'Cause it should be six stars. Totally."

He walked her into his living room, which was very Hopper—clean and tidy, with two brown leather, turned-arm sofas separated by a low-slung, walnut coffee table. Thick oak molding accented every corner, its gleaming dark stain gracing the whole place with a comforting, sturdy permanence. Over the couch, an oil painting of a mountain sunset decorated the space in rich blues, grays and pinks.

He'd made himself a very nice home here.

Yet, there was very little ornament. A couple of candles. A smattering of car magazines he'd been reading. A quilted throw folded neatly on the back of the couch. The quilt was simple, with thick, colorful vertical stripes, but she'd recognize Kathryn's handiwork anywhere. She asked him about it, and he confirmed—Kathryn had made one for everyone in the shop last Christmas.

Otherwise, there was really nothing here in the way of personal mementoes or photos displayed. No pictures of old girlfriends, no family photos, no travel souvenirs. But who was she to judge? Her condo didn't have any signs of life in it either. The thought depressed her. *How much time have we wasted?*

Lila couldn't kick up a brood, though, when she gotta load of Hopper's face. The man grinned from ear to ear as he hit a button, and flames leaped up in the gas fireplace. Remote control starters always were a favorite toy of his. He whipped the quilt off the couch with a theatrical flourish, and she giggled as he tucked her in, propping her legs up over his. They dug into the pint.

Mmmmm. She'd forgotten how much she loved the whole ice cream eating ritual. Cheap takeout and Ben & Jerry's used to be their go-to entertainment on a Friday night. Especially dessert—they'd sit on the couch, feeding each other spoonfuls from the same pint container. He'd feed her the best chocolate bits, and she'd feed him the best cherry bits, each of them getting more of their favorite part. How wonderful it was, to relive such a sweet memory. When it came to her younger years, there weren't very many of those. But then again, the good memories she did have nearly always involved Hopper.

Even while she ate, she couldn't stop staring at his artificial Christmas tree. He'd parked it haphazardly in the corner, half decorated with a homemade construction paper chain—like the kind you might make in grade school. She pointed to it. "So that's your Christmas decorating?"

He rolled his eyes. "A real beaut, huh? I got started on something I couldn't finish. When I first moved in here a few years ago, I bought one of those pre-lit, artificial trees on sale, and then, you know. I just never had the heart to put it up."

Lila snorted. "I get that. I haven't had a Christmas tree since that last Christmas with Mitchell, and that's been at least ten years ago. Felt like a waste of effort for just me. So why did you start this year?"

"The Caine's influence, probably. After I escaped from the Outpost, I came back here, and everything just seemed so lonely and dark. I had a couple of drinks on Christmas Day and pulled this thing up from the basement. I was going to go out and buy some decorations with all the after-Christmas sales, but I ended up checking in at the garage, and guess who showed up, totally wrecking all my plans?"

She got up to inspect the tree, assessing it through narrowed eyes. "So, it's my fault then that you've got this sad tree." Hopper followed, holding up a bite of ice cream and waggling his eyebrows. She giggled and squawked as he pretended to drop it, but finally spooned it in her mouth. "The ceremonial last bite." She wiped her mouth off with the tea towel he offered her. "You always let me have it. If I didn't know better, I'd say you were trying to wear me down, Mr. Vance."

"I am good at that." He grinned, putting one arm around her shoulders and pinching her ticklish ribs with the other.

She snickered again and shoved him off. "No fair! You remember all my tickle spots."

He leaned in for a quick, playful nip on her neck. "*Indeed,* I do."

She shook her head in amusement, trying to be coy. But Lord, it felt good to joke and flirt. She hadn't done that since...since...

Could she even remember when?

While Hopper trotted off to dispose of the pint container, she picked up the end of a half-finished chain. "Construction paper?" she called. "This is the look you're going for?"

Hopper shrugged as he walked back in the room. "It reminds me of you. Of that first Christmas I showed up at Randy's, remember? Other trees, they have all those fancy ornaments and bows. But somehow, when I thought about my own tree, all I wanted were those cheap paper ornaments like what you made. Bells and angels and snowflakes and stuff. Something from nothing, right?"

Something from nothing.

Thanks to the Outpost, that bittersweet memory was close to the surface, tugging at her emotions. She'd been so mortified that they couldn't have a "better" tree back then. And here Hopper stood, a grown man, somehow equating the spirit of the season with those flimsy paper decorations she'd made when she was still a child.

Because every time he'd truly celebrated Christmas, he'd been with her.

She swallowed against her thick throat. *She* had been his Christmas, hadn't she?

Lila turned to him and saw the truth of it in his eyes. No matter what he'd told her, he'd never forgotten her. "Tell me,

Hopper. Did you go out and buy supplies to make all the snowflakes and stuff you wanted?"

"I did."

Lila couldn't stop the smile that spread across her face. "Bring me the scissors."

CHAPTER 22

Blink. Blink. Blink.

Hopper woke to the sight of lights slowly turning red, then green, then blue above him. He wiped at his face, his eyes finally coming into focus. Amused, he realized he'd fallen asleep on the couch after he'd dropped Delilah back off at the Greenbrier.

All his plans to go straight to bed had gone out the window when he'd come back home and gotten the full impact of the decorating they'd done. It was like that day in the studio above Randy's garage, only better. They'd had more supplies, for one thing. And he'd had several rolls of color-changing LED lights sitting around collecting dust in the basement. Now, his house wasn't just done up for the holiday. It was some kind of crazy Christmas fairy land.

He snickered a bit as he laid back, appreciating their handiwork. Maybe they'd overdone it a bit. They'd covered the entire ceiling in ropes of lights, snowflakes and spinners that cast colorful, almost psychedelic shadows on the wall. Who knew you could make so many snowflakes out of the old white file folders he'd dumped in the recycle bin? They'd demolished his construction paper tablets for the tree ornaments. He and Lila had stayed up, giggling, stapling up decorations until one in the morning. Neither of them gave a single damn that it was days after Christmas. They were together, and they were having their Christmas today. Breaking the rules again and being naughty—and it'd been freakin' epic.

He fished his phone out. Damn. Nearly eight in the morning already. He needed to get up and get himself put together. Delilah said she'd be here at nine a.m. sharp. Something about eating hearty and "dressing for the snow," whatever that meant.

Rolling off the couch, he got himself a nice, steamy shower going, memories of last night filtering through his head. Delilah. *God.* The way she'd kissed him when they'd said goodnight…

What if she had invited him in? His cock stirred and his heartbeat kicked up, just thinking about it…his hands roaming over her perfect glowing skin…her moans as he filled her…

Great. Now he was hard. He let out a tortured breath. This three-day thing was going to kill him. Because he wanted her right this minute, maybe more than he ever had.

He got the distinct impression that maybe she was feelin' it too. She'd wanted him when they'd made out in his kitchen. He could feel it. How easy it would have been to peel off those leather pants and bend that perfect ass of hers over the table. She probably wouldn't have stopped him.

Pulling back had taken every last bit of his will. But he wasn't going to give in to his instincts. No, this was about reconnecting with Delilah again, for real. And he wanted to make love to her, not have some random *thanks-for-the-memories* kind of hookup. So he braced himself and turned the faucets all the way to cold. *Augh!* He shivered and swore, sputtering until he got himself soaped up, rinsed off and outta there.

Long game, Hopper, he kept telling himself, as he grumbled, drying off.

The shower sucked, but it worked. He'd managed get his racing libido under control, and his head on straight. By the time she'd arrived, Hopper was ready, dressed in his thermals, jeans and a sweatshirt, and full up on leftover pasta. To his surprise, she hopped out of a rented SUV with an oversized duffel slung over her shoulder.

Delilah came dressed like a snow bunny, wearing clingy, sporty leggings, a toboggan, a matching parka, and rather elaborate snow boots. Suddenly he figured out what their agenda for the day was going to be.

He groaned. "We're going skiing?"

She shrugged herself out of her coat. "Oh my God. You've never gone skiing? Really?"

"It wasn't on the list of offered activities in the pen."

She put her hands on her hips. "You mean to tell me you live this close to the mountains and you've never been? Not once in the years since you've been out?"

"Who was I going to go with?"

She leaned up to give him a quick, sweet kiss. "Well then. I guess I'll have to teach you. And this stuff you've got on won't do. Look at all this absorbent cotton. You'll catch your death out there. Fortunately, I talked to the concierge yesterday, and they got me all the gear you'll need. Consider it a Christmas present."

She shoved the duffel in his direction. *What in the hell?* He opened it and rifled through the contents. Everything was in here—a ski-coat and pants, gloves, goggles, a knit hat, thermal under-layers, wool socks and gloves, and even a pair of ski-boots in his size. Of course she'd remember that. Back in the day, she'd bring him every pair of size thirteen boots that came through the thrift store where she'd worked. He shook his head, but he couldn't help but smile at the woman. "Delilah, baby, come on. There must be hundreds of dollars of gear in here. I can't take all this! Let me pay you back, at least."

She waved a hand. "Vacation money, remember? Yesterday was on you and today, it's my turn. All totally fair. But I'll tell you what. If you decide you like them, and you like skiing, you can buy them back off me. How's that? If you don't like the clothes or the sport, I'll resell them and get the majority of my money back either way. See? No harm, no foul. Go on and try all that on. Chop! Chop! The slope waits for no man!"

He groused a little and made a show of reluctantly agreeing, but secretly, he was kinda blown away by all this. She'd gone to such trouble to get everything he needed, right down to the tiniest detail. He trundled the bag off to the bathroom and laid everything out, shaking his head in wonder at the whole spread. He let out an amazed huff as he realized she'd even gotten him a pair of synthetic boxer briefs for the occasion. In dark gray. Matching his hair, was she?

He held up the silky-looking things and scowled suspiciously. They looked expensive, and like they wouldn't leave much to the imagination, either. "Sports performance" and "moisture wicking," the tag said. Hopper had never been one to give much thought to his unmentionables. He just bought whatever pack of briefs he could find on markdown.

Peeling off all his clothes, he stepped into the briefs. When he turned to check himself out in the full-length mirror, it knocked him back a step. He'd lifted weights for years. Liked to run too. But it'd always been more of a means to an end. So he wouldn't get his ass beat in prison, at first. And then to stay fit and pump out all his frustrations later. But he'd never really taken much time to inspect his physique. Damn. He looked like...*an underwear ad.* For God's sake! He cackled and did a little dance. *Fuck you, Marky Mark!*

The fabric was super soft compared to the coarse cotton crap he normally wore. And the way those seams in the front went…he looked friggin' huge. He turned to the side, checking himself out. Who was he kidding? He *was* huge. Funny how these briefs were so different than what he usually wore—they were low slung on the hips but came down way far on his thighs. He did a slow circle. It was like his whole vibe suddenly made sense. The colorful tats. The silvery undercut. The beard. The scars. Maybe he wasn't such a scary monster after all.

Shaking his head with amusement, he stepped into the jet-black thermals. They were comfortable enough but so clingy, they made him look vacuum wrapped. When he put them together with the snow pants, coat and goggles, everything was black with silver-and-white stripes—exactly what he might've picked out for himself. Yeah, maybe he did belong on the slopes with Delilah. Maybe this day was going to go pretty well after all.

He trotted down the hall to show his outfit to Delilah, doing a couple little runway spins while he was at it. She clapped her hands with delight. "Ha ha! I knew it! I knew this'd be perfect for you! Adventure dude hits the mountain!"

He rubbed his hands together. "You know, I think I might actually enjoy this."

She reminded him he probably wouldn't want to wear the snow pants on the nearly two-hour drive to Snowshoe Resort, so he dashed to his room to grab synthetic track pants and an extra change of clothes, just in case. He came out to the living room, though, to step out of the coat and overalls and into his street wear. As he was peeling off his outer layers, he glanced up to find her tracking his every movement with her eyes.

He swallowed, not able to tear his eyes away from her. The room felt charged, like he'd flipped a switch and the air began to hum. Maybe he started to hum a bit too, his restless muscles twitching as her curious, assessing gaze burned tracks all over him. *Let her look.* He turned to fold his clothes. *Slowly.*

Delilah shook her head. "Good Lord, Hop. You're so fine, you could turn those thermals into lingerie for men. They seem to fit. Do they feel okay?"

It only took a second for him to ditch his "being a gentleman" plan. Because the heat in her eyes? There was nothing planned about that.

"Well angel," he teased, just to see what she'd do. "Why don't you come over here and find out?"

LILA SMIRKED RIGHT BACK at the man. Since when had she ever been one to back down from a challenge? As she began stalking across the room toward him, biting her lip, surprise mingled with heat in Hopper's eyes. Did he really think she wouldn't respond to that tease? That she was too much of a lady to tease him back?

Stupid man. Teasing him was one of her favorite pastimes.

She strutted over, coming up behind him first. "Hmm-mm," she narrowed her eyes, dragging her finger along the wide expanse of his shoulders. "The seams are hitting you right where they should. That's good."

Hopper didn't say anything, just turned his head to give her a lazy, hooded kind of look. Deciding to press her advantage, she traveled both hands down his thick biceps. His muscles instinctively flexed as her fingers skimmed by. Hopper inhaled, deep and slow, turning his head forward again and swallowing hard. But he didn't move. So, she let her fingers play over his strong shoulders, over the jut of his shoulder blades…

"It's snug," she told him, pinching out a snip of fabric and letting it ping back between his shoulders. "But that's the way it's supposed to be. So the cold won't get in."

He threw another teasing look over his shoulder, the corners of his mouth twitching with amusement. "That's a good thing then."

"Mm-hmm. Very good." Lila flattened her hands against him and let them slowly travel down the meaty vee of his back. His skin was so seductively warm under her hands, the fabric seeming to conduct his body heat straight to her fingertips. She stepped closer, no longer afraid to press herself against his back. Her breath hitched at the contact. The pure primal smell of his skin filled her head, familiar like a favorite melody.

Oh yes, she liked the way this fabric felt, liked the way it conformed around every single sinew in his back. She rolled herself against him, her nipples pebbling with the sensation. And she pushed the flat of her hands down over his hips, and his perfect, meaty ass, squeezing hard. The man had never been one for shy, feathery touches, after all.

Hopper moaned, almost inaudibly, and hung his head forward. The sound almost unraveled her. Before she'd even realized she was doing it, she'd pushed one hand up underneath the hem of his shirt, tangling her fingers in the trimmed hair on his taut stomach. And she ran the other hand flat against his hipbone. She rubbed him up and down —not over his cock directly. But *right there*. She hadn't planned on taking it this far. But she…she couldn't stop. Her heart was racing and her core ached, too hot and slippery to ignore. She wanted him.

God, he was hard—*so fucking hard*—and hot as a blast furnace. She could feel the shape of his cock, straining against its confines, tracing along the backside of her thumb. Still she tried to be breezy, as if she had any semblance of control over herself. "See?" she breathed. "They're perfect. No bagging. No sagging. Anywhere."

He rumbled out a low, sexy chuckle and in a flash had her flipped around, so she was in front of him, with her back turned against his chest. He walked her forward a step until she was pinned between him and the back of his couch. "You want to know if I want you? That's what this is about, isn't it?" he rasped, his nose nuzzling her neck.

She couldn't answer him. She couldn't think, or hardly breathe, even. Even lined leggings were no barrier against the long, hard heat of him, pulsing against her ass. She'd forgotten how thick and insistent he felt when he was this close, and it scrambled her brain. He rolled his hips, and she could feel every single thing—the urgent length of him, his blunt tip, pressing…Pure liquid heat unspooled between her legs.

"Oh, I want you, Delilah," he growled, tipping his head close to hers so she could feel the truth of it, rumbling against her ear. "I've wanted you every fucking day for the last sixteen years. Even when I didn't know where you were or who you were with. Still, this *wanting you* was there, like a bullet a surgeon can't ever take out…under my skin. And you want me to tell you why? 'Cause no one could ever be you, angel. No one could ever make me feel like this."

Lila groaned as he wormed his hand up underneath her fleece. Jesus, the feeling of his hands wrecked her, just like always, his calloused fingers rasping up her ribcage and sending pure electrical shocks in their wake. He murmured in pleasure as he circled his big hands around her breasts, his thumb teasing her nipples to needy peaks through her sports bra. Then he pushed his hands underneath the fabric and pinched.

She cried out, pleasure soaking her, and her knees buckled.

He rolled his hips against her harder, faster, the flimsy fabric hardly any barrier at all. He groaned in appreciation as she bucked against him, tipping up her ass up to meet him. "Awww, angel, you're burnin' up. You want some relief? 'Cause I can give it to you."

"God, yes," she gulped out. She pushed his hand down under the waistband of her leggings. "Please."

Hopper growled and wasted no time plunging his hand straight down to her sticky sweet core. And he shuddered, his warm breath stuttering against her neck. He circled the rough pads of his fingers over her clit. He let out a low, pained moan. "You're so wet, angel. *Goddamn,* you're so fuckin' wet for me."

He always knew how to do this, how to make her come apart with just a touch or a filthy word. He ran his hands up and down the seam of her, coating his fingers, pressing as if he might push inside, and then not. She widened her stance a bit, and he began strumming at her clit with short, powerful, fast strokes, the kind that made her lose her ever-lovin' mind. God, she was so turned on, just the feeling of him near her was setting her off.

"Don't stop, baby! You know what to do!" she begged. And he did. He always did. The memory of how he could totally command her body raced through her, the old mixing with the new until she was writhing and desperate. His strokes sped up and intensified with her moans. She hooked her arm around his neck and propped one knee up on the back of the couch. Rolling with him, the pure hit of pleasure sizzled through her veins. Tipping higher, faster…

Then he slid two thick fingers in, grinding inward to hit her right on the one spot that made everything explode into pleasure. He remembered.

Ohhhhhhhh, it was all she needed. Being filled, being pressed in that secret, perfect place. It'd been too long. She was too needy. The climax cracked over her like lightning. She sobbed out his name, shaking in his arms. *Hopper.* He was here again. Making her feel. Making her come so fucking hard, she wasn't even sure what day it was. She trembled, gasping for air, barely able to hold herself upright. But she sure as hell wasn't done with him.

Before he could say another word, she slid out from his grip and flipped him against the couch this time, facing her. She fell down to her knees, ripping his pants and his underwear nearly down to his shins in one sharp movement, baring him to her in all his freaking incredible, manly glory.

"Jesus Christ, baby!" he huffed, half choking, half laughing at the suddenness of it.

She circled her shaky fingers around the beautiful, beautiful length of him, so heavy and hard and primed in her hand. God, he was so big—one hand couldn't hold him. He gazed down at her, his chest rising and falling with his fast breaths, his eyes gone sharp and intense with desire. Her whole body sang at the sight of him—this mind-blowing, masculine work of art. "I have to have you, Hop," she growled, surprised at the feral note in her voice. "Right this minute. I want to feel that gorgeous cock in my mouth. I want to feel your hot cum shooting down my throat. Let me, baby."

Now it was him who was speechless. Yeah, he remembered this, how she'd talk dirty...how she'd always made good on her promises. She could see it in the way his eyes darkened and color slashed along his cheekbones. He nodded, almost imperceptibly, as if he were too dazed to speak. And she proceeded to do just as she'd said. No playing around. No preliminaries. She just took him into her mouth. All the way, opening up the back of her throat to take in every last delectable inch. Then pulling back and sucking until her cheeks hollowed.

Hopper threw back his head with a shout, gasping and swallowing, his Adam's apple bobbing over the tattoo in his corded neck. Yanking off her toboggan, he fisted both hands in her hair as she took him, over and over "Angel, baby... God," he garbled out, squaring his hips to her and meeting her thrust for thrust.

Yeah, she liked it like that, all of him, pounding her

mouth, filling her up with his desire until her hair tangled and her eyes watered. She had it all, right there in her hand. So dirty and wild. So perfect. Just like they used to do.

Normally, he'd draw this out. Tease her back. Hum out the filthiest encouragements. But he was gone. *Just gone,* plunging in deep, his moans coming out almost in shouts. In and out, hard and fast. And she wanted it—all of him, silky skin over hot iron, slippery and thick, over and over until oblivion. She would've smiled in triumph if her mouth wasn't full. Cause she fuckin' loved this. Every second.

His moans...the smell and taste of pure, elemental man. *God,* it made her feel shaky and needy too. Because she remembered...all his secret places, all the things that sent him over the edge, all the pleasure that'd passed between them, once. She hooked one hand around his hip for balance and pushed another between her legs again, her own heat rising with his.

More. Just more. She had to have it. The sharp stab of pleasure over her swollen, sensitized flesh, as her fingers met their target. Oh yeah...he hardened under her hand, and her heartbeat thundered. She couldn't tell whose pleasure was whose anymore...

He shouted her name and stiffened, fisting his hand convulsively in her hair. She strummed herself hard until she tumbled right over the edge with him, plunging her fingers inside herself right as he came, and the taste of his pleasure filled her.

They both shook and spasmed, their release playing out in perfect, filthy harmony. Every nerve tingled and she could barely catch her breath. But after a few long moments, they calmed. With a slow caress of her cheek, he released his grip. And with one last kiss on his tip, she sat on her heels, wiping her mouth with the back of her hand. Hopper quickly pulled up his pants and slid down on the floor with her, propping his head against the back of the couch. His chest heaved, but he was beaming like he'd just won the lottery. Lazily, he grabbed the hand she'd been using on herself and licked her fingers clean.

The little bit of air still in her lungs left her in a rusty chuckle.

He kissed her fingertips. "Well. That got out of hand fast."

She snuggled up under his arm and nipped the side of his sweaty neck. "Consider it an addendum to today's itinerary."

He bent to nuzzle her cheek, and a hank of hair from his undercut tumbled over his face. She succumbed to the urge to trail her finger over his forehead and brush it back. He seemed flushed and wrecked and…happy. "Lord, woman," he rumbled. "I didn't think it was possible, but you might actually be even sexier than you were back then."

"Yeah. You too. Funny how that works, isn't it?"

"Don't do it again."

She tipped her face up to his, suddenly confused. "What?"

He booped her on the nose. "Let me clarify. Don't tease me like that again unless you have hours and hours free. Because so help me God, the next time I get you in my hands, I'm not letting you out of bed for days. Maybe years. I'm thinking we should stockpile food, water, and lubricant. We're gonna need it."

She snickered and rolled her eyes, pulling herself up to her feet. She held out her hand. "Yeah, yeah, yeah. Promises, promises, Don Juan. Assuming your legs still work, it's time to get up. We've got some skiing to do."

He took her hand. "Who am I to keep a lady waiting?"

CHAPTER 23

IF HOPPER HAD BEEN WONDERING if the spark between them was still alive, he had his answer. Being with Delilah was just… Hell, he didn't even have words for it. And they hadn't even gone all the way yet. What would it be like once he had the time and his wits fully about him? The options played out in his head, taking his mind in endlessly erotic directions.

He had so many plans.

So.

Many.

Plans.

Delilah glanced over at him, taking her eyes off the road for a second. "You've been awfully quiet and thoughtful on this trip. Whatcha' thinking about?"

"You." He squeezed her knee. "And the road ahead."

She grinned. "Yeah, I have a pretty good idea what you're thinking about, because I'm thinking about it too. This morning was amazing. You're off to a very good start, Mr. Vance."

"That's the idea," he answered, leaning over to give her a quick kiss on the side of the neck. She giggled as he sat himself back in his seat, a goofy grin on his face.

How odd it was to be in the passenger seat, letting someone else drive. But it was nice. Relaxing. Delilah's GPS was taking them straight up into the mountains, where the temperatures were dropping and snow glittered over everything in view. Accumulation was about a foot thick, but the roads were clear, so driving up was no problem. And it was a beautiful day too, perfect for enjoying the season's delights, with a clear-blue, crisp winter's sky. The sun hitting the pristine powder made everything seem fresh and clean. Like a new start.

He sighed with satisfaction as he considered the world outside his window. It really was a perfect day, with the perfect woman, and the perfect way to celebrate the Christmas week. Still, he was nervous about this skiing business. It'd never occurred to him to try it before. But he'd try anything for Delilah.

He did wonder, though, how she'd gotten to be such an expert at it. Atlanta wasn't exactly the ski capital of the world. He turned to her. "You get one day to do anything you want, and you choose to go skiing."

"Well, the mountains are right here."

"There has to be a reason, though. I don't ever remember you talking about skiing before. How'd you get into the sport?"

Delilah sighed. "My ex. He owned several different car dealerships in Atlanta. But he grew up in Denver, skiing the slopes in Colorado. In addition to five different car dealerships, he also owned a small executive airport and his own two-seater plane. He taught me the sport, and he used to fly us all over to ski—about every other week during the season."

"Wow. That's quite a life."

"No." She turned, giving him a hard look. "It really wasn't."

Chastened, he decided to drop this line of questioning.

He'd promised her they wouldn't talk about "that fucker Mitchell Roby." And he'd abide by that. He let the car grow quiet, concentrating instead on the views and the comforting drone of their wheels on the pavement.

"You said you were there, the day I left him," Delilah finally said. "You saw."

He paused, surprised she was bringing this up again. "That's right."

"Then you know. Anything good or luxurious about being Mitchell's wife was tainted. All that money and comfort became nothing more than a way to control me. If it'd just been a matter of being his trophy wife arm candy, I could have handled it. But the man had rules. And if you broke them, the consequences were something you didn't even want to contemplate."

He stilled. "What kind of rules?"

Delilah bit her lip and tapped her fingers on the wheel, as if she was weighing what she should say. "I'm going tell you, because I can tell that you won't stop asking until I do." She sighed. "But don't judge me, okay?"

Hopper nodded, trying somehow to steel himself against what was coming.

"He knew my schedule and every move I made," she began. "I had to enter it on an electronic calendar he followed, even if I was going on a simple errand. I was allowed no friends of my own and had no freedom of movement." Her fingers tightened on the steering wheel, and her whole body seemed to tense. "You have to understand, Hop. Everything in the house—and I mean everything—was ruthlessly controlled. Every item had to be arranged in a very precise manner, out in the open, but in the drawers and closets too. Luckily, I had staff to help me with this. But it always left you with this fear down in the pit of your stomach. Fear of what'd happen if you set one foot wrong. There were security cameras in every room, and you never knew when you'd look up and see the little blue light on. It'd be a sick reminder that without warning, he could be on the other side of the security system, clocking my every move."

"Sounds a lot like jail," he ground out.

"It was."

"Then why did you stay?"

"I ask myself that all the time," she answered, shaking her head, self-loathing creeping into her expression. "All I can tell you is it's a bit like being a frog in a pot. You don't notice the water is heating up until it's boiling you alive."

It made his stomach churn, hearing her talk like this. Still more, seeing the way her face twisted up, the bitterness twisted inward. On herself—exactly where it didn't belong. He was going to say that, but he decided to wait. He had the feeling she was in the mood to talk about it, so he'd let her.

It took a few minutes of quiet driving. But she did begin talking. And once she started, Delilah couldn't stop. She told him everything about how she and Mitchell had met at the steakhouse where she'd been working. How he'd been so friggin' charming for the six months they'd dated. Taking her on expensive dates. Treating her like a queen. Buying her couture gowns so he could take her out and parade her around on his arm. He'd been twenty years older than her, but he'd treated her so well, she'd overlooked the differences in their age and experience. When one day he'd offered to fly her to Vegas to get married, she said she'd jumped at the chance.

Still, all that too-good-to-be-true behavior seemed odd to him. "There really were no warning signs?"

"There were." She rolled her eyes and shook her head, still more of that self-loathing leaking out. "But I was too young and stupid to see them. He'd been estranged from his ex-wife and teenaged son for years. That should've been my first clue. He'd told me about them exactly once, and then they were never mentioned again. Like they were erased. The man didn't even have a single photo of them anywhere! Can you imagine? I rationalized it all away, figuring he'd just had a messy divorce. I fell back on all the standard excuses—oh, he's just an alpha male and has to call the shots! *Yada, yada, yada.*" She let out a disgusted grunt. "I have to give the man credit—Mitchell did such a magnificent job of managing the details whenever we went out, it never even occurred to me that he was controlling. But he had been, even when he was on his best behavior. Thinking back on it, he never asked my opinion, not once. About anything."

"He never hit you then, when you were dating?"

Delilah turned to him. "You know what? I'm talking too much about all this crap. And honestly, Hop, why do you want me to dredge all this up? It's not exactly fun date material."

He put his hand on her leg and squeezed. "I want to know because I want to know you. I want to be there for you today because I wasn't able to be there for you then. Can you understand that?"

Her eyes rounded in horror. "Hop, trust me. You don't want to hear this."

"I do," he answered, setting his jaw. "I really, truly do."

She threw her hands up in the air and slapped them back down on the wheel again. "All right. You want all the gory details? Here it is. He laid on the rules one by one over the course of that first year, taking away privileges like my car keys or phone whenever I didn't obey. I should've run then. But I was a new wife still, and I tried to write it off as him just being set in his ways and having high standards. I learned to live by his rules. But even that upset him, because I wasn't giving him a reason to punish me. So about six months before I left, he started hitting me. If I ever disagreed about even the smallest subject, he'd backhand me. Right around this time, he was getting into financial trouble. Two of his dealerships were bleeding money. So I gave him a pass then too, chalking it up to stress. But it only got worse. Pretty soon, he'd start threatening me with a knife to make his points. He punched me once, right in the face, for suggesting we start a family. And on Christmas Eve, the day before I left, he'd thrown me down the stairs for asking if we could visit Randy and his new wife over the holidays. There. You happy? Is that what you wanted to know?"

Hopper sat motionless, stunned to silence, his ears still ringing from what he just heard. He shouldn't be surprised by any of this. He'd seen with his own eyes what a prick Roby was. But hearing the story—the beginning, the middle and the end? It gutted him. Just the mental picture of that man's fist connecting with her face. Leaving marks on her perfect skin…defiling her…disrespecting her.

It was just too much.

A furious brand of sorrow formed in his stomach, blazing and angry until it crowded his insides. Heat rose to his face, and his chest got so tight he could hardly take another breath. He didn't notice the tears at first. They seemed to bubble up from some unknown well, deep inside him. He hadn't cried since the day his dad had left. Not even when those cell doors had closed behind him. But now?

His cheeks felt wet. He quickly swiped at them with his sleeve. And that caught Delilah's attention. "Jesus, Hop, you're *crying?"*

"I-I'll be fine," he sputtered. But he wasn't. He was sobbing, like he couldn't stop. *Goddammit!*

Delilah gave him another once over and must not have liked what she saw. She turned the car off onto one of the mountain overlooks and turned off the ignition. He grabbed her then, needing to pull her close. Hot tears poured out of him, and all he could do was rock her against his chest. How could he make her see? The guilt. The shame. For not being there. It was his greatest regret. Losing this woman had been worse than losing his freedom.

Worse than getting stabbed and beaten. And this? This might be the worst of all. He held onto her for what seemed like endless minutes, afraid to let her go, inhaling the flowery scent of her shampoo while she murmured out reassurances.

When he was finally able to get control of himself, he slumped back against the car door in an exhausted heap. He wiped at his face, feeling like a blubbering idiot. Here she was, pouring out her guts, and he was the one falling to pieces.

Delilah fished tissues out of her purse. "I'm sorry, babe. I probably shouldn't have blurted all that out like that. I didn't think about how hard that must be for you to hear."

He took the tissues from her hand and self-consciously blew his nose. "Did you just call me babe?" He blinked shyly from behind his tissue, trying to tease his way to being contrite.

"Yes," she murmured, running her hand down his sodden cheek. "Don't let it go to your head."

He smiled at that, yanking her into his lap again with her back against his chest this time. And they simply sat there for a while, looking out over the horizon while he collected himself. It was beautiful here. The hills rolled off in every direction, all with that distinctive Blue Ridge haze that made everything seem dreamy and out of focus. But there was nothing dreamy about what they'd been through, for either one of them.

He gathered both of her hands in his, idly playing with her fingertips for long moments. "Your old roommate, Jen, she wrote me a letter while I was in prison," he finally said. "Did she tell you that?"

"No. We lost touch after I married Mitchell."

"Well, it wasn't a very nice letter. She basically bitched me out and told me I didn't deserve the information, but you had married a rich man and were going to have this amazing life.

And I needed to sit and think on that while I rotted in prison."

Delilah snorted. "Yeah, that sounds like Jen. Defending me to the end."

"Oh, I didn't take offense to it. If anything, it did me good. It hurt like hell to think of you with another man. But in another way, it kinda calmed me down. It reassured me I'd done the right thing, letting you go. And every time I thought about you—right up to the time I walked into the Outpost—I visualized you with this bright, shiny life. A life with some older man who adored you and gave you everything in the world you deserved."

Delilah popped back into her seat and turned to face him, her eyes flashing fire all of a sudden. "The right thing? That's what you call it? You *broke my heart*, Hopper. Made me question everything I ever thought I knew. And you thought you were being *noble?*"

"What did you want, then?" Hopper barked, alarmed to hear his voice raising a decibel or two. "A jailhouse marriage? Conjugal visits? Hey, maybe if we were lucky, I could've fathered a kid or two, and they could've come to visit too!"

"Oh my God," she gave him an incredulous look. "You really don't understand, do you? I wanted a *choice,* Hopper! If we still loved each other, I deserved to be part of that decision!"

The spike of anger and hurt in her voice was killing him. He took a long, calming breath, trying to figure out the right words. "Okay then. *Fine.* Imagine I told you I was sorry back then. That I was a piece of shit for trying to cheat my way to financial success. That I still considered you the great love of my life, and I wanted you to wait for me, even though they'd handed down a fifteen-year sentence. Imagine, then, if you'd made that choice to stay. You would've spent every day worrying about me getting hurt or worse, all that time. Week after week, year after year, you would've stood by while I wasted away behind bars. So why don't you tell me honestly, angel—if you'd had that choice, what would you have done?"

A long, hard silence fell between them. Delilah narrowed her eyes at him, then looked out the window. Light and dark played over her features as the sun filtered through the trees nearby, dappling her skin. "I have no idea," she eventually answered, her voice so small, it was barely more than a reedy whisper. "Honestly, I couldn't say."

Silently, Hopper felt vindicated. He had given her a choice—the choice to move on unencumbered by the memory of him and the wondering about what might have been. He'd taken the guilt off her and placed it on his shoulders. Which was where it belonged, dammit, given that he'd caused every last bit of this mess.

Except it hadn't been a clean break, like he'd thought. Her pain, her heartbreak? He understood it now—felt it in a way he hadn't appreciated before. His righteousness wasn't much of a reward. What he'd done to Delilah had left its mark and blighted her life in more ways than either one of them wanted to admit. But he'd been given this chance to right all these wrongs. To show her she could believe again, in men. In love. And maybe, if he was really, really lucky, in him.

He lifted his hand to caress her satiny cheek. "There's no tellin' how it would have played out. Let's just leave it at that."

She nodded and leaned her head into his hand.

"I can't say why we ended up at the Outpost," he told her. "But I do know it opened my eyes to everything we had. Made me see it, feel it in a way my poor scabbed-over heart hadn't in years. And I thank God for that. More than anything, I want a chance to feel that again with you. We've been flirtin' and talkin' and kissin.' But do you think we have a chance to start clean again, you and me? For real?"

"Yeah," she answered, right away. "I really, truly do." She took his hand away from her face and gathered it in her lap. His heart leaped in his chest, yet still he braced himself, because she seemed like she was going to say something serious. She smirked at him instead. "But can we get back to this flirtin' and talkin' and kissin' business? Because I was liking that part."

He laughed, sweet relief loosening the bonds that'd been tied around his heart. "Sure, babe. Don't we have some skiing to do?"

CHAPTER 24

AS SOON AS they'd pulled up to Snowshoe Resort and she'd seen Hopper's face, Lila knew she'd created a monster. The man had always had a need for speed. And flying down a mountain turned out to be right in his wheelhouse.

He'd been a good student—at first. He'd grinned at her like a hound while she'd positioned his legs and arms and such. And she may have copped a feel or two as she'd kept showing him how to bend to stay balanced over his skis. But that had been pretty much where the lesson had ended. He'd taken off down the bunny slope before she'd even had a chance to show him how to turn or stop. Or fall properly. Poor guy. It'd been pretty funny watching him twirl his arms out in circles before he'd tottered over like an enormous sack of bricks. Even the kids had pointed and shook their heads. It had been like an episode of *America's Funniest Home Videos* there for a while.

Then there'd been the ski lift. She'd had to sing a little song about when to sit down before he could get it timed right.

But the man was a quick, if stubborn, study. It hadn't taken more than an hour on the bunny slopes before he'd demanded to try something harder. She figured he'd do okay on the blue square, or intermediate courses, so long as she stayed right beside him, keeping him from taking the turns too fast and helping guide him around obstacles.

As they were going down a new intermediate trail, however, she started to see how wrong she really was. Tracking his trajectory down the mountain, she saw a copse of young pine trees and a steep dropoff, right in the way. The turn was too sharp for him to navigate it. She could just tell.

"Hop!" she called out, struggling to get beside him. "When you get to those trees over there, turn hard—up on the sides, okay?"

The man nodded. Unfortunately, he took her instruction too much to heart. Because when Hopper tipped his skis, he ended up turning onto the sides of his boots, sending him spinning on his side, faster and faster until he skidded over the side of an incline and out of sight.

Jesus! Images of him tumbling down to the bottom of the mountain flashed in front of her eyes, and she ended up skiing too damn fast after him. The edge of the drop came up way faster than she expected. She jammed her skis to stop. But she lost her balance and ended up cartwheeling over the side and—*right on top of Hopper*. Turned out the drop was only about four feet.

She groaned as she tried to extricate herself from the tangle of limbs and skis and poles. "Did I hurt you?"

"No," he yelped, wheezing a bit from the impact. "Really, I'm fine." As if to demonstrate, he cupped her ass with both hands. "I think I like skiing. Women just seem to fall out of the sky here."

She giggled as she unwound herself. "I think you've had enough skiing for one day. Maybe next time we'll invest in a real teacher."

He waggled his eyebrows at her. "Next time. I like the

sound of that. Hey, do you think the teacher will grab my ass too?"

They laughed and joked all the way back up the mountain. And together they decided to exchange their skis for a one-hour snowmobiling tour, which turned out to be right up Hop's alley. He'd never driven a snowmobile before, but it was so much like driving a motorcycle he caught on nearly instantly. And, like on his bike, she found she rather enjoyed hanging onto him while he drove. The world was a more beautiful place looking over his shoulder.

It was a gorgeous ride and something she'd never done in all the times she'd spent at ski resorts. Mitchell had always been so obsessed with his skiing technique—and hers—that he'd always refused to do anything else. But this ride with Hopper had been a revelation. They passed through breathtaking trails with towering pines, struggled up inclines and sped over thrilling little bumps and turns. Together they marveled at the sun as it set in the sky, creating the most beautiful combination of blue and gold and purple she'd ever seen. And by the time night had fallen? Well, the moon on the new fallen snow had been the subject of so many poems for a reason. All was peaceful and pristine. Like an unseen hand had sprinkled the whole world with stardust.

When they finally got off their snowmobile, they were famished, and went up into the village to find themselves a fantastic, hearty dinner of artisanal hamburgers and craft beer. Or was it craft hamburgers and artisanal beer? She couldn't remember.

Afterward they lingered a bit in the shops. Hopper bought her a hand-tooled, black leather backpack and square-toed boots. They were late Christmas gifts he'd said, insisting she'd need them when her motorcycle was rehabbed. She'd always told herself she didn't want another man buying things for her, making her feel beholden, or worse, like a child. But when he handed the bags to her, these simple gifts pinged her heartstrings in a way she hadn't expected. They made her feel cared for, and seen. Like a gift should.

By the time they were walking back to their car, they were exhausted, happy, and full up on great food and Christmas feels. She hooked her arm through his, and he smiled down at her with such affection, it almost took her breath away.

"This is the way it's supposed to be, isn't it?" she asked.

He crinkled his brows. "What?"

"This. Going out with a man who cares about you. Someone who wants you to have fun."

He tsked. "Don't tell me you've forgotten that much. It used to be that way with us. All the time. Hell, every time."

"I guess I've just realized how far from that pattern my life has strayed. My memories of skiing in particular were always tense and anxiety-ridden because of my ex. And I hadn't had anything, really, to replace those memories. Just an occasional date that never seemed to go anywhere."

"Until today." He smiled, opening her car door for her.

"Until today." She stopped and turned to him. "You've given me a lot of gifts over the years, Hopper Vance, for Christmas and otherwise. You've helped me rescue Christmas in my mind. Skiing too. Made me remember what I love about it. Thank you, babe."

"There it is again."

She shook her head in confusion. "What?"

"You called me babe again. It's music to my ears." He leaned over top of the door to give her a kiss. "So anytime you want to go skiing, babe, you can go with me. Why wouldn't I want to go?" He batted his eyes dreamily, held his hand over his heart, and let out a school-girl sigh. "Dear Snowshoe…in my mind, it'll always be the place where you just fell out of the sky and into my arms."

She groaned as she laughed, and he just grinned back like

the hound that he was. "Don Juan strikes again," she muttered, not able to resist another kiss. They both got in the car to leave. But before she could put the car into gear, he reached around to stop her.

"Wait—I have one more gift to give you." He handed her an envelope, his eyes sparkling with anticipation. "I hope you want it."

"You don't have to keep buying me things, Hop," she protested. "Just having someone to celebrate Christmas with has been more of a gift to me than you can imagine."

"It's not just for you. It's for us, really. See for yourself."

Opening the box, she found two bright, shiny "season's pass" lanyards. The sight of them did funny things to her insides. It was too much. And it was everything, all at once.

She looked up to see Hopper, beaming down at her with such hope. She felt it too. They'd conquered a mountain today, in more ways than one. Maybe they'd conquer a few more in the future.

He caressed her cheek in a way she was starting to get used to. "I'm going to learn to anticipate those turns, I promise."

"You'd better," she beamed right back at him, and surrendered to another sweet, sizzling kiss. "I'm counting on it."

CHAPTER 25

HOPPER SAT in the main dining room of the Greenbrier, feeling oddly conspicuous. When Lila had dropped him off last night, they'd decided on coming here for brunch this morning. After all, the Greenbrier's brunch was world-famous. There was no way he'd let Delilah end her visit without taking advantage of its amazing culinary traditions at least once.

The only problem was, the main dining room had a dress code. It wasn't too strict, but it did require him to ditch his usual uniform of jeans and motorcycle boots. Tugging at his collared shirt, he couldn't help thinking how ridiculous it must appear up against his neck tattoo. He wore it with a red cable knit sweater. And loafers. God help him. To the casual observer, he probably looked like a soccer dad who's had a bender in Tijuana and woke up covered in tats.

At least he hadn't gone out and bought all this for the occasion. No, this lovely ensemble had been collecting dust in his closet since he'd first gotten out of prison. Back then, he'd figured he should have a "nicer outfit" of khakis and a dress shirt or two, just in case. And he'd never, not once, had an occasion to wear any of it.

He'd actually cut off the tags to wear all this stupid shit today. Honestly, he didn't know how to feel about his choice of wardrobe. On the one hand, he felt like he was wearing some kind of costume that wasn't really him. On the other hand, he wondered what in the hell was wrong with his life that he actively avoided dressing up. He really did need to get over himself.

Because if there was ever a woman who was worth getting dressed up for, it was his angel. He smiled at her over his perfectly mixed mimosa. My, my, she was gorgeous today. She wore a forest-green dress, the wraparound kind that hugged every single one of her curves, and high-heeled tan boots that showed off her legs to perfection. Long, dangly gold earrings shimmered as she talked, brushing enticingly against the sides of her neck.

She looked up from her dainty serving of smoked trout and sweet potato pancakes, her lips quirking with amusement. "Care to tell me what all that staring is about?"

He sighed dramatically. "I was just thinking how nice it would be to be your earring. I could spend all day nuzzled up against your neck."

Delilah giggled so hard, she snorted. "Lord have mercy, that was bad. Would you like a burger to go with all that cheese, chief?"

"Make fun all you want. But it put a blush and a smile on those pretty cheeks. I'll take it."

She just shook her head. "You're a real piece of work, Hopper Vance."

"Damn right."

She pushed back her plate. "Well, I'm stuffed. You polished off that third plate yet?"

He patted his stomach. "Yeah, I think I've hit my limit." And it was a good thing too. The Greenbrier was famous for its breakfast buffet, and for good reason. This was no *get your Cheerios from a plastic tube* kind of hotel breakfast. The dining room, like everything else, was steeped in Southern elegance, with rows of columns and ornament everywhere the eye could see. The buffet seemed to go on forever, with every kind of southern specialty, from grits to country ham. He'd piled the fillings high at the omelet bar. And eaten a heaping helping of every item offered, of course. Anything less would've been wasteful!

Delilah polished off her drink. "So how do you want to spend the day? We did say we'd decide together what to do."

Hopper thought on that for a minute. There were tons of options around here, of course, especially at the Greenbrier. But somehow that didn't seem right. He had the urge to do something different. Something real. "What do you say we make today about real life? We've had enough of the fantasy stuff, that's for sure. And honestly, I'm kind of over this 'digging through the past' business, aren't you?"

Lila shrugged. "What do you have in mind?"

"What do you say we take another stop at Holliday Hot Rods? I can show you around the whole operation, show you how we do things. I've got some cool projects I'm working on that I'd love you to see. And maybe after that I could take you back to Roanoke. You have to go back, right? You said you had plans tomorrow. So why don't I just take you back now and you can show me around? I'd love to see where you live and what your life's like."

Delilah hesitated for a minute, but she finally nodded. "I'm afraid you're going to be disappointed. It's kind of scary how boring my life is."

Grinning lazily, he brought her hand up to his lips, kissing her knuckles. "Angel, there's not a single thing about you that could ever bore me."

Delilah rolled her eyes at all his flirting but agreed to the plan readily enough. Soon they'd finished getting her checked out of The Greenbrier and he'd loaded up all of her newly acquired luggage in the trunk of his newly rehabbed

GTO. It was a showy a little number, painted in sparkly silver with thick white racing stripes Lita had painted down its hood. On the drive over to the shop, he told Delilah all about his plan to resell the car and make a tidy profit before he moved onto the next one. It was a hobby that was working out for him. So far, he'd managed to earn enough profit to pay off about half his house. In five more years, he'd hoped to polish off his mortgage for good, he'd told her.

When they parked in front of Holiday Hot Rods, he wasn't surprised to see Lita hard at work in the back painting the purple topcoat on his latest restoration. And Hunter was there too, with his ten-year-old stepson Wilson, who had a project of is his own: a go cart he was building himself.

Everybody whistled and hooted, of course, once they got a load of what he and Lila were wearing. "What's the matter, Hop?" Hunter called out. "Didn't they hire you for that JCPenney photo shoot?"

Hopper flipped the man the bird, and Hunter just grinned back at him. "I took Delilah to breakfast at the Greenbrier, okay? Certain pleasantries had to be observed," he called back. Hopper walked over to his locker, eager to get this preposterous sweater off. He peeled it over his head and untucked his shirt, rolling up his sleeves. He unbuttoned a couple of buttons so his black undershirt showed. And he switched out his dressy loafers for a pair of motorcycle boots. Already he felt much better.

He joined Delilah over by his project—the Corvair, which was still mostly in pieces. He'd let Lita talk him into painting it a dark metallic purple, and she was on the floor, trying out different samples of leather so they could figure out how the interior should look. "White leather with pink piping sounds all right, I suppose." Delilah stopped and cocked her head. "But what if you left the piping white too? Then you could put big, fat stripes going straight down the center of the seat instead. It would be so pretty in coordinating colors, like turquoise and tangerine and bright green."

Lita turned to him. "That's actually a pretty good idea, don't you think, Hop? We could center the stripes so they go down the middle of the seats, but they'd be asymmetrical. Maybe one stripe would be twelve inches wide, another would be six, another would be two. We'd have to get the colors just right, but when it's done, it'll definitely have its own vibe."

He stood there contemplating the idea for a minute and decided he liked that plan. "Lita, why don't you think on it and you can show me some leather samples in a couple of days?"

"I'm on it." She saluted him playfully. "You should keep this one around, Hopper—the girl, not the car. She's got a great eye for this stuff."

"And I've got an eye for her." Hopper waggled his eyebrows.

Delilah groaned as she shook her head, but she kissed his cheek anyway. She asked him one question after another as he walked her around the shop. It was fun holding hands and giving her a walking tour of what he did on an average day. Actually, it was surprising to hear himself saying it all out loud. Maybe he was a busier guy then he gave himself credit for. After all, he did most of the shop's welding work, helped Ross out with the machining, and handled the lion's share of project management and client relations in this joint. He showed off their vintage car parts business as well, very careful to explain that they only accepted parts with the proper paperwork and VIN.

Delilah squeezed his hand when he said that. She'd caught that detail and understood what he was really saying to her. That he was different. That he'd never get tangled up in anything dishonest again. She'd been there at his trial, after all, and heard everything. How he'd recruited his ring. How they'd used master keys they'd bought from a bail bondsman that could open up any door. He'd had quite the operation, shipping unmarked parts all over the globe. But when he thought back on it, nothing but sick shame bubbled up inside him.

Delilah must have sensed that he was thinking too much about it, because she circled her arms around his waist and squeezed. "I wish my job was half as exciting as yours," she simply said. He kissed her on the top of her head and ruffled his hand through her hair.

Just then, Hunter wandered up, wiping his oil-stained hands with a shop rag. "Exciting is right." He clapped Hopper on the back. "Looks like we got the Carmichael job. We'll be rebuilding that 1961 Ferrari 250 GT, after all."

"Really? Are you serious? They went for it?" Hopper crowed.

"Yep. Carmichael said he considered other shops, but he liked the ideas you had for it the best. We'll have to be careful. The thing is torn to shit. But when it's done? Oh, man."

"Another award winner, maybe." Hopper gave the man a high five. "Not too many people have ever had their hands on that model. It could be museum quality when we're done with it."

"He's bringing it in next weekend, so be ready." Though he surely didn't need to, Hunter thanked him again for making it happen. "Oh, and hey." He gathered Hopper and Delilah and pushed them back a couple of steps, huddling a bit so they couldn't be overheard. "Kathryn and me, we haven't given up trying to figure out what's going on with the Outpost property. I called in a couple of favors from friends working with government databases. And you know what? There's never been a business license or taxes collected for Caine's Christmas Outpost."

"Why am I not surprised?" Delilah drawled.

Hunter held up a finger. "It gets better. We checked into

the land where that building stood. Turned out the acreage was part of a big parcel that'd passed through a few families before it was sold to an oil and gas company back in the 1930s. It was never developed, though. But get this—the last people to own that land were a married couple—Earl and Candace Mayhew. They sold the property in 1938. Then they disappeared. There's no record of children. No record of deaths, or name changes. No other land purchases, either. From a records perspective, they vanished into thin air."

Hopper's couldn't believe this shit. "What is this, some kind of joke? You're tryin' to tell me Earl and Candy were ghosts?"

Hunter threw his hands up. "Well, what else could it be? It's way too much of a coincidence. 'Earl' and 'Candy' aren't exactly the commonest of names. So if they aren't ghosts, do you think they'd be alive, then? They'd be, like, what? A hundred-twenty years old?"

Delilah scowled. "But they were as solid as you or me, Hunter. No way were they ghosts. For God's sake, Candy made us cookies! That couldn't be right. But maybe they really could be alive. What if they were, like, magic people or something like that? People who didn't live on the same kind of timeline you and I do. They did hint about that, right?"

Hopper cocked an eyebrow, but he supposed it didn't surprise him so much that she'd be talking like this. Delilah always did love her fairy tales and paranormal romances. "What? Like a witch or something? That still wouldn't make them immortal."

"Well, whatever the explanation is, we'll never get it," Delilah countered. "Sounds like y'all have already done all the research it's pretty much possible to do. And do we really need all the answers? I kinda like that this mysterious thing happened to us. It was magical. Why don't we just let it stay magical?"

Hunter shrugged. "Guess we don't have a choice, do we?"

. . .

HAVING SHOWN her everything he'd planned to at the shop, Hopper and Lila said their goodbyes to everyone and walked back out to Hopper's car. But Lila had to admit—she was a bit sad to be leaving Lewisburg. She liked it here, especially the warm camaraderie at Holliday Hot Rods. It was easy to see how Hopper could've built a good life for himself here.

Just as they were getting ready to get in the car, a girl's voice rang out. "Mr. Hopper! Mr. Hopper! Don't go!"

Lila spied a blond-headed girl jumping out of an ancient Buick, followed quickly by another tow-headed boy who appeared to be about five. They ran up to Hopper and flung their arms around his waist.

Hopper let out an initial *oof* of surprise but soon smiled fondly down at them and hugged them back. "What are you guys doing here?"

A wiry old lady in a flowery sweatshirt and jeans hobbled out of the car behind them, smiling gamely while she balanced heavily on her three-pronged cane. "Sorry we didn't warn you we were coming. But we were driving past here, and Savannah simply would not rest until we stopped to thank y'all for our Christmas. Well now." She winked and gave Lila the once over. "Who's your very lovely lady friend?"

"This—" Hopper beamed, "—is my angel. Delilah Cook. Delilah, meet Mrs. Casto and her great grandkids Savannah and Tristan. They're neighbors of ours up the road."

Tristan peered up at Delilah speculatively, scrunching up his freckled nose. "Are you really an angel?"

"Naw." Hopper winked. "But she's heavenly to me."

Mrs. Casto groaned and snickered along with Lila this time.

"Mr. Hopper brought us all our food and all our toys and things for Christmas," Savannah said very earnestly, apparently trying to sell Lila on his many merits. "He's better than Santa!"

Hopper frowned at the lady. "I thought we agreed we weren't going to tell them it was us?"

"*You* try not telling them." The woman snorted. "Their mama told them there was no Santa from the beginning. So, they weren't going to believe that nonsense. Savannah caught sight of your truck pulling away and knew it was you."

Hopper put his hands on his hips. "Well, kids, I appreciate all the appreciation. But it wasn't just me. It was the whole shop. We all pitched in."

"Yeah, but it was all your idea. And you got us our tree," the girl replied. "We've never had one of those before. It was so beautiful I just couldn't believe it. It was ma-jes... It was ma-jes... What's that word?"

Lila chuckled. "Majestic."

"That's right!" the girl sang out twirling around in a circle. "It was majestic! Just like my new dress. It spins!"

Indeed, it did. The ruffles on the bottom of her pretty red velvet Christmas dress made a bell at the bottom when she turned. Lila grinned at the girl. She remembered how it felt to spin in a dress like that.

While his big sister was busy spinning around, the boy came up to Hopper and pulled on the man's pants leg. "Mr. Hopper? Do you think you could come by sometime and help me learn how to ride my new bike? Grans isn't very good at it. All she can do is sit on the steps and shout."

"That's because you won't stop trying to run the bike down the hill," Savannah wagged her little finger at him. "You know it's too steep."

"Nuh-uh! I didn't!" Tristan cried.

"You did too!" the girl insisted. "I'm the one who had to fix your wheel when you hit the ditch! And dry it off when you ran it into the creek!"

Mrs. Casto sighed and rested her hand on Savannah's

shoulder to quiet her down. "They've been bickering all week. All the candy, and the excitement, and the new toys I think. Lordy, I can't wait for school to start up again."

"Hey, if you need some help, I'd be happy to come over and teach him some bike safety. Whaddaya think, buddy, maybe we could go over to Dorie Miller Park and try the roads out over there? It's nice and level."

Tristan shrugged. "Nah. That's baby stuff. Let's go out on the trail. I hear they've got a ramp!"

Hopper raised his eyebrows, amused at the kid's bravado. "You're still in training wheels, kid!"

"Oh, now!" Mrs. C clucked. "Mr. Hopper will not do any such thing."

"Seriously though." He nodded to the woman. "Drop them off over here when they need to run off some energy. We can keep 'em busy."

"I'll call you next week. How's that?" she answered, and he nodded in agreement.

"Why don't you kids go on inside?" he offered. "I'm pretty sure Hunter's got a plate of Kathryn's homemade Christmas cookies in there. I think we've got some hot chocolate pods in there too. I bet he'll make you some if you ask real nicely."

"I want coffee!" Tristan whooped as he ran off with his sister.

"Just hot chocolate, young man!" Mrs. C called after him. When they were out of sight, she shook her head and smiled. "I can't even tell you what Christmas has done for these kids. They're smiling for the first time since they've come here. I've got y'all to thank for that."

"The pleasure's all mine." Hopper gave her arm a little pat. "And with you getting up off that walker, you'll be back to chasing around after them in no time."

"That's the idea!" she crowed, straightening herself up proudly. "I've got a garden to plant in a couple of months!"

They chatted about gardens and canning and fun things

to do around the Lewisburg area for a bit, and they left with the promise that Mrs. C would deliver them canned stewed peppers, prize pickles, and apple butter once her crops came in. Just the thought of it made Lila's stomach growl.

Full up on cookies, the Casto family said their goodbyes and rumbled down the road.

Lila linked her hand with Hopper's again as they began walking back to the car. "I never knew you were so good with kids."

"Me?" he demurred. "I wouldn't say that necessarily. I just — I dunno. I just look at those crazy, mixed-up kids, and—"

"You identify."

"Yeah, I can't exactly change my childhood, but it feels good to change somebody else's."

Lila turned that over in her mind, and found she had no argument for that. He said he was trying to be a better man. She supposed doing for his neighbors was part of it. No wonder Kathryn said people in the town loved him. "Did you ever want kids?" she blurted out. She tried to hide her wince. Damn, she hadn't meant for the question to just slip out like that.

He stopped walking and turned to her, cocking his head. He didn't seem angry that she'd pried, just a bit surprised. But she did see a tremor of sadness pass over his face, there and gone so quickly she almost didn't catch it. "Sometimes your dreams get sacrificed to your mistakes. It's not what you want, but it is what it is."

"Yeah. I know exactly what you mean." Their gaze locked for a couple long, uncomfortable beats. But then he squeezed her hand, indicating they should get going.

She changed the subject to small talk about their road trip. Soon they'd buckled themselves in and were heading out.

Once they were back on the road, Lila enjoyed being chauffeured around in this incredible classic car. She couldn't help but admire the way it hugged the road. They called them muscle cars for a reason, baby. She stretched her legs out in the very comfortable leather bucket seat, feeling like she was the sexy sidekick in a Steve McQueen movie.

And they whiled away the day on the route down the Blue Ridge Mountain's famous Skyline drive, alternately oohing and ahhing over the soaring mountain views and chatting about anything and everything—movies, politics, cooking, and favorite books, for starters. They never seemed to run out of conversation. It'd always been always like that with them, from the moment he'd first arrived on Randy's doorstep.

Finally, after a solid hour of deep conversation, she turned to face him. "What is it about you?"

He glanced over and gave her a quizzical smile. "What do you mean?"

"How is it I always feel so safe with you? Like I can tell you anything?"

He hummed thoughtfully. "Is it so surprising? I lived close enough to be a brother, at least for a while anyway, and I saw everything you went through with your mama. I knew you when, an' all that."

Lila resolutely shook her head. "No, that's not it. There was an instant connection between us, from the moment we met. But it wasn't just an adolescent crush. When I had to relive it as an adult trapped in my young body, I had the same feeling, only stronger."

"And do you feel it now?"

"Yeah."

He turned to her with a soft, glowy kind of expression she'd never seen before. "Yeah. Me too."

"I guess I just feel safe with you. I can't explain why."

He harrumphed. "You're just about the only one, sugar."

"What? Are you saying I shouldn't be?"

"Not at all. But I have to say, most people don't feel safe

around me. Not my friends and neighbors, of course. It's strangers I'm talking about."

Lila had a hard time believing this. "Oh, come on."

"No, I'm serious. I'm both tall and broad and I'm not a big smiler. When they see me coming, men tense up, and women hold their purses tighter, even when they don't realize they're doing it. Once I start talking, the reaction fades away, but it takes people a minute."

"It's probably just the tats."

He chuckled bitterly. "Yeah. If they only knew what they were covering up."

She didn't respond to him at first. But finally, she screwed up her courage. "Kathryn told me about the fight at the prison. What you did for the warden."

"I don't like to talk about it." He sighed and gripped the steering wheel a little harder. "So I'll say this once. I'd do it all again. The warden wasn't guilty of anything but doing his job, and I wasn't going to stand by and let a good family man die. At that point I didn't see what I had to live for, anyway. I wasn't some badass. It was a split-second impulse. I threw myself between him and the crowd. For my trouble, I got some scary scars on my neck and four stab wounds up my right side and arm. When I got out, I had a giant phoenix done to cover it all. And trust me, it looks a lot better than those scars do. End of story."

She nodded, letting that sink in. Then she teased her finger up his thigh. "For the record, I like tattoos. And I think your new voice is super sexy. It's gravelly but Southern. Like someone kicked Sam Elliott in the nuts."

He burst out laughing, and the smile spread over his whole face, lighting him up in that way she loved to see. She couldn't wait to put a smile on that face of his a lot more often.

CHAPTER 26

THEY CONTINUED to joke and flirt all the way back to Roanoke. Lila led him through the heart of the city, showing off some of its historic architecture, the main business and entertainment districts, the river walk and such.

When she'd told him she liked it here, she'd meant it. Roanoke was big enough to have great restaurants, attractions, and a decent business community, but small enough that you didn't feel like you were swimming in a sea of people.

She loved the area's cultured, effortless Southern charm. That homey, easy pace was something she'd never had in Atlanta, which had lost all that in its race to become a great southern metropolis.

There was a certain "Virginia-ness" about Roanoke that she'd always admired. The old, square red brick buildings, the turrets, the columns, the low-slung Victorian storefronts. The mild Virginia weather. The history around every corner.

She and Hopper drove around for an hour or so while she schooled him in what she knew of Roanoke's landmarks and history. Lila took him by her office too so he could see where the practice was, which was also in its own antebellum building.

They discussed whether or not to find a restaurant for dinner. But they nixed the idea of a big meal, since they both had eaten so much at the Greenbrier buffet. The grocery store turned out to be their better option, since her cupboards were bare. They chowed down on the store's salad bar and spent a few minutes companionably chatting while she picked out everything she needed. Hopper even managed to make himself useful, actually helping her spot some great after-Christmas markdowns.

Once she'd checked out, he'd insisted on being gallant, loading up the groceries while she waited in the car. When she got back to her condo, he handled all the runs back and forth between the parking garage for her, and helped put everything away, too.

He stowed the last of the items and stopped, cocking his head as he got the first whiff of what she'd set to warm on the stove.

He came up behind her and wrapped his arms around her middle, hanging his nose over the pot. "Uh-oh, is that what I think it is?"

"Yep. It's our famous hot chocolate, just like we used to make every Christmas. Only this time the secret ingredient isn't salted caramel syrup."

"It's not?"

"Nope." She reached into the pantry and did a little shimmy as she pulled out a bottle. "It's Bailey's Irish Cream."

He clapped his hands in appreciation. "Now that's what I'm talking about." She poured out the hot chocolate into mugs and topped it off with the sweet shot of alcohol. When he tipped back the cup, he groaned with bliss. "I like this tradition."

She clinked her mug with his. "It was the least I could do.

After all, Hopper, you're the only man who's ever dared to grocery shop with me."

He crinkled his brow. "Really? It's not like you're a hardship to shop with, Delilah. Why wouldn't a man want to shop with you?"

She shrugged. "Beats me. Guess no one else has ever cared enough."

He smirked and rubbed his chest theatrically. "Face it, woman. I'm boyfriend material."

"Hmm. Yes, I'm beginning to see that."

His whole face brightened and his eyebrows flew up. "Uh oh! Does that mean I've passed the three-day test?"

"Maybe." She ran a finger lazily down the buttons of his shirt.

He screwed his face up in a playful scowl. "Maybe. Is that the best I get? Maybe?"

She shrugged a shoulder noncommittally and bit her lip, determined to make the man sweat a little.

"Well now," he growled, taking her mug out of her hand and placing it on the counter. "It seems I haven't done enough to convince you. And you can bet I'm going to be fixing that, angel. Immediately."

Hopper grabbed her by the hand and walked her backward until he was leaning against her dining room table. Pulling her between his spread legs, he gently cupped both sides of her face in his hands. He searched her eyes for some kind of an answer she didn't have. But she had his. It was written on every line in his face, glowing in the warmth of his eyes, and vibrating through his touch. He'd never stopped wanting her. And he wanted her again, right this very moment.

The promise of that had her head buzzing and her body melting into his embrace.

She let him close the gap, let him press his hot mouth against hers. Maybe she should be getting used to his kisses, but the sensual shock of having him so close short-circuited her senses, making the whole world narrow down to his taste, his heat.

A sweet hint of chocolate...and the warm sweep of his tongue, searching, demanding. His fingers tightened in her hair, and she moaned as his kisses grew harder, deeper.

He opened himself up to her in a way he never had before. She could feel it in the tremble skating over his skin and the way his kisses seemed not just like a demand but...a plea, maybe. Like he'd die if he couldn't have her.

Just when she thought he'd push for more, he stopped. He held a finger up over her lips, the both of them breathing hard. "Wait—do you have some speakers or something I could hook up my phone to, to play music?"

Music?

This was a first. Still dazed from their makeout session, she nodded. "Over there." Lila pointed to the low-slung mid-century cabinet that held her flat screen tv. "There's a white cable."

What is that man up to? He scrolled through his collection, obviously searching for something. Taking note of the darkness outside, she hit the remote that rolled down the blinds throughout the apartment, blocking out the sights and sounds of the city that inevitably came through her floor-to-ceiling, industrial plate-glass windows. She pushed another button, dimming the overhead lights a bit, then used another remote to start the oversized, see-through gas fireplace between her bedroom and living room.

He let out an appreciative hoot. "Nice." One swipe on his phone, and the unmistakable strains of Motown began to play. When the opening notes of "My Girl" rang out, she crossed her arms over her chest. "You want to tell me what this is all about?"

He walked to the center of her living room, grinned from

ear to ear, and held out both hands. "I want to dance with you."

She snorted. "Really? Since when did you become such a big dancer?"

"Since I've got another chance to hold you in my arms, that's when. Now get your sexy ass over here." The gleam in his eye was playful but told her there'd be much, much more to come.

She stalked back over to him, unable to ignore his command. When he took her in his arms, she wanted to make some kind of flirty conversation. But somehow, she just couldn't. Her throat was too full of emotion, and her body was all jangled and stirred up by the feel of him. Her arms, circled around his neck…the warm weight of his hands, cupping the small of her back…

Hopper was quiet too. He simply held her, and they swayed to the beat. There was something perfect about it—the lack of artifice or practiced dance moves. Right here, there was only the two of them, and something thrumming through them both, true and deep. He bent his head and nuzzled his coarse beard against the side of her face. And she couldn't help but breathe deep, wrapped up in the male, elemental scent of his skin and the rhythm of him moving against her.

Not able to hold back any longer, she slid both hands down his chest, taking her good sweet time appreciating every sinew. Leashed energy hummed under his heated skin, vibrating with a need she could feel. Hopper growled, soft and low in her ear, dipping his head for a long, sweet, searching kiss.

And she kissed him back, slowly, taking a moment to sink her teeth into his bottom lip. Hopper moaned his approval.

He began the exquisite, sensual torture of skimming his hands over her then, the back of his knuckles skating soft and light down her side. It was the barest of touches really, trailing over the sensitive underside of her ribs, over her rounded hip, and back again. But it still made her shiver. She closed her eyes, feeling swamped all of a sudden, like every nerve ending in her body had crackled to life. It'd been a while since she'd been with a man—a couple of years, probably. Yet, that wasn't the reason why his touch unraveled her.

No. It was him. His hands—hard and calloused, strong enough to bend metal, yet still touching her like she was the most precious thing he'd ever seen. His desire, his longing, trembling out from his fingertips, coursing in the air around them as if it were some new natural element.

She could barely breathe, but she tipped her head up to kiss him anyway. And when their lips met, it was like the moment a struck match meets the air, and leaps to flame. He crushed his body against hers, and soon they were tangled together, both of them barely able to get their fill.

Hot skin and hard muscle, tongues and teeth. It was hard to tell who was touching or biting or pressing. Dimly, she became aware of one hand on her ass, hauling her against the jut of his erection, the other curled over her breast, squeezing hard, just like she always liked it. Sweet, sizzling pleasure coursed through her, and she cried out, her knees starting to quiver in her high-heeled boots. He gave her no place to hide, tipping her over his arm to ply her chest with scalding kisses and dig his teeth into the crook of her neck.

Lila wasn't sure what song was playing, and she didn't care. She fumbled for his belt buckle, but he stepped back, righting her on her feet.

"Naw baby, we'll get to that. Cause right now? This dress is lookin' like a gift I wanna unwrap." He pointed to the string tie on her hip. "Let me?" And with the hungry, almost feral look he was giving her, she could only nod in response. He never took his eyes off her while he slowly pulled the skinny piece of fabric that held the dress in place. The knot hitched, and in one tug it released, opening wide. He gently pushed aside the panels until it pooled at her feet.

He let out a low, amazed whistle. God, the look on his face. She'd bought red, lacy Christmassy lingerie, just hoping. And it seemed to have hit him broadside.

"Holy shit," he whispered, transfixed.

She resisted the urge to leap into his arms, because he wasn't done appreciating her. He traced a finger over the edge of her bra, tracking the shape of her, trailing goosebumps in his wake. Lila sucked in a sharp breath as he teased her nipples through the sheer lace, the rasp of his fingers through the fabric turning them hard and aching.

"Gorgeous," he groaned as he walked around her, smacking her bare ass with a satisfying ping. "Still hot as hell in a thong, I see."

She would've answered him, but before she even knew what'd happened, he was on his knees behind her, wriggling her panties down her legs. Moaning, she swayed on her feet as he bit that sensitive spot, right behind her knee. Then he began kissing up, up, *God*...a smack and a caress, a spank and the scorching sweep of his tongue...over and over, making her backside rosy and raw and sensitized.

Her core throbbed, aching to be filled. Every nip, every kiss only made the slippery heat between her legs get hotter.

"So beautiful," he murmured, dragging his teeth along her quivering thigh. "So fucking beautiful..."

She shifted restlessly, gasping with every perfect little nip, her knees shaking for real now. By the time that wicked mouth of his licked up her seam, she nearly collapsed from the pleasure of it.

"Goddamn," he growled, burying a finger inside her, "you're so fuckin' ready for me." She groaned helplessly as he pumped his fingers in and out.

Surprising her, he stood up. She whipped around to face him, ready to give as good as she got. But he scooped her off her feet and into his arms. Lord, she was in nothing but her bra and her boots. But she didn't protest as he walked her the short distance through her French doors and into her bedroom. He dropped her softly onto her upholstered bed. Silently, she thanked herself for splurging enough to buy the California king size. They were going to need all the space they could get.

He laid her out on top of her ivory silk quilt, arranging her head on the pillows. As soon as he released her, she popped up to start undressing him, but he waved her hands away. "This turn isn't about me, angel, it's about you. Lay back."

She did as he said, the ache between her legs growing stronger and more insistent as he shucked off his collared shirt and pants. He threw a long roll of condoms onto the nightstand and leaned over her, pinning her arms overhead to the mattress. She hissed with frustration, wishing she could worm her hand under his remaining t-shirt. But one look at his face, and she stilled. Jesus, his eyes were so dark with desire she could practically see the flames dancing in them. Trance-like, he released her and rolled down the lacy cups of her bra to the underwires, leaving her breasts hard and straining up toward his mouth. He huffed out an amazed breath, but recovered himself, grinning wickedly as he traced a trail from her belly button to her nipples with his tongue.

The glide of his wet, greedy mouth on her made her dizzy, the exquisite pull on her breasts a thrill she could barely contain. She tangled her fingers through his hair, holding him to his task as he sucked and nipped and bit like she was his favorite lollipop.

Was she moaning his name? She didn't even know what sounds were coming out of her throat as she squirmed and twisted restlessly.

Lila felt the outline of his brushy smile against her chest. "Mmm, that's right." He chuckled, smoothing his hand down her belly until he stopped at the apex of her thighs. "Is this what you need, baby?"

"Y-yes."

He plunged his hands between her legs, circling the flat of his fingers over her. "Tell me, Angel. Tell me what you want. Like you used to."

She didn't hesitate. "I want your hands on me. Your mouth too, all sweet and dirty. Make me come, Hop." She writhed against his hand. "Come on. Do it."

A devilish smile played at his lips. "Good girl." In a flash he was sitting between her legs, pushing her knees wide. He sucked in a loud breath. "Aww, hell yeah. There you are." He rubbed his hand back and forth, completely mesmerized, soaking up the wetness with his fingers. "So fuckin' sexy… the sexiest thing I've ever… *God,"* he choked out. She bucked, but he simply ran his shaky hands over the hollows of her thighs. "You're beautiful down here. Did you know that?" He hissed as he ran his thumb over the length of her. "Shell pink at first, flaming to the most beautiful coral red once you've come. I had a long, long time to remember you like this. Every day. Every night. You'd think I'd be dreamin' about bein' inside you. But no. When I was locked up, layin' on that concrete cot, all I could think about was putting my mouth on you. That's what I wanted, feelin' you all around me, your spice rising in the air, your slick heat, my face and my fingers all sticky with you, and feeling you come so damn hard when I'm *right there..."*

Lila watched him, unable to look away as he smoothly dipped two fingers inside her, drew them out, and licked them clean. *Slowly.*

It was unbearably erotic, the way his brow furrowed as he lingered…like he'd just been offered a bowl of ambrosia. He shuddered on a strangled moan. "Fuck, it's still the same," he breathed. "Like hot musk and honeysuckle."

Her breath left her in a tortured groan. He bent down to

kiss her stomach, her belly, muttering unintelligible love words all the way down.

Her brain fizzed with the sensation, every touch, every taste.

When he wrapped his arms around the back of her thighs and pulled her tight to his mouth, he cried out, just like she did. Their moans mingled, echoing in the room as he teased and bit and dipped his tongue deep inside. He edged her up and then down, over and over again, his perfect feast. By the time he finally pressed in his fingers and pumped, she practically bawled in ecstasy. She shook in his arms, gasping and begging, her thighs holding him to his task as everything turned to white sparks and heat. And he rolled right with her.

HOPPER POPPED up and wiped his mouth with the back of his hand. His head buzzed. Damn, he was so turned on, he felt like his chest might explode. Somehow, he managed to rip off his underwear and roll on a condom in record time. Delilah started to get up again but he shook his head, pushing her back down on the bed. He spread her legs and unhooked the front clasp on that racy bra of hers. She wriggled it off and threw it across the room.

Holding the crook of her knees in his hands, he buried himself in her—all the way, like a hot knife through butter. So plumped and slippery and decadent…holy fuck…she was still pulsing from her last orgasm. His head spun, but he collected himself enough to start thrusting, hard, harder. Delilah rolled her hips to meet each one, wild and unschooled and demanding her due.

Hell yes, he'd give it her. As much as she wanted, as much as she needed. He circled his fingers around her clit, clockwise, hard and fast, just like she liked it. And yeah, she did like it, her bold, throaty moans music to his ears, driving him higher, closer. "Come on, baby," he growled. "Do it now. Show me. Show me how you come."

She looked him in the eye as she pumped against him, and he looked back, taking in every detail…the flush that crept up her neck, the way her eyes shone, her mouth all red and swollen from his kisses. Then there was the blazing heat of her pussy, pulsing, drawing hard against his cock… *Ahh, God!* The room spun as he felt the orgasm crack over her, and they sped over that cliff together, falling, tumbling, stars exploding behind his eyelids. He held her tight against him as he drove himself inside her, right up to the hilt, and she wrapped her legs around his waist, holding him there.

He struggled for breath, struggled to pull his shit together. He'd forgotten…how perfect and tight she was, how she'd shudder and pull when she came apart in his arms. She'd screamed out his name, like he was the only one who could ever take her there. God, he hoped that was true.

He collapsed back against the pillows with her, sweat rolling off him, chest heaving for air. The room was still sizzling with electricity from what they'd done. Amazed, they both giggled a bit, as if they couldn't believe their attraction was even more explosive than before. But it was. *Goddamn* it was.

Delilah gave him a sweet kiss, and he pushed a sweaty tendril off her cheek with his fingertip. "You're the king." She smiled.

"Damn right." He grinned right back. "And before this night is over, you're going to be calling me holy emperor."

She laughed and shook her head at him. "Cocky much?" He just kept smilin', totally unrepentant, and let her trail her little hands all over him. She stuck her lip out in a pout when she got to his shirt. "I can't believe I came like that, and I didn't even get to see your tattoos. You know my lady parts give out extra credit for that, right?"

Not needing to be asked twice, he sat up, pulled off his

shirt, and tossed the condom in the bedroom waste basket while he was at it. "Well, hell," he drawled. "All this time, and you never told me you have a tattoo fetish?"

He laid back down, stretching out and luxuriating among the pillows so she could examine him to her heart's delight. He thought she'd ask him a bunch of questions about the colorful phoenix tattoo that covered his right arm, his neck, shoulder and half his chest. Or maybe the cuff on his right hand and forearm. They really were something. But he was surprised to see her staring down at him, her eyes wide.

He followed her gaze to his left pec, right over his heart. Her eyes lit with recognition, and a soft, wondering expression stole over her face. Oh, yeah, *of course...*

"The origami angel. You inked it."

"Long ago. So you'd always be with me."

Her eyes shimmered with bittersweet emotion, with years of what had gone unsaid. His probably did, too. "This is why you always called me angel, isn't it?" she whispered.

He paused for a moment, tracing the hollow of her cheek. "Yeah," he whispered back. He wanted to say more, but his heart was in his throat.

She pushed her fingertip along the outline of the crude jailhouse tattoo, done by an old cellmate with pen ink and staples. A happy tear sneaked down her cheek.

He wiped it away and made himself a silent vow. *Only happy tears for you Angel, from here on out. I promise.*

Lila whooped as he rolled her back underneath him. And he kissed her, all over again. It was going to be a long night.

CHAPTER 27

HOPPER STRETCHED his long limbs and cracked his eyes open, startling a bit until he remembered where he was. Delilah's bed. The happiest place on earth. He rolled over and tucked an arm around her waist, drawing the smell of sex, sweat and the remnants of her flowery perfume into his lungs. She curled up against him and sighed in her sleep.

He glanced at the clock on her nightstand. Nine thirty in the morning. Damn. Sleeping in was not usually his thing. An early riser, he'd be up and at 'em by six in the morning at the latest. But he supposed he'd had good reason to sleep. He and Delilah had been up until three in the morning, wearing each other out.

Evidently, reuniting really did "feel so good." Minutes ticked by as he laid there, grinning into the darkness, wide awake but unwilling to tear himself away. She was so warm and soft, a symphony of curves and pure feminine beauty. But it was so much more than that. Delilah was the only person in his life who'd made him feel seen. Understood. Whole, even.

For once, he might be steady enough to deserve her.

Maybe he had a chance to give her what she wanted and needed in a man. He couldn't wait to try. This morning, he'd start by making coffee and rustling up a light breakfast for the both of them.

He carefully slid out of bed, managing not to wake her. And he padded off to her bathroom. It was a nice bathroom with soft gray marble tiles, a double large tub, and pretty sizeable glassed-in shower. He thought about just jumping in but decided he'd wait to see if he could talk Delilah into taking their morning shower together. He smiled over the images *that* conjured the whole time he was brushing his teeth and scrubbing his face. Since he hadn't packed for this slumber party, he decided to go commando and slip on his khakis. It looked weird, but they were slung pretty low and basically cut like jeans anyhow.

He inspected himself in the mirror, chuckling over the love bites Delilah had left behind. She'd marked him in spots that weren't already covered by his tattoos—the right side of his neck, his collar bone, and one right on his hip too. Badge of honor, man.

He tiptoed out of the master bathroom, shutting the bedroom's frosted glass doors behind him. The doors led directly into the kitchen, living, and dining areas, which were all open to each other. He quietly padded around in the living room until he found the remote that opened the living room blinds. Mid-morning sun flooded the space, promising a bright, crisp winter's day.

He sauntered into her spacious kitchen, scanning the white marble countertops to find a coffeemaker. After rooting around in the pantry and the cabinets for coffee and filters, he realized she only had a K-Cup machine. He pulled it out from under the counter and plugged it in.

Since they had one of these things at the office, he knew how to put in fresh water and brew himself up a cup of

Columbian roast, thank you very much. He helped himself to a bagel with cream cheese and cut up fruit salad to serve Delilah when she got up. If she wasn't awake in another half hour or so, he'd wake her. She'd said she needed him out by noon so she could take care of some work obligations. He assumed she'd have to be up and ready by then.

Hopper considered turning on the morning news but nixed that idea. Too noisy. So he stood at the window, sipping his coffee, taking in the sights and sounds of city life. This condo was on a busy urban street within walking distance to the city center. People strolled by with their travel mugs, walking dogs and ducking into shops to catch the New Year's sales. It was a sight he wasn't used to, as he lived in a more traditional, leafy neighborhood. But he could see why Delilah would like condo living. No yard care. A super took care of your maintenance. A rehabbed mid-century factory, her relatively small building only had two floors and no more than fifteen units, so she probably knew her neighbors well.

And this condo was cool. It really was. Tall, soaring ceilings. Exposed brick walls. Floor-to-ceiling windows. Exposed ductwork.

She had this place decorated up super slick, no doubt. And yet, something about it seemed like it was just...*not her*. He thought about the girl who used to decorate the ceiling of her room in origami cranes and butterflies, who used to draw and watercolor the most beautiful things. It seemed wrong that she'd have an apartment with all soft, solid colors, and some deconstructed abstract painting over her couch. Why hadn't she painted something herself? There was absolutely nothing extra in this place. She had four plates in the cabinet. Two pans. Four mugs. Three towels in the linen closet. And one single wreath from the Outpost. That's it.

A solitary life. Kinda stark. But was his any different, really?

He wanted to change that for both of them, more than anything he'd ever wanted before. They'd gotten off to a pretty good start last night, hadn't they? He snickered a bit at the carnage. Clothes and pillows were scattered all over the place—evidence of how they'd managed to christen just about every flat surface…the table, the couch, the kitchen counter, the floor in front of the fireplace. Hopper sighed contentedly. Maybe he should be a good boyfriend and pick some of this stuff up.

He was just reaching down for that sexy red thong when he heard a key twisting in the deadbolt.

What the actual fuck?

He vaulted to the door and put on the chain right as it was opening. He slammed it shut with his hand. "Who is it?" he called out.

"What do you mean, who is it?" an angry male voice bellowed. "Who the hell are you?"

Burning to see what man had a key to Delilah's door, Hopper opened the door wide.

He was shocked to speechlessness to see Randy Jarboe standing there in a Christmas sweater, holding a stack of presents. An attractive redhaired woman about the man's age —his new wife, Amy apparently—came up behind him. Similarly dressed in a Christmas llama sweatshirt and toting a box of doughnuts, the woman batted her big brown eyes curiously. "Honey, who's—"

"You," Randy thundered, barging in through the door. "Of all the people I figured I'd find sniffin' around Lila's door. *You* were the last person I thought I'd ever see. What's the matter? They let you out and you just need a little help to get back on your feet? You tryin' to screw your way out of not paying rent? Huh?"

Jesus. *Randy freakin' Jarboe*. His gut clenched. What could he even say to the man? The last Randy had heard, he'd been sentenced, and had done a pretty cruel job of dumping

Delilah. And now he'd come back into her life, bigger and scarier than ever. Once upon a time, Randy had offered him a hand up and an honest living. And what had he done? He'd spit in the man's face with the horrible choices he'd made. *Of course* Randy would hate his guts. *Of course* he'd be freaking out. He was the last family left to protect her. And he was just doing his job.

"Whoa, Randy." Hopper held up a staying hand, trying his best to shut this shit down. "I think you're getting the wrong idea about all this. I got out early. I've been out for a few years, in fact. And I'm gainfully employed, thank you very much. Delilah and I have just been…reconnecting."

Randy sneered and got right up in his grill, even though the man barely came up to his shoulder. "Reconnecting? Oh *really?* Because judging by those bite marks and this mess in here, you've been reconnecting all over the damn place."

Just then, Delilah came rushing in. "Randy!" she cried. Immediately, her cheeks turned red and she pulled her long silk robe tighter around her. "What are you guys doing here? You weren't supposed to make it to town until one in the afternoon!"

Ah. So *this* was the "work obligation" she'd been talking about. This was why she needed him out by noon—shoving him out of the way before Randy got wind of him. His heart sank.

"Oh, honey." Amy grimaced apologetically and scurried to Delilah's side. "We ended up coming back a day early. We stayed at a hotel last night and thought we'd get over here early so we could have a longer visit. We tried and tried to call your phone last night. You didn't answer."

Delilah groaned and rubbed her forehead. "I'm sorry. I was…distracted. I didn't hear it."

"Distracted." Randy snorted. "Oh, I'll *bet* you were distracted."

"Hey!" Amy wagged a finger. "Delilah's a grown woman. And she can spend time with whomever she pleases, whenever she pleases. Don't you dare forget that."

"Not this one, babe. Anyone but *this one,*" Randy spat.

"Come on," Delilah jumped in. "Don't you think you're being too hard on Hopper? People make mistakes. They can change."

"Awww no no no," Randy countered, his face getting redder by the minute. He narrowed his eyes and stabbed a finger in Hopper's chest. "You can come back from small mistakes. But the kind of mistakes this one made? No, honey. Those go right down to your character, to your soul, even. To be given a chance, over and over again to do the right thing, and to turn those chances down? For years? A man like that isn't worth your trust, Lila."

"I'm not that man anymore," Hopper grated out, trying to breathe through his urge to punch him square in the face. "I haven't been for some time, if you'd bothered to ask."

Randy snorted. "Oh, I see. I have to *ask*. I wouldn't want to offend your delicate sensibilities. *Oh, excuse me, Mr. Vance, are you planning to fuck this family over again?"* He barked out a bitter laugh. "God. That's really what you expect. Total acceptance—just like that, huh? You come waltzing back in here, and we're all supposed to magically trust you? How do we know you're not lying through your teeth, just like always?"

Hopper curled his fists at his sides, willing himself not to take the bait. The angry, defensive rant building in his head would only take this day from bad to worse. "Okay. Alright. I get it." Hopper threw his hands up. "You hate my guts. I'd like to earn your forgiveness someday, Randy, fair and square. But honestly, the only person I need to trust me is Delilah. If there's any trust to be given in this situation, it's up to her to give it."

Delilah walked a step or two closer, appearing to be ready to jump to his defense. "Randy, I—"

But the man just held up his hand again. "No no, sweetie, I don't need any explanations from you. Let's let old Hopper here be a man and explain himself. 'Cause I've got questions. So let's start with the biggie—you want to tell me why you told all those lies to Lila? To me? Hell, to everyone? You want to tell me *why* you had to steal, when you could've earned plenty of money?"

Hopper closed his eyes and briefly considered not answering him. He didn't appreciate the way Randy was making him feel. Like he was small. Worthless. A dirty little secret from Lila's past. But he'd hurt him, and he supposed he owed the man something.

He blew out a breath, knowing how ridiculous this would sound. "I wanted a better life."

Randy looked around the room sarcastically, as if he was waiting for someone else to come in with a better story. "Wait—that's it? You wanted a better life? That's your explanation?" He shook his head in disbelief. "You had a good life! An honest life! Handed to you right on a silver plat—"

"I wanted to go to college, *okay?*" Hopper roared, surprising himself at the self-loathing that rang through his words. "There—everybody happy? You heard my big secret. My *why.*"

His answer hung heavily in the air as everyone exchanged shocked glances.

Lila cocked her head in confusion. "I'm sorry, Hop, I'm not following this. Don't you have a master's degree?"

"Yeah, all online degrees I earned in prison," he answered her. "It wasn't exactly what I had in mind. Oh no, I had it in my head that I was going to get the full campus experience. I'd gotten my GED, and my SAT scores were pretty high. Thought I'd get an MBA and be a stockbroker or some shit. I thought if I only had enough money, I could give Delilah the kind of life where she'd never have to pinch another penny. And you know what's so sad about it all? I was on the short-list for a scholarship at The University of Georgia, but at the last minute, they lost their grant. The financial aid team told me I'd have to find 'alternate funding.' So I did."

Randy just shook his head. "A likely story. Just another line of bullshit he's throwin' out to cover his ass."

And that was pretty much what he would've expected Randy to say. But Delilah? She stilled, wrapping her arms around her middle, her face so blanked with shock, it was like she'd never seen him before. "Wait—you wanted to go to college all that time? You never even told me you'd applied. You never even told me you got your GED! Jesus—you hid that from me too? What you wanted? What you thought *I* wanted? Good Lord, who were you, even?"

A sick feeling roiled in his stomach. He pressed his eyes shut. "I didn't tell you because…I didn't want you to see me fail."

"Well, ain't it just too late for that!" Randy crowed.

No one answered. No one corrected the man.

Too late. Randy's words hit him with the force of a sucker punch. And all his angry replies died a quick death. All he could do was stand there, helplessly.

Randy shook his head, and took a couple of angry, stomping steps before he turned back to him. "All right, all right—let's review, shall we? I took you in, treated you like a son, and gave you everything you needed to get a good start in life. But you decided that wasn't good enough. You cooked up a fantasy in your head that Lila wanted to be some richy-rich housewife, and you found a way to steal your way to your stupid fuckin' dreams. And not only that, you recruited the thieves to do your dirty work. That's five more men in prison 'cause of you. Every day for friggin' years you lied to us. About everything. So tell me, what makes you think you deserve to lay a single finger on a woman like Delilah?"

Hopper wanted to speak up, wanted to defend himself. But the weight of everything he'd ever done clogged his throat. He had excuses. Apologies. But in the end, what good would they be to someone like Randy? Like Delilah? He just stood there, taking the blows.

"God, look at you," Randy snarled, shoving him back a step. "All tatted up. Even more of a lowlife than you were when you went in."

"Hey," Delilah jumped between them. "Don't make assumptions about the man just because of a few tats!"

"Really?" Randy sneered. "I shouldn't make assumptions? Well, everyone else sure will be. Tell me exactly how a man like this fits into the life you've built for yourself. Workin' in an office with doctors. Mingling with the philanthropic set. She's going to a fancy ball tonight. Did she tell you that, Hop? She's on the board of this mental health charity. She's going to stand up in front of the best and brightest of Roanoke and emcee. Boy, just think what that'd look like, you going with her, with all them prison tats on your hands. Wouldn't that be a pretty picture?"

A ball? She hadn't told him. Why hadn't she? He would've gone with her, even if he felt out of place. He would've done it for her. But when Hopper turned to look at his angel, her gaze fell to the floor.

He almost gasped. The realization twisted in his gut, just as sharp as a knife. *Ashamed.* That's why she couldn't meet his eyes. She was *absolutely ashamed* of him. Maybe she should be.

Randy actually had the gall to snicker. "Oh, this is just insane. Boy, what is it about women in this family? Always going after the bad boys. God, you're just like her fath—" Randy's eyes got wide. Panicked, he covered his mouth with a shaky hand and wheeled away from Hopper.

"What?" Lila quavered, her eyes blazing fire as she stepped up to the man. "What were you going to say?"

"I promised your mama I wouldn't," Randy murmured. "I can't."

Lila stuck her hands on her hips. "Oh yes, you sure as hell will," she thundered. "It's *my* information. *Mine.* You've got no right to keep it from me."

Randy trembled, his eyes gone round with dismay. But he didn't answer her.

Lila shoved at his shoulder. "All this time. All this time you knew who my father was? Mama told me it was just some guy she met in a bar!"

Randy let out a long breath, and for just a minute, Hopper felt sorry for him. The man looked like he might be sick. "He is. I mean, she did meet him in a bar."

Lila crossed her arms over her chest. "Go on."

"You gotta understand. The Joneses—your grandparents—they were awful people. Your mama never told you the half of it. There were beatings. Sexual abuse. Drinking. I knew her back then, and I can tell you, all that left its mark on her. She left home real young, and fell into a lifestyle where she was boozing and catting around for a while. She met this guy at a bar—one of those good-lookin' players with lots of charisma. And they hooked up a few times. By the time she figured out he was a real bad dude, she'd gotten herself pregnant. Accidentally, of course."

Delilah narrowed her eyes. "A real bad dude?"

Randy sighed and scrubbed his hands over his face. "He ran drugs, okay? Got involved in shootouts. She never told him about her situation, but he got wind of the pregnancy anyway. She never stopped worrying that he'd come to find the two of you. That's why she was so determined to be independent. And that's why she was always moving around when you were young, too. The guy ended up in jail, though, right around the time your mother came down with cancer and y'all moved in with me."

Lila set her jaw. "What was his name?"

"Jack Glover."

Shock poured like ice down Hopper's spine. Dear God. *Jack Glover...* Hopper made an involuntary, strangled sound and staggered back a step.

Randy snorted with derision when he saw his reaction. "Oh, wait. Don't tell me. You've met."

Hopper grimaced. "I wouldn't say we've been introduced, but he was practically a celebrity in the Georgia penal system. He ran a gang in the state pen. Everyone called him Kingpin. He's a lifer. He set a car bomb that killed two cops."

Delilah looked up sharply at him, the terrible reality of it sinking in. And she wobbled over to her couch, hanging onto the arm like she might fall down if she didn't. Like she might throw up.

Amy moved to her side, rubbing her stepdaughter's arm and thankfully not saying anything stupid like "it's going to be okay" or "it doesn't matter."

Nothing about this was okay. Not a single goddamn thing. Everything Delilah had been through. Everyone she'd been surrounded with. How had she not let it drag her down? And here he was, bringing the criminal element right back to her door again. Upending her perfect life. Throwing her right back down in the dirt again.

He wanted to wrap her in his arms and console her. To take it all away from her. But his feet felt glued to the floor. He just felt...*dirty*. Maybe he was. Hadn't he and Jack Glover shared the same address?

As if he was reading Hopper's thoughts, Randy let out a long-suffering sigh. "Baby girl, I'm sorry you had to find out like this. But don't you get it? Don't you see what I'm trying to tell you? Your mother spent the better part of her adult life trying to keep you healthy and safe. Away from the crime and the insecurity. You can't afford to have someone like this one," he growled, stabbing a finger in Hopper's direction, "back in your life. He'll only bring trouble to your door."

The pall of silence fell in the room. Hopper knew this should be the part where he spoke up. Where he started unrolling his resume, telling everybody all the ways he'd been trying to do better and be better. But what would it matter?

Everyone was so upset, so shell-shocked. Himself included. There was no fixing this. That much was plain to see.

"Dammit, I need some air," Randy finally muttered. The man stormed off and wrestled with the door to the unit's tiny balcony until he yanked it open.

Delilah searched his eyes for a long moment, chin trembling. But she shook her head. "I need to—I need to talk to Randy," she murmured before she slid away. Amy patted his arm apologetically as she followed her.

And Hopper stood there, like an asshole, as miserable as he could ever remember being. Shame curdled in his stomach. He'd done this. He'd brought down Randy's wrath on her. And he'd just keep doing this wherever they went. He'd only hold her back, rubbin' her nose in a past she desperately needed to escape, not embrace.

The past...he closed his eyes, willing the memories to leave him be, and the sound of that bus station bell ringer to stop clanging in his head. Yeah, he was alone at Christmas. What else was new? He had the sudden, overwhelming urge to bawl like a lost little boy. But he wouldn't. No, he squared his shoulders like a man and strode off to the bedroom, before he changed his mind. He threw on his shirt, shoes, and coat, and wrote Delilah a note on a scrap of paper he found.

Angel—

Thinking this would work between us again was the biggest lie

I've ever told myself. I'm sorry, baby, for everything I've ever brought to your door—myself included. Randy's right. You deserve better. And that isn't me.

--Hopper

He left the note on her pillow and quietly slipped out the door. When they came back in, he'd be long gone.

CHAPTER 28

HOPPER PICKED up the biggest piece of rusted metal scrap he could find and hurled it to the top of the pile with all his might. It made a loud metallic squeal before it rolled to the bottom again.

"Hey man," Ross called, ambling out to join him in the scrapyard out back of Holliday Hot Rods. "What's all the racket?"

Hopper winced. They were the only two here today. Everyone else had gone home to enjoy their break. He probably seemed like some kind of lunatic, throwing shit around. Maybe he was, after the morning he'd had at Delilah's. He wiped the sweat off his face with the hem of his T-shirt and tried not to act self-conscious. "Just trying to get some of this in order for the recycler." Inspecting their stores of junk, he pulled out his sledgehammer's next victim—a rusted-out car hood—and teed it up for its flattening.

Ross knitted his brows and sipped a beer while he watched Hopper beat the everlovin' crap out of the thing. After a couple of minutes, the guy finally decided to say something. "Hop, you do realize the scrapyard flattens its own stuff. They got big machines for that."

"Yeah, but," Hop sucked in a breath and swung the hammer again with a resounding thud, "they like it when you get things started for them. They can get more in the truck if it's flat."

"Riiiiight." Ross shrugged. "Whatever you say, man. Want a beer?"

He nodded and thanked the man. Ross was back in a flash with an icy-cold long neck. Hopper guzzled it gratefully. He'd worked up quite a sweat out here, in spite of the cold.

Ross unfolded one of the rickety lawn chairs they kept out back and sat down. "So," he sighed, trying to suppress a wry grin. "You wanna tell me who you're really trying to beat up out here?"

That was easy. Himself. But, seeing as how he couldn't punch his own self in the face, these rusty old pieces of scrap would have to do. He glared and didn't answer him. There was nothing to say. He guzzled down the rest of his beer and sent the empty sailing in the direction of the glass recycle bin. But he'd aimed wide, and it hit the concrete wall instead, busting to a million pieces.

Ross raised his eyebrows but didn't follow up with a joke. Apparently, he could see Hopper was in no mood.

Dammit. Now he felt like an ass on top of it all. He'd have to sweep up the glass later. Not sure what else to do, he went back to his hammering. It hurt, and it wore him down to the bone, but there was something in the painful reverb coursing up his arm that seemed satisfying, like a justified punishment.

And through it all, Ross sat in silence, alternating between discreetly staring off in the distance while he downed his beer, or narrowing his eyes at some fool thing Hopper was doing. The man shook his head. "Wow. Beating up an unsuspecting piece of metal and smashing glass. I'd say all this BS has something to do with that gorgeous woman you had on your arm. Am I right?"

He threw down his hammer and wiped the stinging sweat out of his eyes. "Look—the shit on my mind? It can't be fixed. I just need some alone time. You feel me?"

"Yeah, man." Ross nodded and pushed himself back up to his feet. "I feel you. And I get it, okay? Women are confusing. Believe me, if I'd cracked their code, I sure wouldn't be here on my day off. So, in the spirit of friendship, I'll let you have your demolition derby in peace." As he turned to go inside, he gave Hopper one last, worried look. "If you need me, you know where to find me."

Hopper grimly waved him away and went back to his hammering. He wasn't sure why he was doing this, really.

Wham.

He just wanted to smash shit.

Wham.

Why had he thought he could start over?

Wham.

Just say a few pretty words, make a couple of promises, and all the rest of it would go away? He'd never stop paying for what he'd done. Never.

Wham.

Wham.

Wham.

Wham Wham Wham Wham Wham Wham!

He dropped the hammer, chest heaving, and kicked the door he was pounding on so hard he hurt his foot. He swore under his breath, walking it off and muttering for a minute. But he kept going, piling up every kind of unusable junk you could imagine, all smashed nice and flat, thank you very much. But no matter how much he tried to smash the memory of Delilah in his mind, he just couldn't. Thoughts of her kept swimming to the front of his consciousness…

…how tumbled and trusting she'd been while they cuddled in bed.

…her sexy laugh as she'd made fun of his fractured flirting.

…the shine in her eyes and the wind on her cheeks when they'd been on the open road together.

Goddammit, for just one hot minute, he'd been happy. But the moment was gone.

He bellowed as he brought the hammer down again. This time, he'd actually punched a hole in the rusted metal. He threw the hammer to the ground, and bent over with his hands on his knees, breathing hard. This was pointless.

I love her. And I can't stop.

He could wear himself out and beat himself to pieces. But it would never, ever stop being true.

Ross opened the back doorway again. "Hey, Hop," he called, waving the handset for the shop phone. "You got a call."

"Who is it?" he grumbled, walking up to take the receiver.

"I dunno. Some guy named Randy."

"Ms. Cook?" The catering manager gave her a respectful tap on the shoulder. "Dinner service is ready. Shall we begin?"

Lila nodded, barely even noticing the man. She'd had to struggle to pay attention to this event all evening. But as secretary at arms of Mental Health United, it was her job to see that this evening's run of event went off without a hitch. The ball, it appeared, was going to be a success again—and a moneymaker for the charity. Her efforts tonight would help people get mental health services when they couldn't afford them. And that was the important part.

If only she wasn't so distracted, so *jumbled up.*

She excused herself, walking out of the conference center to the considerably less busy ladies' room off the hotel lobby. Lila appreciated the relative seclusion, taking a few calming breaths while she steadied her hands on the cool, white marble countertop. Somehow, she needed to soothe the jittering unease in her stomach before she was called upon to eat. Searching around in her ridiculously tiny purse, she failed to find anything in there that could settle her. She threw the bag down in disgust. Yeah, she'd need a horse tranquilizer for that job.

Wadding up a paper towel, she doused it with water, turning it into a cold compress she laid against the back of her neck. It was well past time she put Hopper out of her mind. Tonight she had a job to do, and she needed to focus. She ran through her mental checklist again like a touchstone. Cocktails had been served. She'd welcomed everyone. She'd given out the lifetime achievement award. They'd shown the inspirational video about the organization's mission. The hard part was over. All they had to do now was get the meal out and the band on the stage for the "dancing the New Year's away" portion of the evening. No further instructions needed. Everything was pre-paid and on autopilot from here.

So why am I such a wreck?

Lila threw the towel down with a smack. She knew the answer to that question, didn't she? *Hopper.*

She'd only gone out on the balcony this morning so she could address Randy's outburst. She'd been right in the middle of telling the man where he could shove his opinions too. But when she'd come back in, Hopper was gone. Just a little poison pen letter left behind.

Yeah, that ended fast.

Leave it to Hopper to turn tail the minute things got rough. But he'd been a coward about everything, hadn't he? He'd been dreaming of a better life. Yet he'd been too afraid to tell her about it. Then he'd lied to her about his extracurricular activities, because he hadn't had the courage to own up to that, either. And now he couldn't even handle Randy calling him out.

Yeah, he could screw his reasons—all his misplaced

nobility and so-called selflessness. Love should've been his reason. It was the *only* reason. And apparently, he didn't care enough about her to stay.

Hopper Vance could go to hell as far as she was concerned.

Her hand shook as she smoothed on a fresh layer of deep red lipstick and fiddled with the French twist she'd lacquered her hair into for the evening. Heartbreak notwithstanding, she was in top form tonight. She'd found the perfect gown at the consignment store—one that was clingy and made of metallic, dark silver lace. She moved over to the bathroom's full-length mirror for an outfit check, smoothing her hands down her stomach.

The dress really was exquisite, molding to her curves without overemphasizing them. The bodice had a high collar but was sleeveless and largely backless. Even though it was floor length, this gown was slinky, with a show-stopping slit that bared her left leg, all the way up to the middle of her thigh. Strappy sandals with a stiletto heel brought out the definition in her calves, and onyx teardrop earrings glittered in her ears, matching her dark hair. Without a doubt, it was her best outfit yet for one of these things.

Dammit, she looked too good tonight to be a mess inside. She would not be miserable over any man. Especially Hopper.

She. Would. Not.

She'd been doing just fine on her own. And she'd carry on this time, too. She didn't need a man, and she certainly didn't need Hopper. Lila willed herself to ignore the miserable ache in her chest, held her head high, and walked back out into the party.

She slid into a chair at the table her practice had sponsored, relieved to see familiar, friendly faces. Three of the four partners were there—Dr. McKendry and his wife Lauren, Dr. Lewis and her husband Jacob, and Dr. Knoll and her fiancée, Marcus. She envied them. They all seemed so settled in life, so comfortable in their own skin.

She smiled at them and took a long drag of the martini she'd ordered.

Dr. Knoll raised one elegant, perfectly shaped eyebrow at her. The woman never missed a trick. The woman may look like an aging Gucci model, but she was probably the smartest person Lila had ever met. And she could read body language like a member of the KGB. "Are you okay, Lila?" she asked.

"I'm fine," Lila answered her, trying her best to sound smooth and controlled. "Why do you ask?"

"Hmmm." Dr. Knoll reached over and gave Lila's arm a reassuring pat. "Therapist's instinct, I suppose. You're a little pale. Pinched, even. And that's your third martini this evening."

Dr. Lewis took off his tortoise shell glasses, clucking sympathetically as he wiped them clean with his tie. "Oh Delilah, dear. We've been asking an awful lot of you. Keeping our billing straight. Running the office. And running all this, too. You didn't have to, you know."

Delilah knew his comment came from a kindly, fatherly place. But the suggestion still rankled. "Of course I know. I volunteered, remember? Kathryn did so much important work for this organization, and I wanted to see it continued."

They all leaned forward conspiratorially, focusing their attention rather playfully on her. "Well, nonetheless, we don't like seeing you upset. And we don't like mysteries, either. So it goes without saying, we'll be figuring this out," Dr. Lewis trilled. "Lila clearly isn't talking. But didn't Sherlock Holmes have that saying… once you've eliminated all the possibilities, the impossible must be true?"

"Ooo, deductive reasoning. I'll play," Lauren smirked, twirling her glass. "So it's not that she's ill."

"And she says it's not the stress of the event," Dr.

McKendry took his wife's lead, and lifted a pinky to the corner of his mouth like an evil genius. "Very *innnnteresting.*"

"Oh, for God's sake." Lila snorted, but she couldn't help smiling at this endearing crew. "What is this, a game of Clue? Who got to Delilah? Was it Reverend Green with a candlestick?"

"Hmm. I don't know." Dr. Knoll grinned. "For my money, I think Colonel Mustard with a rope would be way more entertaining."

The whole table burst into a riot of naughty laughter.

Until a deep, raspy voice rang out behind her. "Looks like I'm in luck. I guess I've landed me a seat at the fun table."

No.

It *couldn't* be.

But when she turned, her heart tripped helplessly in her chest.

Hopper. It was him, but…

She let out a breath, amazed by the sight in front of her. Not just that he was here, of course. But that he'd come here dressed like *that.* He looked so good—so *different*—she hardly recognized him. His hair was slicked with some kind of pomade, so he had a shock of hair arched roguishly over his forehead. And his beard was trimmed up close to his face, coming down to a precise point at his chin.

But that wasn't what shocked her. It was his suit—jet black and tailored to perfection, trimmed tight enough against his hulking muscles to make him seem…sophisticated. How could this be the same man who'd grumbled about wearing khakis to The Greenbrier? No, this man was a vision in black—with sharp-pointed, black dress shoes, a black dress shirt, and a shiny silk tie in thick, bold black-and-white stripes. Her gaze caught a scrap of black-and-white, polka-dotted fabric. Sweet Jesus—was that a *pocket square?*

"I'm sorry I'm late." Hopper smiled apologetically while

he slid into the seat beside her. "I'm Hopper Vance. Kathryn told me you had an extra seat."

"Ah, yes!" Dr. Lewis clucked. "I totally forgot. Kathryn texted me earlier and asked if we had any spots. She said you had a special connection to the event and wanted to come."

As the lightning bolt of shock started to wear off, anger bubbled up inside Lila, pure and hot. How dare he? How *dare* he tell her goodbye, and then just show up here like nothing had happened? And involving Kathryn in all this too!

Hopper had thrown her away not just once but twice. *Twice!* And here he was, stirring up all this while she was in the middle of an important work event?

Oh, no. Oh, *hell* no.

She turned to him, hoping her face looked as furious as she felt. Hopper blinked uncomfortably as the message was received. Vulnerability flashed in his eyes, but he set his jaw in a determined smile.

"Ah!" Dr. Knoll clucked, her assessing gaze moving back and forth between the two of them. "You've met!"

"Yes," Hopper rushed to answer, before she could. "Delilah and I are old childhood friends. We've recently become reacquainted."

Reacquainted? Is that what he calls it?

Well she was glad he had a word for it. Because the words she had in her head weren't fit for polite company. She turned to him, fury and disbelief pounding through her.

The expression on her face must've said it all. Her coworkers exchanged sly glances with each other, like they were tickled to death to solve the case. Heat rose to Lila's cheeks, and she wadded her napkin in her fist. Oh, she couldn't *stand* this!

"I-I need to go check with the caterer." she jumped to her feet, as smoothly as she could manage. Hopper scowled with concern as she fled, but he didn't go after her.

Lila spent the next few minutes circling the room,

pretending to monitor the catering staff, who didn't exactly need her supervision to do something as simple as putting plates down on tables. She frittered around, waiting until all the attendees had been served and her table mates were well into their entrees. It may have been a petty thing to do. But she wasn't hiding. She was shortening the torture, that's all.

Though she'd tried to keep her eyes on the catering staff, she kept sneaking glances at her table. Everyone seemed to be having a lovely time. Hopper smiled and joked, and the rest of them did too. And honestly, that surprised her. She was so sure Hopper would've been terribly uncomfortable without her there. But he wasn't.

When she finally stopped waffling and slid back into her seat, Dr. Knoll was holding Hopper's hand like a fortune teller and giggling.

Dr. Knoll held up Hopper's hands in her direction. "Oh my gawd, Lila. Have you seen these tattoos on his knuckles? They're Viking runic letters that spell out—get this—L-O-N-E W-O-L-F."

"Yeah." Hopper cringed sheepishly. "I kinda regret that one. I got them when I was inside, thinking it'd make me a badass. But the first rule of intimidation is people need to be able to read the letters. Instead, they'd have to ask me. And when I told them, the guys just ended up laughin', like I was the world's biggest emo idiot. Ended up getting the nickname LW for my trouble."

Dr. Mc Kendry chuckled right along, his gray beard twitching with humor. "My God. What a story. I've always regretted not getting a tattoo when I was younger. But maybe I was wise not to do it, after all. Do you regret any of your other tattoos?"

Hopper turned to Delilah, his expression going soft. "No. And I don't think I ever will."

Delilah would've snorted derisively if she could. He would try to play the angel tattoo card, wouldn't he? The man was making her dizzy with all his see-sawing back and forth. What would his heartfelt profession be tomorrow? And the next day? Dammit, she wasn't strong enough to handle this.

Lila just let the comment go and picked around at the filet mignon and fingerling potatoes on her plate. But her stomach shrank in misery. She hadn't been able to eat a bite all day, and it appeared the knot in her stomach wouldn't be going away any time soon. How could it, when Hopper was there, chatting away to her employers like he'd had some kind of personality transplant?

They asked him one intrusive question after another, and he just answered them, like it wasn't any big deal. His jail time. His offenses. What it was like to be in jail. What inmates had to deal with in there. Why he'd decided to get his degree. The opportunities for inmates, if only they'd take them. And the new life he'd found for himself at Holliday Hot Rods.

When they found out he worked directly with Hunter, the whole table erupted in back pats and congratulations. They loved Hunter, and by extension, they loved Hopper too. And that didn't surprise Lila necessarily. It didn't embarrass her, either. But it did kinda shock her to see him so...*open* about it all. That was new.

Conversation paused with the arrival of the dessert course, and everyone's plates were set with a tall champagne flute of chocolate mousse. Hopper cocked his head quizzically at the tiny, long-handled spoon they'd given him. But he dug in enthusiastically anyway. "I'm sorry if I've been holding court over here and monopolizing the conversation," he leaned over to say. "You've been awful quiet, angel."

She gritted her teeth. *"Don't* call me angel."

Hopper regarded her, silently and steadily, like he was talking himself out of arguing with her. Apparently sensing the tension between them, Dr. Knoll rescued the conversation by peppering Delilah with questions about the event and how much money they'd raised. And she gratefully filled the minutes making small talk about the ball foundation, sharing mundane updates about who was going to be on the board next year, why they'd chosen this new hotel for the event, and things like that.

Lila had just about chatted up all her safe topics when blessedly, the music kicked up. The local band they'd picked was great and specialized in disco oldies that made you want to get up and dance. And the minute the musicians started to cover K.C. and the Sunshine Band, that's what everyone at her table did. Lila suspected it was part of a communal plot to force her and Hopper to sit together like civilized people and hash things out. But she was more or less trapped no matter what they did.

There was a long, painful silence while the two of them sat there, not quite sure what to say. Finally, he turned to her. "Do you want to dance?"

Images of what had happened the last time he'd asked her that flashed through her mind, of him down on his knees...

A stray shot of desire jolted through her, somehow only making her angrier. "No," she growled. She stood up, shaky on her feet but needing to be anywhere but here. Hopper reached out to stop her. The heat of his hand wrapped around her arm, branding her like an iron. She started to pull away, but he just circled his thumb against the tender underside of her wrist, his expression brimming over with a pained kind of desperation she'd never seen from him before. "Delilah...don't go. *Please.*"

A part of her didn't want to. But she yanked her arm away anyway, if nothing but for sheer self-preservation. And she stalked off, barely avoiding a full-out run. Suddenly, it felt like the room was closing in on her, and she had to wrestle free, from the past, from the present...from the pain pressing down on her.

It was too much. She crossed the ballroom and burst into the hallway, stomping off to nowhere in particular. Her vision blurred, but she just kept walking anyway, wiping furiously at her tears. Down a hall. Around a corner. Past waitstaff. She didn't care. She'd walk in circles if she had to—anything to master the heartache threatening to swallow her whole.

She didn't know what to do with it. With *any* of it.

Until she felt a hand dart out from a shadowy, unused alcove and pull her in. She almost screamed until she realized it was Hopper.

"I'm sorry!" he yelped. *"I'm sorry, I'm sorry, I'm sorry.* I didn't mean to scare you. I didn't think you were going to stop any other way. I'm not here to hurt you, I swear. I just...I just...Delilah *please,* I really need to talk to you."

She chuckled ruefully. "You're not here to hurt me. You sure about that?"

He held up his hands in surrender. "Alright. I deserved that. That and a whole lot more, really. Just hear me out. Please? Pretty please?"

Lila hesitated for a long moment, but finally gave him the smallest of nods.

He let out a long breath, clearly relieved that she'd do that much. "I let myself get spooked. I let Randy get up in my head today. And I shouldn't have."

Lila crossed her arms over her chest. "Yet, here you are, doing a total one-eighty from this morning."

"That's right."

She narrowed her eyes. "What changed your mind?"

"Randy did."

Lila blinked stupidly, her mouth hanging open. *"Randy."*

"I could hardly believe it, either. But the man called me. He said he'd talked to you, and you'd told him all about the man I'd become. And he said when he'd left your place, you'd been bawling your eyes out. He felt real bad about that. Said you never made it to your brunch reservations and you hadn't exchanged presents. He was all upset he'd ruined your Christmas."

Lila sighed. "I'm aware. He apologized."

"I can't fault the man. He was just doing his job. If I was your stepdad, I can't say I would've reacted any different. It's a miracle I didn't get punched. Let's face it. I'm not exactly the kind of man most women would take home for Sunday dinner."

Indignation spiked through her. This again? Lila wasn't going to grace that with a response. She was sick of him saying garbage like this. And she didn't have the energy for all the reassuring mantras she'd have to spew. She just crossed her arms across her chest and stared at him.

"Talking to Randy this afternoon…it really got me thinking about why I freaked out and ran." He frowned and shook his head with a rueful certainty. "I've spent my whole life believing I didn't deserve you, Delilah. I've always believed I was tainted in some way. From the very beginning."

She stilled. "Why? Because your dad left you?"

He drew a sharp breath, but finally nodded. "Yeah. And because I didn't have a dime to my name. I wanted you, Delilah, from the first moment I laid eyes on you. But you were so young. *We* were so young. And I believed I needed to turn myself into somebody before I could ask you to love me. Because I felt like you deserved more than plain old penniless me. A street rat. And then a low-level mechanic, making it month to month. I sold myself some stupid dreams—dreams that didn't fit me—all because I could never believe I was enough. That was really it. It's like my self-esteem was some terrible, bottomless pit and I had to fill it up with something before I could have you."

His words hit her hard. They scraped at her soul, poking her in the places that'd hurt the most. *God, Hopper.* It broke her heart that he saw himself that way. She let out a long, shaky breath, and her eyes welled up with tears again.

He had this wound inside of him that wouldn't heal. This belief that he wasn't enough. But it was time he knew the truth.

So she took both his hands in hers. "I owe you an apology too, Hopper."

He lowered his eyebrows, looking fierce. "No, no, you don't owe me one goddamn thing."

"Shh. Don't. Not until you've listened to what I have to say. I have something to tell you, and you're not going to like it." His eyes widened. But he didn't say anything. So she continued. "Like I told you back at the Outpost, I saw what happened with your dad at the bus station."

He nodded, almost imperceptibly.

"You never knew what happened after that. Where he went, or what became of him?"

"No. How could I?"

"Well, Earl showed me what happened...after."

"What?" he breathed, his voice sounding too thin, too pained.

She squeezed his hand. "John was dying, Hop. Kidney failure. Advanced cirrhosis. He even had an enlarged heart. He didn't leave you because you were broken or too much trouble, either. He left because he didn't want his teenaged son to have to go through all that with him. He..." Her voice broke just for a second, the words so weighty, she could hardly speak them out loud. "He *refused dialysis,* Hop. God, I'm so, so sorry. But he was dead in a month."

Hopper staggered backward, completely and utterly stricken. He whipped back around, facing the dark corner, hiding his face. He sucked in a labored breath, and then he slammed the wall with the flat of his hand with all his might. "Goddammit!" he wailed. "Goddammit, goddammit, goddammit!" He pounded it again, the smack echoing loudly in the empty hallway. "I would've stayed with him. So help me. I would've done anything for him. He was my father!" She rubbed his back, feeling him literally shake with grief. "We were supposed to stay together," he whispered.

"He knew that," she murmured. "He knew if he told you, you never would've left his side. And he didn't want that. I saw him go straight from that bus station to the Veteran's Hospital. He went into the hospital and never came out. He never lived on his own again."

He took a couple more breaths. "His grave," he groaned. "Where is his grave?"

"There was no money for all that. He donated his body to science."

"Oh!" He gasped, a strangled, surprised cry coming from his throat. And it was like his legs just went out from under him. He collapsed into the corner, sobbing so hard, she barely recognized him.

Hopper. Oh, baby.

She settled herself onto the floor with him, wrapping her arms around him tight. How could she not? His helpless tears soaked into the lace at her neck, and she held him, simply held him, while great waves of grief seemed to roll off him in big, heated bellows. Guilt stabbed at her. Had she done the right thing, telling him? Or should she have told him sooner? She'd thought knowing the truth might help him understand and heal his wounds. But seeing his reaction, she wasn't so sure.

"I can't even pay my respects. There's nothing left..." He hiccoughed dejectedly.

"Yeah there is, Hopper," she whispered to him. "There's you. *You're* what's left. John's legacy, walking in the world."

She'd meant to reassure him, but it didn't work. He just let out a derisive chuckle in between sobs. Delilah had never seen him like this before—so truly beside himself. But as hard as it was to see his soul-deep tears, there was something good about it. Cleansing. He stood in truth. Hopper's father was gone. And at the end, his daddy had just been doing the best he could.

It took several long, long, minutes, but Hopper finally calmed enough to wipe his tears away. He didn't seem angry anymore. He simply looked…hollowed out. "Why didn't you tell me?"

She gave him her best apologetic shrug. "I was waiting for the right time?"

Hopper shook his head, rueful amusement playing at the corners of his mouth. The absurdity of this situation wasn't lost on either one of them.

"Oh man," Hopper wheezed as he leaned his head back against the wall and gathered her up underneath his arm. "It's going to take me years to process this. But I guess we both have had our daddy issues today. I just wanted to say, for the record, that I'm sorry about all that business with Jack Glover. That was a helluva way to learn about your father, and it couldn't have been good news. But if you're curious, just ask. I'll be happy to tell you what I can."

She circled her arms around his waist and leaned her head against his broad chest. She may be crashed on the floor in a designer gown, but somehow, in Hopper's arms, she didn't feel out of place. Mulling over his offer to tell her more, she seriously wondered if she should take him up on it. She kept waiting for some kind of feeling to manifest, some burning desire to learn about her father. But none came. No, she truly didn't care. "I think I need to keep Jack Glover in my past." She sighed. "I can't imagine what good could come from meeting the man. Mama didn't want him to be part of my life then, and if he's half as scary as what you say, then that was the right call. Let's just call that chapter closed, okay?"

Lila threaded her fingers through his and squeezed. And he raised her hand to his mouth and kissed it, casually and so naturally, it made her heart squeeze. Like he'd done it a thousand times. Come to think of it, maybe he had. When Hopper turned to her, she couldn't look away.

Hopper. He really was like family, wasn't he? The kind of family you made—the kind you gathered to yourself because you couldn't do without them. She tried to reassemble her anger, tried to remember how she came to be in this dark corner with him in the first place. But she couldn't. She was tied to this man. He was part of her—of her past, of the person she'd become. Maybe there was a reason the Outpost had helped her navigate time using gifts. In one way or another, he'd been a gift to her all her life, hadn't he?

Her heart swelled with the realization. She could never, ever leave Hopper Vance. He was essential to her as food, or light, or breathing. He was hers. And she was his.

And there was no running away from that.

She pulled out from under his arm and gathered his hands into her lap. "Does it really matter all the things that happened in our lives? We may be shaped by our past, by our heritage. But the only thing that truly defines us is the person we are today, and the choices we make, moment to moment. And the people we choose to be with us, of course."

Lila's throat got too thick to continue.

But Hopper understood. He leaned forward and kissed her, slow and sweet, and rested his forehead against hers. "I choose you, angel. I'll always choose you."

She cupped his bristly cheek. "Yeah. I choose you too."

"Promise?"

Just then, a distant cheer went up from the ballroom and "Auld Lang Syne" began to play. "Yeah, I promise. I love you, Hopper Vance. I think I always have."

He pulled back to look at her, as if to confirm that she really meant it. When his eyes met hers, he smiled so brilliantly that it lit up her up from her head to her toes. "God, I love you too. So much. I haven't told you that before. But I swear, I'll tell you every day of your life. I'll tell you so much you'll get sick of hearing it."

She dipped her head for more of his decadent kisses, a sensation that was everything good, everything right in this world. Lila fell into the deep of it, tumbling with him. Somehow, she ended up straddling his lap, the slit in her dress turning out to be remarkably handy.

She threw her arms around his neck, arching against him while they scorched each other, one torrid kiss at a time. She rolled her hips, grinding against his lap, and he shuddered as he stiffened up hard.

"Ohhhh, man." He wheezed. "You're killing me."

"I want you." She traced kisses up his neck, fumbling frantically with his tie and the top buttons of his shirt. "I'll never make it until we get back to my place."

But he grabbed her hands. "You know I've never been able to resist the Delilah special. But I've got a better idea." He reached into his jacket pocket and pulled out a room key card.

Lila couldn't help giggling. "You, Hopper Vance, are one classy guy."

He shrugged, and leveled her with a devastating, lopsided smile. "I try."

He got up to his feet and held out his hand to her. They turned toward the elevators, his arm draped proudly over her shoulder. Lila couldn't resist the urge to reach around and pinch his ass. He yelped playfully and gave her a sloppy kiss on the cheek.

Lila smiled up at him. "Nice suit, by the way. You look amazing in it."

He beamed at her. "You like it, huh? It's Hunter's. God bless the man for letting me borrow it. I would've never gotten a suit that fit with so little time to spare. Hunter's a big guy, like me. But we still had to make alterations. Kathryn had to let it out in the leg and the sleeve and—" he waggled his eyebrows, "—in the crotch."

"I don't doubt it." She snickered and slid her hand into his back pocket.

And they disappeared down the hall. Together.

CHAPTER 29

CHRISTMAS EVE, ONE YEAR LATER

HOPPER LOOKED out the back window, and there Delilah was, rumbling up the alley behind his house in that little Corvair he'd finished for her. He grinned. Damn, that old car really did rock its sparkly purple paint and striped seats. But the dog was making way too much noise.

"Shhhh, sweetheart," Hopper whispered, half giggling. "You gotta be quiet. She's almost here. Don't want to spoil the big reveal, do ya?"

The dog just blinked up at him and cocked her head. She woofed again, but softer this time. To his amazement, she laid back down with her nose between her paws, as quiet as you please. He was beginning to think the little bugger really did understand what he was saying to her.

Hopper straightened up the big red bow around her neck and locked the new baby gate firmly in place. "Remember," he held a finger up to his lips. "Shhh. Be cool."

"Honey! I'm home!" Delilah called as she came piling through the back door with all her packages.

Hopper did his best to come strolling casually around the corner. He leaned over the table and gave her a kiss. "I love it when you say that."

She grinned. "Well, if I'm going to be your wife, you'd better get used to it. Come on and help me unload all this stuff."

Dutifully, he helped her drag all the boxes and bags she had with her over to the kitchen table. "This is your last load, isn't it? Surely to God that's it."

She pushed up on her toes, threw her arms around his neck, and kissed him properly this time. *Mmmm*…soft, sweet, delicious. Just like always. She gave him a flirty tug on his shirt before she wheeled away. Opening a box, she pulled out a string of huge origami angels and cutwork snowflakes, each one of them the size of a hubcap. "Didn't they turn out great? Didn't I tell you the kids would do a great job?"

He couldn't help beaming at the woman. "Yes, you did—and they did," he answered her. And it was true. The woman was a genius at creating low-cost strategies for doing up their wedding. She kept saying they were "Pinterest-worthy."

Supersized, backlit origami streamers were the lynchpin of her wedding decor strategy. Delilah had made friends up and down the street. Since one of their neighbors was an art teacher at their local middle school, his brilliant fiancée had been able to broker a deal. In exchange for Delilah teaching free classes in origami art, she'd gotten a legion of interested kids to help them with this project, free of charge.

He was so stoked. After their Christmas dinner tomorrow, they were going to hang them at Holliday Hot Rods, from one end of the shop to the other. The whole ceiling would be covered, and with the enormous size of these things, it'd be just the right scale to turn the place into a winter fairyland. It may be an unconventional place to get married, but after seeing how nice Kathryn and Hunter's wedding had turned out there, it was the only one they'd considered.

They'd put their own spin on the place, though. On the grandest scale imaginable, they'd be making something out of nothing. The day after tomorrow, he'd be marrying the woman of his dreams. And that wasn't "nothing." It was *everything.*

Augh.

The scrabbling sound of doggy toenails on hardwood floor rang out. Apparently, the dog had reached its quiet limit.

Delilah furrowed her brows. "Hop? What's that noise?" She started to move toward the spare bedroom, where he had the dog corralled.

But he jumped in her path and put both hands on her shoulders. "So, babe, before you go look in there, I just wanted to tell you I got us a couple of early Christmas presents. And one of them is in that room. I hope you like it."

She gave him a pouty smile and narrowed her eyes. "What are you up to, Hopper Vance?"

He stuck his hands in his pockets and rolled back on his heels. "Why don't you go see?"

She was screaming and squealing and busting down the baby gate, even before he'd turned the corner. "You got a dog! Oh my God! She's the cutest thing I've ever seen!" The pup leaped straight into her arms and started licking on her. She was an affectionate fluffball, for sure. "Who's the goodest good girl in the whole wide world? You are! Yes, you are!" Delilah cooed.

The dog wiggled her butt all over Delilah's lap, and the woman was loving every minute of it.

He propped his shoulder against the doorjamb, enjoying his front row seat for this new, happy ruckus in his house. "I'd been thinking about getting a dog for a while. I know we hadn't discussed it. I'm so glad you like her. It seemed like the perfect Christmas surprise."

"Like her?" she squawked. "How evil would you have to be not to like this perfect little smudgie mcfee? Seriously, Hop. She's the cutest damn dog in the universe. I wonder what

kind of breeds she's got in her. She's shaped like a Corgi, with the stumpy legs and the pointy ears. But check out her coat, though. White with brown speckles. Where do you suppose that comes from?"

"The pound said she's probably Corgi with Australian Shepherd and Golden Retriever in her. Whatever she is, she's a mutt, through and through."

"And prettier than all the purebred dogs in the land," she cooed. The dog must've agreed, because she licked Delilah right on the eyelid. But Delilah just cracked up laughing and cuddled her more. "What do you think we should name her?"

"Something Christmassy, I think. Snowdrop, maybe?"

Lila frowned and got up to come wrap her arms around his waist. "Not bad, but seems a little too on the nose, don't you think? Like naming a fluffy dog fluffy." She stopped to think for a minute, resting her head on his chest. "I wouldn't be opposed to calling her Cookie. God, I can't wait to be rid of that nickname, and the Cook last name to boot. It was never me. It was just something I was hiding behind."

"You'll be Delilah Vance soon enough."

She smacked him on the rear end and pushed off. "That's right, you sexy beast. And don't you forget it."

He couldn't wait for them to start their new life together. After Christmas break, Delilah was starting a new job in administration at the Osteopath College in town. He'd already gotten all her stuff moved in. And they were headed out for a great honeymoon, to Switzerland—a first for both of them—to stay in a real Alpine village and try their hands at world-class skiing. Who knew? Maybe they'd be lucky enough to get a pregnancy out of the trip. But if they didn't? This dog would do them just fine.

They'd have to name their lil' darlin' first. Hopper rubbed his chin as he thought about it. "I can't get behind the idea of giving the dog your old nickname. Doesn't seem respectful."

She picked up the dog who, he was surprised to see, was

A-okay with being handled and carried. The pup curled up in her arms like she was her favorite purse. "Well." Delilah sighed. "She is as sweet as a cookie, anyway." She paused for a moment, but soon a mischievous grin spread across her face. "Oh my God. I've got it. I know exactly what we should call her. *Candy.*"

He whooped. "Oh my Lord. We'd better hope we don't run into her again. Don't you think the old biddy will be pissed if we named a dog after her?"

"With this face?" She munched up the pup's face in her hands. "It's the world's greatest compliment. We're naming the dog in her honor. Because without her, there's a very good chance we wouldn't have any of this. Our trip through the Outpost might've been the best gift of all."

"How can I argue with that?" He bent over and gave the dog a kiss on its furry head. "Candy it is. With that settled, I've got one more gift to show you. Come on."

He led her by the elbow to the front door while she protested all the way. "Come on, babe, how could you give me anything else? I've got a motorcycle, a car, a house, a dog, and a man."

He opened the door, letting the dog down so she could explore the front yard. And Candy went straight to his present, giving it a proper sniffing.

She gasped. "A rose arbor. Oh my God! It's beautiful!"

He pulled her into the yard, right down to the place where their front door sidewalk teed up to the neighborhood sidewalk. He'd installed the biggest white vinyl rose arbor he could find in that spot, for a very particular reason.

"Come 'ere, come 'ere." He motioned to her. "Isn't it great? Come spring, I'm going to connect a white picket fence to it so Candy will have someplace safe to wander around." He made her stand right in front of him so she could view the front of the house through the frame of the arbor.

Lila stood there in confusion for a moment. But then a

slow smile spread across her face. "My drawing." Her eyes started to mist up. "It's just like my drawing…"

"I never forgot that drawing," he said, wrapping his arms around her from behind. "It was your childhood dream, right on a plate, wasn't it?"

"Yeah." She tipped her head up to smile at him. "It was."

He rested his chin on the top of her head and nuzzled her hair. "I think, on some level I wasn't even aware of, I was thinking about that drawing when I bought the house. I was out here putting up the Christmas lights, and it just hit me. I had to buy the rose arbor then. I even got the roses. They're in the basement under grow lights. They'll be all nice and mature for planting in a few months."

"Oh, really?" She turned. "What kind did you get?"

"They're a red climbing rose variety, with nice big, thick blooms. You're not gonna believe what they're called though." He held up his hands. "I swear. I'm not making this up."

She turned around and gave him a playful little shove. "What?"

"They're Don Juan roses."

She burst out laughing.

And that was a sound he could get used to hearing, for the rest of his life.

The End

SO, WHAT DID YOU THINK?

I'd be so pleased and grateful if you could leave a review. It's easy, and you'll help others find me online!

Review My Book
(https://www.amazon.com/dp/B08GZRYMKS)

And when you're done with that, keep going. More great excerpts and freebies are ahead!

You've Read Hopper and Delilah's story. But have you read Ross and Lita's? Read on, for a free excerpt from Liza's other book in the *Mountain Magic Christmas Series*...

Sweet Like Christmas
a steamy, magical, friends-to-lovers romance
Out now!

CHAPTER 1

Corn+Flour Bakery,
Lewisburg, WV

LITA NOE DIDN'T SHOCK EASILY. She prided herself on that point.

But one look at the text her uncle had just sent, and she nearly coughed up her morning order of Mountain Mud coffee.

Her buddy Ross used his position behind her in line to rub her shoulders in sympathy. "Christ, Lee." He snickered. "What's on that phone? 'Cause seriously, you're gonna cough up a lung here."

Groaning, she sipped her coffee again to correct that swallowed-it-down-the-wrong-way sensation and debated whether she should show it to him. Lord knew, once he saw it, Ross would never let her hear the end of it.

But she flipped the phone around anyway, masochist that she was. "*This* is what Uncle J wants me to wear to his costume ball on New Year's Eve," she told him, pointing to the picture of the barely there proposed outfit—Leeloo, from the movie *The Fifth Element.*

Gah. The "costume" could pass for five strips of Ace bandages, strategically placed. Any one of which, were it to slip by more than a half inch, would leave her functionally naked.

Ross widened his eyes for a second but, predictably, soon launched into a round of way-too-loud whooping and clapping. "Awwww, yeah. Now *that's* what I'm talkin' about. I'd spend good money to see you in that!"

Heat leapt to her cheeks, and she gave him a shove. "Would you *stop* it?"

His bright blue eyes flashed with amusement under his choppy mess of goth black hair. "What?" he smirked.

Lita elbowed him in the ribs. "You know half the town will be wondering what we were talkin' about."

They both scanned the establishment to find that yes, in fact, *all* the people waiting in line for their breakfast had looked up from their phones. Lita cringed. The ambient pop music playing in this quaint downtown bakery bounced loudly off the exposed brick walls, and the chatter hushed. But no one said anything or asked them any questions, though. Just a couple of fond smiles and head nods from the friends and neighbors she knew. And the kitchen staff were way too busy to care.

She blew out a breath.

"See?" Ross nudged her. "This is West Virginia, honey. People care. But they're not gonna get *that* far up in your business."

She supposed that was true. Besides, she and Ross had grown up in this cozy, historic town of about three thousand people, nestled in the shadow of the Allegheny mountains.

Everyone here knew them, if not directly, then by reputation. She was the tough punk chick who did tattoo art on the side and had mermaid-colored braids down to her waist. Ross was the highly talented metalworker and mechanic who liked to party. Of course, everyone had heard of their employer, Holliday Hot Rods—an antique car restoration and collision repair shop that was getting a national reputation for museum-quality work. Most people understood that she and Ross had been tight since high school, too.

They'd been BFFs since sophomore year, and they were twenty-eight now. So that was what—thirteen years now? Messing around with each other like this was simply what they did.

Still. She'd rather it not get around that her uncle was encouraging her to streak her way through Hairball in the Holler this New Year's Eve, thank you very much. No matter how fabulous the man was trying to make the event. She shook her head at her screen. What was that queen thinkin'?

She and Ross leaned a bit more discreetly against the pastry case, and he hung his head over her shoulder to get a better view of the outfit. "Think he'll want you to wear the red wig?" he asked her.

Lita snorted. "And miss the chance to show off his handiwork? Not likely. My head is the best billboard for the salon he could ever have."

Ross broke out another one of his lopsided, sly grins. "You do turn heads, Lee. Thought you'd be used to that by now."

Was she? It wasn't something she even thought about anymore. She'd been the girl with the crazy colored hair and the nose stud since middle school, thanks to having a family in the beauty business. Her mom and Jesús, Mom's brother, had always been hairdressers. But when they'd gotten a tip on a salon that was selling for cheap here in Lewisburg, they'd moved the family up here from Florida. The move had been the right one, allowing Mom and J to truly launch themselves as beauty influencers.

Divalicious was regionally known, mainly because of Uncle J. His before-and-after makeovers had become a legit Instagram and TikTok sensation. And their reputation had been well earned, not only from their work, but from the deep relationships Mom and J had formed in the community. The Hairball in the Holler regularly earned into the six figures for the Greenbrier Valley foodbank system. And they did it by making the event into a spectacle—a parade of hair artistry, costumes, and J's posse from his days on the drag queen competition circuit. Around here, it was *the* place to party on New Year's Eve.

Ross placed his hand over his heart and sighed dreamily. "All I can say is, if I saw you wearing that, I'd be up all night. And when I say *up,* I mean up—"

Lita laughed, cutting him off. "Stop slobbering, dog." That boy never missed an opportunity. But *she* knew *he* knew that act wasn't playin' with her. Eager to get the topic off the prospect of her soon-to-be exposed skin, she wagged her finger at him. "Hey, don't pretend that you didn't get a message too. I heard the alert. So what cosplay is he putting you in?"

Ross smirked and showed her his phone.

Shirtless Neo—from *The Matrix,* complete with black patent leather pants and a matching patent leather trench. Lita had to grin at the perfection of it. Ross may be a little rough around the edges sometimes. He was rangy, and mouthy, and dressed in baggy urban streetwear that didn't suit him. But she'd seen enough snatches of his skin over the years to know he was chiseled under all that, with the palest of complexions and a collection of some seriously cool, black-and-white surrealist tats.

Ross Mason had a certain something about him. A presence, maybe. He could *totally* pull off Keanu. But she wouldn't be telling him that anytime soon. The boy's ego was big enough.

Lita was about to lob a joke about patent leather and rashes when the door whooshed open, and she lost her train of thought. A blast of cold wind and glittery snowflakes skittered over the threshold as two new customers stepped inside. The middle-aged man and old woman caught Lita's attention, mainly because she'd never seen them here before. The woman was a tiny little thing, bent with age, but with long, wild, curly white hair and fiery, brilliant blue eyes. Despite her determined bearing, she hobbled, leaning heavily on the man she was with.

Her son, maybe? Grandson? It was hard to tell. When you considered the man in one light, he seemed like a guy in his twenties. In another, he seemed ageless and weathered, his hair radiating a faint, silvery hue. The man was tall, well-muscled and dressed in expensive camo pants and military-grade boots, a black long-sleeved tee, and a black pea coat. Like he was three different military branches at once, and yet none of them at all. She studied the way he patted the old lady's hand. He clearly was catering to her, and helpful, but she didn't see the warmth of a family bond there. A bodyguard? Or a caregiver, maybe?

"Here, get in front of us." Lita waved to them. "We're in the front of the line. You won't have to stand so long."

The old woman sized them up, and for a second, Lita almost moved back a step at her penetrating gaze. Then a smile broke across the woman's well-lined face, sweet and surprised. She hobbled over in their direction. "Oh! Aren't you kind? You see so little of that these days."

"It's no trouble ma'am," she murmured, letting the old lady pat her arm.

Suzie, the bakery's owner was working the rush today, and she waved to get her attention. "Hey Carmellllliiita!" she sang out, as she rushed around behind the counter. "Your breakfast bowls are all done, and I put those two extra coffees in the carrier for the rest of the crew. But the tray of cinnamon rolls for the shop just came out of the oven. It's cooling on the counter. Give me a minute for the icing, okay?"

Suzie hustled up, all smiles and warm welcomes, and handed the bags to Ross. Lita grinned gratefully at her. Suzie was a sharp businesswoman, and smart enough to know to have the same Holliday Hot Rods order ready every Monday. She and Ross were a bit early today, so they settled in to wait, checking their phones.

Lita listened with half an ear while Suzie took the order for the old lady and her companion, only glancing up briefly when the man excused himself to the back of the restaurant to take a call.

Resigned to her romantic fate, Lita grumbled under her breath as she opened her Tinder app. If she wanted to find a *date*-date to a complicated costume bash like the Hair Ball, she was cutting it a bit too close.

Honestly, she felt a little weird about opening the app up outside the confines of her apartment. The last thing she needed was for someone to spot her standing there, scrolling through Tinder, looking desperate. Yet, considering her last boyfriend in a long line of crappy boyfriends had ghosted himself away six months ago, "desperate" was pretty much exactly what she was.

Okay, maybe not desperate.

Option deprived.

She thumbed through her latest string of choices and stifled a curse. *Really?* All these matches were guys she either knew or in many cases, had dated at least once already. *That's small town life, isn't it?* She hovered over the button to increase the search radius when she heard Ross snort overhead.

"What's the matter, Leeeee, have you kicked the local dating pool already?"

"You're one to talk," she huffed. *"P-snap."*

Ross reddened up at the mention of his old nickname, and he shuffled on his feet. "Man. You get a tongue piercing for *one year* in high school, and all of a sudden you've got a rep with the ladies."

Lita rolled her eyes. "Not that I'd know."

Ross leaned an arm on the pastry case and gave her another long, lingering perusal, like he was about to make another one of his standard flirty jokes. But it was a feint. The man snatched the phone from her hands instead.

"Hey!" she yelped.

"Well now," he crooned as he tapped the screen. "Let's see who's up in queue here. There's Bo-hunk Gaither." He shook his head. "You don't want him. He's an even bigger dog than me, and that's saying something. And gawd. Here's Marcel French. Seriously, the guy who assists at the podiatrist's office? What a nerd!"

"He's an intern!" she protested.

"Even worse. He's *interning* to learn how to saw people's bunions." He shuddered theatrically, still smirking. "Ugh, he's a total mama's boy. And haven't you heard? Marcel has a secret stockpile of size-five high heels that he likes to lick in his spare time. Not that I'm proud to know that 'lil tidbit. Next!"

Lita crossed her arms over her chest and glowered at the man. But Ross kept thumbing.

It didn't take long before he stopped and raised a pierced eyebrow at her. "Uh-oh. Lee? What's Cam Longstreet doing in here? Didn't you catch him cheating on you last fall?"

"Last summer, actually, not that it's any business of yours. He keeps showing up in my matches. What can I say?"

Ross wiggled the phone between his fingers. "*Why* are you putting yourself through this?"

"I need a date for the Hairball, *okay?* You happy? Now can I please have my phone back?"

His eyebrows slammed down into a flat line, and he scowled. "Well, *duh.* You don't need a date. *I'll* be there."

Now it was her turn to snort. "You can't be serious."

"Why not?"

"Because. I need a *date*-date." She swiped at her phone, but he jerked it away.

"Why, Lita?"

"Because!" She lunched for it again, this time jumping up a little against his surprisingly hard chest, but still missing.

He grinned and held it up higher. Which was totally not fair. He was only five foot ten, but that was still ten inches taller than her. "Nut-uh." He cackled. "Not until you tell me why you'd rather go with..." He scrolled to the next choice. "Oh, now here's Mr. Gassaway. Our old high school guidance counselor! He *definitely* wants to know if you'd like to match with him. I could just see it. 'Oh, Lita, I think we should schedule a session to talk about your future with my pants...'"

She jumped for it again. And again. "Oh my freakin' God! Would you *stop?*"

But Ross kept right on giggling every time she jumped for her cell, and if she didn't know better, she'd swear he was enjoying all their squirming and bumping. Finally, she popped a foot on his knee and levered herself over his shoulder. She got her hands on her prize, but he stumbled backward, *hard.*

And right into that sweet old lady in front of them.

The woman didn't fall—*thank little baby Jesus*—but the sudden nudge made the poor dear lose her balance enough to drop her tray. Her breakfast sandwiches and drinks went flying.

Their *"Oh no!"* was so similar and simultaneous, it came out sounding like stereo. They leaped forward to help the woman.

"Ma'am, we are so, so sorry. Are you hurt? Is everything okay?" Lita patted the woman down, checking for injuries, while Ross gathered up her tray and snatched paper towels to soak up their spilled hot chocolates. Ugh! Now the whole place was seeing what goobers they'd been. Oh man, little marshmallows were floating across the floor.

"I'm fine," the old woman chirped, though to Lita's ears, her voice sounded thready and frail. "Can't say the same for my breakfast."

Well. Hadn't they made royal asses out of themselves. And now this poor woman... Lita just about died of embarrassment as everyone stepped out of their way. She helped the old sweetheart toddle over to the window side bar, and hike herself up rather rather painfully onto the high stool. By now one of the employees had stepped up with a bucket and mop —yet more trouble they'd caused.

Ross ran off, got a clean tray, and set it down on the table. "Ma'am, this is awful. We can't let you pay for new food." He motioned over to Suzie. "Hey, can you remake her order? I'll pay for it."

"Okay." Suzie shrugged. "But all these people will be ahead of you. And we have more phone orders. It could be a few minutes."

The old woman grimaced. "Oh no! I guess we'll have to keep going without anything to eat then. My traveling companion said we're on a tight schedule. We can't afford to wait. And I was *so* hungry too."

The poor sweetie had the most hangdog expression Lita had ever seen. She and Ross exchanged a helpless glance, until Lita spotted the bags of food they'd ordered, all warm and ready to go on the counter.

She pointed it out to the lady. "You know what? You can have ours."

Ross nodded in agreement and jumped up to fetch the bag. He unloaded it into another fresh bag for her to take, while the old woman murmured protests like "Now-now, I couldn't" and "But you'll miss your breakfast." But Lita could tell from the way the lady's eyes sparkled that she was secretly pleased. Finally she agreed to the idea, and thanked them over and over.

Ross held up a hand. "Don't thank us. This never should've happened in the first place. I was the one messin' around like a moron, and that's on me. I'm *so* sorry ma'am."

The woman glanced over her shoulder to confirm that the man who'd brought her was still on the phone, and then turned back to give them both a good, hard look.

And that struck Lita as odd. Because the strangest expression passed over the woman's face. An odd twist on a knowing grin, like all that bumbling sweetness had been a mask, and it'd slipped for a hot second. But then the lady was back to smiling at them with such a helpless, elderly guilelessness, Lita felt terrible for even having the thought. Come on. The woman really was a lil' old darling.

As if to illustrate that thought, the woman smiled down at the slim bag of cookies she'd managed to hang onto, even after all the mayhem. It appeared to be all that remained of her original order, and she held it out to them, motioning to them to take the two seats on either side of her.

"Here," she insisted, pushing the cookies into Lita's hands. "You're going to have to wait a long time for your order now. No sense you bein' hungry too."

Lita couldn't help protesting at that. She and Ross bickered back and forth with the woman, not wanting to take anything from her after they'd ruined her meal.

Finally the old lady put her hands on her hips. "Hasn't anyone ever told you it's rude to refuse an old biddy's hospitality? Now, you go on and eat those while you wait for your food."

That earned a sheepish chuckle from both her and Ross. All contrite now, he took the bag from Lita and pulled out a cookie. He handed the remaining one back to her.

Lita hadn't realized how hungry she was until the cookie hit her lips. And it was delicious—an oversized sugar cookie shaped like a round Christmas tree ornament, with a little heart stamped out of the middle. Oh, it was a sandwich cookie—Linzer style with red jelly peeking through on the heart part. Whoever decorated it had mad skills. The icing was brilliant green—glass smooth and covered and tiny edible silver-and-gold balls in elaborate scrolling designs. Honestly, this cookie was really too glittery and gorgeous to eat. When it caught the sun coming in the window, it glowed in her hand.

"Mmm." Ross licked his lips as he chewed. "This does hit the spot. I can't remember when I've had a better cookie."

Lita couldn't help giving Ross a little side eye at that. It wasn't like him to get so excited over a frilly cookie. But then again, she couldn't deny what he was saying, because she felt it too. The cookie was addictive—perfectly golden crisp and tasting like vanilla and almonds. Yet, it wasn't like anything else in the Corn+Flour case today, or any other day that she'd seen. Which was odd, now that she thought about it. But she kept chewing anyway.

The old lady grinned with satisfaction as they ate, and she reached up to touch Lita's face. The woman did it in such a warm, wonderful, grandmotherly way, Lita didn't think to stop her. "Now look at you," she crooned, patting Lita's hair now. "Aren't you sweet? The sweetest girl I ever did see."

That earned a bark of laughter from Ross. "Trust me. Lita's a lot of good things, but *sweet* ain't one of them."

Haha muy gracioso, idiota, Lita wanted to say, and probably give him a pinch too while she was at it. But she couldn't. No, she was too busy locking eyes with this odd old bird. As if she was pinned somehow—captured by strange blue eyes that, like the cookie, almost seemed to glow.

The old lady cackled a little, still cupping Lita's cheek. "Oh, but you *are* sweet, darlin.' You're sweet like Christmas, and between now and the New Year, you'll see exactly what I mean. There won't be a single, lady-lovin' man in this whole town who'll be able to resist you."

Ross's eyes rounded in shock, and he stopped chewing. "Wait—*what?*"

"And you!" the woman clucked, rubbing her hand on Ross's arm now. "You're sweet too. Sweeter than you'll ever let anyone know. But just for the holiday season, you won't be able to hide it anymore."

And then came the freaky part. The *oh-my-God-am-I-really-seeing-this?* part. Ross stared at the woman like he was mesmerized, too. And right where the old woman was touching him, his arm glowed with that same strange pixie-dust sparkle from earlier. It hadn't been the snow. It was that woman. She was *doing* something.

Lita's intuition flared, telling her to smack woman's hand off him right now. But this whole thing was so fucking bizarre, she was stunned, frozen, like her brain couldn't get the signal through.

And it was getting worse. Now his eyes were glowing silver, then gold! Lita suppressed the urge to scream. Frantic, she scanned the rest of the restaurant to see if anyone else was seeing this, but everybody was acting completely normal.

When she turned her head back in his direction, Ross seemed totally fine. He polished off the last bite of he cookie with a grin. And now, Lita was shocked to find herself sitting there, holding up an empty hand where her cookie used to be. *Dios mio. Have I really eaten it all?*

She must've. But why couldn't she remember eating it?

Was she losing her mind? Had she really seen all this glittery glowing business? And what would all this *mean,* anyway? That a nice old lady gave them a present and said nice things to them?

Lita rubbed at the back of her neck, wondering how her

day managed to take this weird turn. She really needed to get a grip. She must be seeing things.

The old lady smiled again with an expression so sweet and innocent, Lita was beginning to question her own senses. This old biddy was harmless, wasn't she?

Lita wanted to ask the woman some questions. But just then, the old lady's companion came back. She and Ross explained what had happened with their breakfast and apologized all over the place. His gaze darted between two of them, then he narrowed his eyes at the old lady, looking suspicious.

"What?" The old biddy grinned. "We were having a nice talk!"

The stranger didn't bother to introduce himself or the old lady, he simply apologized for being such a bother. She and Ross insisted they had been the problem, not her. Still, Lita watched the way the man's eyes darted around the room, and he clenched his jaw. There was something he wasn't saying.

The stranger shook their hands and thanked them for breakfast. But he seemed to be in a big hurry. He quickly propped the old woman back on her feet again, and as he walked her out, Lita could swear she heard him say something like "You need to stop meddling" and "It's their business" and "You can't make them lo-"

Ugh! The door closed behind them, effectively cutting off any chance of hearing what the man was saying. So, Lita simply watched the two of them and every mincing step they took as he helped her over the snowy sidewalk. They disappeared around the corner.

She and Ross exchanged wide-eyed expressions.

"Did you feel that?" she asked him.

Ross shrugged. "What?"

"That tingling, when she touched you!" Lita insisted. "I did! It didn't hurt, exactly. But I swear, when she touched my cheek, it felt like she was pushing glitter through my bloodstream."

He snorted. "She made you *feel like glitter.*"

"Hey, you weren't able to see my face because she was blocking your view. But I could see you. When she touched your arm, your face got all..." Her words drifted off. The way he reared back and furrowed his brow, she could see he had no idea what she was talking about. Concern was written all over his face, and she'd been friends with him long enough to know what he was gonna say next. Probably some dumbass thing like she needed to get more sleep, or stop watching *Twilight* reruns or something.

"Got all *what?*" Ross asked her.

She shook her head and waved a hand at him. "Yeah, you know what? Never mind. Must've been a trick of the light or something."

Ross cracked a smile, like he was gonna say something, but Suzie flagged him down again. She pointed to the bag of cinnamon rolls she'd just put up on the counter. "Cinnamon rolls are up and your new orders too. You're good to go, guys."

Ross pushed himself to his feet to go grab the food.

Lita stood up too, brooding as she gathered up their mess. Dammit, she just couldn't shake the creeping suspicion that *something* had happened.

She gave herself a little shake. *C'mon. Don't be ridiculous.*

This was just another ordinary Monday. Just their standard Monday-morning breakfast run for Holliday Hot Rods.

But somehow, there didn't seem to be anything ordinary about it at all.

CHAPTER 2

THEY WERE LATE, of course, bringing breakfast in for the crew. Ross knew they were going to get an earful about it as soon as they rolled in. He loved his boss, Hunter Holliday, who was generally pretty chill. But the man could get awful hangry if he wasn't fed.

And Hunter's number two, Hopper Vance? *That* man nearly tackled them at the door.

Hopper snatched the bag right out of his hands. "God you two—what took so long? I'm about ready to eat my arm!"

Ross couldn't help grinning at how this big, bad biker in front of him could be undone by cinnamon rolls. He nodded to the man's enormous guns. "And that arm of yours could've fed you for a week."

"Very funny, squirt." Hopper grinned back and ruffled Ross' hair just to piss him off. It was the sort of thing the man was always doing, mainly because Hop stood head-and-shoulder taller than him, and the two of them were pretty tight. An ex-con with no family of his own, it had taken Hopper longer than most to become a part of the Holliday Hot Rods family. But when Hopper had married his wife Delilah a couple of years ago, he'd opened himself up to everyone and everything. Now, the man had decided their role in the Holliday Hot Rods family was big brother-little brother. It'd become the running joke between the two of them, and it never failed to make them both smile.

Ross slapped the man's hand away, laughing.

They walked everything back to their breakroom, and Ross took a careful inventory of the cars waiting to be worked on as they did. He shook his head at the sight. The place was packed. Seemed like half the town had brought in their cars to get the dings and rust fixed before they traveled for the holidays.

The shop was full up on orders for custom classic car design, too. They had four stripped-down vintage car bodies laying in pieces right now, one of which had to be finished so it could be given as a Christmas present. He had a stack of Hunter's Auto CAD drawings to put up on the laser metal cutter this morning, and a whole afternoon of welding work that would realistically take him well into the night.

But it was all good. He loved this place, his job, his coworkers, his home. He grinned at the Chipmunks Christmas album thumping through the speakers, and the Polar-Express-themed mural Lita had painted for the Christmas party they were sponsoring for families in the local foster care system. From the smell of the paint, it was still drying.

And that's what Ross loved about the place—that spirit of creation, of possibility, that seemed to hang in the air. Holliday Hot Rods was more like a big, mechanical makers space than your typical grimy garage. It was a huge, rehabbed shirt factory that Hunter had inherited from his dad when he'd retired. Ross loved the mayhem of it—the sparks, the classic car parts stacked up in every corner, the noise, and especially Lita's funky artwork, painted large and in charge on every wall like a tangle of refined graffiti. Hell, he even lived here, in the studio apartment Hunter had built in the old supervisor's mezzanine. Seemed like everyone at the shop but Lita had taken a run in it, for one reason or another over the years. And at only two hundred dollars a month rent, Ross had been taking his turn for three years now, so he could save up to buy property of his own one day.

He'd worried it might be weird living above the place where he worked, but it hadn't been. It was simply home to him. And he was making real progress on his dreams here. Buying a house and paying it off. Having acreage and some space to call his own. It was so close now...

Hunter ambled up, attracted no doubt by the big tray of cinnamon rolls Lita was setting out. He snatched one out of the box and jammed it in his mouth before he could even get a plate. "Ummmm," he closed his eyes. "Ah, man, they're still warm."

Lita pinned him with one of her no-nonsense looks that was one part den mother and one part smartass, and handed the man a proper plate. Then a napkin. Hunter gave her a sugary, unrepentant smirk, and wiped the icing from his close-trimmed beard. Now two big flannel-wearing gear-heads were officially undone by baked goods.

"Jaysus," Hunter groused, as he stuffed the last of the roll in his mouth. "I thought you guys would never get here."

Lita snorted. "You know what? You can thank Ross for that."

"Me? I think we both created that accident."

"Yeah, right," Lita rolled her eyes. She reached in the bag and passed Hunter his breakfast bowl. And a fork. And another napkin. "It would've never gotten so out of hand if you hadn't been actin' up. You should've seen him, guys. First, Ross is reading my phone over my shoulder. Then he steals it! *And* makes fun of my love life."

What love life?

The words jumbled and crowded in his mouth, ready to rush out. But his lips slammed shut. Like some unseen hand had shut his mouth for him. He tried to open it again, ready to follow up with some epic burn that they could joke about. Maybe stick a pin in the tension that always seemed to simmer between them. Well, the simmering, *I-wish-I-could-tell-you-how-bad-I-want-you* tension that was on *his* side, at least.

But his mouth wouldn't open. He took a deep breath.

And another one.

The total silence got his coworkers looking up from their biscuits, waiting for him to give it right back to her.

And he wanted to. But when he finally was able to pry his lips apart, "You're right" came out.

Huh? Wait a minute, wait a minute...

He opened his mouth again, and "It was totally my fault," came out. "I never should've butted in like that. I think maybe I picked on your dating life because mine isn't any better. Can you find it in your heart to forgive me?"

Ross had the sudden, overwhelming urge to clap his hand over his mouth, or even holler, maybe.

He hadn't meant to say that. He hadn't meant to say that! Those words—those thoughts—they weren't even his!

He'd actually intended to say the exact opposite, but what could he do now? Admit he didn't have any control over the verbal diarrhea that came out of his face?

Lita, for her part, simply sat back in her seat and narrowed her eyes at him.

"What?" he managed to say, trying his best cool, *I meant to say that* pose.

A disbelieving smile spread across her pretty face. "Yeah, Ross, I can forgive you. And thank you."

"For what?"

She shrugged. "For admitting when you're wrong. It's...nice."

"Mark your calendar," Hopper called. "It'll never happen again."

Ha-ha. You're fuckin' hilarious, dickhead. He thought about saying it. But somehow the moment felt wrong now, so he kept his mouth shut. And that was *his* decision this time.

"I still don't get how Ross horsing around held you up so long," Hunter mused.

Lita jumped in and answered him, giving the guys a pretty accurate description of how they'd messed around until she'd basically ended up pushing Ross right into that odd old lady. When she went into the bit about the old woman patting her hair and saying she'd be irresistible, he expected the guys to crack up laughing.

But they...*didn't.*

Ross and Hunter both stopped chewing and slid each other a glance. Like a *did-you-hear-that?* kind of glance. For crying out loud, they weren't taking this whole thing seriously, were they? The men actually seemed concerned. To his shock, Hunter and Hopper both started digging for details and peppering them with questions.

What did she look like? And the guy she was with?

Did she say she'd be back?

Did she say where they lived, or where they were going?

Did anyone else see what was happening?

You're sure they were strangers, and nobody knew them?

Ross went slack-jawed with amazement. From the way they were carrying on, you'd think their brush with a strange old biddy was the mystery of the decade. He was so blown away, he must've been a little dazed, because Lita put her hand on his arm and shook him a little.

She turned those big, green doe eyes in his direction. "I don't know about the old woman's touch. I think I definitely felt tingles, like sparkly kind of tingles, when she touched me. What about you, Ross?"

Ross sighed. She was at this whole thing again, and he wasn't sure where she was going with it. And now this weirdness with the blurting. He couldn't even say what that had been. He sure as shit wasn't admitting to that. What, that he didn't have control over his own mouth? That was *nuts.*

Honestly, he couldn't quite remember much about what the old woman had said to him. He'd been too worried about what she'd said to Lita, about all the guys she was going to attract. That's some next-level freaky right there. "*Something, something, sweeter than anybody knows,*" was all he could remember the woman saying to him. And he couldn't remember whether he'd "tingled." But he could say one thing for sure. His arm was tingling now because Lita was touching him.

That, unfortunately, was nothing new. He'd always felt that way, jittery and warm, even when the girl gave him a friendly pat.

Ross let out a long sigh. "What's this about tingling? I don't even understand what you're getting at, Lee. Are you tryin' to tell me we were visited by a witch who put some kind of spell on us?"

Lita's exasperated expression seemed to say *you got any better ideas, dumbass?* She sighed resignedly. "You have to admit, the whole thing was strange."

He sighed too. "Yeah, on that point, we're agreed."

Hunter chucked his wrappers in the trash can and stood up. "We may never know what that old lady was going on about. That said, I'd suggest the two of you be extra careful and keep a close eye on each other. There's no telling what could happen."

Hopper frowned. "What, you don't think that—"

Hunter held up a staying hand and shot the man another one of those weird speaking glances of his, like he was willing Hop to stop talking. What were these two not saying? "I'm *saying,*" Hunter continued, "the mountains around here are full of legends and ghost stories and magic of all kinds. And it wouldn't be the first unexplained thing to happen in these parts at Christmastime. You know, strange pulls of the moon and the lay lines and all that. So…watch yourself. Okay?"

Lita gave Hunter a wise little nod, like she'd bought into this whole line of bullshit lock, stock, and barrel.

What the actual hell?

Ross laughed. He couldn't help it. Whether he was nervous, or incredulous, or what, he couldn't tell. But the fact that everyone was so serious about this was plain ridiculous, and that's all there was to it.

No one laughed with him. "Wait up." He waved a hand at them. "You mean to tell me that every last one of you believe what that old woman said? That Lita is somehow gonna become the siren of Greenbrier Valley? Like a bunch of men are going to follow her around like the friggin' Pied Piper or something?"

Hunter and Hopper didn't answer him because Lita beat them to it. Her eyebrows slammed down, and she waved her finger at him. "Oh no, you did not say that. Whassa matter, ese, you don't think I could?"

Shit. How was he supposed to answer *that?*

He'd been crazy about her for so long, he could totally see how any guy would want her. Lita Noe could be any man's wet dream—with those big green eyes, and hair he wanted to dig his hands in, and a body so dope it put him in a sweat just thinking about it. But it was more than that. It had *always* been so much more than that. He was crazy about her spirit, and intelligence, and that fiery, take-no-shit 'tude of hers. He loved being with her, and working side by side, and laughing at the same inside jokes .

No matter how many times she'd friend-zoned him, he'd loved her since the day she'd sashayed into his homeroom like some badass unicorn. He was just trying not to be too pathetic about it.

If there was any magic affecting him right now, all these mushy thoughts he was having must be triggering it. His mouth was tingling like a beyotch right now. And that scared him. What inconvenient truth was he going to say this time? He clamped his mouth shut, desperate not to embarrass himself again. Unfortunately, Lita took his silence for an insult.

She stiffened and reared her head back. "Oh, really? Why not? I'm not pretty enough?"

"No! *God,* no. It's not that—"

"What then? I'm not smart enough? Don't have a college degree? Too bossy? Too loud? Come on, what is it, then?"

Hunter and Hopper watched him with bated breath, cringing. Both of them had enough experience with women to know how badly he'd stepped in it here.

Ross knew it too. And he had that sensation again, like words were backing up like train cars in his head. All the things he would probably say:

Because you always pick the wrong ones.

Because you don't suffer fools lightly. And there's a shit-ton of fools around here.

Because you're not every man's cup of tea.

And they were all true, every one. But instead, when he opened his mouth, "'Cause you're too amazing for all of them!" blurted out.

That was true too. But he'd surely never meant to say it.

Far from being disgusted at that way-too-gushy remark he'd made, Lita smiled, her whole face softening into a wry, surprised, lopsided grin that made his heart ping helplessly. "Huh. There it is. Proof there's magic in the world, after all."

Ross couldn't do anything but grin back stupidly at her. Damn, her smiles. They were like a ray of sunshine on a cloudy day, weren't they? He was addicted to them, and always playin' the fool for them too. If he couldn't have her love, he could have *those* anyway, like a little gift that was just for him.

Hunter must have taken note of how awkward this whole

situation was getting, because he was grinning from ear to ear at the two of them.

Hopper snorted. "Something was definitely in those cookies, man. I doubt Ross has ever called anything *amazing* in his life. The boy's getting' so basic he'll be giving out meme wisdom on YouTube pretty soon."

Ross laughed, happy for the out Hopper had given him. "Don't tempt me, man."

And just like that, that was the end of it. They could all get back to reality and put all this weirdness behind them. Ross breathed a huge sigh of relief as everybody shuffled off to their workstations.

Ross was busy picking off the last bites of his breakfast when the front door clattered open. When he poked his head back around the corner to see who it was, he swore under his breath.

It was Pervis Langdon, II. Or Pervy Junior, they used to call him in school, coming in with another friggin' repair on his POS vintage Jaguar. Perv was every bit as much of an uppity asshole now as he'd been in high school. He'd been two years ahead of them but had always acted like his shit didn't stink. *He* was on some special kind of upscale track the rest of them couldn't possibly understand, let alone aspire to. His dad was the president of the local bank system, and he'd made good and sure Junior here was Vice President at the Lewisburg branch, straight out of college.

Lita was the closest to the intake desk, so she trotted up to talk to the man. But Ross didn't trust this prick. He decided to watch Pervis from the relative safety of the break-room, which was on the other side of reception. He'd step out there if the boy got into any of his typical entitled bull-shit with her. Ross stood, hands on his hips, waiting for the moment Perv would treat Lita like a servant or, worse, some separate life form—the crazy lil' woman with the rainbow hair who couldn't possibly have a brain in her head. Ross could set his watch by it.

But the minute the man's eyes landed on Lita, that wasn't the reaction she got at all. Oh no, Perv's eyes got wide, and he stood up to attention in his expensive loafers. His gaze raked over her from her head to her toes, and that little sumbitch actually wiped his hand over his mouth, as if he'd spied the most delicious morsel on the buffet.

"Well, well," Pervis crooned, grinning like a fool. "If it isn't Lita Noe, all grown up. Why don't you come on over here and talk to me, darlin'?"

Darlin'?

Ross growled. Maybe that old biddy at the coffeeshop was up to something, after all…

CHAPTER 3

Ross could tell Lita was suppressing an eye roll and trying to put the customer first. Given how much she loathed this poser, it was almost funny to watch.

Almost.

They'd moved around to the driveway now, where Perv's car sat in a glowing green puddle of power steering fluid. Ross propped a shoulder against a shadowy corner and watched in case she needed help with this guy. And that boy was *definitely* acting strange today.

Perv was the kind of guy who was all about appearances. Starched shirts with cufflinks. Real silk ties. Designer horn rims and short blond hair slicked back from his forehead. He had a modern, mountainside house bought with Daddy's money, and a lemon of a vintage Jag that unfortunately, made him a frequent flyer at Holliday Hot Rods.

Every time he'd come here, Perv had barely spared a glance at Lita. When he did, the man had always regarded her like she was some kind of zoo exhibit—the crazy Hispanic with the rainbow hair, devoutly to be ignored.

But today? Perv must be smokin' something. The man was acting like some kind of switch had been flipped, and now Lita was the most appetizing woman on the planet. He leaned up against the car, all loose limbed and smiley, and dangled his keys out of front of him. When Lita curled her hand around them, he yanked them backward, making her almost fall against him.

Scowling, Lita planted her feet, pried the keys from his grip, and gave that asshole a dirty look. Perv snickered but opened the door theatrically for her so she could pop the hood. She did, only taking a minute to find the release.

Hop ambled up behind him, sipping his coffee. "This is what we're doing?" he murmured. "We're letting Lita handle Mr. Personality today?"

Ross crossed his arms over his chest and narrowed his eyes, never taking his focus off the scene. "She hates it when we butt in. All that business about the customers needing to take her word for it. She may not be a mechanic, but she can estimate as well as us, you know."

"Yeah, well..." Hopper snorted. "Not too hard to see something's wrong."

True that. When she came around front and popped up the hood, they both grumbled. Somehow that dipstick had let one of the fuel hoses crack too. Wisps of smoke rose from the engine block.

But that wasn't what Ross was watching. Lita leaned over the engine to get a closer look. And Perv, true to his name, stepped back, leering at Lita's fine ass in those low-slung jeans.

Oh-ho-ho *no,* buddy. His whole body stiffened with anger, and his hands itched to punch this oily motherfucker.

Lita popped up, pulled a rag out of her pocket, and wiped her hands. Ross could see her pointing to the engine and trying to explain something but Perv didn't seem too interested in her words. The guy stepped right up in her space, smiled dreamily down at her, and twirled one of her long pink braids around his finger.

Lita was so surprised, she seemed to freeze for a second.

But Ross didn't.

Blood fuckin' boiling, he shot out of the garage and pushed that creep back in two seconds flat. "Hey, man." He stepped between them. "We have a no-touching policy around here. No harassment, either."

Ross glowered at Perv. Eye to eye. Man to man. And it was the strangest thing. Any other man would've been all puffed up and defiant, spoiling for a fight. But Perv? Confusion flashed over his face, and he blanched, seeming disoriented.

He leaned over Ross' shoulder to keep ogling Lita, though, and started smiling stupidly again. "Awww now. Harassment? I was only trying to be a gentleman. Can't a man ask a lady out on a first-class date? I've got tickets to the Charleston Symphony, Lita. The Christmas Pops concert. I'm going with Mom and Dad, and we've got an extra front-row ticket for a pretty lady like you."

"No, Perv!" Lita barked. "What's gotten into you today? I'm not going to the symphony with you today, or any other day. We're here to talk about this completely undriveable car, and it's gonna to cost five thousand bucks to fix it."

Relief rolled over Ross in a sweet wave, and he smiled at the way Lita'd shut Perv's ass down. He wondered if Perv would pivot to his default setting—negging and haggling over the price.

But the argument never came. No, Perv kept grinning at Lita. "Sure." He sighed. "Whatever you need to make it right, Miss Noe. You've got a blank check, as far as I'm concerned."

Hop, who'd been standing there too, let out a concerned-sounding harumph. "I want to make sure we manage your expectations here. What you're bringing us is a major repair. These parts are going to be tricky to source. And the repairs themselves will require us to take the engine apart to check for leaks and clean it. The shop is jammed with work already.

Realistically, I don't think we can get your car done until the middle of February, maybe."

The man didn't even blink. "No problem." He kept grinning, never taking his eyes off Lita.

"Pervis!" Hopper snapped his fingers. "Hey! You heard me, right? Mid-February! And I'll need to be paid twenty-five hundred upfront so we can order the parts."

Pervis nodded blankly and handed his whole wallet to Hopper so the man could run his card. Frowning at the weirdness of it all, Hopper shook his head and trotted off to get the man his receipt.

Pervis stood there, silently checking out Lita's ass as she closed up the hood and rolled the car over to their secured lot. And Ross stood there, grinding his teeth, watching *him*. Like a hawk.

Hopper came back and handed the man his wallet. Pervis took out his phone, muttering something about calling an Uber.

Pervis started to walk off but whipped around like a marionette on a string when Lita came back to the garage. "Lita, darlin', I'll be back!" he called out, giving her a double-guns finger point. "I'm going to convince you to go the symphony! It'll be the best night of your life! I promise!"

"No, Pervis!" she called back. "We'll call you in February—when the car is done!"

"February, right," he muttered, still grinning like a damned idiot. Pervis wandered off down the road, presumably to hail an Uber. It could be a long wait around here. Holliday Hot Rods was in a little bit of a desolate spot on Route 60, with no sidewalks, and no nice little cafes to wait in. The man was literally walking in a three-piece suit in the scruff on the side of the road.

Hopper and Ross watched him go, shaking their heads in wonder. "You think we should give him a ride into town?" Hopper sighed.

"After harassing Lita like that? Hell no." Ross glowered.

"All right then." Hop snickered. "But you have to admit that was a whole lotta cray-cray right there. I mean, have you ever seen Pervis act like that? I haven't! If you ask me, that little old lady *totally* put something in those cookies."

"Yeah, right." Ross snorted. He still wasn't willing to admit anything was happening here.

Ross and Hop strolled back into the shop, and everyone went to their stations to dig into their day. Soon Hunter was back at his desk, drawing out designs for the custom grill plate designs their shop was known for. Hopper was busy attaching an engine block to an old Model T, and Lita was in the process of painting an American Eagle and Chuck Norris onto the hood of a restored Trans Am.

For his part, Ross was loading more of Hunter's drawings into the laser cutter. Or at least, he was trying to. Truth be told, he couldn't tear his eyes away from Lita today.

She seemed rattled. She'd dropped her airbrush gun twice now and had blasted herself with paint—something she'd normally be way too sure-handed to do. When she wasn't scowling, she was pacing and chewing her bottom lip ruby red. On a regular day, she would've been finished and putting the clear coat on by now. But she'd been spending so much time staring into space, she'd only managed to draw back over her guidelines.

There was no doubt about it. She was bothered by everything that had happened this morning.

And honestly, maybe he was too. There was no denying, between that mess with Pervy Junior and the weird tingling sensation he'd gotten when that old biddy had touched him, Ross was beginning to suspect maybe something strange was at work here. And then the business about him not being able to get his words out…

If that kept happening, things could get crazy around here quick. He shuddered.

Realizing he wasn't going to get any work done until he'd checked on her, Ross sauntered over to her station, dodging a couple of pneumatic paint guns dangling from the ceiling. Ross stood behind her, checking out the half-finished Chuck Norris.

When she realized he was there, she jumped in alarm. "Jesus!" she yelped and gave him a little shove. "Don't sneak up on me like that!"

Ross backed away and found a safer spot leaning against the car. "Sorry. Didn't mean to scare you. I couldn't watch you pacing around anymore. Hey, I get it. You're still wound up over that whole thing with the old lady, and Perv, and—"

She held up a hand. "No. I just am really sick of drawing Chuck Norris."

He laughed. "Bullshit!"

"How can you not see it?" She swept her arm in poor old Chuck's direction. "I've got his eyes so wrong he looks like an alien!"

He snickered. Okay, so the man's cheekbones were probably a little too high, but otherwise, it was still Lita's best work. She needed to get her head back into it. "Then he'll be the bad-assinest alien in two quadrants." Ross leaped into a bad crouching-tiger karate pose. "I laugh at your photon blaster."

She smiled ruefully, when she normally she would've laughed at the joke and probably said *pew pew* back to him. His own smile faded.

"Hey," he rubbed the tops of her arms. "You know you've got enough talent to beat this project into submission. You're the best there is. You're the most amazing woman I've ever met. You're incredible, actually—"

"Oh, *gawd*. Not you too," Lita shrugged out of his hold. "Just stop."

Ross felt that sting right in his gut. But after a second, it dawned on him what was happening here. She believed he didn't mean what he was saying. That *he* was hexed too.

Not wanting to confirm or deny that, he simply shook his head. "Lita. You know this isn't about me. Or Chuck Norris, even. You're letting all that weirdness with Perv get into your head. Come on, a man you don't like flirts with you, and now you're off your game for a whole day? Since when have you ever let the assholes get you down?"

"All right." She shook her head and held up her hand in testimony. "I'll give you that. This isn't like me. Any other day, I would've slapped some sense into that creep, right upfront. But I couldn't. You didn't see him as close up as I did. When he was looking at me, he was there but… I dunno. Was he? It was like he wasn't calling his own shots. You know what I mean?"

"No, I don't."

She opened her mouth again, like she was about to argue with him.

But he beat her to it. "Maybe he saw a beautiful woman and decided to make his move."

Lita snorted. "I'm not beautiful."

Ross snorted right back. "Seriously? You mean you can look in the mirror at all this—" he waved his hands in her direction, "—and not think, *damn,* girl!"

She grinned and gave him one of her little play shoves. "That's not what I meant! I mean, I'm not beautiful *to him*. Have you ever seen Perv with a girl who resembles me in any way? Every last woman he's dated has been blonde, tall, skinny, cultured, and from money. And then that bit about wanting me to go out in public with his parents on a first date? I mean, how crazy is *that?*"

Ross shrugged. "I dunno. It's a little intense, I'll give you that. But maybe he was trying to impress you."

"Ha! Everything Pervis does is to impress. But never, not once in all the years I've known him, has he ever looked my way. I don't care how long you stand there and tell me otherwise. You will never get me to believe Pervis would want to be seen in public with a girl with a nose ring and mermaid hair."

Ross suppressed the urge to growl. He hated it when she put herself down like this. Why was a conversation with that pretty boy bothering her so much? And what in the hell was he doing here, defending the man?

But then, he wasn't really defending Pervis, was he? He was defending Lita and the way she saw herself. He couldn't let her think she wasn't good enough for some dick like Pervis Langdon.

So as usual, he cracked a smile. "What—you weren't born with mermaid hair? I hear the pink-haired people of Mexico are the world's most legendary beauties. The chickarellas—sirens of the bodega."

She laughed and shoved at him again. But this time, she stopped, wrapped her arms around his middle, and totally shocked him with a hug.

Lita buried her face in his chest and squeezed. And for a second, the loud music didn't seem so loud, and there were no smells of grease or paint, only the smell of lavender and almonds that seemed to cling to her, no matter where she went.

Sweet Lita. He dropped his hands slowly around her back and swallowed hard. What he wouldn't give to be able to hold her like this, any time he wanted. He rested his cheek against the top of her head and let his eyes fall closed, reminding himself she'd only meant to give him a friendly hug. Still, she seemed to melt against him just a little, their bodies fitting together far better than he would've guessed. When was the last time she'd hugged him?

High school?

But she was all grown up now…

“Thank you,” she murmured against him. “You always know what to say, Ross.”

Because I see you. I’ve always seen you for who you are, Carmelita Rose Noe.

The words were crowding up in his mouth again, bursting to be said. And given his weird tendency to blurt shit like this out today, he wasn’t in the mood to take chances.

He clamped his mouth shut long enough for the tingling to pass. “So.” He grinned. “You really weren’t born with pink hair?”

She pushed out of his embrace and stalked off for more paint, smiling and shaking her head. Her braids swayed as she went.

Someday, he told himself like he had a thousand times before. *Someday, I’m going to tell her...*

But it wouldn’t be today.

To Paul, my darling husband, who always leaves the last bite of the ice cream for me. You teach me the true meaning of love, every day.

ACKNOWLEDGMENTS

When you're reading a great story, it's so easy to imagine that an artist labors away in solitude, and out pops a masterpiece. In reality, it takes a whole team of people to create a worthwhile book, and I am blessed to the best team a writer could ask for at my back.

I'll start off with Rhonda Merwarth, my editor, who's never steered me wrong, even when she was telling me to start over. And I'd like to give a special shout out to Elizabeth Turner-Stoakes, who created the amazing illustrated covers in this whole series, as well as quite a lot of my author branding. And the team at Wildfire Marketing has been doing a great job of helping me spread the word.

I'd also be remiss if I didn't mention Geno Zulisky, a friend and police officer who was willing to hang out on the phone with me for a couple hours, talking about the ins and outs of chop shops and the criminals who run them. The characterization and story lines of Randy Jarboe and teen Hopper have much to do with his influence.

Then, of course, there's the readers who don't have the glory assignments—the intrepid crew whose criticisms and eagle eyes ferret out those pesky problems and typos. My undying gratitude would not be enough to thank my proofing posse, Stephanie Knott, Nan Cayton, and Cathy Stadler, as well as my beta readers, romance author Ava Cuvay (avacuvay.com) and fan number one, Stacey King Smith. I love all y'all, more than I can say.

I'd also like to thank the marketing staff at The Greenbrier in White Sulphur Springs, West Virginia. They've been consistently lovely to me throughout the writing and research process, and it has been a true pleasure to feature one of the nation's crown jewel resorts in this series. Check out their website at greenbrier.com, and you'll see, I didn't exaggerate!

The same holds true for the other real locations in this book including The New River Gorge Bridgewalk (*https://bridgewalk.com/*) and Snowshoe Ski Resort (*https://www.snowshoemtn.com/*). And yes, even Helen, Georgia (*https://www.helenga.org/*) is real, too. Regrettably, Holliday Hot Rods is entirely fictional. But Lewisburg, West Virginia, is not. (*http://lewisburg-wv.com/*) And I'd like to think that bucolic town would be the perfect place for that kind of business.

West Virginia is a beautiful place with many natural wonders that often don't make the headlines. I hope you'll give it a visit sometime. It was a great place to grow up.

ABOUT THE AUTHOR

Liza Jonathan is a writer of big, sexy contemporary romances with a magic mountain twist. A West Virginia native, she now lives in the flat, flat lands of Indiana. But as she's discovered, you can take the girl out of the Appalachia, but you can't take the Appalachia out of the girl.

When she's not haunting the house at all hours working on her books, she has a life as a marketing content writer on all things IT, and is wife to her long-time husband, and mother to two very nearly adult-aged sons.

She is the 2020 Winner of the HOLT Medallion for "Best First Book" and a finalist in the contest's Paranormal Romance category.

Connect with Liza on:

Her Website, www.lizajonathan.com. Here, you can sign up for her enewsletter, which can link you to free books and sales from the industry's most exciting authors, among other things.

There's plenty of places to be friends, including her reader group, Liza Jonathan's Mage Page, https://www.facebook.com/groups/2228890480570180/ where she regularly posts exclusive content, great deals from her author friends, and new release information. She's also on Goodreads!

And don't forget to be friends on Facebook and follow her on Bookbub, linked below. There's so much more to come.

facebook.com/liza.jonathan.351
bookbub.com/authors/liza-jonathan

CPSIA information can be obtained
at www.ICGtesting.com
Printed in the USA
LVHW031640181121
703740LV00002B/127

9 781951 209049